MY
TEMPTATION

ALSO BY T L SWAN

MY TEMPTATION

KINGSTON LANE

T L SWAN

 Montlake

Published by Montlake, Seattle

www.apub.com

Amazon, the Amazon logo, and Montlake are trademarks of Amazon.com, Inc., or its affiliates.

ISBN-13: 9781662512735
eISBN-13: 9781662512742

Cover design by @blacksheep-uk.com
Cover photography by Regina Wamba of ReginaWamba.com

Printed in the United States of America

GRATITUDE
The quality of being thankful;
readiness to show appreciation for and to return
kindness.

I would like to dedicate this book to the alphabet, for those twenty-six letters have changed my life. Within those twenty-six letters, I found myself and live my dream. Next time you say the alphabet, remember its power. I do every day.

Map Key:

Number 6 – The Navy House

Number 7 – Winston Brown's House

Number 8 – Ethel Davidson's House

Number 9 – Antony Deluca's House

Number 10 – Rebecca & John Dalton's House

Number 11 – Juliet Drinkwater's House

Number 12 – Carol Higginbottom's House

Number 13 – Henley James' House

Number 14– Blake Grayson's House

KINGSTON
LANE

Chapter 1

Juliet

"Will you relax?" Chloe says.

Ugh. I look around the huge ballroom. "How did I let you talk me into coming here? I feel so out of place."

"I bribed you, that's how. Stop whining. You look hot."

"True, and you are paying up. Dinner anywhere I want next week, remember?"

"McDonald's sounds good."

"Tight-ass." Chloe is my best friend, whose magical talent is talking me into doing things that I don't want to do.

"Remind me why we are here again?" I ask her.

"Because I want to have sexual intercourse with Dr. Grayson," she whispers as she rearranges her boobs in her dress. "You know this already."

I giggle. "I thought you just wanted to fuck him?"

"That too."

Chloe is in lust with a doctor who works at our hospital. The problem is, so is most of the female population, and he doesn't even know who we are.

"Who is that slapper he is talking to, anyway?"

I glance over to the beautiful redhead talking to Dr. Grayson. "I don't know, but she's hot."

"I could take her."

"Totally."

The night is a glamorous event, auctions and celebrity trivia, and while I would love to tell you that my mind is on charity, that would be an appalling lie. This is so far from my thing, but I do admit that something *has* caught my attention: the stranger across the ballroom.

I noticed him the moment I walked in. Wearing a black dinner suit, he's laughing and talking with a group of people. Dark-brown wavy hair, square jaw, and the biggest dimples when he smiles.

"I'll get us some more drinks. Same again?" Chloe asks.

"Yes, please." I watch her walk off to the bar, and then my eyes drift back over to him. He's very tall, maybe six foot four. Broad shoulders and built, but there's something about the way he's talking to his group of friends. He's all animated and laughing, and they're hanging on his every word as he commands their attention.

I look around the beautifully decorated ballroom. I've never been to anything like this before. A fundraiser for the children's medical-research wing at the hospital I work at. Nurses don't usually get invites to things like this, but I've become friends with one of the doctors, and he invited Chloe and me to come along. I glance back over to the gorgeous stranger, and for the first time, we lock eyes. We stare at each other for a beat longer than usual, and then, as if perplexed, he tilts his chin to the sky as he takes a sip of his amber drink. Even the way he holds the glass is hot. His legs are wide and his back is straight, dominance oozing from his every pore. I snap my eyes away, embarrassed that I was caught perving. His wife is probably loitering around here somewhere.

I pretend to look around and then glance back to see Dr. Grayson walk over to him. They begin to chat like old friends, laughing and animated.

I bite my bottom lip to hide my smile. They know each other. *It could be double date heaven.*

Chloe arrives back with our drinks. "I just saw Helen at the bar, remember her?"

"Not really," I reply without even trying.

"Yes, remember, she worked in our wing a few years ago." She continues on this long-winded story. But I hardly hear her. My attention is lost. I can feel his gaze on my skin, sense that he's looking at me.

Over the next two hours, more of the same.

Every time I casually glance over, he's staring at me. And the thing is, when I catch him, he doesn't look away. He holds my gaze in a silent dare, as if willing me to do something . . . just what that is I'm not too sure.

Can a look give you goose bumps? Because I swear his is.

I can't even say anything to Chloe because the reason we are here, the dick Dr. Grayson, hasn't even looked her way.

"Is he going to talk to every fucking woman here tonight?" Chloe whispers angrily with her eyes locked on him. "I'm over here. You haven't talked to me yet, you giant dickhead."

"Right?" We watch Dr. Grayson for a moment. "What's his first name again?" I ask.

"Blake."

"Blake Grayson." I twist my lips. "Hot name."

"The name isn't half of it." Chloe eyes him. "He'd be great in bed."

"What makes you say that?"

"Look at him, how could he not? He could just stand at the end of the bed naked, and I would orgasm."

I giggle. "True."

Dr. Grayson looks more like a model than a doctor, with sandy-brown hair and a square jaw, fit and buff.

"And he's a pediatrician." She sighs dreamily.

"That's the killer, I have to agree."

I glance back over to the handsome stranger to find him staring at me again. My stomach flutters. I can feel the air between us swirling, sexual tension so thick that you could cut it with a knife.

This man is a walking temptation.

"Lord have fucking mercy," Chloe whispers.

"What?"

"Have you seen Dr. Grayson's friend?"

Seen him? I can't take my eyes off him.

"Who?" I act dumb.

"Oh fuck," Chloe whispers, wide eyed as she looks over my shoulder. "He's coming over."

"Who?"

"The god."

"What god?" My eyes widen.

"Act cool."

"What?"

"Ladies," a deep and husky voice purrs from behind me.

Oh crap.

I turn around to come face to face with piercing dark eyes.

Yep . . . he's even better close up. "Hi," I squeak.

What the hell is that mouse voice?

"I mean, hi," I say lower.

Chloe smirks. "Hello."

"I don't believe we've met," he says as he holds out his hand. "I'm Henley James."

Henley James.

"Chloe Willcox." Chloe smiles as she shakes his hand.

4

He turns his attention to me, and I stare at him, tongue tied.

"And you are . . ." He raises his eyebrow.

"Juliet." I force a shy smile. He takes my hand and shakes it. His thumb dusts over the back of my hand as he maintains eye contact.

Oh . . .

"Juliet who?" He gives me a slow sexy smile, knowing full well the effect he is having on my poor deprived hormones.

I swallow the lump in my throat. "Drinkwater."

"And do you?" he replies, his eyes still locked on mine.

"Do I . . ." I frown, confused.

"Drink water?"

"Yes, I do." I fake a laugh that resembles a six-year-old's.

Help.

Okay . . . what the hell? Please go away. You are too good looking for my brain to work.

"Would you like to go out with me, Juliet?" he asks.

My eyes flick to Chloe and then back to him. *Did I hear that correctly? Huh?*

"Well?" he prompts me.

"Um . . ." I take a sip of my champagne. "Like . . . on a date."

His mischievous eyes light up. "Yes, like a date."

"Oh, um." *Answer him, fool.* "Okay."

He gives me that slow sexy smile again. "Shall we say . . . Friday night?"

A goofy grin begins to come over my face, and I inwardly stop myself.

Act cool.

"I'll have to check my schedule," I reply.

He chuckles as if knowing my game. "Sure." He pulls out a business card and passes it over. "Call me." Then without warning he leans over and kisses my cheek; his lips linger for a beat on my skin, and the smell of his aftershave wafts around me. Then he turns and walks casually across the room back to his friends.

Chloe and I stare after him, shocked.

"Oh. My. Fucking. God," Chloe whispers. "Did that just happen?"

I glance down at the card he gave me.

HENLEY. JAMES
ENGINEERING
044 289 0777

"He's an engineer," I whisper.

"Who gives a fuck. I would sleep with him if he was homeless."

I giggle and turn my back to him. Can't seem too interested.

Chloe clinks her glass with mine and winks. "Well done."

It's Thursday night. I'm on my couch, and I need to get my act together. I've been nervous about this all week. I chew on my thumbnail as I stare at the business card.

"Just call him," Chloe says. "What's the worst that could happen?"

"He could be a dick, that's what."

"Listen to me," she says, deadpan. "He's fucking gorgeous, and gorgeous men are an endangered species, practically extinct. So when you find one, you need to grab him with both hands. Not to mention that he asked you on a date and gave you his card. He wants you to call him. You're not just some random chick off the street."

"You're right."

"Here's the plan: you call him, you two fall madly in love, and then you set your friend up with his friend, Dr. Grayson."

I roll my eyes. "It's so simple when you put it like that."

She passes me my phone. "Just fucking do it."

"I'm way overthinking this, aren't I?"

"You are."

I dial his number and quickly hang up.

Shit.

"Okay, what do I say again?"

"Oh my god, you're killing me," she gasps.

For the tenth time, I run through the conversation in my head: casual . . . concise, and make the date. Don't be nervous. Who cares if it doesn't work out—he's probably a dick anyway.

Right!

I dial his number and hold my breath as it rings.

"Hello," a woman's voice answers.

My eyes widen. Who the hell is this? "Aah . . ." I hesitate. Is this his girlfriend or something?

"This is Henley James's phone," she says, all professional-like. "I'm his assistant, Jenny."

"Oh." Relief fills me. "Can I speak to Henley, please?"

"He's not available right now. May I ask who is calling?"

My eyes widen. Is this a trap? Maybe he has a girlfriend, and this is her pretending to be his assistant to catch him out and plot my murder. "Um." I hesitate as I try to think on my feet. My eyes flick to Chloe's. "It's Juliet."

"Juliet Drinkwater?" she asks.

"Yes." I frown. How does she know my name? "I am."

"Juliet, Henley has had to take an unexpected trip overseas for a site inspection, but he left me with instructions if you were to call."

What?

"Oh," I reply, surprised.

"Yes, unfortunately he won't be back until Friday, but he wanted for me to arrange a time on Friday night for dinner."

What?

This is weird.

"Um . . . sure." I shrug.

"Is seven thirty okay?"

"Yes."

"May I have your address so that Henley can pick you up?"

This is weird. I am not giving some random woman my address. She could be his bunny-boiling serial-killer wife. "I'll meet him there."

"Are you sure?"

"Positive."

"Okay, I've booked Monsieur on Riley for seven thirty."

"You've already booked it?"

"I knew you'd call," she replies, a twang of sarcasm in her voice.

I roll my eyes at my predictability. *Of course you did.* "Okay, thank you."

"Goodbye, Juliet."

"Goodbye."

I hang up the phone and stare at Chloe in shock. "Friday night, seven thirty."

"Fucking boom." Chloe laughs. "And that's how you do it."

At 7:10 p.m. on Friday night, I get out of the Uber with a spring in my step.

I'm early, I know, but I want to get there before him so I get to watch him walk in and not the other way around. I'm nervous enough already.

I'm wearing a sexy black date dress that's strapless and fitted, along with new high heels; I even had a blowout today at the salon.

I've got a good feeling about this . . . he was handsome and so nice; I mean, he even told his assistant about me when he had to travel overseas. It sounds like he's as eager as I am.

I walk up the street and see the swanky gold sign:

Monsieur

Wow, what a place to have a first date.

I've wanted to come here for forever. This place is legendary. I've tried to get a table here before, but it has always been booked out for months in advance.

I push open the heavy doors and walk in. The waiter at the front desk smiles. "Hello. How may I help you?"

"Hi, I have a booking for seven thirty tonight?" I smile nervously as I look around. Wow, this place is something else. French furnishings. Big, beautiful murals are painted on the walls. Lamps with warm glow bulbs are everywhere.

"What was the name?" he asks.

"Um." I shrug, unsure of the answer. "Henley James?"

"Yes." He smiles. "Your table is right this way." He leads me through a hallway and out to another area, then down some stairs, and we arrive at a quaint garden courtyard. It's a different feel out here, more playful and intimate.

Music is playing, and the sound of jovial chatter floats through the air. Beautiful murals are painted on the brickwork. There are huge plants in terra-cotta pots, and fairy lights are strung up above, creating a canopy.

Wow, touchdown on the location.

He knows his stuff; this date is a ten already.

And then I see him . . . and my stomach flips. He's sitting at a table for two in the corner as he waits.

He's early too.

I had a sneaking suspicion that this was all an elaborate hoax. He glances up. Our eyes meet, and he instantly rises out of his chair to greet me.

He's wearing a sport coat and pants, a black shirt with the top button down. I can see a peek of his chest.

"Hello." He smiles as he kisses me on the cheek. "You look lovely."

Oh, he smells good.

"Hi." I swoon.

He pulls my chair out, and I slip into it. "Thank you." I can feel that my face is a nervous shade of red.

Okay, scratch that: this date is a twenty.

I roll my lips and rearrange my cutlery on the table as my heart races. I'm so nervous it's ridiculous.

He sits back in his seat. "So . . ."

"So . . ." I smile.

"Can I get you something to drink?" the waitress asks.

Tequila, bitch . . . all of it.

I pick up the drink menu. *Quick, pick something.*

"What would you like, sir?" she asks him.

"I'll have what she's having," he replies in his deep sexy voice.

"Of course." The waitress smiles.

Oh . . . the pressure.

"Do you like margaritas?" I ask timidly.

"I love them." His eyes hold mine, and he bites his bottom lip as if to hide his smile.

"I'll have a margarita, please," I tell her.

"How would you like it?"

"Shaken and salted."

"Make that two," Henley says.

The waitress disappears, and my eyes meet his. "Do you really like margaritas, or are you being smooth?"

His eyes dance with delight. "I'm trying to be smooth, but I do actually like margaritas. So, good choice."

"Oh." I smile goofily.

"How am I doing?"

"With the smooth?"

"Yeah."

"Like a baby's bottom."

He chuckles and I do too.

"I was actually nervous coming here tonight." He smiles.

"You?" I scoff.

"Yes, me," he scoffs back. "Why wouldn't you think I'd be nervous?"

Because you look like that.

"You just don't seem like a nervous type of person," I reply casually. "*I* was nervous coming here tonight, but . . ." My voice trails off as I stop myself from elaborating.

"But what?" He smiles.

"But I don't go on many dates, so . . ." I shrug.

His brow furrows. "You don't go on many dates?"

"No."

"Why not?"

"Men are dicks."

He chuckles. "That we are."

I look around at our surroundings. "I give your date place a ten, though."

"It is nice, isn't it?" He looks around too.

"Come here often?"

"First time."

I nod, feeling suddenly out of my depth.

"I don't date often either," he adds.

"You don't?"

"No."

"Why not?"

He shrugs. "I don't know—it's a lot of hassle."

"Here you are." The waitress puts our drinks on the table, interrupting us.

"Thank you."

She leaves us alone, and we both pick up our drinks, and I hold mine up for a toast. He holds his to mine and waits.

"To smooth hassles," I say.

He gives me a slow sexy smile. "I never said it was going to be smooth."

The air between us is electric.

"I like some bumps." I smile, feeling a little braver.

"Something tells me this date is going to be anything but a hassle."

"Until I turn into a psychopath tomorrow."

He throws his head back and laughs out loud, and I smile goofily over at him.

He thinks I'm funny.

A million margaritas and laughs later.

The restaurant has gone quiet. Everyone cleared out. But our conversation is still running hot.

Henley James is funny and charming, not to mention utterly gorgeous. I find myself hanging on his every word.

"So . . ." He sits back in his chair as he acts serious. "How do you rate our date so far?"

"So far?"

He smiles mischievously into his drink.

"So far . . ." I narrow my eyes as I pretend to think hard. "Like a two."

"A two?" he gasps. "This date is not a two."

"I know." I laugh. "It's a ten."

He gives me that look, the one he does so well. "Twenty."

"Twenty?" I raise my eyebrows: it's like he's reading my mind. "That's a high score."

He twirls his glass on the table. "I think this is my best first date ever."

Your last first date.

"What's so good about it?" I smile as I play along.

"Well . . . the scenery." He gestures to me.

I giggle and lick the salt from my glass.

"That." He points to me with my tongue hanging out. "That is a definite high point. Every time you do it, I feel it in my loins."

I burst out laughing, and he does too.

"Loin or groin?" I ask.

"Both."

We laugh again. I'm sure the waitstaff all hate us by now—nothing is this funny.

"I love that you're understated," he says.

I flick my hair around and bat my eyelashes.

"Your wanting-to-renovate-a-house thing is a little concerning, though. Don't know if I would trust you with a nail gun."

I giggle. *He is so fun.*

"I love that you're a nurse."

"Have you lost somebody?" I ask.

"Why do you say that?"

"Well." I shrug. "Most people who appreciate nurses have spent a lot of time in a hospital."

"My mother."

We fall serious.

"I'm sorry. Recently?"

"No." He sips his drink. "When I was fifteen."

I watch him, unsure what to say next.

13

He looks out over the restaurant as if miles away. "It was a catastrophic event in my life."

Oh . . .

I hold my hand out over the table to him, and he places his in mine. I rub my thumb over his fingers. "She would be very proud of you."

His eyes meet mine, and he rolls his lips as if annoyed. I instantly know that I've overstepped.

"But she said you better up your game because this date is definitely slipping down to a two."

He smirks and picks up his drink. "Really?"

"Yes." I nod, acting serious. "She said you should walk me out to my car and kiss me good night if you want to raise the score tally."

"Oh, she did, did she?"

"Yep." I smile into my drink, feeling proud of my crisis-management-while-being-flirty skills.

We stare at each other as the air between us swirls with an energy that I haven't felt before.

"Can I see you tomorrow night?" he asks.

"Yes."

"Where do you want to go?"

"Grocery shopping will do."

He bursts out laughing and sets us both off again.

"I'm sorry, we are closing the restaurant," the waiter says as he places the check wallet onto the table.

"Yes, of course."

I go to grab it, but Henley snaps it up. "I'm paying."

"No, you're not. We will go halves."

"Shut up."

"No."

"You can pay tomorrow night," he offers.

14

"When we go to buy my groceries?"

He laughs and sets us off again, and the waiter rolls his eyes from the corner.

"Stop it." Henley tries to act serious as he gets his wallet out. "The waiter hates us."

"Because we're funnier than him."

"This is true," he agrees. "We are."

He pays the bill and takes my hand in his. Electricity shoots up my arm, and as if he feels it, too, he lifts my hand to his lips and kisses the back of it as we stare at each other.

What's happening right now?

We walk out through the front doors, and suddenly the pressure is on again.

Do I be a good girl, or do we go home together?

"Did you drive?" I ask.

"No, Uber."

"Me too."

He stares down at me, and I know the very same questions are rolling around in his head. Be a gentleman or throw me across a park bench and have his wicked way with me?

I'm voting for option two.

"Cab?" he asks.

"Sure."

Damn it, he's going for option one.

Gentleman.

He puts his arm around me as we walk and pulls me close, and there's a familiarity between us. This feels like the most natural thing in the world.

"I had a good time tonight," he says as we walk.

"Me too." I smile goofily. "I'm already excited about going grocery shopping tomorrow."

He arrives at a busy corner and stops at the traffic lights, and he turns me toward him.

"Is this where you kiss me?" I ask.

"I don't know, is it?"

I nod. "Probably."

Right here, in the middle of everyone, he takes my face in his hands. His lips softly brush against mine, and my feet float off the ground. We kiss again and again, and it's like a wave of perfection comes crashing over us.

The lights change. People are rushing . . . but it's the two of us lost in the moment. It's not awkward, like a first kiss should be. It's intimate and tender, something more.

He smiles against my lips and pulls me close, and we stand in each other's arms for a moment.

"Henley."

"Yeah." He kisses my forehead.

"This is my best first date."

"Until the next one."

I giggle, and he gives me a sexy wink.

Butterflies flutter in my stomach because, holy crap, *this is something*.

We arrive at the taxi stand, and damn it, one is there waiting. He opens the back door for me and kisses me softly as he brushes the hair back from my face. "I'll call you tomorrow."

"Okay." I smile shyly and get into the back seat, and he closes the door behind me.

I wave, and then before the car can drive away, he opens the car door and pulls me out by the hand. "Change of plans: you're coming home with me."

"What?"

He cuts me off with a kiss, and everyone in the cab line groans in disgust.

Lips locked, hormones in overdrive, we burst through the door of his apartment like animals.

Gone is the polite first-date Mr. James; we left him in the restaurant.

I like this version better.

All the way home in the Uber, he had his hand up my dress, and I think it's fair to say that we are both very good to go.

"Get this fucking dress off," he whispers as he struggles to unzip it. The zipper snags, and he tugs it hard.

I giggle at his impatience. "Who said I am a sure thing, anyway?"

"I did." He tears my dress over my shoulders and throws it to the side.

"I don't fuck on first dates." I smirk as I put my hands on my hips, acting indignant.

"You do now." The mood changes as his dark eyes sweep down over my body. Suddenly I'm nervous.

Because hell, this has been the best night, and I want it to have an even happier ending and blow his mind.

He puts his hand around my throat, steps forward, and puts his lips to my ear. "You are going to take my cock so fucking good," he whispers. His breath brushes my ear and sends goose bumps up my spine. "Like the bad girl I know you want to be."

My eyes widen. *Fuck.*

He talks dirty. . . shit, shit, shit.

With his hand in a viselike grip around my throat, he licks up the side of my face. "Are you creamy for me, baby?"

Adrenaline and arousal scream through my bloodstream. The feeling of his large hand around my throat is both terrifying and euphoric. I've never been with a man like this.

He's different on so many levels.

My breath quivers as I try to calm myself enough to reply.

His teeth drop to my neck, and he grazes me with them. "Answer the fucking question, Juliet."

Jeez.

Charming Henley James is nice, but choke hold Henley James is next level.

"Yes," I whimper.

He pulls back and stares at me. His eyes hold mine. "Yes what?"

"Yes sir."

Satisfaction flickers in his eyes. "Good girl."

Okay, what the fuck is going on here?

I am not into kinky sub-dom bullshit, but somehow this is off-the-radar hot.

With my heart pounding hard in my chest, I stand still as he undoes my bra. His thumbs dust over my nipples as he stares down at them. He bends and slides my panties down and kisses me there.

My breath quivers.

Fuck.

He stands, and we come face to face again. "Don't be nervous," he murmurs. He kisses me, his tongue swiping against mine as he holds my face in his hands. "I won't hurt you." He puts his lips to my ear. "Much . . ."

I close my eyes. *Fucking hell, fucking hell,* fucking hell.

"Get on the bed on your hands and knees."

I stare at him for a beat. "You're very bossy."

"Hungry." His eyes are blazing, and damn it, I *am* prepared to supply the feast.

I get onto the bed and go onto my knees.

"Lean onto your elbows."

"Are you going to undress?" I fire back.

Slap.

He smacks my behind.

"Behave," he growls.

For some sick twisted reason his discipline starts a fire between my legs, and I know in that moment . . . I'm about to do anything he wants.

What the actual fuck is going on here?

I go down to my elbows, and he stands behind me, and with our eyes locked in the mirror, he takes his shirt off over his head and then in slow motion unzips his jeans and slides them down his legs. His body is rippled with muscles, and his large cock springs free. I swallow the lump in my throat.

Okay . . . that's a lot of man meat.

His eyes drop to my sex, and I watch in the mirror as he pulls my lips apart with his fingers and strokes himself a few times. His eyes are dark and flickering with arousal.

Fuck.

He drops to the floor behind me, his tongue taking no prisoners as he licks me there.

Deep adoring licks, as if I'm the queen and he's my servant, on his knees for my pleasure.

Oh . . . dear god . . . my body begins to build, and I shudder. I see stars.

I scrunch the sheets up in my hands as I try to deal with him. "I'm going to . . ."

"You'll come on my cock."

"Then hurry the fuck up," I demand.

He chuckles, and it's the first time I see a glimmer of my playful date. He rolls on a condom.

He wraps my hair around his hand as he holds me still and then slowly slides the tip of his thick cock through my lips. Back and forth, back and forth.

Hurry up.

He positions himself and slowly eases himself in. The air leaves my lungs, and I whimper out loud.

Oh . . . he's big . . . and . . . way too good at this.

"How's this?" He slowly slides himself in and out, warming my body up to his size.

I nod, unable to make a coherent sentence.

"Answer me."

"Good." I close my eyes as I try to deal with him. "Really good."

The scent of his aftershave, his grip on my hair, his cock so deep inside of me that I can't breathe.

He's all around me, in a perfect sensual 3D experience.

He withdraws completely and slides back in. He does it again, completely out, and then slides right back in.

What's he doing?

"I'm fine," I tell him.

"I'll be the judge of that."

"You're not going to hurt me."

His grip on my hip tightens, and he slams in hard, knocking the air from my lungs.

Ow . . . okay, maybe a little.

Then he is riding me hard, the sound of our skin is slapping loudly, echoing through his room.

I try to hold myself up, but it's hard when you are being fucked by a Mack truck.

I can't hold it, and I scream into the mattress.

"Fuck," he pants. "Oh yeah, just like that."

I smile as I listen to him come undone. Is there a hotter sound on earth?

He hisses, holds himself deep, and comes hard inside me. I feel the telling jerk of his cock as it releases.

I'm wet with perspiration as I hear him gasping for air behind me.

And then he kisses me on my behind. "Fucking hot," he whispers against my skin.

I smile into the mattress.

Completely and utterly ruined.

Chapter 2

He pulls the car over to the side of the road. "I'll see you." He leans over and, taking my face in his hand, kisses me softly. "Tonight . . ."

I smile against his lips. "Tonight."

Seriously . . .

The

best

night

of

my life.

We had the best date ever, went home and fucked like animals, then had a shower and made tender sweet love.

I woke up to more of his oral skills this morning, and then he made me breakfast.

Now that's what I call a date well done.

This is it . . . he's the one.

I am walking on fucking air.

"I have to work today, but I'll call you later?" he asks.

I want to punch the air, but I won't because I'm being cool and all that. "Have a good day."

I open the car door, and he pulls me back for another kiss. I laugh against his lips. "I have to go."

"Maybe I have to come."

"You're a sex maniac." I laugh. With another quick kiss I jump out of the car, and he gives me a slow sexy smile. "Bye." I float inside. I'm on cloud nine.

I change my sheets and bundle up the old ones at double speed.

In among the walking-on-air thing, I've been on cleaning crack today.

I've tidied. I've washed. I've bought fresh flowers. I've vacuumed and mopped. I cleaned the bathroom. I bought new underwear and even got a few groceries, just in case things go really well tonight and we don't make it out to dinner.

With my hands on my hips, I look over my apartment to try and see it with new eyes. The living room rug looks a little tired. *Hmm.* I mean, I have had it for a few years. Maybe I should take it down to the garage?

I really want to put my best foot forward with Henley tonight.

I slide my coffee table over and roll up the huge rug. I try to pick it up and strain. Oh hell, this thing is heavy.

I drag it to the door and struggle out into the hall, dragging it as I go. I turn toward the elevator, then remember that it's closed for maintenance today.

Fuck.

Six flights of stairs it is.

I drag it along, sweating, huffing, and puffing. It takes me ten minutes to get down only two levels.

Hell, this date will have to be another sleepover, simply because I'm going to be so exhausted that I'll fall asleep before dinner.

I get halfway down and have to sit for a few minutes and rest. I take out my phone and check it.

No missed calls.

I finally get to the bottom of the stairs and drag my rug into my garage.

Right . . . now to make myself simply irresistible.

I pick up my phone and check it for the thousandth time today. I'm sitting on my couch, primped, primed, with nowhere to go.

It's 7:00 p.m., and Henley hasn't called me yet.

Where the hell is he?

I have this uneasy feeling in the pit of my stomach. What if something's wrong?

Stop it.

He's going to call; I know he is.

So why hasn't he already? It's 7:00 p.m. He would have called by now if he was going to.

I flick through Netflix in search of a distraction.

Maybe he's lost my number?

I sit up, suddenly interested in that theory. Yes, that must be it. If he did lose my number, then he has no way of contacting me.

Maybe I should call him?

My phone rings. "Hello," I answer.

"Did he call yet?" Chloe asks.

"No." I sigh.

"Fuck."

"Do you think I should call him?"

"No."

"What if he lost my number?"

"Then he's a dickhead. Anyway, your number will be in his call history. He hasn't lost your number, Jules."

My heart sinks. "Something is wrong. I know he's going to call me."

"Why, because he said he would? Wouldn't be the first man to ever lie on a date."

"Chloe, I'm telling you. We had something; I know he's going to call me."

"Okay," she replies in an unconvinced voice. "The girls and I are going to Club 70, if you want to come."

"No." I exhale as I lie down on my back. "I'm going to wait for him."

"He's not calling."

"He is." I roll my eyes. "He had to work today. Maybe he's going to just show up here any minute. Goodbye."

I exhale heavily and look around my spotless apartment. He better fucking call.

8:00 p.m.

Ring, ring . . . ring, ring . . . I screw up my face as I wait for him to pick up.

"You've reached Henley James. I can't come to the phone right now. Leave a message."

Shit.

"Hi, Henley, it's Juliet." I pause as I try to think of the right thing to say. "I was just . . ." Fuck. "I thought we were catching up tonight?"

Damn it. I sound desperate.

"Just called to see what's happening. Anyway, bye."

I put my hands over my eye sockets in disgust. Oh god . . . that sounded so pathetically needy. Why didn't I just wait for him to call? Now I've ruined it.

Ugh . . .

My phone vibrating on the side table wakes me. "It's too late for your drunken phone calls, Chloe," I grumble as I answer.

"Guess who just turned up at the club?" she yells through the loud nightclub music.

I rub my eyes to try and focus on her voice. "Who?"

"Henley James."

"What?" I sit up, suddenly wide awake. "What time is it?" I glance at the clock on my phone: 2:00 a.m. "Who's he there with?"

"Two guys."

"Are you serious?" I get out of bed.

"You get down here and tip a fucking drink on his head for standing you up."

I drag my hand down my face. "What's he wearing?"

"Who cares. He looks like a walking vibrator in whatever he's wearing."

"Are you sure it's him?"

"I'm sending you a video." She fumbles with the phone for a few seconds. "I'll call you back." She hangs up, and I go to the bathroom and walk out into my living area. My phone beeps a text, and I hit play.

Henley is talking to two men. He's wearing jeans and a T-shirt and talking and laughing. He's looking all relaxed while drinking a Corona beer. A hot girl walks past, and his eyes drop to her behind. And then he says something to his friends before turning his attention back to her behind.

My heart sinks.

Wow . . .

My phone rings again. "Hi," I answer.

"See it?"

"Yep." I sigh.

"He's a fucking asshole," Chloe spits.

"Whatever, I don't care what he does." I act unruffled.

"Can I tell him what I think of him?"

"No," I snap. "Forget him like I have. I'm going back to bed."

"I'm sorry, babe."

"Don't be. I'm not," I lie.

"Breakfast in the morning?" she asks.

I can't believe this.

I really don't want to spend all day tomorrow listening to disco tales of Henley James, and seeing Chloe tomorrow will open the gates for that. "I can't. I'm seeing my parents," I tell her. "Catch up next week?"

"Sure, babe." She hesitates. "You okay?"

No.

"Of course I am." I smile sadly. "Bye."

I hang up, and with my heart in my throat, I torture myself and watch the video of Henley again.

The way he's all relaxed and happy. The way he looks at that girl's behind.

The way it makes me feel.

As reality sets in, an old proverb runs through my mind: *If something seems too good to be true, it usually is.*

Asshole.

We walk down the crowded footpath. "So then, I wait at home all night, and Chloe calls to tell me he's in a club at two a.m.," I continue on my rant to Liam.

"Why did you sleep with him? That's not like you to give it up on a first date," he replies, uninterested.

"Because he was the best date of my fucking life, that's why. And maybe I just wanted to be a bad girl for one night, you know?"

"No. I don't know."

"Because you're my brother, that's why. If you had the best date of your life, would you play Mr. Innocent to prove a point?"

He rolls his eyes. "Are we going in here?" He gestures to a restaurant.

Poor Liam. I made him come to lunch with me so I can vent all about my weekend from hell.

"Yeah." I sigh. "This will do." I push the heavy door open, and we wait in line to be served.

"How do you know it was even him in the club? Chloe was probably wearing beer goggles."

"Because she sent me a video of him."

"She took a video of him?" He screws up his face in disgust. "That's not creepy at all."

"Look." I bring up the video that I know by heart by now because I've watched it ten thousand times.

I hit play, and he watches the footage. "He's a douche, Juliet."

I exhale heavily. "It was the best night of my life."

"No, it wasn't. Look how he made you feel. He's a fucktard. Forget him."

I sigh heavily. "I guess."

"What's his name, anyway?"

"Henley."

"That's a weird name." He curls his lip in disgust. "Hen as in chicken?"

"Hen as in cock, I would say." I widen my eyes.

He winces. "Yuck, too much information."

As we wait, he watches the video on my phone again. He passes it back in disgust. "If I ever see him, I'll knock him out for you," he mutters dryly. "Deal?"

"Okay, deal." I smile, feeling a little bit better that my younger brother is also one of my best friends.

We get to the front of the line. "Hello, can we have a table for two, please?" I ask.

The hostess looks over the booking sheet. "I just have to get the table cleared. Can you wait for five minutes?"

"Sure."

She gestures to a waiting area. "Just wait in there, and I'll call you when it's ready. What's the name?"

"Juliet."

We make our way into the bar area to wait for our table, and I watch the video of Henley again. I don't know why I keep watching the damn thing. It's as if I'm hoping to find evidence that this actually isn't him.

If only.

Liam's hand comes up over my back, and I frown as I stare at my phone. "What are you doing?"

"Teaching him a lesson."

"What?" I glance up to see Henley approaching us.

What the fuck?

"Hello, Juliet." He fakes a smile. Looking like he just stepped off a runway, he's wearing a gray suit, white shirt, and blue tie. His dark hair is all just mussed to perfection, and *Oh my god, what the hell are you doing here?*

"Henley, hi."

Henley turns his attention to Liam. "Who are you?"

Liam smiles like an evil Cheshire cat. "Liam." He gestures to me. "Juliet's fiancé."

He did not just say that.

Henley's eyebrows shoot up in surprise as he puts his weight onto his back foot. His jaw flexes. "Fiancé?"

No, no, no.

29

No!

"That's right." Liam continues with his lies. "Do you know her well?"

Just shut the hell up!

Henley's eyes come to me, and he rolls his lips. Fury oozes out of him. "Perhaps not."

Please, earth, swallow me whole.

He glares at me, and I want to tell him this is all a lie, but what's the point? He's a douche and wouldn't care anyway.

"Have a nice life, Julietttt." He accentuates the *T* in my name. "With"—he looks Liam up and down and smirks as if amused—"your cute little fiancé."

Arrogance personified.

"Hey, what's that supposed to mean?" Liam asks as he acts dumb.

Henley brushes past and purposely miscalculates the distance between them. He bumps Liam with his shoulder so hard that he nearly goes flying over. He pushes the heavy door open and storms out.

Liam stares after him. "Interesting."

"Interesting?" I gasp. "Why the fuck would you say that? Now he thinks I'm a ho bag."

"It takes one to know one." He drops his shoulders as if pleased with himself. "He liked you."

"How can you tell?"

He smiles broadly, feeling very pleased with himself. "He was pissed."

"And this is funny because . . . ," I gasp, infuriated.

"He had his chance, and he blew it. Touché, fucker."

Chapter 3

"Congratulations." Tim the real estate agent smiles as he hands over the keys. "It's all yours."

"Thank you." I open the door, and we walk into the foyer. My parents and Liam are here to help celebrate this momentous occasion.

He looks around the old, dilapidated house. "Have fun renovating."

"I will." I beam. "Renovator's delight, remember?"

Tim chuckles at his own sales pitch. "I remember."

My grandmother, God rest her beautiful soul, left me and my brother a large inheritance each, and with my savings I have somehow snagged a house in the best neighborhood in Half Moon Bay.

This is my ideal suburb, but it was never even close to my price bracket. Somehow—and I'm guessing it was Grandma organizing this in heaven—the stars aligned.

I received her inheritance, and in the first week I was looking, this house came up.

It was a deceased's estate with no beneficiaries, so the will trustee made the call that it would be sold to the first person who made an offer, any offer. By some miracle, I was the first to look at it, I fell in love, and I was the first to make an offer.

I nearly fainted when they accepted it.

It's a total dump, but it's on a beautiful street. Well, it's not really a street. It's a cul-de-sac, Kingston Lane.

"Bye," Tim says as he walks down the front steps. "Call me if you need anything."

"I will. Thanks again. Bye."

I do a little jig on the spot in excitement. "Can you believe this?" I gasp.

My mom kisses me. "We're so happy for you, Jules." She grabs her phone from her bag. "Hold up your keys—I need a photo." I hold up my keys and smile goofily as my mom snaps away.

"It's bittersweet. I wish Gran was here."

"She's watching." Mom smiles. "I know she is."

"The worst house on the best street." My dad smiles. "You've bitten off a lot, that's for sure."

"I'm up to the challenge." I smile as I look around. "There's no rush. I have forever to do it."

The old house is clapboard and two stories. It's white with a green tin roof. It has a wraparound veranda and an overgrown yard. It's going to be a lot of hard work to bring it back to its original glory.

"And when does your puppy arrive?" Mom asks.

I do a little dance on the spot. "I pick him up from the shelter tomorrow. He's actually the most exciting thing about finally buying a house. I can have my own dog. And he's not a puppy, Mom. Remember, I adopted an older dog."

"But I thought you wanted a puppy."

"I did. But when I got there, he looked so sad and timid. He's the one for me."

"What are you going to call him?"

I shrug. "I don't know. I guess we'll work it out together once he gets here."

"What time does the moving truck arrive?" Dad asks.

I glance at my watch. "We have three hours."

Mom walks into the kitchen. "Let's get cleaning."

It's 11:00 p.m., and after the longest day in history, I trudge up the stairs.

Liam left a little earlier for a hot date. Lucky him.

"Good night, Jules," Dad calls from the spare room.

"Good night. Thanks for everything today."

He and Mom are staying so that I'm not alone on my first night here. I've only ever lived in apartments since moving away from home. If I'm being honest, being here in this big old house may be a little scary. That's one of the reasons I decided on getting an older dog. He can be my protector as well as my best friend.

I walk into my bedroom and look around. The walls are different colors, one green and one cream; the other two are a dusty pink.

Hideous.

The former owner did do a bit of a renovation at some point many years ago. An en suite bathroom was added to the master, although its brown tiles leave much to be desired. At least it's there, I guess.

I shower, throw my pajamas on, and turn off the light. When I go to close the blinds, I notice that the neighbor's upstairs bedroom window is in full view; I can see straight in. It's luxurious looking, with expensive furnishings. There's a four-poster bed with a couch at the end.

The bedroom looks huge.

Jeez.

"Swish." I smile. There's a giant artwork behind the bed, and I narrow my eyes to try and zoom in on it. I think it's an abstract painting of a naked woman?

Hmm . . .

A man walks into the room with a towel around his waist, and I quickly grab the cord to pull the blinds down. I don't want him to think I'm a Peeping Tom. I yank the cord, but nothing happens.

"Shit." I struggle with the cord, but it's stuck solid. I glance back up to see the guy is now in black briefs. He's pulling the blankets back on his bed.

"Fuck." I duck behind the wall. I don't want him to see me. I'll struggle with the cord after he closes his blinds.

I wait and wait . . . and wait. What the hell is he doing?

I peep around the corner and watch. And the man in the window walks over to close the blinds, and for the first time, I see his face.

My eyes widen.

No . . .

I quickly duck back behind the wall in horror. With my heart hammering hard in my chest, I peer back around the corner. This cannot be happening.

What are the chances?

It's that asshole bastard, Henley James.

3:00 a.m., the witching hour

I lie on my back and stare at the ceiling.

Fuck. Him.

How dare he ruin this for me?

Is it not enough that he's ruined sex for me forever?

34

Is it not enough that I compare every damn date I go on to that stupid fucking horrible, amazing, wonderful nightmare date that we went on?

I bet you he's married.

I bet you his wife is gorgeous and smart and probably a lawyer or something equally impressive.

She's probably going to prance around here every fucking Thursday in a little white tennis skirt.

With their two point five perfect children that go to a private school. She probably vacuums her car every Saturday and weeds the garden on Sunday.

Bakes pies and shit.

Ugh . . . I roll over, infuriated, and punch the pillow.

God, I wish I never met him.

And the worst part is, my mind still goes there. It lingers on that night when he was throwing me around in bed. The way we laughed at dinner, the way he kissed me.

The way he made me feel.

But worse than that, it lingers on how I wasn't enough for him.

And how badly it hurt.

A click sounds through the kitchen as the toast pops. I take it out and juggle it between my fingers. Ouch, that's hot. I put the scrambled eggs onto the plates. "Mom, Dad, breakfast is ready," I call.

They come down the stairs and sit at the makeshift card table in camp chairs. "This looks good." Dad smiles as he picks up his knife and fork before digging in.

After tossing and turning all night, I've decided I'm not going to let that horrid man next door spoil my new-house glow. He's nothing to me, and I don't care where he lives or how beautiful his wife is.

Fucker.

Our date never happened. That was a lifetime ago. I've moved on.

"Maybe I'll get a round table for the kitchen area," I think out loud. On the ground floor there is a foyer with a big, rickety timber staircase, a formal living room, and then a dining area, and in the back of the house is a big kitchen and informal living area. It's all horrible, of course. I can't wait to dig in and make it my own.

"Maybe a bench built into the corner would look good too," Mom says as she looks around.

"Maybe." I smile. "So many possibilities."

"I can't wait to see what you do with the place," Mom says as she begins to eat. "Are you sure you're going to be all right here on your own?"

"Yes. Go on your trip. You've had this booked for over a year." Mom and Dad are leaving for Europe tomorrow for their trip of a lifetime, four months of sightseeing. "I get my dog today, remember? We will be fine, just the two of us."

Mom exhales heavily. "I wish we could stay for a few more days. It just feels so . . . empty. You don't even have furniture for most of the place yet."

"Mom, I'm fine. My girlfriends are around, and if I need anything, Liam is here, and I have enough furniture to get by until the new stuff arrives. I came from a one-bedroom apartment, Mom. Of course this big old house looks empty right now."

"I guess," she agrees.

"Besides, I want to live here for a few weeks before I decide what I want. This house is different. I want to really get a feel for it and buy just the right things."

"What time do you pick up your dog?" Dad asks.

"As soon as you guys leave." I hunch my shoulders. "I'm more excited about getting him than I am about the house." I've wanted my own dog for years.

36

"It's not vicious, is it?" Mom says. "I always worry about grown dogs in shelters being vicious."

I roll my eyes. "He's not vicious. He's as sweet as pie."

"Did you think of a name for him?"

"Not yet; I'll see what suits him when he gets here." I can hardly wipe the goofy smile from my face. "I have to go by the store and get him some food on the way." My mind goes into overdrive. "I wonder what he likes to eat?"

Knock, knock sounds at the door.

We look at each other. "Who would that be?" Mom frowns.

"Not sure." I go to the front door and open it to see a little old lady. She's holding a tray with a red-checked tea towel over it.

"Welcome to the neighborhood." She smiles as she passes me the tray. "I saw the truck yesterday, and I made you some scones."

"Oh." I smile as I take them from her. "Thank you so much. How lovely. I'm Juliet."

"I'm Carol Higginbottom. I live just across the road." She points to a house across the cul-de-sac. It's a stately home with perfectly manicured gardens.

"Hi, Carol, it's lovely to meet you." Oh my gosh, so sweet.

Carol looks over my shoulder and into the house as if she's going to walk in. "Is your husband home?"

"No." I step in front of her. I don't want to invite her in until I get more things put away. It looks like a dumpster fire in there. "I'm not married."

"Oh." She looks at me in surprise. "Engaged then?"

"No. Single. I bought the house and will be living here alone." Her face falls. "Oh dear."

I fake a smile. Hmm, sweet Carol is annoying.

"What do you do, then . . . to be able to afford a home in this neighborhood?"

Scratch that, Carol is really fucking annoying.

"I'm a nurse."

"Oh . . ." Her eyes hold mine, and I can see her brain ticking at a million miles per minute. "I see."

"Who do you live with, Carol?"

"I'm a widow. Mervin passed a few years back."

"I'm sorry."

"Me too."

Actually, I can pick her brain a bit as we walk out onto my veranda. "Tell me about the street."

Carol smiles broadly. "It's a wonderful place to live, dear. It's like a big family."

"So, you know the neighbors, then?"

"Oh yes, we all know each other very well."

"Who lives where?" I ask.

"Well"—she points to her house—"I live in the white house. Next door to me is Blake Grayson; he's a doctor. Wild as they come, that one."

"Oh."

Chloe is going to fucking freak.

"Then you have Antony Deluca. He lives next door to you."

"Alone?" I ask.

"He has a different girlfriend every week." She rolls her eyes. "He's a lawyer and isn't home very much. He works on big fancy cases all over the state."

"Oh." I glance over to the gray house. A fancy lawyer, hey? Hmm.

"On the other side of me, in the cream house, is Ethel." Carol smiles. "She's elderly and a little frail. We all look out for her."

I smile. I have to admit, this does sound like a nice place to live.

"Then on the corner"—she points down the street to a huge house on the corner and rolls her eyes—"that's the military house. Best to avoid that one at all costs."

"The military house?" I frown.

"Six Navy SEALs live there together. I don't know, special ops or something."

My eyes linger down the road . . . my interest piqued.

"Sordid things happen in that house, dear."

"Really?" I bite my lip to hide my smile. Special-ops sordid things sound hot.

"Women coming and going at all hours. Real playboys, those ones." She leans in to lower her voice again. "I wouldn't be surprised if they're swingers."

"Oh . . ." I nod as my eyes roam over their house. "Are they married?"

"No." She frowns. "What makes you say that?"

"Swingers are married, aren't they?"

"No, no, dear, it just means that they have sex with a lot of people. Look it up on the Google."

The Google.

I bite my lip to hide my smile. Carol thinks she knows everything, and it is clear that she doesn't.

"Anyway," she continues, "they are huge and all muscly and go running and all types of crazy extreme activities."

My eyes linger on their house.

Interesting.

"They rent and don't really involve themselves with us. The boys don't like them much."

"The boys?"

"Oh, the men on this street are all tight. They hang out together."

"What men?"

"Well, next door to you on one side lives Henley James."

"What's he like?" I act clueless.

"Beautiful man." She leans in and lowers her voice. "Owns a huge engineering company, very successful."

"Is he?" I nod as I listen. "What's his wife like?"

"He's not married. Although every woman he meets falls madly in love with him."

Ugh . . .

"I see."

"And then in the white house on the other side of you is Bennet Stark."

"What's he like?"

"He's some IT whizzbang, develops apps or something." She shrugs. "It's all well over my head, but he's the bee's knees at what he does apparently. He's single too. Actually, I think he's got a girl-friend now. There's a strange car there at night sometimes."

"Oh, I see." I look around the small cul-de-sac. There seems to be a lot of men who live here. Chloe is going to be so jealous when she finds out that Blake Grayson is one of them.

"Rebecca and John are across the street. They are lovely too. They got married a few years ago."

"What do they do?"

"John is a surgeon, and Rebecca is a teacher."

"Sounds great." I smile, grateful for the intel. "Thanks for the rundown."

"I do hope you like scones, dear," Carol says as she walks down the front steps. I walk with her as we talk.

"I do. Thank you so much." I peek under the tea towel and see steam rising. "Oh, they're still hot." I smile in surprise as we arrive at my mailbox.

"No store-bought rubbish in my house, dear. I bet you're a good cook too."

"Sure am," I lie with a fake smile. Can't cook for shit, Carol, but whatever.

A black Range Rover pulls onto the street. "Here's Henley home now," Carol says.

Fuck.

He drives in and waves and parks in his driveway. His house is big and fancy looking.

He gets out of the car and waves. "Hi, Carol." He begins to walk into the house. "Lovely day." He walks toward his front door and stops on the spot.

He just realized who I am.

He turns back to us and frowns as his eyes lock on mine.

Shit.

"Come and meet our new neighbor," Carol calls.

He twists his lips as if angered and walks over with his hands in his fancy suit pockets. "We meet again."

Hearing his familiar sexy voice snaps the sanity band in my brain, and I just want to lash out and be a bitch.

"Sorry?" I smile sweetly as I pretend to forget him. I hold out my hand to shake his. "I'm Juliet. Nice to meet you."

He narrows his eyes in confusion as he shakes my hand. "Henley James."

"Juliet just moved in; I've made her some scones."

Henley's eyes stay fixed on mine, his face emotionless. "The best scones in the land, Carol."

Carol lets out an overexaggerated giggle. "Oh, Henley, you tease me so."

I inwardly roll my eyes as it becomes blazingly clear that Carol is one of those women who is in love with him.

"The owners must be renting this house out while they get a permit approved for the new build," Henley says.

You wish.

"No, Harry," I reply.

"Henley," he corrects me, unimpressed.

41

"I bought it."

"What?" He frowns. "What do you mean, *you* bought it?"

He means, How could I afford a house on this street? Judgy prick. I begin to hear my angry heartbeat in my ears. "What else could I mean, Harry? I bought the house."

"Henley," he spits through gritted teeth. "Don't call me Harry again." His eyes hold mine, and it's really hard not to burst out laughing. This forgetting-him plan is a hoot.

God, I'm brilliant.

"Nice to meet you," he lies before storming off. "Goodbye, Carol," he calls over his shoulder.

"Bye," Carol calls. "I'll make you some scones on Sunday, Henley."

"Not necessary." He waves his hand in the air and keeps walking.

Carol stares after him, perplexed. "He must be very busy. He's usually so warm and welcoming; he's never abrasive like that." She raises her eyebrows as she contemplates his reaction to me.

Only friendly on first dates when he wants to get his dick wet . . . asshole.

I'm infuriated just by seeing him again.

"Thanks for the scones." I smile. "It was lovely to meet you. I have to get going."

"Goodbye, Juliet."

I wave and walk back into my house and feel a little proud of myself as I close the door.

That went okay. I'll probably never run into him again. Maybe this won't be the disaster I thought it was going to be.

An hour later, I fold a T-shirt and throw it into Mom's suitcase as it lies on her bed. "Now remember," I tell her as I pack her things, "if anyone tries to grab you or you feel unsafe, call the tour guide immediately."

"I know."

"And if Dad gets too chatty with people, don't let him tell them all his details. You know he's an oversharer, and you can't trust everyone that you meet overseas. It isn't the same as home, Mom."

"Yes. Yes, I know." Mom rolls her eyes at my lecturing.

"And if Dad's ankle gives him trouble, it's okay to have a few rest days at the hotel."

"Oh, Juliet, stop worrying." She sighs.

I exhale heavily. With all the house stuff I've had going on, it's only just hitting me that my parents are traveling alone for the first time overseas. It's a little terrifying. "If anything medical happens, just call me, and I'm on the first plane."

"Yes, yes."

"Someone's at the door," my dad calls from the bathroom.

"Who would that be?" Mom asks.

"I think it's the delivery man." I throw the sweater into the case and bound down the stairs. I open the door to see Henley. "Oh," I stammer, taken aback. "Henry."

He stares at me deadpan.

"Yes?"

"If you call me by the wrong name again, there will be hell to pay."

"Sorry." Unable to help it, I smile. "Forgive me, but what was your name again?"

"You *actually* don't remember me?"

I wince as I act worried. "I'm so sorry, should I?"

He twists his lips, unimpressed.

"When did we meet?" I shrug. "Was it at work? I'm a nurse, so I meet a lot of people, and I'm terrible with faces."

He leans in. "I don't know what you are playing at by pretending not to know me," he whispers angrily, "but I do not appreciate you bombarding your way into my street."

"*Your* street?"

"That's right." His jaw tics as he glares at me.

"I mean, I do know the cul-de-sac is called Kingston Lane, but I didn't realize it had its very own king. How lucky we are."

"You are *not* funny," he snaps.

I so am.

"Please tell me what your problem is?" I ask impatiently.

"I think you know."

"I don't. You keep saying we met, but I have no idea where. So unless you are willing to tell me what the issue is, we have nothing to talk about."

"Don't shit me," he sneers. "I know you remember me. Don't play dumb."

I feel my temper rise. This man is an infuriating fucking pig.

"I'm not sure where we know each other from, but it has become very clear why I've chosen to forget you. Still practicing being an asshole, are you?"

"Not practicing." His furious eyes hold mine. "Perfected."

Good comeback.

"What do you want? Do you want me to congratulate you on becoming a perfected asshole?" I whisper angrily.

"I want you to move, that's what I want. Our street does not need someone like you living here."

"Tough shit, King Henley the Fucking Great, I'm not moving, and nobody judges me but me, so stay out of my way."

His eyes bulge. "You stay out of my way."

"No prize for seconds, dickhead. Don't copy my comeback."

"I swear to fucking god . . . ," he whispers angrily.

"Juliet." My father's voice rings out as the screen door opens. "Who is your friend?"

Crap.

Henley and I step back from each other. "Dad, this is my neighbor. He just stopped by to say hi."

This is awkward. I told my parents about my letdown of a date back then when it happened. And although I never told them his name, if Henley asks where my fiancé is, I'm screwed.

"Dad, meet Henley." I gesture to Henley. "Henley, meet my dad; Henley was just leaving," I blurt out in a rush.

Oh my god, leave.

Leave now.

"Hello." Dad smiles as he shakes his hand.

Henley fakes a smile. "Nice to meet you."

"Beautiful place you live in," Dad replies. "It's like heaven here."

Henley's eyes flick to me as if he's about to say something. "It was—is," Henley corrects himself.

"We're going to Europe tomorrow, the missus and I. Excited is an understatement," Dad continues.

"How long for?" Henley asks.

"Four months."

"Henley was just leaving, weren't you?" I widen my eyes as a buzz-off sign. "You really don't need to make me scones. Thank you for the offer, though."

He begins to walk down the four front steps.

"Henley," my dad calls.

Henley turns back. "Yes?"

"Keep an eye on her for me, will you?"

Henley's calculating eyes meet mine. "Shouldn't her husband be doing that?" he sneers sarcastically.

Kill me now!

Fucking Liam. I'm going to kill him.

"Juliet isn't married." Dad laughs. "Perhaps you have a friend to set her up with."

For the love of god. *Shut up, Dad.*

I open the door and gesture inside. "You really need to pack."

Get inside right now before I beat you to death with the front door mat.

"Goodbye, Henley. Nice to meet you," my dad calls.

Henley waves and continues walking back to his house. I watch his broad back as he disappears across the lawn.

"What a nice man," my dad calls loudly as he walks inside. Surely, Henley heard him.

He's not, Dad. Nowhere close.

"Just this way." The attendant leads me down a corridor.

"I'm so excited." I nearly dance along behind her. "I've been wanting this dog for forever."

"He's a beautiful dog. He's had all his shots and is ready to go."

We get to his enclosure, and he looks up at me. His eyes are sad, and my heart breaks. "Hey, you." I smile as I bend down. "What breed of dog is he again?"

"Not sure. Definitely a springer spaniel in there somewhere." She opens the gate, and he stands, unsure of what's about to happen.

He's brown and perfectly spotty. "And how old is he?"

"Judging by his teeth, we think around three. Although he could be a bit younger or older. He's not super old—put it that way."

"And how did he come to be in the shelter?"

"His owner died unexpectedly."

"Oh." My heart sinks. "Poor baby."

"Out you come, Barry," she says.

"Barry?" I frown.

"Yes, his name is Barry. Of course, you can change it if you want to."

"Did his last owner call him Barry, or did you just make that up since he's been here?"

"He's always been called Barry."

Oh, I don't really want to have a dog called Barry. I was thinking something more noble and cool.

Hmm, I'll have to think on this.

"He was an outside dog at his last home."

"But . . . does he like inside?" I ask.

"Show me a dog who doesn't." She puts the leash on him, and he tentatively walks out.

I hold my hand out for him to smell. "Hi." His tail gives a weak wag, and I smile. "Let's go home." I carefully lead him out the doors, and he looks back at the attendant as if to say *I'm allowed to leave?* We walk out to my car, and I help him climb into the back seat. He sits quietly, and I shut the door behind him. "You're a good boy." I smile at him in the rearview mirror. This is so wonderful to be able to do this. It doesn't get any better than this.

1:00 a.m.

"Woof, woof, woof" echoes through the entire neighborhood.

I wait.

"Woof, woof, woof."

I roll over in bed. "Fuck's sake, Barry."

Silence for a few moments.

Owoooooooooooooo.

47

"What the hell? He's howling like a werewolf now?" I flick back the blankets and march downstairs. I open the back door. "What?" I whisper angrily. "What do you want?"

Barry wags his tail, ready to play.

"Come inside. You're keeping the entire street awake."

He barrels into the house past me, and I close the door behind him. This has been going on for hours. He barks when he's left outside, and then I let him in. Five minutes later he barks to go back outside.

I have no idea what he wants or what to do.

I lie on the floor, exhausted, as Barry runs around in circles. Woofing at me to play, he jumps and nips at my hair. He picks up a ball and drops it next to my hand.

Oh god . . .

"It's not playtime," I murmur sleepily. He picks up the ball and drops it again.

I doze for a moment, and he goes to the back door and begins barking to go out.

"What are you doing?" I sigh in frustration. "I just let you in."

He begins to scratch on the back door to go out.

Hell, this was not in the brochure.

I get up and let him out, and he runs back out to the backyard all excited.

"Go. To. Sleep." I close the door and march back to the living room. There's no point even going back upstairs. I'm only coming down again in two minutes. I grab the throw and snuggle up on the floor with some cushions.

Bang, bang, bang.

I wake with a start.

Bang, bang, bang.

Huh? I sit up all disheveled. I fell asleep. Is someone banging on the door?

Owooooooooooooo, I hear from the backyard.

Crap, Barry is howling again.

I open the front door in a rush to see Henley standing at the door, wearing navy satin boxers. "Are you seriously this selfish?" he spits as he marches past me into my house.

"Huh?" I'm squinting as I try to focus my eyes. "What?"

"Your dog is keeping the entire neighborhood awake," he spits angrily.

Owooooooooooooo, the werewolf cries from the backyard.

"I'm so sorry," I stammer. "He's new and just settling in. I just got him today."

"He's a literal fucking nightmare."

Owooooooooooooo, sounds the werewolf.

Henley marches over and opens the back door in a rush. "Shut. Up!" he yells so loudly that it could be heard from the next neighborhood.

Barry quiets for a moment and then barks again.

Henley marches out into my backyard. "Listen, you," he yells as he points to Barry's kennel. "Get in your bed, and you go to sleep. Right. Now."

Barry walks into his kennel and curls up.

Henley marches back into my house and slams the door.

"You are taking that dog back to wherever he came from tomorrow," he demands.

This man is the most self-entitled asshole of all time. I scratch my head and feel my hair standing on end.

"Do you understand?" His eyes drop down my body, and his eyebrow rises. "And what the fuck are you wearing?"

Chapter 4

I glance down at myself and cringe. What *am* I wearing? "Well . . . obviously . . ." I search for something to say, some divine intervention that offers an excuse for me. I glance up at his muscular body in only boxer shorts, and I hold my hands up toward his body. Of course he looks photoshopped. "What are *you* wearing is the question," I splutter.

He puts his hands on his hips in a silent dare. "Pajamas."

"Well . . ." I'm tongue tied and can't find the right words. Why the hell does this guy make me so dumb? "How dare you come over here in the middle of the night and start ordering me around half-naked in your pajamas. That is not how this works, Henley. I do *not* know who you think you are, but I can assure you that you have no say whatsoever in anything that goes on in this house."

His demeanor changes, and he steps forward, causing me to take a step back.

His closeness causes my heart to somersault in my chest.

"I came over here to control your mutt."

"The control of my mutt is none of your concern, Mr. James."

He steps forward again, his eyes darkening. I instinctively step back until I am cornered against my fridge.

"Your *mutt* is all of my concern."

How does he make the word *mutt* sound hot?

I swallow the lump in my throat as we stare at each other, the air swirling between us.

He picks up a piece of my hair and holds it between his fingers. His breath tickles my skin. "Your pajamas are ridiculous."

"I like them," I spit. That's a lie. I want to die a thousand deaths right now.

Without another word, he turns and leaves through the front door. I stare at the back of it as it closes behind him.

My heart is beating hard in my chest. I glance down at my Minnie Mouse underwear. "Fuck you, Minnie."

"Oh my fucking god, I cannot believe Blake Grayson lives here," Chloe whispers as she peers through the curtains. "This street is the mother ship of orgasms. The holy grail, even."

I roll my eyes, unimpressed. "They're dickheads. All men are giant dickheads."

"That's exactly what I'm after, so it's a win-win," she replies as she keeps up her spying. "Who put that putting green there, anyway?"

"Ethel's husband was a greenkeeper. Apparently, he loved golf, so he turned the center of the cul-de-sac into a putting green, put a grill over there with a table and chairs. He died, but everyone else uses the park area he created now."

"So they all just hang out in the middle of the street? This is seriously brilliant. We can see what they do right from your window. Pole position."

"Ugh, I really didn't think this through."

"Okay, so give me the rundown," she says as she keeps peeking through the window. "Who's who?"

I get up and join her. The men are all sitting at the table and chairs, and a few are putting golf balls.

"So there's Henley putting the golf ball, and obviously Blake Grayson is beside him."

My eyes linger on the shoulder muscles twitching beneath Henley's shirt as he putts the ball.

Flipping hell . . .

"Fuck, Blake's hot," she murmurs, her eyes glued to them. "I hope he takes his shirt off."

"Why would he take his shirt off?" I frown.

"Because he's hot from all the golfing." She widens her eyes as if I'm stupid.

Seriously?

"Then there's some lawyer guy, but I forget his name. I haven't seen him yet," I continue. "And I don't know, but I'm assuming that one of the guys sitting at the table is my next-door neighbor on the other side, Antony or something." I shrug. "And beside him is . . ." I shrug. "I don't know. I haven't met the others yet."

"Well, get out there."

"What?"

"Let's go out there and meet them."

"Let's not. I've already had a fight with King Henley the Great, and I do not want a rematch."

We continue to spy out the window.

"This is excellent viewing," Chloe whispers, her eyes glued to the street. "This is my new seat, twenty-four seven. Got any popcorn?"

Nighttime, beholder of secrets. Instigator of sins.

I stand in the shadows of my bedroom. My light is off; his bedside lamps are on.

Front-row seats at the best show in town.

I have a new hobby, one that I'm not proud of. Spying on someone I shouldn't: the self-proclaimed God's gift to women, Henley James.

The golfing was bad enough, but this is taking it up a notch.

I shouldn't be doing it. I am well aware of how creepy it is, especially since we hate each other, but somehow that makes it so much more delicious.

A wicked temptation.

A drug that I shouldn't want, and I don't . . . I swear I don't.

Henley is walking around in his bedroom wearing only a towel. He leaves his blinds open, and I'm beginning to wonder if he's purposely showing me what he's got. What he thinks I'm missing out on. Baiting me to think deviant things about him while I'm alone in bed.

Not that I ever would, of course.

I bite my thumbnail as my eyes roam over his cut muscles. Tanned broad back and a scattering of hair on his chest and a thin trail that disappears down under his towel.

Damn it, why does he have to be so great in bed?

Stop it.

There is nothing about him to like, yet I find myself going over our little kitchen exchange the other night. On some level I kind of wish he ripped off my Minnie Mouse panties and bent me over the counter.

He pulls back the blankets, and I hold my breath; he drops the towel, and I get a bird's-eye view of his perfect ass. My stomach flutters.

There it is.

He climbs into bed and picks up a book from the side table. He puts his glasses on and sits up against his grand headboard.

What's he reading?

I wish I had binoculars.

I smile at the thought, and after one long last look through the window, I climb into bed and snuggle into my pillow. "Good night, Barry," I say as I look over at my housemate.

But he doesn't hear me; Barry's fast asleep.

"Good morning." I smile as I walk into the nurses' station.

"Hey, you're back." Leonie smiles as she hands me the huge stack of patient files. "How's the big homeowner doing?"

"Great." I laugh. Today is my first shift back at work after a week off. "Thanks for letting me do day shift for the next few weeks. My new dog is still settling in, and I can't leave him at night just yet." I open the first folder and begin to read the notes.

"What's his name?" Karen asks.

"My dog?" I move to the second folder. "Barry."

"Barry?" Warren frowns. "Why the hell would you call your dog Barry?"

"I didn't. He came with it."

"So . . . tell us all about your house. We've been dying for updates," Leonie puts in.

"Well." I shrug. "The house is terrible, but the street is nice."

"And the neighbors?"

"Are . . . great."

Warren turns to the computer, and Leonie widens her eyes at me behind his back.

"What?" I mouth.

She scribbles on some paper.

Karen told me that Warren is going to ask you out on a date today.

My eyes widen. Shit. I have felt him being super friendly for a while now, and I really don't know how to handle it because I treasure our friendship. We work together nearly every shift; it's just going to be awkward between us if he asks me out. Renee scribbles another note.

Tell him that you have a boyfriend or something.

"Are you kidding me?" I mouth.

Before he asks you out or it's going to be fucking awkward.

True.

"I have a garden, and my dog is great. I really think I'm going to like it there." I ramble on.

"I'm really looking forward to Deb's bachelorette party on Saturday," Leonie says.

"Me too," I reply. Not really. There's that small problem of Barry being home alone. It will be fine; he'll be settled in by then, surely.

"So what made you buy in that area?" Warren asks. "It's a fair way from your old place."

Um. I try to think on my feet. I need to buy some time. "I got back with my ex," I lie.

Warren looks up from the computer, horrified. "What?" He glances between Renee and me. "Since when?"

"Well . . ." I pause. Oh no, please don't question this. I can't lie for shit.

Leonie cuts in. "Ages ago. He lives next door, doesn't he? You found the property while you were staying at his house."

What?

That is the worst lie of all time.

"Yeah." I shrug. "So . . . it just made sense . . . to stay in the area."

Jeez.

Warren nods and fakes a smile. "Sounds great."

I rub Warren's shoulder, feeling guilty for lying, but he needs to trust me on this one. This is better for us. "Let's get to work, buddy. I missed our friendship while I was away."

"I missed you too." Warren drags himself off the chair. "Let's go."

Warren walks out of the room, and Leonie wipes her forehead. Phew, that was close.

"You ready to go, big boy?"

Barry runs to the front door, his tail wagging wildly. We've made our own little morning routine, and it seems to be going great.

Turns out that if Barry goes for a run in the morning, then he's quite content for me to go to work while he lies in the sun in the backyard.

Taking care of this damn dog is like having a baby.

I mean, I knew dogs were hard work, but I didn't realize he would be quite such a handful.

I put his leash on and walk out the front door. There's a method to my madness. I've worked out that if I leave at exactly 5:40 a.m., I happen to run into the asshole engineer from next door as he leaves for work.

I really need to get ahold of myself. My spying is turning into a full-time occupation, and I really don't know why because I don't even like him.

It's just that it would be a lot easier to ignore him if he wasn't so easy on the eyes . . . and the memory.

We walk down the front sidewalk, and Carol is watering her garden with the hose. "Morning, Juliet," she calls.

"Good morning, Carol." I beam. "Beautiful day, isn't it?"

"It sure is. You hitting the pavement again this morning, dear?"

"Uh-huh."

"Run for me, too, will you?"

I laugh and stretch my legs as I hold on to my mailbox. Honestly, this cul-de-sac is like living in a dream. I'm basically a Stepford wife, but just without the husband and the being-rich-and-perfect part.

Right on cue, Henley's front door opens, and he walks out in his suit, navy blue today. He glances up and waves to Carol and me. And like the dirty perverts we are, we both wave back.

He puts his briefcase into the back seat of his Range Rover and answers his phone. He stands beside his car as he talks to someone, and my eyes linger over the fine specimen. Perfect posture, six foot four, dark hair, square jaw, and built like a well-oiled machine.

A sex machine.

And I should know, because I see him near naked every night.

I think he secretly wants me to look, and I mean, if I was half as hot as him, I would leave my blinds open too. Hell, I would just walk around naked all the time.

Ugh . . . get a grip, Juliet.

He's a giant dickhead . . . remember?

He keeps talking on the phone, and he needs to hurry up and go, or else I'll have to start running in front of him. That's awkward. What will I look like from behind? Usually, I only catch a quick glimpse of him, and then he drives away.

I keep stretching, trying to bide my time.

Drive away now . . . go on. Get in your car, and drive away.

I glance back over to him as he talks on the phone. The sleeves on his jacket are hitched up a little, and I can see his expensive chunky watch. I don't know what kind of watch that is, but it probably costs more than my car.

Damn it, I can't loiter any longer. It's so obvious what I'm doing. Here goes nothing. "Let's go, buddy." I begin to jog with my trusty friend beside me, trying my hardest to look perky. I get fifty yards up the road and am about to collapse. *Drive past already. I can't keep up the pace for this long.*

As I approach the military house, the front door opens. A big buff guy with a crew cut appears with two girls.

He kisses one girl and then turns and kisses the other. Carol was right; they *are* gangbangers.

Oh . . .

I keep running past, fascinated.

How exotic . . . my mind boggles. How does that work? Does he finish one off completely and then move on to the other, or do they keep swapping the entire time? I think on this scenario for a moment. I don't think I would like to share with another girl; that's not hot to me. I would want to be the one with two men.

Barry suddenly cuts across in front of me. I stumble and fall and just catch myself in the nick of time in the most unladylike of ways.

The black Range Rover pulls up beside me, and the passenger-side window comes down. "What happened, Juliet, distracted? Can't keep your eyes on the road?" Henley asks as he raises his brow, and I don't know if he's being playful or judgy.

"Just keeping an eye on things around here, Mr. James," I reply as I keep running.

"And as the newest member of Carol's neighborhood watch program, what have you worked out?" he asks.

"That the military house is definitely one to watch."

Mischief flashes across his face as he drives along at a slow pace beside me. "I thought you would run faster than this."

You thought wrong.

"Is critiquing elite athletes a hobby for you?" I puff. *Please drive away. I'm about to go into cardiac arrest.*

"Only the clumsy ones." He smirks.

How could a smirk be gorgeous?

Get a grip, Juliet.

He's a jerk.

"On your way, then." I try not to puff.

Dying . . . no air.

His car stays slow with me. "Am I annoying you?"

Drive away, motherfucker!

"Yes, and you're very good at it," I puff. "Go and do whatever it is that you do."

He smiles as if his mission has been accomplished. "Have a good day." He drives off, and I watch his fancy car as it disappears around the corner. I stop and put my hands on my knees while I gasp for air.

Maybe he's being nice to me because he feels sorry for me because of my pajamas.

I get a vision of myself in Minnie Mouse underwear and what he must think of me, and I pant in disgust.

"Keep running, bitch."

Everyone wearing white at a bachelorette party.

What next, a black wedding?

I step back to look at myself in the full-length mirror. "Hmm."

I turn and look at my behind. This dress is a lot shorter than I would usually wear.

My minidress is fitted and strapless, and I'm wearing nude stilettos with a clutch in the same color. I'm fake tanned, my blonde hair is down and full, and my makeup is trying to be sexy.

"Not bad."

I'm going to let my hair down tonight, have fun with the girls, maybe dance with someone to take my mind off everything. And by everything, I mean my out-of-bounds twat-face next-door neighbor Henley James.

That damn man is distracting.

I've been in my house for over two weeks now, and instead of painting and planning my renovations, all I'm doing is plotting and spying . . . on him.

It's counterproductive and getting really annoying.

I get Barry's huge bone out of the fridge and take it out back. "This should keep you busy," I tell him. He just looks up at me, completely uninterested in my gift.

"You eat it," I tell him.

He ignores it.

I go to walk back inside, and he tries to follow me. "No, you be a good boy and amuse yourself tonight. Momma needs a night out."

He immediately begins to bark and scratch on the door to be let in.

"No," I tell him.

"Woof, woof, woof," he carries on.

"Seriously." I glance at my watch. "I have to go." I walk away from the back door. Maybe if he can't see me, he'll calm down. He's quite happy to stay outside if I'm home.

I reapply my lipstick to the sound of him barking in the distance.

Fuck's sake.

I don't want Henley to go postal again.

"Barry, stop it."

I hold the cards in my hand and take a drag of my cigar. My eyes flick around the table.

Poker night.

And I am kicking their asses.

Blake puts down a stack of chips. "I'll raise you fifty."

I narrow my eyes. "You sure about that?"

"Positive."

"Looks like you boys are making another deposit into the bank of Henley James." I smirk.

Blake holds the cigar between his teeth as he looks through his hand. "That bank is fucking corrupted." He throws his cards down.

I chuckle. "What about you, soft cock?" I ask Ant.

"Fuck off," Ant mutters, deep in concentration, a pen strategically placed behind his ear. "Hold."

"Full house." I smirk as I lay the cards down.

The table erupts. "Fuck off," they all cry. "You are one hundred percent cheating."

I laugh as I begin to shuffle the cards.

A knock sounds at the door.

"That's the pizza," I say. We all throw twenty dollars onto the table, and Blake goes to answer the door.

"Who wants to double the stakes?" I smirk as I look around the table.

"Triple them," Antony says.

I laugh as I lean back on my chair. "Begging to be bent over again, I see."

"Well, hello there," we hear Blake say in his trying-to-be sexy voice. "Who are you?"

"Is Henley home?" I hear Juliet's voice, and I glance up to see her dressed in white and looking like Aphrodite herself.

Next minute I'm standing at the door. "Juliet." My eyes drop down her tanned and muscular legs, and I imagine them around my ears.

I feel myself twinge with arousal.

Hmm.

"Sorry to interrupt," she says.

Suddenly all the boys are standing behind me, waiting to be introduced.

Fuck off.

"Hi, I'm Bennet." He steps forward and shakes her hand. "It is *great* to meet you."

I stare at him deadpan. *Don't even think about it.*

"Hello." She smiles. "I'm Juliet." She points to her house with her thumb. "I just moved in next door."

"That's great," Antony says in an overexaggerated way. "We are neighbors. Excellent."

I give him a swift elbow to the ribs.

"I'm Blake." He shakes her hand and turns her so that her back is facing me. "You look fabulous, by the way. White really sets off your eyes."

"Oh . . . ," she says, embarrassed. "Thanks, I guess."

I step behind her and slice my finger across my throat at him.

"Juliet, come inside and play cards with us."

"She's here to see me," I snap. At least she better be. I lead her down my front steps and away from the animals in the zoo.

"So sorry to barge in," she says.

"No problem." I concentrate on keeping my eyes on her face. I remember those great tits.

They bounce . . .

"I'm heading out tonight, and I just wanted to warn you that I have a problem with Barry," she replies.

"Who's Barry?"

"My dog. You know, the one you hate."

I screw up my face. "You named your dog Barry?"

"He came with the name. Anyway, I have a date tonight, and . . ."

She's going on a date . . . looking like that?

Owoooooooooooo. The dog howls from next door, and I instantly feel my hackles rise.

"Has there ever been a worse sound than that?" I ask her.

"He just doesn't like me going out."

That makes two of us.

"I'm not babysitting for you. I can't help it if your dog is a wimp, Juliet. What were you thinking getting a mutt named Barry, anyway?"

"I know . . . but"—she hunches her shoulders up and tries to be cute—"if you could just—" She holds out a piece of paper with a phone number on it.

"Call the pound to come and take it back?" I reply dryly.

"No," she snaps. "He will calm down when I leave. I'm sure of it."

"And if he doesn't?"

"Call me and I'll come home."

Owoooooooooooo, cries the wimpy dog over the fence.

Hmm . . . I take the paper from her. "You better come straight home if I call because I am not listening to that carry on all night."

"You won't even hear him; you're playing cards with your friends."

"I'll be bored of them soon."

"Fuck off," I hear the chorus of them all yell inside, and I roll my eyes. Of course they're listening.

"So, if he doesn't calm down, you'll call me?"

"This is a major inconvenience."

"Please?" She does a jig on the spot.

I exhale heavily. "I guess I'll have to. I don't want the entire street disrupted."

"Thanks."

My eyes hold hers. "Have a good night."

Not too good.

"You too."

A car pulls up. "That's my Uber. See you later. Thanks." She turns and walks away, and I watch her sexy little ass wiggle as she walks.

Hmm . . .

Infuriating.

I walk back inside to find the boys all standing at the window, peering out through the curtains at her.

"Holy fuck, she's hot," Blake gasps. "Like real fucking hot."

"Eyes off," I snap as I sit back down at the card table.

"What does she do?" Bennet asks.

"She's a nurse."

"A nurse," Bennet gasps. "Oh fuck, she can give me a sponge bath anytime."

"There isn't enough soap for your dirty dick," I mutter as I shuffle the cards.

"What hospital?" Blake asks. "I've never seen her before."

"I'm not sure."

"The bank of Juliet is getting a deposit from me very soon," Bennet says.

"Not happening." I begin to deal the cards.

"Give me one good reason."

"Because she doesn't take deposits from the bank of tiny cock."

They laugh.

"And besides." I pick up my cards and rearrange them in my hand. "I already have an account open at the bank of Juliet."

"What?" They all gasp. "You do not."

I smile as I pick up my cigar.

"Details, we want the details."

"A gentleman never tells."

"True, but you're not a gentleman."

I smile as I stare at my cards. My mind wanders to the delectable Miss Drinkwater. "Double or nothing."

Juliet

The music is loud, and I dance in a circle with the girls. I am tipsy, tipsier than tipsy. The cocktails are going down way too easy tonight, and I'm having the best time.

"Bathroom?" Leonie shouts.

I nod, and she grabs my hand and leads me through the club to the bathroom. I stumble in and sit down as the stall begins to spin. Oh man . . . no more for me.

I take out my phone and see a missed call.

"Whose number is this?" I call to Leonie in the stall next to me.

"Huh? What number?"

I click on the number, and it calls it back.

"Took your time," a deep voice snaps.

"Is that you, Harry?" I pretend to forget his name.

"Don't push your luck, Juliet. I'm on the verge of poisoning your dog."

His grumpiness makes me giggle. "Is Barry being bad?"

"What do you think?"

I smile. "On my way."

"Hurry up." The phone goes dead.

I stand and pull my dress down. "I've got to go home," I call to Leonie.

"Why?"

"Because Harry is going to poison Barry," I call.

"Huh? Who's Barry?"

"My dog."

"Who's Harry?"

"My neighbor who is actually not named Harry, but it's fun to call him Harry."

"I'm so confused right now," some random girl calls from the stall on the other side of me.

"That makes two of us," calls Leonie.

I giggle. "Is anyone else's stall spinning?" I ask.

"Yes," everyone cries in unison.

I hug the girls goodbye and totter to the front door and call an Uber as the ground moves beneath me.

Oh man . . .

The car pulls up. "Thank you." I open the door and put one leg out and then the other.

How the hell did I get so tipsy?

The cul-de-sac is quiet, not a peep to be heard. I look up at Henley's house, and I smile. I imagine going inside and surprising him with my very own peep show.

"You have a good night," I tell the Uber driver.

"You too."

"Don't pick up any drunk and disorderly people," I tell him. "There are some real troublemakers out there."

He smiles. "Are you all right to get out on your own?"

Boy, I'm so tipsy.

"I am. Thank you for driving me home." I smile goofily. "I had fun."

"This isn't a fucking date, Juliet," Henley's voice growls.

Huh?

He grabs my arm and pulls me from the car, and I come face to face with Mr. Holy Hotness himself.

"Oh." *How convenient.* "It's you."

Chapter 5

Henley

"Go inside and control your mutt."

Juliet smiles up at me all sexy-like. "Stop saying *mutt* like that."

I twist my lips. "I'll say *muttt*"—I accentuate the *T*—"any way I want to."

"Hmm." She smiles. "Always so bossy, Mr. James."

You have no idea.

She sways on her feet. She's really quite inebriated. "You're drunk."

"Am I?"

"Do you make a habit of offering yourself to seedy Uber drivers?"

She giggles and turns toward her house. She bends and slips her stilettos off. I watch her ass in that dress as she does. "Are you jealous, Henley?"

As fuck.

"Go inside," I warn her.

"Or what?" she teases.

Get bent over your letterbox, that's what.

"Don't play with me, Juliet."

She turns back toward me and smiles sexily as she bites her bottom lip. Our eyes are locked, and she walks back to me. We come face to face.

Her perfume surrounds me. My cock twitches in appreciation at her close proximity.

Don't even think about it.

"Henley," she whispers.

My eyes drop to her lips. "Yes."

"If I was playing with you, I would tell you something sordid."

"Such as?"

The air crackles between us.

She leans in close and puts her mouth to my ear. "I haven't had sex in eight months," she breathes.

I inhale sharply. Damn it, tell me anything but that.

Throb, throb, throb . . .

I hear the blood rushing from all over my body to fill my cock.

This isn't good. Abort mission.

I get a vision of her riding me, good and deep, her perfect tits bouncing as they do. Eight months to catch up on. She'd be fucking fire.

She's an adultering witch, remember?

Stop it.

I step back from her. "You should probably tell someone who cares. Do you want me to call the Uber driver back?"

She smirks. "Maybe I do."

"Get inside." I point to her house.

Before I do unspeakable things to you . . . or murder an overhelpful Uber driver.

"So bossy, Mr. James."

"You have no idea."

Her eyes hold mine, and I know she's imagining the exact same thing as me.

Fuck.

Why is she so hot?

Last time we had sex, she changed my fucking DNA. There is no way in hell I'm doing that again.

"Go inside," I demand.

She smiles up at me all sexy-like, and damn it, I just want to kiss her.

"Go inside right now, Juliet," I growl as I struggle with the last inch of control. "And shut your fucking dog up."

She shrugs. "Okay." She turns and walks into her house and gives me a wave with her fingertips before closing the door.

I stare at the door. My cock is rock hard, and fuck's sake, I do not need this temptation living right next fucking door.

I march into my house and up to the bedroom. I open my side drawer and take out the lube.

A man's got to do what a man's got to do.

Juliet

The sun is shining, and I am weeding the garden next to my front steps. The perfect Saturday afternoon.

Time to focus.

No more thinking about the world's biggest prick. I've been overanalyzing everything. He's been so rude this week, hasn't even waved in the mornings when he drove past. In fact, he glares at me as if I am his mortal enemy.

I'm living in a world of regret for possibly being flirty last weekend, although I'm not entirely sure. I think I told him I haven't had sex for a long time, or maybe it was a nightmare. Either way, I'm never drinking again.

He hates me, which is fine with me, because I hate him more.

I'm going to concentrate on the important things, like renovating my house.

First step, this garden.

I hear Carol's voice. "Hello, Juliet."

I glance up. "Hi."

I keep weeding. *Go away, Carol, I am so not in the mood.*

"Did you hear that Ethel's daughter is coming to live with her?"

"Is she?" I reply, but my mind is off on a tangent.

"She's coming to seduce Henley, if you ask me."

"Wait, what?" I look up at her. "Who is coming to seduce Henley?" I ask, suddenly interested in the conversation.

"Oh, Ethel's daughter, Taryn. She's always had her eye on him, that one. And now that her marriage has broken up, of course this is the first place she comes."

"What's she like?"

"Gorgeous." She widens her eyes. "Real supermodel material."

Fucking great.

I begin to dig with vigor. I don't care. *He's nothing to me,* I think as Carol walks off.

Poof to him.

He's the gift that keeps on giving. Dreaming about having sex with him is bad enough; watching him actually do it with everybody else is going to be a frigging nightmare.

I need to get a boyfriend, and I need to get one quick.

A procession of cars pulls up and parks out front. And I look up to see all my work friends. A heap of them.

Oh no.

"What are you all doing here?" I gasp.

"Surprise!" they all call. Some are carrying plants; others are carrying platters of food or bottles of wine. "It's a surprise housewarming."

"What?"

Oh god, no.

"Great," I lie. This is the very last thing I want to do today.

Chloe told me she was bringing over her mother to visit this afternoon. I had no idea that they planned this.

"Come in, come in." I stand. "I look a wreck."

Chloe kisses my cheek. "Happy housewarming, babe."

I put my arm around her as we walk inside. "I'm going to kill you—you know that, don't you?" I mutter under my breath.

"Totally."

Henley

I rub the chamois over the trunk of my car as I finish drying the last of it off.

A loud burst of laughter comes from the front porch of Juliet's house, and I glance over.

What's going on over there?

She better not think I'll be putting up with another Saturday night of her noisy-dog shenanigans.

My mind goes back to last weekend and her little white dress.

It's the only thing I *can* think about.

I rub the car trunk so hard the paint nearly peels off.

She's nothing but a pain in my ass. Why she would have the audacity to move here is beyond me. I mean, what's she playing at? Who does she think she is?

I keep drying my car at double speed.

Kingston Lane is ruined forever.

Unbelievable.

I rub the trunk harder.

I feel my phone vibrate in my pocket, and the number comes up.

Vanessa.

Hmm. "Hi." I smirk.

"Hey, you," a seductive voice purrs down the line.

"Whatcha doin'?" I smile.

I love hearing from this woman. She never demands a relationship. Uncomplicated, hot, and doesn't have an annoying dog or live next door.

"I'm working until nine, but maybe I'll swing by tonight on my way home? I haven't seen you in a while," she replies.

If anyone can fix my mood, Vanessa can. "Sounds good." I smile. "See you then."

"I'll look forward to it."

I stuff my phone back in my pocket and get back to work.

"Hi," a man's voice sounds from my driveway.

"Hello," I say. "Can I help you?"

"Yes." He smiles and holds his hand out to shake mine. "I'm Warren."

"Henley." I frown. Do I know this guy?

"I'm Juliet's friend," he says. He's a good-looking blond guy, around my age, early thirties. "I'm just visiting her next door and wanted to come over and meet you."

Why?

"Okay."

"I know that you and her are together now," he continues.

I frown. "Excuse me?"

"She told me all about you and how her boyfriend lives next door."

"She did?" I raise my eyebrows in surprise. "Did she?" I rub my car as I think of something to say. "So she told you this because . . . I'm guessing you asked her out?"

"I was going to." He shrugs sadly. "But she told me about you and her first."

I inwardly roll my eyes. Of course she did. Uses me as a scapegoat for rejecting this poor pathetic bastard.

This woman is the living end.

"I just want to make sure you know how special she is." He shrugs.

"She's definitely special, all right." I smile through gritted teeth.

Especially fucking annoying.

I widen my eyes as I keep drying the car.

Unbelievable.

"Look after her, hey?" he asks.

I fake a smile. "I will. Thanks for coming over. Nice to meet you, Warren."

Go home, loser.

"Goodbye," he says. I watch him walk back to Juliet's house as smoke begins to steam from my ears.

I sit in the golf garden in the middle of the cul-de-sac while the boys play cards and have a few beers. I'm too angry to play.

"What's up with you?" Blake asks.

"Nothing." I sip my beer, distracted by the laughter coming from Juliet's house.

What's so fucking funny in there, anyway?

"Please tell me you've nailed Juliet again?"

I roll my eyes. "No, I have not nailed Juliet again, because *she* is my neighbor. And everyone in the civilized world knows you do not give the bone to your neighbor." I sip my beer, disgusted.

"I don't see the problem; we all fucked our neighbors in college," Bennet replies.

"It was a frat house," I mutter dryly. "And we were completely out of control."

"Well, if you're not going to make a move . . ."

"Forget it," I snap. "She's off the table."

"But if she isn't on your table?"

"She isn't on yours either." I glare at him. "Last warning."

"Fucking hell, calm down," Blake scoffs. "What's the issue with this girl, anyway?"

I screw up my face in disgust at this conversation. "Nothing."

We sit for a few minutes in silence.

"I have a situation with her," I eventually reply.

"Like what?"

"We've met before."

"When?"

"We went on a date once."

"And?"

"And she was the girl who fucked my brains out, and then I saw her with her fiancé two days later."

Bennet's eyes light up. "This is the girl?"

"You're fucking joking me."

"Oh . . . she just got a lot hotter." Blake smiles darkly. "I like them slutty. I especially like giving them what their boring partners can't." He pumps his hips. "Show them what they're missing."

I roll my eyes. "Or dodging the bullet."

"No . . . ," Bennet scoffs. "That can't be her. Juliet is all sweet and innocent."

"Is she really, though?" I narrow my eyes. "That's the million-dollar question."

"Happy to find out for you." Bennet winks. "Do some market research."

"Fuck. Off," I spit. "I'm going to knock you out in a minute."

Bennet frowns. "I'm confused. What's the problem? So she lives next door, so what?"

"The problem is," I whisper angrily, "that I don't want her but I can't stop thinking about her, and Vanessa came over this weekend, and I couldn't get the fucking job done. Ended up telling her I had a migraine."

They both frown.

"And Juliet the pain in my neck lives next door to me, and I have to look at her sexy little ass run up and down my street and listen to her dumb dog bark all fucking day, and all I want to do is bend her over my car and give her what for."

I drag my hand down my face in disgust.

"Hmm." We fall silent.

"And now it gets worse. Her dumb friend just came over and warned me to look after her, seeing we are dating now."

"Huh?"

"She lied to him and told him I was her boyfriend so she didn't have to go out with him. This woman is a manipulative, venomous, cheating witch."

"Who you should totally fuck."

"Exactly." I sip my beer.

"So what are you going to do?" Bennet asks.

I think for a moment. "The only thing I can do."

"Which is?"

I sip my beer. "I'm going to teach her a lesson."

"With your dick?"

"Not with my dick," I scoff in disgust.

A roar of laughter comes from Juliet's house, and I look in as a new plan rolls around in my head. "Maybe Juliet's boyfriend should crash her party."

"You wouldn't."

I smirk. "Watch me."

Juliet

It's just getting dark, and my visitors are making themselves at home. Some are in the backyard playing with Barry. Some are on the front veranda. Hopefully all are leaving soon.

I'm in the kitchen making tea when the front door opens. "Where's my girl?" a deep voice calls out.

Huh?

I peek around the corner and see Henley standing in my living area. The room falls instantly silent as everyone stares at the god.

What's happening right now?

"Just had a good old chat with Warren." He winks sarcastically.
Oh no.

He walks into the kitchen and takes me roughly into his arms in front of everyone. "Thought I'd better come over and see how my *girlfriend's* doing."

Aah!

He bends me over backward in a dramatic fashion and looks down at me.

"It's so good to see you, sweetheart," he sneers.

My eyes widen at his sarcastic tone, the hatred for me dripping from his every pore.

Dear god.

Chapter 6

"Henley," I gasp. "What are you—"

He cuts me off with a kiss. His lips linger over mine, and then he nips me with his teeth before pulling me back up to my feet.

Leonie's and Chloe's mouths drop open. They're as shocked as I am. They know we aren't really dating.

Oh hell. The blood drains from my face. He's here to ruin my life. There can be no other reason.

This is bad.

I fake a smile. "Honey, what are you doing here?"

"Couldn't keep away." He grabs a handful of my behind aggressively, and I jump.

My life is over.

"Where have you been keeping him?" Gisele smiles as she looks him up and down.

"Tied to the bed." Henley winks, and the undertone of animosity is crystal clear. "She's a real nympho, this one."

Kill me. Kill me right now.

"Can we . . ." I smile at my work friends all watching us. "Excuse us for a moment." I grab Henley's hand and pull him into my laundry room and shut the door behind us. "What the fuck are you doing?" I whisper angrily.

"What the fuck are *you* doing?" he whispers right back. "If you think you can use me as a scapegoat to dodge your loser friend, you can think again," he growls. "I have never been so infuriated."

"Keep your voice down," I whisper. "The girls made up the story, not me."

"Bullshit," he spits. "You lied to him about having a boyfriend, and I will not stand for it."

"So go home," I spit. "I didn't ask you to come here."

"And I didn't ask to be a victim of your lies. Tell me the truth or else."

"Or else what?" I fume.

"Or else I'll fuck you on the table in front of your guests."

"What?" I explode. "That's the most ridiculous thing I've ever heard."

Although . . .

He grabs me by my two arms. "You're a liar."

"Don't touch me." I struggle to get out of his grip. "You sleazebag."

"Coming from you, that's laughable."

"How dare you."

"Oh, I dare, all right. I'm going out there to tell everyone what you're really like. Fucking me while you were engaged to another man. You couldn't lie straight in bed."

"Don't." I panic as I grab his two hands in mine. "You can't," I beg. "I know I lied to Warren, and he'll be upset. Please don't hurt his feelings to get back at me."

He narrows his eyes.

"Please." I put my hands in a praying gesture. "Just pretend to like me for ten minutes, and then you can go home and never speak to me again."

He raises an eyebrow.

"What does that mean?" I whisper.

Without another word he storms out. My heart is thumping hard in my chest. I can't believe this. Why the hell would Warren go over to his house?

This is the worst. I look like an even bigger loser now. What must he think of me?

"Who wants a drink?" I hear Henley ask everyone in a super-sweet voice.

"I'll have one."

"Me too," I hear them all chime in.

Oh no . . .

He's up to something. I just know it.

I go to the bathroom and splash water on my face and shake my hands around to try and calm myself down.

It's ten minutes. Realistically, how pear shaped can things go in ten minutes? I'll play along, and then he'll go home. And next week I'll pretend to break up with him. Problem solved.

I stare at my reflection while I prepare myself for battle; my heart is hammering in my chest. I tentatively walk back out to the living area to see Henley sitting in the living room with everyone.

He's on the chair, legs wide with his dominant stance, a glass of champagne in his hand.

He looks up and smiles warmly. "Puppy, come sit with us." He taps the couch beside him.

Puppy?

"What did you just call her?" Leonie asks, wide eyed.

"That's my sexy-times name for her." Henley's eyes twinkle with mischief, and he rubs the seat beside him. "Sorry, I should save that for private, shouldn't I, sweetheart?"

What the fuck is happening right now?

I drop to sit beside him, and he puts his arm around me. He slides his fingers up over my shoulders and skims my neck.

I stare straight ahead as I consider swallowing my tongue.

"I would die if my boyfriend called me puppy." Leonie twists her lips as she tries to keep a straight face.

Not funny, Leonie.

"Well." Henley sips his champagne. "She likes being called puppy, don't you, baby?" He holds up his hand as if to whisper. "You know, with her doggy kink and all."

What the . . .

Everyone's eyes widen, and I take his glass of champagne off him and take a gulp.

"Now, now, sweetie." He snatches the glass back from me. "Don't want to choke yourself on that leash tonight when you go potty out back."

Leonie coughs as she tries not to laugh.

I see Chloe disappear into the kitchen to snicker in private.

Help!

"So, how did you two meet?" Warren asks as he looks between us.

"She was"—Henley raises his eyebrows—"sleeping with my father, after she broke up with my brother." He continues with a straight face. "I guess I just didn't want to miss out on the action." He slides his fingers up the back of my neck and grabs a handful of my hair.

What the fuck?

"Ha ha. You're so funny." I untangle his fingers from my hair and swat his hand away. "Not exactly." I fake a laugh. "The truth is . . ." I look over at him as I try to think of something to say. "Henley's never had a girlfriend, and I felt sorry for him."

Everyone in the room stares at us in silence, unsure what to say.

"Oh," Warren replies as he looks between us. "I see."

"He's socially awkward, and the good person in me was feeling charitable." I stand. "I'm trying my best to show him the way."

Henley lets out a chuckle, and I know the psychotic part of his brain has just been activated.

He's about to blow.

"So you probably all should get going now." I march to the kitchen and begin washing up coffee cups in double time.

Henley's mouth goes to my ear from behind. "You are *fucking* kidding me," he sneers in a whisper before nipping my earlobe.

His hands slide up my arms, and he realizes that he's given me goose bumps. I feel him smile against me.

Oh no.

"You like that, Juliet?" he whispers darkly.

"No."

As if being egged on, he pushes his hips up against mine, pinning me to the sink.

Okay, what the hell is happening right now? This man is sick and twisted and about to fuck my working-life friendships up.

"Need any help cleaning up?" He pulls my hair around one side of my neck and licks me up the length of it, and my knees nearly buckle beneath me. "My little puppy." He pinches my stomach.

I give him a swift sharp elbow to the ribs. "Stop calling me that."

He kisses me again on the neck. His teeth graze my skin, and I begin to feel it to my toes. "What about this? Do you like this?" He pushes forward harder with his hips, and I begin to feel faint.

It has become disturbingly apparent that I would, in fact, actually do doggy kink for this man.

Whatever the hell doggy kink is.

The guests slowly collect their things, and Henley grabs my hand as we walk them out. We stand on the curb, and as I'm talking to them, he dusts his thumb tenderly over the back of my hand as if forgetting that he hates me.

I glance up at him, and something shifts as we stare at each other.

What exactly that is I just don't know.

"You must come to my wedding next weekend, Henley." Debbie smiles as she kisses us both.

Wait . . . did we just have a moment?

"He's busy," I reply.

"Thank you, Debbie." Henley smiles, completely ignoring me. "That would be lovely."

I look up at him in horror. *You are not coming; this has been the most stressful day of my life.*

"Goodbye," Warren says. He kisses me on the cheek and then shakes Henley's hand. "Nice to meet you, Henley."

"The pleasure was all mine," Henley replies in his smooth voice.

I wave as the cars all drive away, and as they slowly turn around the corner, Henley drops my hand like a hot potato. "You are not forgiven," he snaps.

"*I'm* not forgiven?" I gasp. "Your father *and* your brother?" I fume. "My work friends think I'm a crazy ho. Thanks a lot."

"If the shoe fits, Juliet." He storms off toward his house.

"And don't you ever call me puppy again," I call after him. He marches through his front door and slams it with a bang.

Ugh . . . infuriating.

Asshole.

It's 10:00 p.m. I hear a car pull onto our street and look out the window to see it pull into Henley's driveway.

Who's that at this hour?

I peer through the side of my curtains, but at just that exact moment, the lights go off in the car and I can't see into the car. I quickly go out the back door and sneak around to the front through the side gate.

In the darkness, I can see someone sitting in a sporty white Mercedes, and I peer over the hedge.

Who is it?

I stand up for a closer look, and the car door opens, and I quickly duck back down. I hear high heels clicking on the driveway.

A woman.

He has a woman over.

Of all the nerve . . .

I crane my neck as I try my hardest to see what she looks like, but I can't see a thing.

His front door opens. "Vanessa," his deep voice says.

"Hello, darling," she replies before going inside. The door shuts behind her.

I step back, shocked. Yet not surprised. On autopilot, I walk back inside and empty the trash with vigor. "I hate that man."

I shake the new bag aggressively in the air. "He's such a fucking asshole." I stuff the bag into the trash and struggle around with it and then kick it for good measure. "I wouldn't go out with him if he was the last man left on earth."

Barry looks over at me from his bed. His face is flat and unimpressed.

Even he knows I'm talking shit.

"If he came over here right now and begged me for sex, I would slam the door in his face." I go back over to my front window and peer through the curtains over to Henley's. "What's going on over there with fucking Vanessa the Undresser?"

I peer through the curtains some more. "With her fucking Mercedes. So what? You have a fancy car and high heels. Big whoop. You can have him. He's a giant dickhead."

Barry sighs and gets up and leaves the room.

I march to the freezer and open it in a rush. "I need ice cream."

I sit at my kitchen counter as I write myself a to-do list. I'm not wasting any time today. I'm getting straight to it.

I open the kitchen blinds and look out into the backyard; the sun is just coming up. I've been waiting for it to get light enough to be able to see where I'm going. "Let's go, Barry." I put his leash on, and he dances around all excited. Our morning run has become the highlight of both our days.

We walk out the front door. I lean on the mailbox and curl my foot up behind my bottom and hold it as I stretch my quad. I glance over to see that Vanessa's car is gone.

Stop.

I don't care what he does. Good for him.

I stretch my other leg and then put my headphones on and begin a slow jog up the road. I've been running for a few minutes when from the corner of my eye, I catch sight of something and glance over to see Henley drive past. He doesn't slow down. He doesn't try and talk to me, and I know it shouldn't matter.

In fact, it doesn't; I hate him.

Chloe walks back into my kitchen. "So . . . tell me?"

"Tell you what?" I roll my eyes. Just like I knew she would be, Chloe was here bright and early this morning to find out the gossip.

"What happened last night?" she asks.

"With what?"

"With Henley." She screws up her face as if I'm stupid.

"Nothing." I act casual as I go to the fridge. "Warren went over there and warned him to look after me, and Henley, being the dick that Henley is, thought it would be comical to mess with me." I pass her a glass of water.

"It was pretty funny for us too." She smiles.

"You think?" I mutter, unimpressed.

"I mean, when he started calling you puppy because of your doggy kink and then about going potty out back."

"Don't," I cry as I put my hands over my eyes in horror. "Makes me embarrassed just thinking of it."

"And the sleeping with his dad after dating his brother bit." She laughs. "He's fucking funny, if you ask me."

"Oh hell, kill me." I cringe. "What the hell made him think of that?"

"So afterward?" She smiles hopefully.

"Nothing." I shrug. "He's just my neighbor, and there is nothing there, and that's the end of that."

"Except it's not."

I need to defuse this situation and stop thinking and talking about stupid Henley James.

I picture him and Vanessa rolling around in the sheets last night, and I let out a deep sigh. "Believe me, it is."

It's Sunday afternoon, and Chloe and I stand back to look at the color patches on the wall.

"I mean, this white on the end looks fresh," I say as I point to the paint sample.

"True"—she twists her lips—"but the cream looks warm and homey."

"Also true." I try to imagine how it's going to look with the furnishings.

"So what style are we going for?" she asks.

"Like, expensive country."

"Then the cream?"

"But I also love expensive Hamptons," I add.

"Then the duck-egg blue."

"But the outside of the house is going to be white."

"Hmm." Chloe thinks for a moment. "I feel like you should get an interior designer's input. I mean, you don't want to put all this work into it for it to look like shit."

"Maybe."

Henley

"Morning." I step onto the crowded elevator and push the button before turning to face the doors.

11TH FLOOR

Silence hangs in the air as we rise. Monday-morning blues. Seems everyone has it today, not just me.

My mind goes back to the weekend and its turn of events.

The doors open, and I stride out and walk through the reception area.

"Good morning, Henley." Jenny smiles.

"Morning, Jen."

"Is everything all right?" she asks.

"Yes, why?"

"Blake called looking for you, said you were supposed to have a late breakfast with them but are now not answering your phone."

"What?" I dig my phone out of my pocket.

DO NOT DISTURB.

"Fuck." I flick off the Do Not Disturb button and call him as I walk into my office.

"Where are you?" he answers.

"Sorry, I forgot." I shake my head in disgust and dump my briefcase on the desk.

"Since when do you forget anything?"

"Since now, okay," I snap. "Shut up."

"Just ordered your breakfast—get down here."

I exhale heavily. "Fine."

"You want a coffee?"

"They serving espresso martinis?"

He chuckles. "Good weekend?"

"The fucking best," I mutter dryly. "See you soon."

Juliet

I scroll through Google.

> Martello Interior Design
> Ariana Interior Design
> Joel Marcel Interiors

I'm on my lunch break and trying to get my renovation project underway. I think Chloe is right—I do need a professional opinion.

I click on Joel Marcel, and it dials his number. He answers on the first ring.

"Hello, Joel speaking."

"Hi, Joel," I reply. "It's Juliet Drinkwater calling."

"That's an unusual name." He sounds like he's smiling. "Hi, Juliet."

"Hi." I scratch my head while I try to think of what to say. "I'm not sure if you're the person to call, but I have an interior design dilemma and was wanting some advice."

"Okay, sure. Design dilemmas are my thing."

I smile, feeling a little more at ease. "I've just moved into a house, and it needs a full renovation."

"Okay."

"And I'm doing it myself, so I need to be really budget conscious."

"Right," he replies as he listens.

"I want to . . ." I stop myself to try and articulate my words.

"You want a plan?" he asks, reading my mind.

"Yes. I just don't want to start something one color and then realize six months down the road that it doesn't go with anything else."

"Good idea. What you need is a color consult to start with. That way we can get an overall vibe of the feel you want for the house, and then we can pick the colors and go from there."

"Exactly." I smile, excited. I like this guy. "How much does that cost?"

"Well, my first visit is free, and we just talk about your wish list, and then after that for small projects like this, I charge an hourly rate."

"That sounds great. When can you fit me in?"

"Hang on, I'll bring up my schedule." I hear him type on his computer. "What suburb are you in?"

"Half Moon Bay, Kingston Lane."

"Oh, nice street. One of my colleagues did a house in there."

"It is." I smile proudly.

"Okay, I can come two weeks from Friday."

My shoulders slump. "That long?" Damn it.

"Too far out?" he asks.

"It's just that I don't even have a couch, and I wanted to order my furniture and start painting."

"Hmm." He thinks for a moment. "My last appointment this afternoon isn't far from there. I could stop by on my way home. It will be late, though, around six thirtyish."

"That would be great." I smile.

"What house number on Kingston Lane?"

"Eleven."

"And I can reach you on this number?"

"Uh-huh."

"See you tonight, Juliet."

"Bye." I hang up feeling very accomplished. *Let's get this party started.*

It's 7:00 p.m. when his car pulls onto our street. His car creeps past my house; there's no number on my mailbox. I turn on the porch light and walk out front and wave. He sees me and parks his car and gets out with a bunch of folders. "Juliet," he says.

"Hello." I smile as I shake his hand.

Oh . . .

Joel is hot.

Ha, who knew?

He looks up at the old two-story house. "So this is her?"

"Uh-huh." I laugh. "It's really in need of everything."

"I did a little digging today, and did you know that this is the oldest house in the neighborhood?"

"Is it?"

"Yeah, and originally the entire neighborhood was this house's meadows."

"Oh." I smile up at my big old house. "I knew she was special."

"Very special." He smiles. "What are your plans for her?"

I love how he calls my house a her.

"I want to try and keep the old-world feel as authentic as I possibly can."

He listens.

"You know when you go away for the weekend to a really well-kept country house and everything is modern but with an old-fashioned design?"

"You want to keep the integrity of its age?" he asks.

"Yes."

"You want it to feel like the luxurious house that it was back in the day."

"Exactly." I smile. "That's exactly what I'm after. I want to walk in here and feel transported into . . . another world. I don't necessarily want modern, but I want beautiful."

Joel smiles dreamily up at the house. "Sounds perfect."

The black Range Rover comes creeping up the road, and Henley looks at us as he drives past. He glares out, and I glare back.

"How long have you been here?" Joel asks as we walk up the front steps.

"Three weeks. I'm ready to get started. If we can at least work out a color design and what couch I need to order, that would be amazing."

We walk through the front door, and he looks around at the dreary, sparse space. "Wow," he says in surprise.

"It needs a lot of work, doesn't it?" I wince.

"This is going to be so beautiful when it's finished, Juliet."

I go up on my toes with excitement. Finally, someone who sees in it what I do. He gets out a pad and pencil. "I'm just going to walk through the house and take some notes and make a quick floor plan."

"Sounds great."

He wanders around for a little while. I hear a knock just as we are standing in the foyer, and I open the front door.

"Henley." I frown.

He's wearing his navy suit, and instantly his dominance is felt in the room. "Hello." His eyes flick to Joel. "Who are you?"

Chapter 7

I widen my eyes at him . . . *rude*.

I introduce them. "Henley, this is Joel." I smile awkwardly. "Joel, this is my neighbor Henley."

"Hello." Joel puts his hand out to shake Henley's hand.

"What do you do, Joel?" Henley asks, arrogance personified.

Joel's eyes flick to me in question. "I'm the interior designer."

"Are you really?" Henley's assessing eyes hold his.

What the hell?

"Henley, can I help you with something?" I ask.

"Yes, I need to speak to you."

"Okay." I frown. What about? "I'll come over and see you when Joel and I are finished."

"No, it's fine." He walks past us into the house. "I'll wait."

"It's going to take forever."

"I'm happy to wait," he says. He casually pulls up a stool to the kitchen counter and takes a seat.

My god, what is he doing?

Go home, Henley. I want to dream about my house in private.

Joel walks around downstairs and scribbles on his notepad. He draws a floor plan and takes some notes.

I peer out to the kitchen to see Henley scrolling through his phone. I have no idea what he's doing here, but it must be important.

"I'll show you upstairs," I say to Joel.

We take the rickety stairs. "This staircase is original," Joel tells me.

"No, it's not," Henley calls from the kitchen.

"Are you sure about that?" Joel calls back.

"Positive," Henley snaps.

"I'm sorry," I mouth to Joel as we walk up the stairs. "Ignore him."

"Who is he?" Joel mouths back.

"My neighbor."

We get upstairs, and Joel winces. "It's in a lot worse condition up here."

"I know." I bring him through to my bedroom. "There is an en suite, though."

"Nice brown tiles." Joel chuckles as he looks around. "I'll have my work cut out in here."

"Pfft." We hear a tsk from the doorway. Henley is now upstairs and looking unimpressed.

Seriously?

"Henley." I hold my hands out. "What is it?"

"Nothing." He puts his hands in his suit pockets as he looks around. "Just interested in what Joel has to say, that's all."

"Wait downstairs," I reply.

"No, I'm good." He stands beside Joel and looks around the bedroom, legs wide, with his dominance overpowering the room.

Joel scribbles on his notepad, and I can tell that Henley has rattled him. "I think that should do me," Joel says as he makes for the stairs. "I'll call you tomorrow, and we can discuss."

"Or you could just be professional and email her," Henley says from the top of the stairs.

I bite the side of my mouth to stop myself from smiling as I follow Joel down the stairs.

He's jealous.

Joel glances up at Henley, and I see him come to the same conclusion. "I'll be doing that after our discussion," he fires back. "So what colors are we thinking, Juliet?" Joel asks me.

"I really like white, but then I want it warm, so perhaps cream would be a better option?" I shrug. "What do you think?"

"I'm going to make some mood boards up for you, and we can really dive deep into the essence of the property."

I glance up and see Henley roll his eyes in an overexaggerated way.

"Fantastic." I smile as I open the front door. "Thank you so much for coming."

"It was really great to meet you, Juliet." He shakes my hand; he glances over to Henley as he stands on my stairs. "Henley."

"Goodbye, Joel." Henley smiles sarcastically.

I close the door behind Joel, and I turn toward Henley, who is standing halfway up the stairs. "What are you doing?"

"Walking down the stairs."

"No, you're not. You are trying to annoy me. That's what you're doing, and let me tell you—it's working."

He holds his hand out in surrender. "What?"

I walk into my kitchen and flick the kettle on. "What did you want to see me about?" I snap.

"I came to talk about Saturday night."

I frown, confused. "What about Saturday night?"

"The wedding."

"You're *not* coming to the wedding," I scoff.

"Yes, I am. Debbie invited me."

"You don't even know Debbie."

"It would be rude of me not to go after I said I would."

"No."

"I'll be on my best behavior."

"You don't have good behavior, Henley, let alone best." I hold up a coffee cup. "You've perfected assholism, remember?"

"Got any wine?"

"No," I snap. "Do you want coffee or not?"

"Fine."

"What do you want, Henley? And before you say anything stupid, think very carefully about your reply because I am sick of your childish tantrums."

His eyes hold mine.

"If you want to have an adult conversation, let's have it," I say as I make the coffee and then sit at the kitchen counter. He slouches onto the stool beside me. We sit in awkward silence for a while, and I can tell that my lecture is rolling around in his head.

"When you moved onto the street, it's possible that we got off on the wrong foot."

"Possible?"

"Probable," he agrees.

I sip my coffee as my body goes into fluttering overdrive. Just sitting beside him makes me want to do dirty things. Damn it, why is he so gorgeous? It would be so much easier to be repelled by him if he was hideous.

"Anyway, I just thought . . . Saturday night we could come out to your friends and pretend to"—he pauses—"be together . . . for the story's sake, one last time. Before we spectacularly break up."

"What would Vanessa say about that?"

A frown flashes across his face. "Who's Vanessa?"

"I was outside the other night, and I saw her arrive."

"Oh." He thinks for a moment. "Not that it's any of your business, Vanessa and I have an agreement where neither is bothered by what the other one does."

"She's a booty call?"

"She's a very nice lady"—he smirks—"who does offer her booty."

"Oh." I fall silent. What do you even say to that?

"I'm a very sexual person, Juliet. I have needs." He sips his coffee. "I do what any highly sexed single person does to get by."

I remember.

After a while he says, "Vanessa won't be visiting me again."

"Why?"

"I'm no longer interested in her."

His eyes drop to my lips, and he gives me the best come-fuck-me look of all time.

I nervously sip my coffee.

"And there lies the problem," he continues.

I frown as I try to keep up with the conversation.

What problem?

"I like to keep my dating life and my home life separate, and especially with you being you."

"Me being me? What's that supposed to mean?"

"Come off it." He rolls his eyes. "The night we spent together wasn't exactly an earth-shattering moment."

It was for me. My heart sinks.

"You were engaged to another man, for fuck's sake."

It wasn't exactly an earth-shattering moment.

Our night meant nothing to him. He hasn't thought about it again since.

"You're right." I look up, determined to get over this dick. "I was."

His cold eyes hold mine.

98

Awkward . . .

"What?" I sip my coffee, feeling like an errant child.

"So . . . let me get this straight. You were engaged to be married while fucking other men."

"We had an open relationship," I lie.

He tilts his chin to the sky, angered. "I don't know much about marriage, but I can be pretty fucking sure I wouldn't be sharing my future wife."

I swallow the lump in my throat, feeling uneasy with his contempt. "What do you want, Henley?" I snap. "Did you barge in here to make me feel like shit? Because mission accomplished, you've done just that."

He stands. "I will pick you up on Saturday for the wedding."

I stare at him, and I know that I should stay far away from this selfish bastard forever.

Move house even.

But the thought of being on his arm just one more time sends me into overdrive.

"Three o'clock," I murmur.

His eyes hold mine. "Three o'clock."

It's 5:40 a.m., and I am on the front porch, stretching for my run. Right on cue, Henley's front door opens, and he walks out in his suit.

My heart somersaults in my chest at the mere sight of him.

Where does he go so early every day?

His office doesn't open until nine. I mean, I know he would have to go in early sometimes, but every single day, even on weekends?

He glances up and gives me a sexy smile. We stare at each other for a beat longer than necessary, and then he gets into his car and drives out.

He gives me a casual wave as he drives past, and like the fangirl I am, I wave right back.

I watch his car disappear around the corner and make a mental note of what I have to do today.

Buy a new dress, the hottest one known to man. Book a hair appointment for Saturday and get everything waxed.

I mean everything.

A knock sounds at my door. It's Saturday, after the longest week in history.

He's here.

I'm regretting this before I even go. Stupid, stupid. What am I thinking? Just get it over with.

I open the door in a rush. "Hi."

His eyes drop down to my toes and back up to rest on my face. "Hello." He gives me a slow sexy smile. "You look"—he inhales sharply—"good."

I try to hide my smile; he likes the dress. "Hello, Henley." I grab my purse and shawl.

We get into his car, and he pulls out onto the road. "How was your week?" he asks.

Long.

"Good, thanks. How was yours?"

"Busy."

I twist my fingers in my lap and stare out the window as we drive, and I go over the game plan for today.

Stay distant.

Whatever I do, remember that this is just a game to him.

I can't be too chatty or friendly. I just have to let the day pan out.

We drive in silence for the rest of the way and finally pull into the parking lot.

The wedding is at a big country house estate. The gardens are beautiful, and I can see the white chairs lined up in rows near a floral arbor. That must be where the vows will be exchanged.

I internally count the ways that this could end badly. "This looks nice," he says as he parks the car.

"It does." My nerves are pumping, and suddenly this doesn't seem like such a smart strategy.

He opens my car door and takes my hand and pulls me up into his arms, our faces only millimeters away from each other's, and my breath catches.

His eyes darken and drop to my lips. "Today, you're mine."

I inch back from him. "*Pretending* to be yours."

He smirks before licking his lips. And somehow, I think his conquering me has become the world's greatest challenge. "Let's go, sweetheart," he says as he takes my hand in his. "Invitation?"

Sweetheart.

I dig in my bag and pass it to him. And he reads it as we walk. "Just so you know how to act today, I like my women submissive."

Ha . . . you wish.

"Just so you know how to act today," I reply as we walk across the parking lot, "I like my men submissive."

His hand is big around mine, and it's giving me all the flutters. There's like this electrical current that's running through his body and into mine.

Does he feel it too?

He doesn't seem to. He's as unaffected by me as you could possibly be.

Seriously, what was I thinking?

So fucking dumb, Juliet.

We walk through the giant archway doors of the atrium, and I look around in awe. "Wow."

Everything on the round tables is white, with fancy silverware and candelabras and huge bouquets of white and cream flowers in big beautiful vases. Oversize chandeliers are hanging down in a dramatic fashion on silver chains.

Henley's eyes roam over the space, and he smiles. "Very nice."

"Great place for a wedding reception."

He puts his hand on my behind and pulls me close as he puts his mouth to my ear. "Great place for our first fake date." His breath tickles my senses, and goose bumps scatter. I smile bashfully.

Stop it.

Fake date . . . this is a fake date.

Don't forget that for a moment.

He's already said we can never eventuate into something, due to us living next door to each other, and to be honest, he does have a very valid point.

Henley pulls the invitation out of his pocket and glances down at it. "The service is out on the lawn." He pulls me by the hand. "This way."

He's so tall and intentional. As he pulls me through the room, people turn and look at him. And suddenly, I remember.

I remember what it's like to have someone take charge.

I haven't had it for so long, and I didn't realize how much I missed it.

He leads me through the garden to the perfectly lined up chairs. "Which side?" he whispers.

I smile up at him.

"What?"

"How many weddings have you been to?"

He smirks, embarrassed by his obvious inside knowledge of weddings. "I'm thirty-three—nearly everyone I know is married. Some of my friends twice."

"Left," I reply.

He ushers me through. And we sit to the left. He picks up the program and flicks through it. "How did these two meet?" he asks.

"Who, the bride and the groom?"

"Yeah."

"Um." I lean into him to talk softly. "They met on Tinder and went on a date but hated each other. He wore her down for a second date and then redeemed himself."

He smirks.

"She wasn't interested at first." I want to elaborate on my story a little. "But he has a really great dick, and she couldn't resist."

Naughtiness flashes across his face. "And so she shouldn't—great dicks are hard to find these days."

"That's what I said."

He leans back and puts his arm around the back of my chair. "What else did you say to her?"

I try and think of something sexy to say. "I asked her what position her groom preferred."

He smirks and glances up at the groom, who is standing at the altar with his groomsmen as he waits. "Hmm . . ."

"I think missionary," I whisper.

"No." He twists his lips as he looks him up and down. "Reverse cowgirl."

"Reverse cowgirl?" I frown. "Why do you think that?"

He leans in and puts his lips to my ear. "He looks like a nerd, which means he would have watched an exponential amount of porn in his youth."

I frown in question.

"The very best way to watch your own girl in a porno is reverse cowgirl." He winks. "Front-row seat to watch your cock slide in deep to make her moan."

Oh . . .

I get a visual of what he's just told me. I flutter down below and swallow the lump in my throat. *Jeez.*

"What's your favorite position?" he whispers into my ear.

Reverse cowgirl sounds pretty good.

"Um." I try to think of a sexy answer, but he's fried my brain, and I've got absolutely nothing. "It's private," I whisper back. "Why, what's yours?"

"Lots of favorites." He circles his finger on my shoulder. "I do like sex swings."

I frown. What the hell? He has a sex swing?

"I love the uninhibited submission it gives me." His finger circles lower down my back. His breath dusts my skin, and he may as well be trailing his finger over the lips of my sex, because that's exactly where I'm feeling it.

A slow pulse begins to throb.

I get a vision of him naked and hard, tying me into a sex swing, dominating me in the most depraved way, and I clench to try and get some friction down there.

This man is a master seducer. I'm about to blow in just three whispered sentences.

Fake date.

The chairs begin to fill, and Henley looks around as his finger circles my shoulder. After a while he leans in and murmurs in my ear, "What panties are you wearing?"

What?

"Why do you want to know that?" I whisper.

"Because as I feel your skin beneath my fingers, I'm imagining myself being on my knees in front of you, peeling you out of them with my teeth. I want a visual of what I'm about to take off right here in front of everyone."

Hold the phone . . . hold the fucking phone, because I am dead.

I look up at him, and he gives me the best come-fuck-me look of all time.

The air between us is thick and heavy.

"Henley," I breathe.

He bends and softly nips my ear with his teeth. "Yes," he whispers. His breath is quivering. He's as hot for this as I am.

"Behave yourself," I whisper.

"Give me a color."

"White," I reply before my mouth-to-brain filter kicks in.

Satisfaction flashes across his face as his dark eyes hold mine.

The wedding waltz begins, and I'm snapped out of my arousal fog as the bride begins to walk down the aisle.

My body watches the nuptials as I hover way in the sky, watching Henley and me from above. He holds my hand in his lap, and I'm melting into a puddle at his touch. Imagining cowgirls in sex swings and public oral orgasms with legs over shoulders during weddings.

This bad man makes me think about bad things.

Four hours later

"So, Henley," Warren asks across the table, "tell me, what do you do?"

"I'm an engineer." Henley smiles, but his smile doesn't touch his eyes, and I get the feeling that Warren annoys the shit out of him.

The reception is dragging. We've had dinner, and Henley has been answering a barrage of questions from my work friends. He's charming the pants off all of them, of course, and they are officially hanging on his every word. And me, well, I just want the wedding to be over . . . but then, I don't want the wedding to be over. Because then my one date with him will be over, and to be honest, I'm really into him being all over me.

Henley picks up my hand and puts it on his lap under the table.

"What do you do, Warren?" Henley asks him.

"I'm a nurse."

"What's your favorite part of the job?" he continues as he discreetly slides my hand up over his crotch. I can feel that he's hard, and it takes all my strength not to wrap my hand around it.

Fuckity fuck.

I pick up my wine as I act casual. No big deal I'm feeling up my fake boyfriend who I hate in front of my work friends.

"I like walking out of my shift knowing that I gave my all to my patients," Warren continues.

"It must be very rewarding," Henley replies. He flexes his hardened dick under my hand, and I nearly choke on my wine.

"We should dance, puppy," Henley says.

Chloe's and Leonie's eyes widen with excitement.

I roll my lips to hide my smile. "Should we?"

"Uh-huh." He stands and takes my hand and leads me to the dance floor and takes me into his arms. And we begin to sway to the slow music.

"I thought I told you not to call me that," I say as I act serious.

"Well . . . it's your fault that I call you that."

"How is it my fault?" I gasp.

"You shouldn't have such great puppies."

"Puppies?"

"Yes, you know. Breasts. The things I should be sucking on right about now."

My mouth falls open as we sway. "If you say these things on a fake date, what on earth would you say on a real date?"

He pauses as if thinking for a moment. "I would tell you that you look beautiful. Like a dream come true."

I smile up at him as we dance. "You charmer, you."

"And I would tell you that it has taken every inch of my strength not to kiss you tonight."

I swallow the lump in my throat.

"And I would tell you that you should be thankful that you are dodging a bullet."

My heart swells.

"What would you say to me?" he asks softly.

"I would tell you to shut up and kiss me anyway."

His eyes hold mine, and something shifts. We move from the pretend world to a real one.

In slow motion, his lips drop and softly brush mine.

Oh . . .

Our kiss deepens, right here on the dance floor for all to see.

And every cell in my body lights up as if this is my first kiss . . . maybe it is.

Because I've never been so swept away in the moment with anyone.

We kiss again, and we are no longer swaying to the music.

Time has stopped.

Goose bumps are all over my skin, butterflies are dancing in my stomach, and the ache between my legs has built to a tsunami.

He pulls back and looks down at me, a frown crossing his brow.

"What's wrong?" I whisper.

"Nothing." He steps back from me. "We should get going."

"What?"

He takes my hand and leads me off the dance floor.

"But I'm not done kissing you yet," I stammer.

He glances over his shoulder at me and then turns and marches down the corridor, pulling me behind him.

"Where are we going?" I ask.

"I've got something to show you." He opens a door and closes it again. We keep walking down the corridor, and he opens another door and peers in and then pulls me inside and slams the door shut behind us.

I look around. We are in a library of some sort. Antique-looking books line the walls. There's a fireplace and formal, expensive-looking chairs.

Henley pulls me over to a chair and sits down and rearranges me over his lap to straddle him.

We fall silent as our most private parts touch.

He's hard. I'm soft and wet.

The air crackles as we stare at each other.

One night. I just want one night. Is that so bad?

"Kiss me," he whispers darkly.

My lips take his, and his hands slide up under my dress to cup my behind.

Oh . . .

He moves my body to grind over his hardened cock, and I begin to build.

Back . . . forward. Back, forward.

His tongue delivering the perfect kiss.

His hands move to my hip bones, bringing my body down harder onto his.

Fuck.

I glance up at the door. What if someone walks in?

I begin to lose control as he grinds me onto his erection, my breath quivering as I try to hide my arousal. His grip on my hip bones is near painful, and I shudder and moan into his mouth as an intense orgasm tears through me.

He inhales sharply and holds me still and pushes forward, and I feel the jerk as he comes hard, right there in his pants.

We pant as we kiss, coming down from our high.

Tenderness falls between us. That wasn't supposed to happen.

"Did you just fake an orgasm?" He smiles against my lips.

"Totally," I pant. "Did you?"

"Of course." He lifts me off his lap and we both stand, totally disoriented.

He runs his hand through his disheveled hair.

Holy shit . . . did that just happen?

"I need a bathroom." He smirks as he grabs me aggressively and bites my neck.

"You do." I giggle as I try to get away from him. "You're a disgusting hot mess."

"You can talk," he mutters as he pulls down my dress and rearranges it. He takes my hand. "We should get back before we are banned from this place."

I giggle as I imagine someone busting in on us. "Okay."

He leads me back out into the corridor, and we walk back to the reception hall.

What the fuck?

Did that just happen?

The festivities are ending as the night comes to a close. Henley looks around. "I'm going to the bathroom. Back in a minute."

"Okay." I count the ways I'm going to eat this man whole when we get home.

One night can't hurt.

I'm here for it.

I go to the bathroom and wash my hands; I smile goofily at my reflection in the mirror. I'm flushed and disheveled and feeling on top of the world.

"Holy shit." Oh my god, this is going to be so fucking good. I take my time as I try to calm myself down from having a full fangirl moment over him. And eventually, I make my way back out.

Henley is saying goodbye to everyone at our table and shaking hands. "Lovely to meet you." He smiles. He kisses Chloe and Leonie on the cheek, and I think they are fangirling him harder than I am.

Not possible.

I say my goodbyes to everyone as he watches on.

Henley takes my hand, and we walk back to the car. The tenderness we just shared isn't there anymore, but perhaps I'm just imagining it.

He opens the car door, and I slide in. He gets in behind the wheel and pulls out onto the road, and we drive for a while. Curiously . . . he's not touching me. Which is weird because he's been all over me all night. "So, what are you going to tell them?" he asks casually as he drives.

"Huh?" I frown over at him in confusion.

"The reason why we're breaking up—what are you going to tell them?"

"Oh." My mind begins to scramble. That's the last thing I thought was going to come out of his mouth. "I'll think of something," I say softly as I look out the window.

What?

We drive home in silence. Gone is the playful, sexy god who was my date.

Henley James is here in all his bastardly glory.

He stops the car outside my house, gets out, and opens my car door. He helps me out by my hand. "Good night, Juliet," he says casually, as if I'm a stranger he met on a bus.

I frown.

"Have a good night." He smiles.

I stare at him. What the hell? "You too," I whisper distractedly.

He gets back into his car and circles around the cul-de-sac and drives off down the street.

What?

He's going out?

I stand on the end of my driveway watching as his car disappears out of sight.

What the fuck was that?

Chapter 8

The hot water runs over my head as I lean up against the tiles.

I don't understand this man at all. He was into it. I know he was because I was right there with him.

And then he flipped a switch—just like he did when we went on our first date.

Perfect when in the moment, and then he turns into something cold. It's like he's two different people. I've never met anyone like him.

Nor do I want to.

I run my hand down my face in disgust. And now to make matters worse, I have to see him every damn day—when I know he doesn't like me—knowing that I like him.

My blood boils, and I'm infuriated with myself. He knew exactly what he was playing at, and I was like putty in his hands. Doing everything that he told me to do like a pathetic little puppy.

He's probably at Vanessa the Undresser's house at this very moment.

Giving her the steak that I preheated.

Ugh . . .

I roll into bed and toss and turn and kick myself for going there in the first place.

One thing I do know now for certain is that I'm not cut out for fake dating; all those romance books are full of shit.

This sucks.

The sound of a car wakes me from my sleep, and I sit up straight like a zombie.

He's home.

I glance at the clock: 5:00 a.m.

Where the fuck have you been all night, asshole?

Unable to help it, I scurry to the window and spy through the sheer curtains. I watch as Henley slowly drives into his garage and gets out of his car.

He's still wearing the suit that he wore to the wedding. I roll my eyes at my idiocy. *What do you think he's going to wear home, a bathrobe? You fucking idiot.*

That is it!

I storm to the bathroom enraged with myself.

That is fucking it!

I dig my gym clothes out of my closet and put them on with fury.

Well . . . I've got news for him.

He can't reject me . . . because I am rejecting *him*.

Who the hell does this jockstrap think he is? I'm going to be so damn hot that he will be begging, *begging*, for a speck of my attention, and I will be too busy dating hot men to give him the time of day. I'm going outside to wake up Barry, and then we are running fast, maybe even sprinting.

Screw him.

I march downstairs in my gym clothes, ready to fight a tiger and then chase a bear.

You want to play, fuckface?

Let's go.

"Do you have an estimate of the costs?" I ask. It's Wednesday, and Joel has sent me his notes and mood images for my house inspiration. I love everything about them.

"Well, depending on how quickly you want the work done, and the quality of the fixtures, I would estimate anything between thirty and sixty thousand," Joel replies.

"Dollars?" I gasp.

"Heritage luxury is expensive, Juliet."

Jeez.

I puff air into my cheeks as I think.

"Unless you want to change the brief and go for a less expensive quality."

"No." I think for a moment. I'll find the money somewhere. "I want the best. This is my forever home. I guess we will start with one room and work our way through as the funds allow. Would that be okay?"

"That's what I was thinking. Good idea. What room do you want to start with?"

"Definitely the living room. It's the heart of the home and where everyone sees first. And besides, I really want a comfy couch to sit on."

He chuckles. "Great, okay. I'm going to email you a selection of the couches that I feel would suit our style. Go through them, and see if you gel with anything. If you want to order it through me, I can get my thirty percent wholesale rate from these particular suppliers."

"Oh, fantastic."

"But of course you may find something similar at a cheaper price at another store. These suppliers are top end, but I feel like this shape of couch is what we are after."

"Awesome. Thanks so much for your help. I really appreciate it."

"Send anything that you find to me, and I'll just check the color and dimensions. You don't want to order something and find it's too big or small for the space when it arrives."

"Good thinking."

"Let's touch base next week—maybe Tuesday I can come over on my way home from work."

"Can't wait. Thanks so much, Joel. Have a great week."

"Bye, Jules." He hangs up, and I smile at him calling me Jules. He has that kind of personality where you feel like you know him already.

I hang up and slump onto the stool. I really wanted to get this house perfect as quickly as I could. I need more money, much more money.

I think for a moment. I wonder if I could get an extra shift a week at a nursing home. They are always looking for nurses. Hmm, that's a good idea, actually.

I'll make some calls today. I could squeeze in one shift a week, two some weeks.

Operation Hot Bitch is on. Don't mess with me, world, because I will cut you.

I grab Barry's leash, and he and I go out front. I'm so sore from running extra fast all week that I have to stretch a little extra. Being in a bitch mood sure does up the ante on my training schedule. I hold on to my mailbox and pull my foot back to my behind. I feel the stretch all the way through my quad. Henley's garage door goes up.

I pretend not to look as he drives out in his Range Rover.

I glance at my watch. It's 5:40 a.m.

Surely he doesn't work a sixteen-hour day every single day.

He pulls onto the road and catches sight of me. He waves as he drives by as if we don't even know each other, as if Saturday night didn't even happen.

Did it?

Or was I just so high on his pheromones that I invented the entire thing in my head?

His car turns the corner, and I exhale heavily.

Ugh, I hate men.

"Juliet." I hear Carol's annoying voice from behind me, and I close my eyes.

Give me strength. Not now, Carol.

"Juliet," she calls in her singsong voice. I turn toward her and fake a smile.

"Morning, Carol."

"Hello, dear." She comes bustling across the street. "What are you doing next weekend?"

Decapitating Henley James's voodoo doll.

"Nothing much." I smile. "Got to get going on my run."

"Oh, that's good, because I've taken the liberty and organized a little welcome-to-the-neighborhood party for you."

"What?"

"Just the street family—we want to welcome you."

"That's not necessary."

The king of the street already welcomed me on Saturday through his pants . . . with his dick.

"I wanted to give you a few weeks to settle in, and time has gotten away, but now it's already organized. I'm going inside right now to print out the invitations."

"I don't want a fuss, Carol."

"Nonsense." She smiles. "You're a part of the Kingston family now."

Actually, Carol, I'm a dirty dry humper who has no shame.

"Five o'clock on Saturday afternoon on my front porch."

Feeling like the biggest bitch in the world, I smile. She's being so nice, and here I am dreading talking to her. What the hell is wrong with me? "Thank you, Carol."

Suddenly I'm feeling all emotional, and I hug her. "You really don't need to throw a party, though."

"Nonsense." She smiles into my shoulder. "Go run that marathon."

"Okay." I begin with a slow jog. "Have a nice day."

My brother Liam smiles as he looks around the house. "I love it already."

"Do you really?" I smile hopefully.

"Uh-huh, it's perfect." He holds open a rickety door and closes it. "You need to replace these hinges."

"The interior designer has come up with a plan, and we're doing up one room at a time. This room is first, so I guess we will get to it."

"You're paying an interior decorator?" He frowns. "Isn't that shit expensive?"

"No, he's not too bad. Charging me by the hour. But he does think it's going to be between thirty to sixty thousand dollars to complete."

"Fuck." His eyebrows shoot up in surprise.

"I've got an interview at a nursing home this week."

"I thought you liked your job?"

"I do. This is a second job, just one or two shifts a week so I can try and save faster."

"Don't kill yourself for a house renovation. It's not worth it."

"It's fine. I'm just going to stack my shifts at the hospital, and then on my days off, I'll just do one shift at the nursing home. The money is really good."

He nods. "Okay."

"So, how did your date go?"

He exhales and flops back onto the chair. "Yeah, okay, I guess."

I watch him for a moment. "So . . . I'm guessing from your reaction that you had dinner and went home alone."

"No, we got busy." He seems bored.

"And?"

He shrugs as if uninterested. "It was . . . mediocre at best."

"Oh."

I fall silent, unsure what to say. Liam's girlfriend died in a car accident three years ago, and he's never been quite the same. "Maybe you're not ready yet, babe."

"I don't care anyway," he lies. "I just needed to—"

I cut him off. "I get it."

I need to find the right girl to kiss him better. Because he deserves better, much better.

"Maybe we're destined to be single for forever." I smirk.

"Suits me." He smiles. "I've got my tools in my truck. Want me to change the hinges?"

"Really?" I sit up, excited. "You have time?"

"Yes, but you're making me carbonara for dinner."

"Deal." I beam.

"You want another beer?" I ask as I stand.

Antony lies on a deck chair by his pool, eyes closed. "Yeah, that'd be good." He yawns, half-asleep. "Grab us a snack or something while you're up."

"Like what?"

"I don't know, cheese." He shrugs, eyes still closed. "Biscuits."

"You're going to turn into fucking cheese and biscuit soon."

"Probably," he replies, uninterested.

I called over to see him this afternoon and somehow have now been out here lying by the pool for three hours. I walk inside and grab two beers and a packet of chips and walk out the back door. From the high balcony I glance up and see Juliet's house.

Whose vehicle is that in her driveway? I stand still as I watch for a moment.

Whose fucking car is that?

Who cares? It doesn't matter.

I take the beers and chips down to the pool area and put them onto the table between the deck chairs, and then before I can even sit down, I turn and walk back to the house. "Where are you going now?" Ant asks.

"Checking something out."

"Like what?"

"Back in a minute." I stand on the steps and stare over to Juliet's. The front door opens, and a guy walks out. He's shirtless.

What?

Who the fuck is this?

I narrow my eyes as I try to hone my vision in on him. I've seen him somewhere before. He looks familiar somehow.

He walks out to the truck and grabs a toolbox.

Who is he?

He turns so I can completely see his face. Where have I . . . the penny drops.

Get fucked.

That's the fucking fiancé.

She's still with him. That's it! I storm down to the deck chair, infuriated.

"She has got to be fucking kidding," I spit.

"Who?"

"Little Miss Innocent from number eleven."

Ant exhales heavily. "What now?"

"You know who's at her fucking house right now? I'll tell you who," I fume. "It's that dopy prick fiancé."

"Huh?"

"She's still with him." I begin to pace. "So she's dry humping me at the wedding in public, forcing me to go back to my apartment because I can't be trusted being next door to her and not jumping the fence. Get blisters on my hand from wanking so much, and the whole entire time she's still going to marry him," I spit.

Ant stares at me.

"Oh . . . she's good, I'll give her that. Plays me like a fucking fiddle." I walk back and forth on the deck as my mind races. "You know what she is?" I point at him. "She's venomous. She's a lying, poisonous, voodoo-pussy wolf in a lamb suit. That's what she is."

Ant thinks for a moment. "Sneaky woolly muff?"

I smirk at his analogy. "Exactly."

"What are you going to do about it?"

120

I drop to sit down and exhale heavily. "Nothing."

"Nothing as in wank over her some more?"

I roll my eyes, disgusted at myself for wanting her. "Pretty much."

I glance at my watch as I drink my coffee. Shit, I've got to go. I'm late.

I'm on struggle street this morning. Exhausted after tossing and turning over the witch next door.

I'm over it. I'm over her.

Fuck this.

I put my toast in my mouth to hold it, grab my coffee to go, and walk past the glass back door, and something catches my eye.

Huh . . .

I step back and stare into my backyard. My face drops in horror. *"What the fuck?"* I explode. I open the sliding door to see carnage like you've never seen before.

Mud.

Everywhere.

Potted plants tipped over and chewed up.

My white Italian outdoor couch cushions covered in mud. "Someone has broken in and vandalized my entire backyard." I look around. "I've never seen anything like this."

From the corner of my eye, I see something move and turn to see Juliet's mangy dog up on my white outdoor couch as if he owns the place, fast asleep on his back and snoring. He's covered in mud from where he dug under the fence to get into my yard.

I inhale sharply and clench my fists at my side. "Motherfucker."

Adrenaline surges through my body.

I walk over to the snoring dog and glare down at him as I imagine his grisly end. "What did you do?" I growl.

He keeps snoring, and I see red.

Calm down.

I inhale deeply as I look around at the disaster zone.

I'm livid.

"Barry," I hear Juliet call from next door. "Barry, where are you?"

The dumb dog lifts its head up when it hears her voice and then flops it back down to sleep again.

My eyes flicker red as thermal nuclear energy threatens to steal my control.

Before I can stop myself, I find myself marching to Juliet's. I push open her side gate.

"Barry," she calls from her back steps.

"Juliet," I scream as I lose all control. "Get your fucking ass over here!"

Chapter 9

Juliet

"What?" I screw up my face.

"You heard me," Henley growls from his place at my side gate. "Get the fuck over to my house now and see what your fucking fleabag has done."

"You are so dramatic. Are you going for an Oscar or something?" I huff. I march past him through the gate and over to his house. The gate is open, and I walk around into his backyard.

My eyes widen in horror.

Oh no.

Mud as far as the eye can see, tipped-over pots, chewed plants, torn-up couch cushions.

I put my hands on my hips, indignant. "Well, how do you know it was Barry?"

Henley looks at me deadpan. "Open your eyes."

I glance around to see Barry asleep on his back on the white couch.

Fuck me dead.

"Barry," I scold him.

Barry sits up and pricks his ears, all happy-like.

"Don't smile at me, young man. You are in trouble." I try to sound tough and convincing.

"First of all, he's not a man, he's a mutt. And second of all, clean this shit up. Right fucking now," Henley demands with his hands on his hips.

"Do not use that tone with me, Henley. I will not take it," I fire back.

He steps toward me, and we come face to face, only inches apart. "You'll take whatever I fucking give you," he growls.

"Like hell I will."

"I bet you take whatever he gives you."

Huh?

"Who?" I scrunch up my nose as I try to follow the conversation. "Barry?"

"Don't act dumb, Juliet. It really doesn't suit you."

"What the hell are you talking about, you nutjob?"

"You can stop fucking lying now."

Okay, what the hell is he talking about? Have I missed part of the conversation?

"What are you talking about, Henley?"

"Why don't you ask your fucking fiancé what I'm talking about?"

"I don't have a fiancé."

"I saw him with my own fucking eyes," he explodes.

Oh . . . Liam.

I roll my lips to hide my smile.

"You think this is funny?" he whispers angrily. "You're riding my cock at that wedding and engaged to be married the whole fucking time?"

"Okay, let's get something straight here." I hold my hands up, trying to calm him down. He's about to pop an artery. "Are you angry about my dog, or are you angry about Liam?"

Full of contempt, he steps forward, and I step back. "I'm angry that you're a liar," he sneers.

"Well . . . you are right, I am a liar."

"I knew it," he spits.

"Liam is my brother, you fucking idiot."

"What?"

"He lied to you back then because I was upset at how you treated me and he wanted to get you back."

"What?" His eyes nearly pop out of his head. "How I treated you? How the fuck did I treat you?"

"I waited at home all day for you to call me, and you stood me up and never called me again."

"I was working," he yells.

"Bull fucking shit you were working. I saw you at the club. I saw you being a sleazebag, you lying asshole."

"That's bullshit." He frowns and puts his weight onto his back foot. "What the hell are you talking about?"

"Oh." I have proof. I swipe through my phone, and I know exactly where the video Chloe sent me is saved because I've watched it a million times. I bring up the video and hit play and hold my phone up to show him.

He frowns as he stares at the screen. He watches himself laugh and talk and then turn his attention to the girl's behind.

I'm so angry that the whole sky has turned crimson.

"So you just fucking lie to me?" he growls. "I thought you were engaged this whole fucking time."

"You were never going to call me anyway, Henley. What does it matter?"

"I might have."

"Who on earth do you think you are? You might have . . . pfft. Fuck you," I huff. I turn and storm toward my house, infuriated.

"Get back here and clean this mess up."

I flick him the bird and keep walking.

Clean it yourself.

Ugh, why did I agree to this stupid welcome party?

It's Saturday, and I can see everyone walking across the road to Carol's house with their platters of food.

I'm dreading this with a passion.

I haven't spoken to Henley since our fight over Barry. And now I have to go and pretend to everyone that I like him when all I really want to do is tip a drink over his entitled-asshole head.

I take one last look in the mirror and exhale heavily.

All right, I look good.

Feminine while not trying to be sexy. I'm done with being sexy on this street. The appropriate outfit for me right now would actually be a straitjacket, but whatever. This pink maxi dress will work just fine. It's full and flowing, long, with spaghetti straps.

I grab my platter of hors d'oeuvres and, with my heart in my throat, make my way over to Carol's house. The sound of chatter echoes through the street, and everyone seems to be in a jovial mood. Carol's front veranda is full of people, some I've never seen before, and they all turn to look at me as I walk across her front lawn. I contemplate turning around and running back home.

Awkward.

"Here she is"—Carol laughs—"the guest of honor."

"Hi." I kiss her on the cheek and smile at everyone.

"Hi, Juliet." One of the boys smiles. Everyone waves. "Hello, hello," they all chime in.

"Hi." Oh crap, this is awkward as hell. "Where would you like me to put this?" I gesture to the plate of dips and cheeses that I've brought.

"Just inside on the table, sweetheart."

"Thanks." I open the screen door and walk inside and smile at Carol's house. It's like a step back in time. Photos in frames are all over the walls, and the furnishings are all in perfect condition but date back forty years. There are even three flying ducks on the walls, like you see in the movies. I put my plate onto the table and take my time to rearrange it. Seriously, I just want to go home. This is not enjoyable.

"Hi," a voice from beside me sounds.

I look up to see a girl with light-brown hair. She's around my age and pretty. "I'm Rebecca. I live a few doors down; I've been meaning to come over and introduce myself, but time has gotten away from me."

"Oh hi, nice to meet you." I smile as I shake her hand. "You're in the blue house?"

"Yes, that's it." She gestures to a man across the room and waves him over. He's blond and good looking and probably in his late thirties. "This is my husband, John."

"Hello." I shake his hand. "Nice to meet you."

"Sorry I haven't been over yet. Time flies," he apologizes.

"Oh no, please, I totally get it." I shrug. "I'm busy too."

"What do you do?" he asks to make conversation.

"I'm a nurse."

"Fantastic," he replies. "Another medical professional on the street. That makes three of us now. I'm an orthopedic surgeon."

"Wow." I smile. I turn my attention back to Rebecca. "Do you work or have children . . . or?"

"God no." She winces as she pours herself another glass of wine. "I'm a teacher—best contraceptive in the world." She crosses her eyes as she tips her head back to drink.

I giggle. I like Rebecca already.

"Have you met everyone?" she asks.

"Some." I shrug. "I work a lot, so I miss most people."

"Come on"—she takes me by the hand—"I'll introduce you."

"Ugh, do you have to?" I whisper.

She giggles. "Unfortunately." She drags me by the hand over to a group of men. "Boys, this is Juliet. She's the homecoming queen of today. This is Blake Grayson." She introduces me. "Blake is a doctor."

I feel like I know a creepy stalker amount of information about Dr. Grayson already, not that I'll ever let on.

"Hello."

"Juliet is a nurse," Rebecca tells him.

"Are you?" He smiles. "Where do you work?"

"At Lady of Rosemary."

"You've been busy lately; I hear they are at capacity."

"All the time."

Rebecca pulls me by the hand again over to an elderly man. He looks to be in his eighties. "This is Winston. He lives in the white house."

"Hello." I smile as I shake his hand.

"Hello, dear." He smiles and has a southern drawl. "Lovely to meet you. I see you running around in the mornings with your dog."

I giggle. Poor thing. What must I look like? "Nice to meet you too."

"And this fine specimen is Antony Deluca. He's your next-door neighbor."

He smiles, and I feel it to my bones. He's European and utterly gorgeous. "Hello, Juliet." He kisses my cheek. "I've heard all about you. Nice to finally put a face to the name."

"Henley, Blake, and Antony are childhood friends."

"Oh, right." I smile, surprised. "That's great."

"Where's Henley?" Rebecca asks as she looks around.

"Here I am," he calls out as he comes through the front door.

"Come and meet Juliet," Rebecca replies.

"We've met." Henley smiles casually, as if he isn't the biggest prick in the world.

I'm onto you.

He kisses Rebecca on the cheek and then turns to me. I'll play nice because we are in public.

"Hi." I smile.

He smiles warmly and kisses my cheek. He's wearing a cream linen jacket and blue jeans. Looks like he just stepped off a *GQ* modeling shoot or something. "Hello. Good to see you both."

I flutter with nerves at the smell of his heavenly aftershave.

"Where have you been?" a man snaps. "We've been waiting for the bartender to arrive."

Henley rolls his eyes and goes over behind the bar. "Who wants what?"

Everyone huddles around the bar and puts their drink order in with him. And I smile at their familiarity. I have to admit, it is a nice street to live on.

A little old lady walks in through the front door.

"Hello, Ethel," everyone calls.

"Party's here." Ethel smiles as she puts her tray of cakes onto the table. "Sorry we're late."

"Va-va-voom!" one of the boys calls from the bar as he looks toward the door. "Who is this stunner?"

I turn to see a drop-dead gorgeous woman walking in—long dark hair and a figure to die for. A perfectly well-done face of makeup and perfectly pouty big lips. She's wearing a black fitted dress and looks like she's a famous Instagrammer or something.

"Great, Taryn's here," Rebecca whispers.

"Is that a bad thing?" I whisper.

Oh no, this is the Taryn that Carol told me about. Surely not.

Rebecca fakes a smile. "Depends on who you are," she mutters under her breath.

"I'm back, darlings. Have you missed me?" She puts her hands in the air and tries to be cute. Actually, there's no trying. She's totally nailing it.

"Yes," the boys all cry in unison. "Taryn." They all line up to kiss her, and she hugs each one of them as if she's their long-lost love while totally ignoring all the other females in the room.

"Everyone on the street is in love with Taryn," she whispers. "Including Taryn."

I giggle. "Not me." I hold my glass up. She clinks hers with mine.

"Me neither."

"Henley, darling," Taryn says in a sexy voice. "Where have you been all my life?"

Henley chuckles and pulls her in for a hug. "Right here where you left me."

My eyes meet Rebecca's, and she raises a see-I-told-you-so eyebrow.

Yes, I see it now. Ugh, give me a break.

Rebecca grabs my hand. "Let's go out front."

"Good idea."

The night has been fun, and I really, really like Rebecca. We've just clicked. It's as if I've known her forever.

We are sitting on the park-bench seat in Carol's front yard. Everyone is chatting, and the boys are well on their way to being tipsy.

"So are you in a relationship?" Rebecca asks.

"No. I broke up with my ex a year ago."

"Were you with him for long?"

"About twelve months."

"Is that a good thing or a bad thing?"

"Good. It was my doing." I shrug. "I don't know, I always seem to attract the wrong kind of guy."

"You have a type?"

"Not really." I smirk. "But maybe I turn them into that type." She laughs.

"We just weren't on the same page. He wanted to party and go out all the time, and I'm past that. I mean, the occasional night out is fun, but clubbing every Friday and Saturday night is not my ideal place to be."

"Yeah, I get that. How old are you?"

"I'm twenty-seven, and you?"

"I'm thirty-one. How amazing that you bought that house by yourself." She smiles.

"It is." I smile, proud of myself. "I've just got to pay for the renovations now. The quotes are coming in, and I'm floored how expensive things are."

"Oh, I know. We just did our kitchen, and it was more than double what we thought it was going to be."

A loud and husky laugh comes from the veranda, and Rebecca and I glance up to see Taryn draped all over Henley. My stomach twists with jealousy. She's been all over him all night. "Are those two dating?" I ask.

"Henley and Taryn?" She screws up her face. "God no."

My eyes linger on the two of them. "How do you know?"

"Because he's super friendly with her."

"Huh?"

She lowers her voice so that nobody can hear. "He and John are quite good friends. Don't tell anyone this, but he has some major baggage."

"Like what?" I whisper. At last, some intel.

"He will only sleep with women that he doesn't like."

I screw up my face. "What do you mean?"

"He is so antirelationship that if he meets someone he likes, he won't date them again for fear of falling into a trap."

I stare at her, shocked. "Since when?"

"Since his mother died when he was in his teens."

"Has he been to therapy about this?"

"He saw someone in his early twenties, but it didn't work." She shrugs. "I think he's just accepted that this is the way he is."

"Oh." My eyes rise to watch him. Taryn laughs out loud and puts her hand on his chest in a flirty way.

Fuck off, Taryn.

"And get this," she whispers. "He even has a burner phone."

"A what?"

"He has fake business cards with another phone number on it that his PA answers."

"Why?"

"So that the women he dates don't have his actual number if he wants to disappear."

I sit back, shocked.

Adrenaline surges through my blood. That's exactly what he did to me.

"Wow," I whisper. "I've officially heard it all now."

Taryn laughs out loud again, and I imagine myself pushing her head into the punch bowl until she chokes on the frozen strawberries.

"So I imagine he must ghost a lot of women, then," I reply.

"No. That's the thing—he hardly ghosts anyone."

"What?"

"He just dates for sex. It's super rare that he actually likes someone and ghosts them."

He ghosted me.

"But if he's having sex with all these women, he must like them?" I frown, confused.

"Attraction and feelings are two very different things to him. John says he just dates them until it runs its course, and then he moves on to the next without looking back."

"Oh." I watch him across the room. "So in other words, he just breaks hearts wherever he goes."

"I guess he's pretty fucked up."

"I'll say." Henley glances up, and our eyes lock. We stare at each other for a beat longer than we should, and I tear my eyes away. "I have to work in the morning, so I should get going."

"Yeah, me too." She screws up her nose. "Taryn is probably about to start dancing for the boys."

"She dances?" I wince.

"Like a stripper on crack."

I giggle. "Don't, I'm getting a bad visual."

Rebecca laughs too. "Do you want to grab a coffee sometime?"

"Yeah." I smile. "I'd like that." I kiss her on the cheek. "It was so lovely meeting you."

"You too."

Somehow I feel like I made a friend tonight.

I kiss Carol. "Thank you so much for tonight."

"So good to have you here, my dear." Carol smiles.

"Bye, everyone." I wave. "I have to work in the morning, so I'm heading out."

"Goodbye," everyone calls.

Henley's eyes lock on mine, and we stare at each other across the room for a beat longer again. As if not remembering that we hate each other.

Stop it.

With another small wave, I walk back across the road to my house, and just as I step onto my veranda, I hear Taryn's annoying voice echo through the street. "Let's get some music going."

Ugh, Rebecca is right.

I lie in bed, wide awake.

The beat from the music is drifting through the neighborhood.

The party has moved from Carol's house to Antony's backyard. They are now sitting around a campfire. I don't know who's over there, but I can still hear Taryn's annoying voice over everyone else's.

My mind keeps going over Rebecca's words about Henley tonight. And I know I should be angry at him and resentful because he has a burner phone, but . . .

He's damaged.

I feel sad for him. I can't imagine what it must be like to hold no hope of meeting the one. Or not even wanting to.

I thought he would have tried to talk to me tonight . . . but then, based on his crazy up-and-down behavior, I didn't.

I mean, everything Rebecca said all makes a lot of sense.

I knew we hit it off on that first date. And I knew he liked me. Damn it, I liked him. I was so shocked when he didn't call me.

But did he want to?

Even last weekend, we made out in the most perfect of ways, and then he acted like it meant nothing.

What happened to him to make him so closed down?

I hear Taryn's annoying laugh, and I roll over and punch my pillow. "Go back to your ex-husband, Taryn. You're pissing me off."

I run around in a fluster. Joel is going to be here any minute to talk about the couch and colors, and I got home late from work.

I hear a knock at the door, and I quickly throw my clothes into the laundry hamper. "Fuck's sake, this place is a mess," I whisper en route to the door. I open it in a rush. "Hi." I smile. "Come in."

"Hello." Joel smiles. Damn, he's good looking. Not in a Henley-king-of-the-world way—more like a prince kind of guy.

"Would you like a coffee or something?" I ask.

"Oh yes, please. After the busy day I've had, I need an upper." He follows me into the kitchen, and I make our coffees. He opens all his books on the kitchen counter and begins to flip through them. "So you liked this Hopewood line?"

"Yeah. I love it, but I don't know if I should get a two-seater or two three-seaters."

"Hmm." He thinks for a moment. "Let me measure the room again." He takes out his tape measure, and we walk out into the living area.

A knock sounds at the door.

"Who could that be?" I roll my eyes. "Excuse me."

"Sure," he replies as he begins to measure the room.

I open the door to see Henley standing there. "Hi." He gives me a lopsided smile.

I frown. What is he doing here? "Hi."

"Can . . ." He hesitates. "Can I come in?"

He only wants to come in because Joel is here.

"No, I'm busy." I cross my arms. "Can I help you with something?"

"Um." He puts his hands into his suit pockets. "I . . ."

I glance back into the house; I can't leave Joel alone too long. "What is it, Henley?"

"I need a favor."

"Like what?"

"I have a thing for work this weekend, and I need a date."

My eyebrows shoot up in surprise.

"One of my clients is trying to set me up with his daughter, and I kind of . . . told him that I have a girlfriend."

"You want another fake date?"

"Yes."

"No."

His face falls. "No?"

"Hard no."

His eyes search mine.

"Do you really think after what happened last week and the way you treated me that you deserve another fake date?"

"I was doing you a favor." He frowns. "It was . . . you wanted the fake date?"

I lower my voice so that Joel can't hear us. "I never wanted the fake orgasm."

"You didn't fake it," he whispers angrily.

"Yes, I did," I lie.

"You owe me."

"I do not owe you anything, least of all my time."

He steps back, affronted. "You're angry with me."

"Yes, I'm fucking angry with you," I spit. "You didn't talk to me all weekend, and you're only here now because Joel's car is out front."

His jaw tics as he clenches his teeth. "That's not true. I was coming over anyway. I didn't even see his car."

Bullshit.

I lean into him. "Let's get one thing straight, Henley. I am not the backup plan. I am not someone you call on when there is no better option. Ask Taryn to fake-date you."

"I don't want to go with Taryn."

"Tough shit. I don't want to go with you."

He puts his weight onto his back foot, annoyed. "So it's a no?"

"It's a hard no."

His eyes hold mine, and I know he's trying to think of something to say.

"Good night, Henley." I close the door in his face and walk back inside to Joel. "Sorry about that."

"Let me guess, your neighbor?"

I give a heavy sigh.

"He likes you."

"No. Trust me, he doesn't."

"I'm telling you; I know when a man likes a woman. He likes you."

"Yeah, well . . . it's not happening." *And I really don't want to discuss this with you.* "Where were we?" I ask him.

"The couch. I think two three-seaters."

Thursday morning, 6:30 a.m., I walk up the corridor of San Sebastian Nursing Home. My first shift at my second job has been a delight. I'm going to do three nights a month, and that should free up some funds for these stupidly expensive furnishings.

"How was it?" Sonya smiles.

"Great, actually." I'm relieved. I had no idea what I was signing up for. "Everyone was so nice."

I glance up the long corridor and see a familiar figure walk into one of the rooms and close the door behind them.

Was that . . .

"Who was that?"

"Who?"

"I just saw a man walk into the room at the end?"

She looks at her watch as we walk up the hall toward the room. "Oh, that would be Bernard's son."

"Bernard?"

"One of our patients."

We stop in front of the door in question and peer through the window. Henley is dressed in his suit and laying out clothes on the bed.

I frown, confused.

"He is the most gorgeous man," she whispers. "He comes every morning and feeds his father breakfast and gets his clothes out for the day."

I watch as Henley smiles and chats with the old man. He cups his face in his hands and says something and then goes and gets a pair of clippers from the bathroom to help him shave.

"Breaks my heart." She smiles sadly.

"Why is that?" I frown as I watch the pair.

"Because his father doesn't even know who he is."

Chapter 10

My heart sinks. "How long has he got?"

"Not sure."

Henley says something and whips his father with his T-shirt. The old man laughs out loud as they play.

I feel my heart constrict as I watch on. "The son comes every day?"

"Never misses one."

"How long does he stay?"

"He gets here just before seven a.m. and leaves around nine. Feeds him breakfast, helps him shave, and then keeps him calm as the nurses help him shower. Reads him the morning paper too."

"There are no other siblings?"

"No, I don't think so."

I get a lump in my throat as I watch on.

Henley stands, and I duck behind the wall. I don't want him to see me. "Thanks for showing me the ropes." I smile. "See you next time, eh?"

"Sure thing." She saunters off, and I peer back in through the window in the door. Henley is now flicking through the television channels to put the morning news on.

As my heart constricts, another piece of the Henley James puzzle clicks into place.

He's a good man.

You know that feeling when you're about to do something stupid, but you don't care and want to do it anyway?

That's me right at this very moment. I knock hard on the door. Something about seeing Henley at the nursing home this week has opened a huge gaping hole of enchantment in my heart for him. I know I don't know him, but I do have more of an understanding as to why he is the way he is.

I need to know more.

Knock, knock, knock. This is undoubtedly the most stupid thing I have ever done, yet it's all I can think about. Henley opens his front door. "Juliet."

"Hi, Henley." I force a smile. "I've reconsidered your offer."

His eyebrows shoot up in surprise. "For?"

"The date."

"Oh."

"Yes." I shrug as I try to act casual. "Turns out I can be your date this weekend after all."

"Why is that?" he asks flatly. "You were repelled by the idea when I asked you."

"Yes, well . . . I don't like you barging over every time I have a man come to the house when you can't be bothered to even acknowledge me if you see me anywhere else."

"Like where?"

"Like at Carol's party."

"You were talking to Rebecca all night."

"Yes, while you were talking to Taryn."

He rolls his eyes. "I'm single, Juliet."

"So am I, so I don't appreciate you barging in on Joel and I."

Ugh, why am I such a smart-ass around him? He brings out the worst in me.

"Isn't dating your designer going against some code of ethics or something?"

"Who cares. So is it a date?"

He glares at me.

"Hurry up and make your decision," I snap.

Take the bait.

"Don't try and tell me what to do, Juliet. I don't like it. And, yes, it *is* a date. A fake date—don't get any ideas."

Anger bubbles just under the surface. He really is infuriating in the flesh. "Believe me, ideas are the last thing I'm vibing from you right now, Henley."

He crosses his arms, and it's then I notice he's shirtless and in boxer shorts.

Eyes up.

"Seeing Joel this week, are you?" he asks.

"Not sure," I lie.

His calculating eyes hold mine, and I inwardly smile. Maybe he does like me, even if it's only a tiny bit.

"What time on Saturday?" I ask.

"It's in the city and will be a late one. We will probably have to stay the night in a hotel."

"What?"

"You'll have your own room, of course." He rolls his eyes. "I'm not stupid, and there is no way I'd share a room with you."

There's a reason Henley James doesn't date; nobody would put up with his shit. "Goodbye, Henley." I walk down the steps.

"It's black tie," he calls.

I turn back. "What?"

"The function, it's black tie."

Fuck it, now I have to spend money that I don't have on a stupid dress. "Great." I smile. "Can't wait."

I storm back to my house while inwardly kicking myself for agreeing to this.

What did you do?

Vroom, vroom, vroom.

Laughter echoes through the street, and Barry's ears prick up.

"Huh." I glance toward my front windows. It's nearly 6:00 p.m. on Thursday night.

"What's that sound?" Chloe asks from her fold-up chair. Damn it, I wish my new couch would arrive already.

Vroom, vroom, vroom.

More male laughter. A girl screams.

"What is it, Barry?" I get up and walk to the front window, and my eyes widen in horror. "What the hell?"

"What?"

"You better come look at this because you wouldn't believe me if I told you."

Chloe gets off her fold-up chair and comes and stands beside me to spy through the sheer curtains.

Taryn is roller-skating up and down the street. She's wearing electric-blue biker shorts and a matching sports bra. Her hair is in two pigtails, and her huge perky boobs are hanging out on display. She has white knee and wrist guards on.

"Are you kidding me right now?" Chloe snaps. "Who the fuck is that?"

"Taryn, the one I was telling you about."

The neighborhood men are all on Blake's front lawn chatting, while secretly eyeing her.

"She obviously saw them and then came out to put on a show," Chloe scoffs. "Has she no shame?"

"Does it look like she does?"

We both watch as Taryn is over-the-top flirting and being dramatic as she skates. I roll my eyes. "Give me a break."

She touches Blake's tie and says something to him, and he laughs out loud.

"Fuck off, you silly show-off witch," Chloe snaps, her eyes glued to them.

Henley's car pulls around the corner and slows right down. He says something to her through the window of his car, and she laughs out loud. "Oh, Henley, you're so funny."

No, he's not.

"He's a grumpy shithead. Goes to show how little you know about him," I whisper angrily.

Henley doesn't bother driving into his garage. He parks his car in the driveway and gets out and goes to talk to the boys on the curb. They stand around chatting as they enjoy the show.

"Of course he does that," Chloe snaps, infuriated. "He's a fuck-tard too."

He eyes her up and down, and I fume.

"We have established this already."

She starts to try and spin with her arms out wide, and I roll my eyes. "This isn't fucking *Xanadu*, you silly bitch."

I spy through the sheer curtains, and I watch Henley watch her. I don't like him looking at anyone else.

Rebecca walks across the road. "Who's this coming?" Chloe asks.

"Rebecca. I met her on Saturday night. She's nice."

She steps onto my lawn. "Why is she coming over here?"

"I don't know. Quick, act natural." We both run and dive onto our fold-up chairs.

"Taryn better fuck off. I'm really going to lose my shit. I have not liked him for three years for her to swoop in and steal him at the finish line," Chloe whispers angrily.

"Blake won't like her," I whisper. "Henley will like her. I just know it."

"We need to take this bitch down."

Knock, knock sounds at the door.

"Come in," I call.

Rebecca opens the door, "Hi." She smiles. Her face falls when she sees Chloe. "Sorry, I didn't realize you had company."

"No, no, come in. This is my girlfriend Chloe."

"Hi, Rebecca." Chloe smiles.

"Umm . . ." Rebecca looks between us and then closes the door behind her. "Have you seen that idiot on roller skates?"

"I'm going to throw some ball bearings on the road so she falls ass over tit." Chloe rolls her eyes.

Rebecca sits down nervously, and I get the feeling something is wrong. "Are you okay?"

She shrugs. "So . . ." She pauses as if choosing her wording carefully. "If I needed a confidential, unbiased female opinion on something in my house, could you two keep a secret?"

Chloe and I exchange glances. "Yeah." We shrug.

"You promise you won't tell anyone? It's just that . . ." She pauses again. "We moved interstate to live here five years ago, and I'm so busy working that I haven't made any friends. Well, I do have friends," she explains. "But they are all couple friends, if you know what I mean. Like . . . I can't trust them with a secret."

"Of course. What's going on?"

"I need to show you something." She stands. "It's at my house."

"What?" I frown.

"Come on." She walks out, and we follow her past the roller-skating idiot and the sidewalk perverts.

"I swear to god, if she makes a move on him, it's go time," Chloe huffs as she watches Blake talk to Taryn. "This street is like fucking Tinder on crack."

"Who are we talking about?" Rebecca frowns.

Chloe hesitates.

"Hey, I'm about to show you something that you promised not to tell. Your secret is safe with me."

Chloe exhales. "I have a thing for Blake Grayson."

Rebecca smiles as she marches across the lawn in front of us. "Who doesn't."

"I know, it's so annoying," Chloe huffs. "I wish he were ugly."

"Then you probably wouldn't like him," I reply.

Rebecca walks us up the stairs to her front porch and into the house. She flicks the dead bolt on the front door behind us.

I frown. "What's going on?"

"So . . ." She pauses. "This is so random, and I feel I might be going crazy, and I hope you are going to tell me this is all in my head."

"Right . . ." Chloe frowns. "Go on."

"So John's back tire has been going down, and it was booked in for a service today to get repaired."

"Who's John?" Chloe frowns.

"Her husband," I reply.

"He had to work, so I offered to take it in for him, and he took my car to work," Rebecca replies as she leads us through the house.

"Right." I frown. Where is this story going?

"And I took it in and got the tire fixed, and then I thought I would clean and vacuum his car out as a surprise." She opens the internal garage door, and we see a gunmetal-gray hotted-up Audi SUV.

"Okay."

"I want you to tell me I'm crazy." She opens the back door of the car.

"Spit it out."

"Get in."

"What?"

She gestures to the car. "Get in, and don't touch anything."

Chloe and I climb into the back seat.

"Do you see anything abnormal?" Rebecca asks.

Chloe and I look around the car. "No . . ." We frown.

She turns on the flashlight on her phone and shines it on the window. "What about now?"

Two perfect foot marks come up on the inside of the door window: a woman's footprints.

"I've never been in the back seat of this car," Rebecca says.

Our eyes widen as we stare at the footprints.

"You see them, right?" she asks.

We both nod.

One footprint is at the side, as if someone has been lying in the back seat; the other one is on the other side of the window, as if they have been spreading their legs.

"You think he's cheating on you?" Chloe whispers.

Rebecca shrugs. "How the fuck do women's footprints get in the back seat of your husband's car?"

"I don't know." I stare at the footprints. "They're definitely there, though. You are not imagining this at all."

"Fuck."

We all stay silent as we think.

"You know what we need?" Chloe replies. "We need one of those black light semen detectors."

"What?" I frown.

"Yeah, you know. Like the police use."

Chloe begins to look in the pockets in the backs of the seats. "Did you check everything?"

"Yep, I didn't find anything."

Chloe gets down onto the floor and begins to feel around under the seats.

"What are you going to do?" I ask Rebecca.

"I don't know. This isn't concrete evidence enough to prove anything, but if he thinks I'm onto him, he'll be super careful, and I'll never know the truth."

"You really think he would cheat on you?"

"He cheated once in college."

I frown.

"He was drunk, and we were doing the long-distance thing, but he called me distraught half an hour after it happened, crying his eyes out, racked with guilt. He's not the lying type. At least I don't think."

"Is this yours?" Chloe pulls out a small pink bulldog clip from under the seat.

Rebecca stares at it in Chloe's hand. "No. It's not."

I put my hands over my mouth in horror. "Fuck."

"Men are such fucking idiots," Chloe whispers angrily.

"Get out. We'll talk about it out there in case he gets home," Rebecca whispers. "I don't want him to know I'm onto him."

We climb out of the car and close the door, and we walk back into the house. "Who wants wine?" Rebecca fumes.

"Yeah, sure," Chloe and I reply, both scared for our lives.

This is so weird, sharing something so personal with someone we hardly know.

Rebecca pours three glasses of wine and heads out to the back garden. There's a beautiful pool area with a cabana, and she leads us down there. We sit at a table.

"Have you had any inkling that something was off?" I ask.

She twists her lips. "Our sex life has been nearly nonexistent, but he's been working so much that he's been tired."

"But has he really been working?" Chloe whispers. "I mean . . ." She shrugs.

"Who fucking knows." Rebecca puts her hand over her forehead. "I can't believe it."

"Look, it may not even be what we're assuming. It could be completely innocent," I try to reassure her. "Innocent until proven guilty, right?"

"How could this be innocent?" she huffs. She drains her glass and fills it again.

"I don't know." I try to think of a logical explanation. "Have you ever parked this car in valet parking?" I ask.

"All the time."

"How do you know that one of the parking attendants hasn't been getting busy with a waitress in your car?"

Rebecca stares at me.

"Or the car wash?" I shrug. "Or the mechanic. The mechanic may have fucked his receptionist in the back seat of the car just today."

Chloe twists her lips. "Maybe."

"I don't know, but don't just assume the worst until we have proof."

"Oh, get off it," Chloe snaps. "Coming from you, that's a joke. Why don't you give Henley the same forgiveness?"

"Henley?" Rebecca frowns as she looks between us. "You're on with Henley?"

My eyes widen at Chloe. *You did not just say that.*

"I mean . . . what I was saying . . ." Chloe trips over her words as she tries to cover up her mistake.

"Chloe," I snap. It's too late now. "I went on a date with Henley a few years ago, and I didn't know he lived here when I bought the house."

Rebecca's eyes widen. "What happened?"

"We had the best night ever, and then he ghosted me with his burner phone."

Her eyes widen as she puts the pieces together. "Oh . . . fuck, that means . . . he liked you."

"And now Taryn is out there rubbing her big boobs all over him, and I'm totally screwed because I still think he's gorgeous when, in fact, he is actually a fucking asshole."

She rolls her eyes into her drink. "Amen."

"Listen, on to more important things," Chloe interrupts. "Can someone just think of a plan to make Blake Grayson fall in love with me? I cannot date one more mediocre man."

We all fall silent, lost in our own thoughts as we drink our wine.

"What are you going to do?" I eventually ask Rebecca.

"Keep my eyes and ears open, I guess. If something is going on, he'll catch himself out. They always do."

I put my hand over hers. "I'm sorry."

She exhales. "Not as sorry as he's going to be if I find something out."

"I'm choosing to think innocent until proven guilty." I smile hopefully.

She squeezes my hand. "Let's hope."

I look at my reflection in the mirror. "How much is it?" I pray as I wait for her reply.

"Four hundred and twenty."

Fuck.

I puff air into my cheeks. I'm trying on formal gowns in a boutique. This one is a deep red; the top is like a corset with boning and the bottom a flowing skirt.

It is sensational.

"What look are you going for?" the shop assistant asks.

"I want to knock someone's socks off."

She smiles as she looks me up and down. "Then you have to buy this one."

"I didn't want to spend this much money."

"You can't fake quality, dear. You'll have this for years. It's timeless."

"True."

"And this may be the only chance you get to knock him dead."

"Also true."

"And if you wear something else, are you going to be kicking yourself that you didn't buy this one?"

"Probably."

She shrugs. "I think you've answered all your own questions."

Damn it. Why did I come into this shop when I knew it had over-the-top prices?

If I buy it, then it will put me back another week with my renovations.

New lamps or a possible night with Henley James . . . hmm.

It's a tough decision.

Lamps . . . Henley . . . lamps . . . Henley.

I twist my lips as I stare at my reflection.

Fuck it. You only live once. "I'll take it."

Saturday afternoon and I am rushing around like a madwoman. Chloe is coming over to stay with Barry after she finishes work. I have my bag packed and ready to roll. We are checking into the hotel early and getting ready there. My nerves are at an all-time high. My phone rings.

Why is he calling me? Don't tell me he's canceling. "Hello?"

"Hi."

"What's wrong?"

"Are you ready?"

"Yeah, why?"

"Any chance you could sneak over here?"

"What?"

"If Carol sees me pick you up, we will never hear the end of it. But if you sneak over here, she will be none the wiser."

"Um." I think for a moment. "Yeah, okay. But I have my overnight bag."

"Throw it over the back fence."

"You want me to climb the fence?" I gasp.

"Can you?"

"No."

"Too high? I thought you were an elite athlete."

"I am, and boxing is my specialty, Henley."

He chuckles. "Okay, throw your bag over the back fence, and then sneak around to the front."

"Are you serious?"

"Yes. Trust me on this. Neighborhood watch is alive and well."

"We went out two weeks ago, and she didn't see us."

"She was out when we went to the wedding."

"How do you know?"

"Because I asked her what she was doing the day before."

I roll my eyes. "Fine, come out back now." I hang up and take my bag out to the backyard, and Henley's arm comes over. I pass my bag over to him.

"Fuck, what have you got in here? It weighs a ton."

"A body bag," I whisper. "To dispose of the evidence."

"What evidence would that be?"

"A body."

"Mine?"

"Who else's would it be?"

"I told you not to get any ideas," he replies. "Now sneak around to the front."

"Yes."

"Are you coming now?"

"Yes."

"Hurry up."

"Henley," I snap. "Shut up."

I go inside and lock my house up. Then I walk out the back door and around to the side gate. I look left and right, and I slip behind the bushes and sneak into Henley's yard.

Hmm, not bad. Stealth mode at its very best. Those bushes come in handy.

I run around to his backyard and slip through the side gate. Voilà . . . I did it.

I'm in.

Henley is waiting at the back door. "Well, well, well, look what the cat dragged in." He smirks.

"Reason five hundred why I bought a body bag," I mutter as I walk past him.

And suddenly, I'm inside his house, his personal space. My eyes look around in awe. It's modern, gorgeous, and totally spotless. It sort of has a European feel: lots of marble and white walls. Textured furnishings and abstract art.

"Wow." I smile as I look around. "Henley, it's beautiful."

"Thanks." His eyes linger on my face, and I get the feeling he wants to say something else.

It's there between us; the electric current is back. It's actually more like lightning, but whatever.

Butterflies flutter in my stomach. "What have you got in store for me tonight?"

"Lots of things."

And I already know from the look in his eye what *lots of things* means.

At least I hope I do.

"Let's get there and get ready," he says. "We can have a cocktail or two before we have to go."

I smile. "Sounds like a plan."

He leads me out to his garage, and he unlocks his Range Rover.

We climb into the car, and the garage door begins to go up. He begins to reverse.

"Fuck, duck down," he splutters.

"What?"

"Carol and Taryn are out front. Get down."

I put my head between my knees. "Aah, they're going to see me."

"They won't." He pulls out at high speed. "Keep down."

I actually wish Taryn would see me. That would teach her show-off, hot, roller-skating ass.

Henley pulls out and, with a quick wave to the neighborhood watch program, speeds past them. "Stay down," he tells me.

I'm crumpled up in a ball. "Are we past them yet?"

"Stay down." He grabs the back of my head and pushes me farther down.

"Aah." I swat his hand away. "You'll break me in half."

"Not yet," he mutters under his breath as he drives.

"What did you say?" I sit up.

"Nothing."

But I heard him, and I roll my lips to hide my smile.

Please.

We drive along in silence for a while. My mind is running at a million miles per minute.

I have a plan, and I know it's not a smart one.

But it's a plan.

I want to get to know Henley better, and he's afraid of commitment. I'm thinking that if I can just create a safe space for us to get to know each other . . . Without the pressure of expectation, who knows what may happen?

"So"—his eyes flick over to me—"what's the deal with your interior designer?"

Really? We're getting to this already?

"I don't know." I shrug. "He asked me out, and I'm considering it."

"If you like him, why didn't you just say yes?"

"I'm not looking for a relationship."

His eyes flick over in question.

"I've actually been thinking about getting on Tinder to try and find a friends with benefits situation."

"What?" He frowns, shocked.

"I just don't want a relationship." I act casual. "I want to focus on work and fixing up my house," I tell him in my practiced speech.

What I really want is time to try and figure him out, but I can't tell him that without scaring him off.

"No," he snaps.

"What do you mean, no?"

"I don't want you to have a regular booty call."

"Why not?" I frown. "You do."

"That's different."

"How is it?"

"Well . . ." He shrugs as if searching for the right words. "It's just sex to me, and you aren't like that."

"How do you know? You thought I was an engaged adulterer a week ago."

"I wonder why." He widens his eyes.

"Well, I don't see another option. I don't want a boyfriend, I don't want to fall in love, but I miss sex."

His eyes flick over to me. "I know what you're doing."

"What?"

"You want me to offer you my dick for your own personal use. That is not happening, Juliet."

"What?" I act horrified.

That's exactly what I want.

"Don't be ridiculous—we're neighbors." I look out the window as I act casual.

He twists his lips as he stares through the windshield.

"Anyway"—I shrug—"I'll work it out. Joel thinks it's a good idea."

His eyes flick over to me. "You've discussed this with him?"

"We were just talking about sex, and it came up."

"You were talking about sex with your interior fucking designer?" he barks.

"Why not?" I snap back. "I'm talking about it now with you."

"That's different."

"How is it different?"

"Because." He wobbles his head around as he searches for the right words.

"We went on a date and made out and stuff."

His eyes flick over to me. "You fire him. He's not to come back to your house. Ever."

I roll my eyes. "We did not make out. We pretended to make out, Henley."

He narrows his eyes as he stares back at the road.

"Anyway." I smile sweetly over at him. I put my hand on his thick thigh. "It's okay. I'll figure it out."

"What did he say?"

"What did who say?"

"When you told that dickhead that you wanted a friends with benefits situation, what did he say?"

"He told me that if I ever asked him, he would be more than happy with that arrangement."

"I bet he did," he sneers.

"I'm not going to ask him," I add. "I have work with him. It would be weird." I try to dig myself out of the hole. Oh crap, I really am going to have to fire Joel now. Henley can never see him again.

"Anyway." I squeeze his thigh. "It's not your problem. You're probably saving yourself for the love of your life to come along. And so you should too."

His jaw tics in anger, and I roll my lips to hide my smile. It's a wonder my nose isn't a foot long, with all the lying I'm doing.

We drive the rest of the way in silence. I'm secretly high-fiving myself for sticking to the game plan and being so brave. And he's probably thinking about ways to stuff me into the body bag.

The car pulls into the circular driveway, and the doormen rush to open our car doors. "Are we getting out here?"

"Yes," he mutters distractedly. He passes the keys to one of the doormen. "Be careful with it, please."

"Of course, sir. We will bring your bags to the room."

"Thank you." Henley takes my hand in his and leads me through the lobby. The hotel is fancy and over the top, with marble everywhere. "Two rooms in the name of Henley James, please."

"Yes, sir." The male concierge smiles. His eyes linger a little too long on Henley, and I feel my stomach twinge with jealousy.

He's holding my hand, you know?

Jeez, some people.

He types into his computer and then passes over two keys. "Here you are, two rooms, as requested."

"Thank you."

"Have a nice stay."

Henley leads me to the elevator, and we get in and turn toward the doors.

"He was checking you out," I whisper.

He raises an unimpressed eyebrow. "I don't think so."

"I know so."

"How would you know what checking me out is?" he mutters dryly. "You don't do it."

I giggle. "Does it bother you?"

"No."

"It does."

"I just don't understand why you would tell an interior designer that you want friends with benefits."

"Because I do, Henley."

"I'll buy you a vibrator."

"Fine." I hold my hands up in surrender. "I shouldn't have said anything. I don't know how to make it any clearer: I need a man to take care of my needs. Nothing more and nothing less. You are reading into it too much."

His dark eyes drop to my lips, and then, as if remembering where he is, he turns back to face the doors; his face is solemn. "When are you seeing him again?"

"Who?"

"The designer," he spits.

"Oh my god, will you drop it?" I whisper angrily.

We get to our floor, and we walk down the wide and fancy corridor. He passes me a key. "Six o'clock."

"Uh-huh."

"I'll come and get you."

"Okay."

We stare at each other; an unspoken feeling runs between us. He's battling with jealousy and wants to explode, and I have to say I'm totally into it.

"See you at six."

He steps forward, forcing me to step back. "What are you wearing?"

"Clothes."

"Shame."

I do love it when he's naughty.

I turn to my door. "Goodbye, Henley."

"See you at six."

"Holy fuck," Chloe whispers as she looks at my reflection over FaceTime. "This poor bastard doesn't stand a chance tonight."

I giggle. "That *is* the plan."

Knock, knock sounds at the door. "I've got to go—he's here."

"Text me updates. Love you."

"Bye." I take one last look at myself: deep-red corset, plunging neckline, and a flowing skirt. I smile, happy with what I see. This dress was worth every penny.

I open the door in a rush, and there he stands. His messy dark hair and black dinner suit, and a smile that could blow up the world.

"Hi," he breathes. He steps forward, taking me into his arms.

"Hi." One touch and my hormones are in overdrive.

His eyes drop down my body and then darken. "You look fucking delicious."

I smile up at him as the air crackles between us. Without saying a word, he takes my face in his hands and kisses me. A gentle brush of his lips, a little tongue, and a whole load of promise.

Dear god.

Chapter 11

Henley

Just a taste . . .

"Henley." Juliet pushes me back. "What the hell are you doing?"

Pulled out of my momentary dick fog, I look up at her. *What am I doing?*

Fuck.

She takes a step back as she pulls out of our kiss.

That was a brain snap and a half. "Well, you shouldn't look so gorgeous. I am only human, Juliet. There's only so much a man can take."

She smiles up at me, and I feel it all the way to the tip of my dick. Unable to help it, I take her in my arms. "We should practice kissing some more."

She smirks. "Should we?"

My lips dust hers, and a tidal wave of desire rips through my very core. We kiss again, and my eyes close as I pull her closer. What is it about this woman?

Every touch is magnified.

We kiss again and again, and I step forward, pinning her to the counter.

Thump, thump, thump throbs my cock.

I want more.

"That's enough." She breaks the kiss and pulls out of my arms.

"What? We haven't even started yet."

"This is a fake date, Henley; we don't need to practice kissing in private. I think we both know that we already have it perfected."

I stare at her. With no blood left for it, my brain is having a hard time functioning. "Right."

Get it together.

I drag my hands through my hair. My eyes drop down her luscious body in that red dress. And I swear, I'm two seconds away from blowing.

Which is not in the plan.

"We should get going," I tell her.

"Okay."

My eyes drop to her lips, and I imagine them around my cock. I feel myself harden to an almost painful level.

In slow motion she licks them, and I clench as if I feel it. My eyes rise to meet hers.

"Everything all right?" she whispers. She runs her hands over her breasts and down to sit on her waist. She gives a playful wiggle of her hips. "Henley?"

Is she playing with me?

"I'm fine," I reply sharply. "We should get going."

"Okay."

I open the door, and she sashays past me; I follow her down the corridor with my eyes on her ass.

I imagine bending her over and giving it to her from behind. I wouldn't need any practice for that one. I know what to do.

We get into the elevator, and she takes my hand in hers. "I'm looking forward to tonight." She smiles casually.

"Me too," I lie. I have no interest in the event tonight. We are only going so that I have a legitimate reason to touch her.

"Our second fake date." She smiles up at me.

I smirk, and then in slow motion she lifts my hand to her lips and kisses the back of it tenderly.

Uneasiness falls over me.

Don't do that.

"I'm eating all the dessert tonight." She smiles casually. "I wonder what the main course will be." She kisses my hand again, completely distracted. "I'm hoping we can order whatever we want. I'm craving carbs."

I stare at her as the walls close in around me. This feels very *real*-date-like.

The way she looks. The way I feel.

"You should stick to protein," I mutter.

She giggles and nudges me with her shoulder. I nudge her back. She nudges me again.

"Juliet, don't push your luck, or you will find yourself being fucked in the foyer of this hotel."

She giggles. "You wish."

I do, actually.

I clear my throat, annoyed by my body's reaction to her. "A date is a date, and all date entitlements should be made readily available."

"What?" She laughs. "So you think because we are on a fake date that we could actually have sex tonight?"

"Who knows."

"Hen . . ." She goes up onto her toes and kisses me softly. My hands instinctively snap around her waist. "I'm looking for something more regular."

"With him?"

"No, not with him."

"Then with who?"

"Someone I have chemistry with."

I stare at her, choosing my next words wisely. The elevator doors open, thankfully cutting me off.

Hand in hand, we walk out through the foyer and head down the street. She chats away while my mind is running a million miles per minute.

This feels off.

I'm not on my game. Something is seriously wrong with this picture.

No.

Abort mission.

There's to be no sex with Juliet Drinkwater under any circumstance. Take it off the table, right now.

She's my next-door neighbor, for fuck's sake.

The only thing that's sure to come out of this is a neighborhood disturbance.

We walk past a storefront window display; it's a tower of fresh flowers, and she stops to look at it. "Hen, look how beautiful." She slides her arm in under my coat jacket and puts it around me. She pulls me close as if it's the most natural thing in the world.

The disturbing thing is, it feels like it is.

I feel Henley straighten beneath my arm and pull away from me. I glance up at him in question. "What?"

"What, what?" he replies curtly.

"Why did you just do that?"

"Do what?" He stares straight ahead at the window display, seemingly annoyed.

"Never mind."

"Did you still want to grab a drink before we go?" I ask.

"If you want."

"Where shall we go?"

He looks down the street. "There's a bar over there."

"Looks good."

We make our way over to the bar and take a seat at the bench table by the window. It's eclectic and moody, with a huge bar in the middle.

"Would you like a drink?" he asks.

"Yes, please."

He raises an impatient eyebrow. "Such as?"

Gone is the playful and touchy man that was just here. Mr. Mercurial is now in his place.

"A margarita, please."

Moments later he returns with two drinks, a margarita for me and an amber fluid for him. "Oh, what's that?" I ask as he sits down at the table.

"Scotch."

"Hmm, didn't imagine that you'd be a scotch drinker."

Amusement flashes across his face. "What did you think I would drink?"

I twist my lips as I think. "The blood of small children."

He chuckles. "Tempting."

"Actually, as far as alcohol goes, I would guess Jägerbombs."

"And why is that?"

"You explode."

"When have I ever exploded?"

"When my dog barks or makes a mess."

"Ah yes, Barry the *mutt*." He smirks.

I smile and take a sip of my margarita. "Oh, this is good, and don't say it like that."

"Say what?"

"*Mutt*."

"Why not."

"It sounds hot." I smile. "Does things to me. Gives me tingles."

"*Mutt*," he mouths.

I smile goofily. "You should put that on your Tinder profile."

"What?" he scoffs.

"'I sound hot when I say the word *mutt*.'" I widen my eyes, and he chuckles.

I feel a little of our chemistry return.

"Actually, that's a good idea," I tell him.

"What's a good idea?" he asks.

"You can help me write my friends-with-benefits Tinder profile."

"No." He screws up his face in disgust.

"Why not?"

"Because it's the most ridiculous idea I've ever heard of, that's why. You'll have every weirdo sex maniac on the planet applying."

"One can hope." I smile into my drink.

He rolls his eyes. "It's not going to work, you know."

"What's not going to work?"

"You won't be able to do it. You're going to fall in love."

Would that be so terrible?

"No, I won't," I lie.

"I know how women like you are wired, Juliet."

"Oh please." I roll my eyes. "Do you now?" I sip my drink. "For the record, I have had a friends-with-benefits situation before, and it was perfect."

"When?"

"In college."

"With whom?"

"My roommate."

He stares at me as if completely perplexed . . . or maybe it's because he can sense that I'm lying through my teeth. Well, I'm not really lying. I did have a booty call with my roommate a few times in college, but then he got creepy and I panicked and moved out . . . so yeah, kind of friends-with-benefits-turns-into-serial-killer thingy.

"How long did you see him for?" he asks.

"A few months."

"How did it end?"

"We mutually decided that we didn't want to do it anymore."

"I don't believe that for a second—no man would give up sleeping with you."

"Maybe I'm shitty in bed."

Shut up. Aren't you supposed to be selling the dream to him, you fool?

"Quite the opposite." His eyes hold mine, and the air swirls between us.

He's back.

"And what do you want from your man?" he murmurs.

Shit . . . think of a hot answer, and quick!

"I like to be challenged sexually."

His eyes darken. "Do you . . ."

Just come out and say it.

"That's why I was interested in doing this friends-with-benefits thing with you."

He steeples his pointer finger up the side of his face as he leans on his hand. "Go on."

"Well . . ." I pause as I try to get the wording right in my head. *Don't fuck this up.* "You said that you are not looking for a relationship."

"Correct."

"You like to dominate in the bedroom."

He stares at me for a beat before replying, "You'll get attached."

I sip my drink. "I think that if anyone is getting attached, it would be you."

"I can assure you it won't be me."

Poor deluded fool.

"Good." I smile. "That settles it."

"Settles what?"

"You're going to be my friend with benefits. There's no reason we couldn't have a business arrangement."

Amusement flashes across his face as he listens. His pointer finger is still up the side of his face as he leans on his hand. "No."

"Yes."

"No, Juliet. I'm not negotiating a body fluid business deal with you."

Time to play hardball.

I lean in close and put my mouth to his ear. "Are you trying to tell me that you wouldn't like me on my knees sucking your cock," I whisper.

His eyes darken. "Not one bit."

Liar.

"I like to swallow, you know."

He holds my gaze, and something tells me I'm playing with fire.

"I know you do," he murmurs.

Every cell in my body is screaming for me to stop, telling me how irresponsible and stupid this is. He wants sex with no strings attached. He's telling me this straight to my face.

Yet I know that deep down on some level he likes me, even if it's just a little bit, even if it's only for one night. I can't let it go without seeing what there is between us. I know I can handle this.

"I like the way *you* make me feel, Henley."

His eyes drop to my lips.

Fuck, sleeping with him is either going to be a major regret or a major achievement.

Either way, a definite heartbreak.

I slide my hand up his muscular quad.

"You could jump over the fence in the middle of the night and have your wicked way with my body and nobody would ever know."

Fire lights in his eyes, and I know he's imagining it. "It's not happening," he whispers distractedly.

I try to think on my feet. *Offer something that I know he wants.*

I lean in close again and run my teeth over his earlobe. "Do you want me to beg?"

The door busts open as we kiss, tongues exploring each other, hands in the hair, and off-the-hook chemistry erupting between us.

Shoes are kicked off, his jacket goes flying, and Henley's lips are locked on mine as he walks me backward toward the bed. We didn't even make it to his work thing, and I think I may have found his one weakness.

Dirty talk.

A few depraved things whispered in Henley James's ear, and his dick was so hard that it nearly ripped through his suit pants.

"Get it off," he murmurs against my lips as he fumbles with the ties on my dress.

I undo the buttons on his shirt and tear his shirt over his shoulders.

My eyes drop to his chiseled body, down over his abs to the trail of dark hair that disappears into his pants.

Aah . . . he's so ridiculously hot, I can't stand it.

He spins me away from himself and begins to unlace my corset. "Get that fucking thing off," he whispers. He pulls it with a tight jerk, and I smile at the wall. He's desperate to get me naked.

He gets to work unlacing my dress. If only he knew that I had to call a hotel cleaner into my room earlier to lace me into the damn thing. Not one of my coolest moments, but I had faith that the dress would pay off, and it turns out that it certainly has.

He slides my dress down over my hips and takes my hand to help me step out of it. His eyes drop down my body, and when they rise to my face, they are blazing with desire.

My heart somersaults. I don't think anyone has ever looked at me like that before.

Stay out of this, heart. Tonight is none of your concern, and don't go getting any ideas. This is a physical intel mission only.

He drops to his knees and kisses me there through my panties. My breath is quivering as I struggle to breathe. Without another word he slides them down my legs and takes them off. He looks up at me from the ground, and suddenly the mood of the room has changed, no longer desperate and horny.

There's a silence, a deep ache, and longing. Perhaps even an understanding that this is more . . . or maybe that's just my wishful thinking.

He stands, and his lips drop to my collarbone. And he slowly kisses up my neck as he reaches around and undoes my bra. I can't string two words together, so I stay quiet and let him lead the way. My body's reaction to him is out of this world.

It's like I can feel something shifting deep within my DNA, a longing that has never been met, a thousand goose bumps, a million senses waking from a dormant sleep.

He holds his arm out from his side and drops my bra onto the ground in a dramatic fashion, and I stand before him, naked and vulnerable.

His eyes roam over my skin and down over my sex and come up to linger on my breasts as I hold my breath.

Say something.

"You're more beautiful than I remembered," he murmurs as his eyes meet mine. "And trust me, I've remembered that moment a lot."

There it is—a glimmer of softness.

"I need you naked," I whisper.

He holds his hands out wide. "I'm all yours."

Mine.

I step closer and run my hands up over his broad chest, and if I'm not mistaken, he's not breathing either. I bend and kiss his chest as it rises and falls. I put my hand over his heart and feel it race beneath my fingers.

My eyes search his. And what the hell is going on here?

Focus.

I undo the buckle on his belt and slide it out of his pants. And then I undo the button and fly. My god . . . my heart is hammering in my chest. Have I ever been so nervous?

I slide his pants down and see his white briefs.

Tanned and toned, his abs and thick quad muscles are just so masculine. I've never seen such a virile man.

"All of it," he breathes.

My eyes shoot up. That's right, I'm supposed to be undressing him, not standing here ogling in my very own fantasyland. "I'm taking my time," I whisper as I softly kiss his big pouty lips. His eyes close as he gets lost in the moment. And damn it—I don't care how the sex goes. The night is already perfection.

I slide his briefs down, and my breath catches. *Fuck.*

He's huge and hard. The engorged head of his cock is shiny and red, weeping with pre-ejaculate.

That is one beautiful dick.

Unable to help it, I bend and lick the pre-ejaculate from his tip, and he inhales sharply. I take him into my mouth and slide him down my throat. His knees nearly buckle from beneath him. "You taste so good," I whisper around him.

His hands tenderly swipe my hair back from my face as he watches. I clench my legs together to try and control my urges.

"Enough," he murmurs before pulling me to my feet. "I need you." He pulls me over to an armchair in the corner of the room. "I need it to be here."

I frown.

"You have no idea how much you riding me the other night on that chair is burned into my brain."

"You want it like that?"

He nods and goes to his suit and takes a condom out of the pocket and then sits down.

I stare at him as my brain misfires. "But . . ."

"I don't want foreplay. Not this time."

My eyebrows shoot up in surprise.

"I want to feel you struggle to take in every inch."

"Oh."

Fuck, there are a lot of inches.

He rolls the condom on and holds his hand out to help me as I climb over him. Then, in another unexpected move, he positions my legs over the arms of the armchair.

"I . . ."

"You what?" he asks softly as he brushes the hair back from my face.

I'm not on my knees. I have no leverage, no safety net. "I have no control like this. What if . . ."

"What if I hurt you?"

I nod.

He kisses me softly, his tongue slowly plowing through my open lips. "I will hurt you, Juliet." He kisses me again. "But it's a good pain." His lips linger over mine. "It's a pain that I need."

I stare at him—confused, aroused, and completely terrified. It's not even about the pain. It's the fact that he wants to get off on it.

Our kiss deepens, and once again he steals my thoughts. "Can you do that for me, baby?" he whispers.

Baby.

I nod nervously. I'll do anything to have him call me that again. "Okay."

He lifts me and places the head of his cock at my entrance. It's like a cement wall.

No give at all. His size has scared me.

"Relax," he whispers up at me. His voice is soft, cajoling. "Work your way down on it." His lips take mine, and I push down a little. "That's it." He smiles against my lips.

I rock forward, and he eases in an inch more. Ow . . . it smarts.

A sharp sting that makes me wince.

"Slow down," he demands with a strong kiss. He rubs some saliva into my sex.

We go slower, kissing and taking our time, and eventually my body loosens a little.

"That's it, sweetheart." He eases his body up a little; his breath is quivering. "Can you feel how badly I need you?"

"Yes." I nod, because I can.

Our combined need for this is almost primal.

We stare at each other as he slides in another inch, and I whimper.

"That's it," he coaches me. "Good girl, just like that." He takes my nipple into his mouth, grazing it with his teeth. His eyes are locked on mine as he watches my body react to him, reading the cues that he's getting.

I begin to see stars.

Sure, it's the magical cock, but it's also the way he wanted to do this. Staring at each other while his body breaks mine in. His soft coaching. His tender touch.

Intimacy taken to another level.

Not at all what I was expecting, and to be honest, I know I'm in unsafe territory.

If he can own my body after only being half in, I don't know if I'll survive what comes next.

He slides in more, and I shudder, stretched to a new level. "Hen," I whimper.

"I know." His kiss is getting more aggressive as he struggles with control. "So fucking good. I can feel every muscle inside of you."

He grabs my ass cheeks and pulls them apart; I slide down a little more, and it smarts. "Aah," I cry out.

"Shh," he soothes me. "You need to relax."

"You're so big." I plead my case.

"And you're so tight." He smiles up at me in wonder. "We fit together perfectly."

We stare at each other, and I feel this warmth run through me. It's like liquid honey, sweet and sensual. Nothing like what this night is supposed to be.

He splays his palm over my lower stomach. His thumb pressing against my clit, he circles with just the right pressure, and I smile against his lips. "Yes." I roll my hips. "Like that." He keeps circling as we breathe hard. Our bodies are desperate for the hard fucking they deserve. I push down hard, and he stops me.

"Slow down," he demands. "You'll hurt yourself."

"Hen," I whimper into his mouth. "I need more."

"And you will get it." He pulls my cheeks apart again, and he slides in slowly to the hilt.

I'm so full and stretched, my body is rippling around his, half in panic, half in ecstasy.

We stare at each other, hearts racing.

He puts his arms under my thighs and lifts them. At this angle I'm completely at his mercy.

My hands are on his strong shoulders as I hold myself up.

I've never had a sexual experience like this before, and I don't use the word *experience* lightly. It's obvious he has a ton, and I have next to none. It's only now that I realize my past lovers have all been a bit vanilla.

He lifts me and brings me back down onto him with a sharp snap, knocking the air from my lungs. My body finally recognizes what she's supposed to do, and I get a rush of moisture.

"That's it." He smiles as he feels the lubrication finally arrive. He lifts me again and slides in deep, so deep.

The last of his control snaps. He lifts me and begins to ride me, his hips rising to meet mine, slower at first and then working up to deep, punishing pumps, the kind that make your eyes roll back in your head.

The sound of our skin slapping together echoes throughout the room.

I cry out as I begin to spiral.

"Not yet." He lifts me higher and higher, his hips working at piston pace, desperate for the orgasm his body is demanding.

I clench down as I come hard, and he holds himself deep, and I feel the hard jerk of his cock.

We pant as we stare at each other.

A beautiful, perfect clarity runs between us, something that is foreign and new.

I cup his beautiful face in my hand.

His eyes are wild. His body is still inside mine, yet I can feel him pulling away from me by the second.

He's panicking . . .

Without a word he lifts me off him and throws me onto the bed.

He flicks off his condom and throws it in the trash and then crawls between my legs and pulls them open. He licks me there, his eyes closing in pleasure, and I shudder and shake, my body still reacting to the orgasm I just had.

Then he's eating me like I'm his last supper. His stubble is burning my skin. His hands are all over, and I get the feeling that he's blocking me out. Instinct has taken him over.

He's feeding his body now; I have nothing to do with it anymore.

He licks me deeper and deeper, and aah . . . What the hell is he doing? We just had sex. This is perverted.

But it's not, not even close.

This is dirty and hot, just like I knew he would be.

He takes me there again, licking me until I can't stand it, until I'm writhing on the bed. And then he flips me over onto my knees and pulls my hips up with a sharp snap.

I hear the condom wrapper tear, and he grabs a handful of my hair and pulls my head back as he slams in hard. My knees nearly buckle from underneath me, and he slaps my ass. "Get on your knees and ride this fucking cock. I'm nowhere near finished with you." He slides his thumb into my ass. "My dirty girl next door."

Excitement runs through me, and I smile.

Hands down, best night of my life.

I wake up sleepy and put my arm out for Henley. The bed is empty, and I look around the darkened hotel room. Is he in the bathroom? "Hen?" I call.

No answer.

I sit up. "Henley?"

Silence . . .

The energy is different. Fuck it. He's gone.

I reach over and grab my phone to check the time: 6:00 a.m.

Did he leave last night after I went to sleep?

He broke me in on the armchair. Then we had rough sex. Then we had a shower, and somehow that turned into sex, too, and eventually, we rolled into bed exhausted. I don't remember much after that, but I do remember him holding me close as I drifted off to sleep.

Shit.

I get out of bed and go to the bathroom. On the way back to bed, I see a scribbled note on the bedside table.

Gone to the gym,
back soon.
X

Relief fills me. Okay . . . he's only at the gym, and he left me a note.

Crisis averted.

I lie in bed and smile goofily up at the ceiling. Last night was the most incredible sexual experience of my life.

He's so . . .

Wow.

I feel sated and alive. And damn it, I want more.

Henley James is one addictive drug.

I know he's not at the gym. He's visiting his father, being the wonderful man that I know he is deep down. He'll be back soon.

Fuck, he'll be back soon, and I look like roadkill. I need to be simply irresistible from here on out. I jump up and bounce into the shower. Time to get back to my hard-to-get plan.

Focus, bitch.

"Another coffee?" the waitress asks.

"That would be lovely. Thank you." I smile. I glance at my watch. 7:45 a.m.

Where is he?

I'm sitting in the hotel restaurant, trying to play hard to get. I'm waiting for him to call me to see where I am when he gets back.

He better fucking call me.

What if this plan backfires and he just leaves without me?

It won't. He won't.

If I want more of this man, I have to make him think I'm not attached and clingy.

But right at this moment, I feel serial-killer clingy toward him.

My phone beeps a text.

Where are you?

I smile. Yes!

I text him back.

I'm in the restaurant having breakfast.
Join me?

I hunch my shoulders up like a little kid. Everything is going according to plan.

Okay, see you soon.

I open my prop newspaper, and with my heart thumping in my chest, I prepare myself for battle.

Ten minutes later. "Hello."

I glance up to see Mr. Gorgeous sliding into the seat opposite me. I want to jump up and kiss him, hug him so tight that he pops, but I won't.

"Hi." I smile casually. I turn my attention back to my paper. "How was the gym?"

"It was okay." He looks around. "Is it a buffet, or are we ordering?"

"I've already eaten," I lie. "I was hungry."

"Oh."

"I'll wait with you while you eat if you like." I glance up from my paper as if he's an inconvenience.

A frown flashes across his face before he quickly hides it. "Don't let me keep you."

"No, no." I glance at my watch. "I've got half an hour."

His eyes hold mine. "Before what?"

"I'm going shopping. My girlfriends are meeting me. We have a full day planned."

"Really?" He rolls his lips as if annoyed.

"You didn't expect me to go home with you, did you?"

His jaw tics in anger. "Not at all."

The waitress comes over. "Can I take your order, sir?"

"Yes." He looks over the menu. "I'll have the big breakfast, please, with a latte and an orange juice."

"Sure." She scribbles down his order before leaving us alone.

I keep reading the paper, and I can feel Henley's eyes fixed on me. "You don't have to stay," he says.

"Actually, I might get going. I do have a lot to do." I fold my paper in half and drink the last of my coffee.

His eyes hold mine.

I bite the inside of my cheek to keep myself from smiling. "You were a great fuck."

He blinks, shocked.

"Until next time, Mr. James." I blow him a kiss and, without another word, walk away; I can feel his eyes on my back, and I want to jump and punch the air.

That was so cool that I can't even stand it.

Let the games begin.

Chapter 12

I walk into the café and smile and wave as I see Chloe waiting at the table for me. I bounce over. "Hi." I beam.

"Hi." She smirks up at me. "You look like you've been well fucked."

"Not even close." I giggle and fall into my seat. "I've been spectacularly fucked, actually."

She giggles and holds her hand up for a high five. "Yes."

"Your coffees." The waitress smiles as she puts them down on the table.

"Thank you."

"So?" Chloe widens her eyes. "Tell me everything."

"Oh my god." I sigh dreamily. "Picture the best night in all of history, and that's what I had. He is . . . unbelievable."

"What, good in bed?"

"Good at everything, and he's sensual and sexual and hung like a horse and, gah . . . I'm addicted."

Chloe twists her lips as she looks at me. "I thought this was an intel mission only."

"It was . . . is," I correct myself.

"Hang on a minute—you said you just wanted friends with benefits with him."

"I do," I lie. "But . . . I'm just going to see how it goes."

She rolls her eyes. "Whatever you do, don't fall for this guy. He's emotionally fucked up, and the last thing you need is a man with colossal baggage."

"I know, I'm not."

"We'll see." She sips her coffee. "So did you stick to our plan this morning?"

"Yep. I was as cold as ice."

Chloe raises her coffee cup to me as a silent salute. "And what did he do?"

"He was too shocked to speak." I shrug. "I think"—I contemplate that for a moment—"at least I hope that's why he wasn't speaking." I shrug. "Anyway, I said I had plans, and when I was leaving, I told him that he was a great fuck."

Chloe chokes on her coffee. "You said what?"

"I was telling the truth." I laugh. "He was a *great* fuck. The best, actually."

Chloe laughs out loud. "Oh man, I am so living vicariously through you right now."

We fall silent as we drink our coffee.

"So what's the next move?" Chloe asks.

"Cockteasing."

"Cockteasing?"

"I'm going to be all sexy-like but unavailable for sex."

"Yeah, well, that could majorly backfire."

"How?"

"If you give him an appetite and then close the restaurant, he'll go somewhere else to eat."

"True." I contemplate this theory for a moment. "But I also know that years of a self-destructive pattern can't be broken easily. If I want more time with him, I have to play the game."

Chloe's calculating eyes hold mine. "You're already in love with him, aren't you?"

"Don't be ridiculous," I scoff. "I'm in lust with him."

"I don't know about this." Chloe lets out a deep sigh. "This has the potential to end very badly. I can feel it in my gut."

"Relax, I've got this." I fake a smile. "I'm not getting invested."

I don't know much about life, about love, about anything, really.

But one thing that I do know for certain is that I don't have this . . . not even close.

Henley James has me.

It's Tuesday, and I walk out front to stretch by my mailbox for my morning run.

I haven't seen Henley since I left the restaurant on Sunday morning, and I'm getting a little bit jumpy.

I thought he would have knocked on my back door well before this. Maybe my body isn't as addictive as I thought?

Maybe he's moved on to eat at another restaurant already.

Damn it. Why did Chloe say that to me? Now it's all I can think about.

"Morning, Carol," I call.

"Morning, dear." Carol smiles. She walks across the road toward me in her fluffy pink dressing gown, coffee cup in hand. "Good morning, Barry." She smiles down at my little best friend.

Henley's garage door slowly goes up, and I try not to look.

"Did you see the boys are having a bonfire on Friday night?"

"What?"

"We all got invitations."

"I didn't." I feel a little dejected.

"Check your mailbox."

I open it to see the invitation, a hand-scribbled note.

Bonfire.
My house, Friday night.
Antony.

Phew . . . oh shit, I'm working.

Henley's car pulls out of his garage, and he slows down as he passes us and lowers the window. "Morning, ladies."

I instinctively go up onto my toes in excitement. "Morning."

"Morning, dear Henley." Carol smiles. "How are you today, darling?"

"Better now that I've seen you two." He gives a playful wink, and I feel it down to my toes.

Get into the back seat of your car . . . right now!

"Have a good day." I smile.

"You too." His eyes hold mine for a beat longer than they should, and then he drives away. Carol and I stare after him like the groupies we are.

"Such a good man." Carol smiles as she watches his car turn the corner. "I bet Taryn is already planning her next move."

My eyes flick to Carol. "What?"

"She came over to my house yesterday and told me that she knows that Henley is the man for her. Plans on making a move."

"Is that right?"

"I guess this bonfire on Friday night will be the perfect opportunity. A few drinks, romantic fire, and music."

"Hmm," I reply, distracted by the angry heartbeat sounding in my ears.

"Anyway"—Carol shrugs—"good for her, I guess."

"Yeah, good for her."

It would also be especially good for her to meet a grisly end. "Anyway, I've got to get going." I begin to run. "Bye, Carol."

"Bye, dear."

I run up the street and around the corner and immediately take out my phone and dial.

"Hello."

"Hi, it's Juliet."

"Hi, Juliet."

"I have a huge favor to ask."

"What's that?"

"Can you cover my shift on Friday night?"

It's 8:00 p.m.

My second shift at the nursing home and room 206 is calling me.

And I don't know why. If he doesn't remember his own son, he's definitely not going to talk any sense to me. But for some reason, I can't stop thinking about meeting Henley's dad.

I knock quietly. "Come in," a deep voice calls.

I poke my head around the door. "Hello."

He looks over at me sternly from his bed. "You'll have to be quick; my wife will be here soon."

"Okay." I walk in and replace his water jug. "My name is Juliet."

"Hi." His eyes stay fixed on his television.

"What's your name?" I ask.

"Bernard," he replies curtly.

"Well, it's nice to meet you, Bernard." I clean his room as I talk. "Are you having a nice day?"

"Was all right before you started jabbering and interrupting *M*A*S*H*."

"Oh." I glance up to see that his television is on the ad channel. "You like the show *M*A*S*H*?"

"Yep." He keeps watching the ads. "You better hurry. Caroline will be here to bring me home soon."

My heart sinks. "Okay." I clean a little more while I think of what to say. "Is Caroline your wife?"

"Yep."

"Do you have any children?"

"A son and three angels."

I stop still. "You've lost three children?"

"Before they were born."

"Oh . . ."

Fuck.

"What's your son's name?"

"Henley."

I smile. He remembered his name.

"He's four."

"Four?"

He nods.

"Tell me about him?"

"He'll be back soon." He smiles wistfully. "He's at camp right now."

"Camp?" I smile. "What kind of camp is it?"

"I don't know." He rolls his eyes. "Caroline takes him to these silly things. He prefers to stay home with me."

Sadness rolls in. His long-term memory is still firmly intact. He's lost track of time. He thinks it's back then.

"What's Henley like?"

"He's a good boy." He nods. "Smart like his mother."

"I bet he is."

"Can build LEGO for hours. You've never seen a kid concentrate for so long."

185

I smile as I listen.

"He'll be back from camp soon; we'll build something big."

I nod.

"Caroline is coming to take me home."

My heart sinks.

She's never coming back.

"And I'm sick of the scratching in my closet," he continues. "You need to get someone to look into that."

"What scratching?" I frown.

"That damn cat won't leave me alone—scratching and scratching on the door to get out."

I smile. "Do you want me to check on it?"

"You'd better," he replies seriously as his eyes stay focused on the ad channel.

I open the closet door to humor him, and I see a pile of photo albums. "What are these?" I ask.

"Oh, they're the photos."

"Can you show me?" I take them out and put them on the bed.

He shuffles through them until he gets to the red one. He opens it to the first page. "This is Caroline." It's a picture from their wedding. She looks like Henley: same dark features and big eyes. "She's pretty."

He nods. "The most beautiful woman you've ever seen."

I smile and turn the page to see her pregnant. "She's having a baby?"

"That's Henley in there." He points to her stomach.

I smile as I turn a few more pages and see a little boy laughing in his mother's arms.

He's probably two. He's wearing cute little overalls, and his dark hair has a curl to it.

The way his mother is looking at him is pure adoration.

I turn the page and see another photo of him on her shoulders, holding her two hands and leaning down to kiss his father, who is standing beside them.

So much love.

My heart constricts, and I feel suddenly emotional for all that Henley has lost. I blink away the tears.

Why am I crying?

I don't want Bernard to see my tears, so I close the book. "We should do this another time. I don't want to keep you."

"Okay." He turns back to the television. "Caroline is coming to take me home soon."

"I know she is."

I return his photo albums to the closet and pull his blankets up over him and restraighten his bed linens. I fill his glass with water. "Can I get you anything, Bernard?"

"Shh with all the jabbering. I'm watching *M*A*S*H*."

I glance up at the television to see a Wonder Mop being advertised. "I'll leave you to it." I walk to the door and look back at Bernard. He's concentrating on the television, totally engrossed.

With a heavy heart I walk up the corridor and get back to work.

Sometimes life just isn't fair.

I peer out the upstairs window of my spare room.

It's Friday night, and I'm spying into the backyard of Antony to see if Henley has arrived yet. I don't want to get there before him, but the longer I stay here, the more nervous I become. The whole street seems to be there, but so far, no sighting of Henley. He better be coming; these come-fuck-me jeans cost me one hundred and twenty damn dollars.

Just as the salesgirl told me to, I'm wearing a boosty bra and white T-shirt. My hair is up, and I am trying my very best to be the fuckable girl next door.

Okay, I need to just go before I give myself a heart attack.

I grab my bottle of wine and the cheese platter that I made. "Wish me luck, Bazza."

I make my way over, and the front door of the house is open. I can hear chatter coming from inside.

Shit.

Why am I here? I feel as awkward as all hell.

"Come in, come in," I hear a deep voice call from the kitchen.

Antony meets me in the doorway. "You came." He laughs as he pulls me into a hug.

"Thanks for inviting me." I hold out my platter. "I brought cheese."

"Excellent." He takes the platter from me. "Everyone is out back, and the wineglasses are in the kitchen. Help yourself. I'll put this out on the table."

"Okay."

"There you are," a familiar voice says from behind me before kissing my cheek.

"Rebecca." I smile. "Thank god, you're here."

She links arms with me, and we walk into the kitchen. "Of course I'm here. Had to come and watch tittsy Taryn make her move." She gets out two wineglasses, and I open my bottle of wine.

"What do you mean?" I frown.

"Apparently she's been tuning Henley all week."

"Tuning . . . as in?"

"I don't know, probably sucking his dick, knowing her."

I stare at her, horrified. "Wait, has this actually happened or speculation?"

"Speculation, of course." She rolls her eyes. "But who knows."

I sip my wine as my mind races.

If he's touched a single hair on her head . . . then that's it.

I'll go postal.

There are no words to tell you how postal I am going. And I'm also murdering him and burying him in my backyard.

Jail would be worth it.

I drain my glass. "Another one?" I put my glass on the table.

Rebecca's eyes widen. "Thirsty?"

"Extremely."

"Hi, girls," a sexy voice purrs from behind us. We turn, and Taryn breezes in. Hair out, wearing a full face of makeup. She's in a tight, stretchy pale-pink dress that leaves nothing to the imagination.

Damn it. She looks amazing, and why are her boobs so good? Huge and perky.

My tight jeans suddenly feel very mom-like.

"Where are the boys?" Taryn asks as she looks out the back door. "Is everyone here? I've been so looking forward to tonight."

Rebecca crosses her eyes as she sips her wine, and I bite my lip to hide my smile.

"We're here," Rebecca replies.

"But what about the fun people?" she asks, distracted, as she looks into the backyard.

"Rude," Rebecca mouths as she flips off Taryn to her back, and I drop my head to stop myself from laughing out loud.

Could she be any more obvious?

"Ladies," Henley's sexy voice says from behind me.

My stomach flutters at the mere sound of his voice, and I turn toward him. He gives me a slow sexy smile, and I just want to hug him.

Is it possible to miss someone you hardly know?

"Henley," Taryn gasps in an over-the-top way. She runs toward him and hugs him, doing exactly what I wanted to do. "I'm so glad you're here, darling. It's not a party without you," she coos.

Henley smiles. "Taryn." He unfolds himself out of her arms. "I'm heading out back."

"I'll come." Taryn smiles as she links her arm through his. They disappear out the back door.

"Fuck you, Taryn," Rebecca whispers. "Seriously, she's a vulture. If he sleeps with her, I will never forgive him."

That makes two of us.

"What's going on there?" I ask in a whisper.

"I know she wants him. Word is that she left her husband for him."

I stare at her, horrified. "So they have slept together?"

Rebecca shrugs. "I don't know, surely not."

"She is hot." I sip my wine, distracted.

This is a disaster.

"She's not as hot as you," Rebecca whispers. "Make a move."

"I already did," I whisper back.

"What?"

"We slept together on the weekend."

Rebecca's eyes widen. "Oh my fuck, tell me everything."

"Ladies," a male voice says from behind us. We turn guiltily to see three of the military boys standing in the kitchen. Huge and overpowering the space.

"Hi," I squeak.

"Hi, boys." Rebecca smiles. "About time you finally came to something."

They chuckle.

"This is Juliet. She just moved in next door," Rebecca says as she gestures to me.

"I'm Mason. This is Austin and Scott." He's tall, with a buzz cut and muscles for miles. Not handsome and cultured like Henley, more like I'll-fuck-you-through-a-brick-wall kind of hot.

"Everyone is in the backyard," Rebecca tells them.

"Thanks." The three giants walk out the back door as Rebecca and I stare after them.

"Carol tells me they're gangbangers," I whisper.

"God, I hope so," Rebecca whispers. "Can you imagine taking the three of them at once?"

I get a vision of them using my body for their pleasure. "Don't, it's making me flutter," I whisper.

Rebecca giggles. "You didn't call me for that coffee yet."

"I know. Let's do it next week. Time got away from me. Did you say anything to John?"

"No, I'm hoping your car-valet theory is right." She shrugs. "I don't know what to think."

"It will be okay." I smile as I try to reassure her. "I'm sure it's innocent."

"Hope so. Come on, let's go socialize." I follow Rebecca out into the backyard. There's a fire, and everyone is sitting around it. Some people are chatting in groups, and to the left, Henley is sitting with Taryn. She's talking, and he's listening intently.

Jealousy simmers in the pit of my stomach.

Rebecca begins to talk to John, and I'm standing to the side.

"So, Juliet," Mason says as he walks over to me, "how are you liking the street?"

"I'm still settling in." I smile. I glance up to see Henley's eyes flick over to us. "How long have you lived here?"

"It's been a year, but I was deployed for six months of that time."

"Oh, really?" From my peripheral vision, I can see Henley watching us. "Where were you deployed to?"

"I'm a Navy SEAL, so I was at sea."

"A Navy SEAL." I smile, fascinated.

Hot.

Taryn laughs out loud like the attention seeker she is. "Oh, Henley, you're a scream."

Fuck off, Taryn.

Mason gestures to two chairs. "Do you want to sit down?"

I glance over to Henley, who is still talking to Taryn, and my blood boils.

"Sure thing."

We sit down, and Mason chatters on and on. I'm not listening, of course. I'm too focused on the bimbo across the fire flirting with my man, and of course, Henley is loving every minute of her attention.

Fucker.

"Do you think we could poison her drink?" Rebecca whispers.

"Probably not."

It's late. The night is drawing to an end, and after we watched Taryn Titties flirt with every man at the bonfire, our patience is well and truly used up.

I've chatted and laughed with most everyone here, too, and had a great night. Not a single word has been spoken to a certain person, though.

"Henley, come and dance with me," Taryn purrs as she curls her finger up to him in a come-hither gesture.

That's it.

Enough!

I can't take one more minute of watching her fawn all over him. If he wants her, he can fucking have her. Good riddance to both of them.

"I'm going to get going." I stand.

"Oh really?" Rebecca sighs. "Don't leave me here."

I smile. "You're married—go talk to your husband." We both look over to see John playing chess with Bennet, and she winces. "It looks very boring over there. I'll come with you. Give me a second to say goodbye." She disappears over to the chess table.

"Bye, everyone." I smile with a wave. "I'm heading home."

Henley glances up as if taken by surprise. "Already?"

Yes, fucker. I've been here for six hours, and you haven't said a single word to me.

I give a wave and make my way out front.

"Wait up," Rebecca calls as she runs to catch up. She links her arm through mine. "Screw Henley, I think we should set you up with Mason."

"No." I scrunch up my nose. "Definitely not."

"What's wrong? Don't you like huge hot men who give you their undivided attention all night?"

I giggle. "I mean . . . he seems nice and all, but I don't know."

"Taryn's probably making a move on my husband right now." Rebecca rolls her eyes. "What if it's her? What if he's sleeping with her?"

My blood boils at just the thought.

"He wouldn't. It's not her. She's shameless, though. I wouldn't put it past her," I huff. "Seriously, if it's her, I'm going to bomb her house."

"I'll help." We get to the middle of the street, and she gives me a hug. "Tonight was fun."

"It was."

"And we need to organize our coffee date."

"I know. I'm on day shift next week. Next weekend maybe?"

"Sounds good."

With another wave I stomp to my house and march inside. "Hi, Barry."

Barry looks up from his bed all sleepy-like.

"Henley James is a giant fucking dickhead," I whisper angrily.

Barry looks at me blankly.

"He didn't even look my way, let alone speak to me," I tell him. "Ugh . . . I don't know why I started this dumb thing with him. Chloe is completely right. I am going to end up hating his guts. I kind of do already."

Barry sighs.

I'm now forcing my poor dog to listen to my dating-hell crap. I flick on my kettle in disgust.

"I paid all this money for these stupid jeans. Well, I shouldn't have bothered. He wouldn't have noticed if I was wearing a garbage bag."

Fucking jerkface.

I make my tea, and Barry comes out into the kitchen and stands at the back door. "You want to go out?" I open the door, and with my hot tea in my hand, I sit on the back steps in the darkness as I wait for him to go to the bathroom.

Barry looks up at the fence and starts wagging his tail. I hear a noise in the darkness in the far corner.

What's going on out there?

I get up and walk toward the noise. I see two hands holding on to the top of the fence; then a leg swings over. With a lot of huffing and puffing, Henley comes into view. He's climbing the fence. He swings his other leg over and then jumps down.

"What are you doing?"

He jumps, startled to find me standing here. "I'm coming to visit you."

He honestly thinks he can ignore me all night while flirting with Tittsy LaRue?

Ha. Of all the nerve.

"No, you're not," I reply blankly. "Go home, Henley. I'm not in the mood tonight." I turn and storm back toward the house. He's hot on my heels.

"Since when?"

"Since you're a giant flirt."

"I was not flirting," he scoffs. "I was talking about very important things."

I roll my eyes, and I march into the house. "Like what bra size Taryn wears? Give me a fucking break."

"Are you jealous?"

"No," I explode. "Why would I be jealous of her? And . . ." I gesture toward him in disgust. "You." I put my hands on my hips to try and look convincing. "Go home."

"No, we have an arrangement," he fires back. "I would like my night tonight."

"Oh, would you now? The answer is no."

"You cannot be jealous; this is not a relationship. We talked about this, and you said you were fine with it."

"I know that," I whisper angrily. Why did I agree to this stupid fucking arrangement anyway? "What I am not fine with is watching you flirt all night right under my nose."

"So you *are* jealous."

"Oh my god. I am not fucking jealous. What I am is pissed off with you."

Does he really think that he can ignore me all night and then turn up here for sex?

No way in hell. The man is an idiot.

"Because you are jealous."

"Shut up and go home."

"Not until you kiss me."

195

"I'm not kissing you," I spit. "I wouldn't kiss you if you were the last man on earth."

Lies!

"Go and kiss Taryn. I'm sure you've negotiated an arrangement with her already."

"You cannot be jealous; you have no right to use that card. We have an arrangement. Nothing more and nothing less."

Knock, knock sounds at the door.

We both fall silent. "Who's that?" he mouths.

I shrug. "I don't know."

I open the door to the closet under the stairs. "Get in," I mouth.

"No," he spits.

I push him into the closet and close the door behind him. I open the front door to see Mason standing there. "Mason." I frown.

Shit!

"Hi."

"Hi . . ."

He hesitates. "I was wondering if you wanted to go out sometime . . . on a date."

"Oh . . ."

Shit, shit, shit.

"I just haven't met anyone quite like you. I know we would hit it off."

"I'm . . ." I pause. Henley's words from only two minutes ago come back to me loud and clear.

You cannot be jealous; you have no right to use that card. We have an arrangement. Nothing more and nothing less.

I know that from his place in the closet, Henley can hear every word we're saying. Maybe it's time for some payback.

"I'd love to go on a date with you." I smile sweetly.

A bang sounds from the closet, and Mason looks over toward it. "What was that?"

"My clumsy oaf of a dog."

"Oh . . . so it's a date?"

"Uh-huh."

"Great." Mason smiles.

"I'm working nights all week, so I'll call you?" I offer.

"Sure." He lingers, and I think he's fishing for a good night kiss.

"Bye then." I give him an awkward wave and close the door in his face.

Fuck . . . I'm going to have to get out of that one.

I wait for a moment, and another bang comes from the closet. I smile. That couldn't have gone better if I planned it myself. I open the door. "Ready to come out of time-out?" I ask sarcastically.

His face is murderous. "You are not going on a fucking date with him."

I act innocent. "You just told me that we cannot be jealous of anyone and that this is an arrangement, nothing more and nothing less."

He narrows his eyes, knowing full well that I've got him.

"I don't trust him."

"Good thing that you're not going on a date with him, then, isn't it?"

"No." He steps forward, forcing me to step back. "You are not going out with him."

I cross my arms in a sarcastic manner. "You can't tell me what to do, Henley."

"Watch me. Get upstairs, get those clothes off, and open your legs on that bed, because you're about to get some sense fucked into you."

Excitement runs through me. *I like this game.*

"Make me."

He grabs my hand and drags me up the stairs and throws me onto the bed. "You will do as I fucking say from here on out. Do you hear me?" he whispers angrily as he rips his T-shirt off over his head.

"Or what?" I bait him. My eyes drop down his rippled abdomen and the V of muscles that disappears into his jeans.

"Or you're going to get that sarcastic mouth of yours fucked hard . . . until you choke."

"You couldn't handle my mouth."

"Watch me." He unzips his jeans and pulls out his already-erect cock. It seems Henley likes this game too. He grabs my head and guides his cock into my mouth. He then pushes my head down onto him. I feel him slide deep down my throat, and my eyes close instinctively as I try to deal with his punishment.

Hmm . . . he tastes good. My insides begin to liquefy.

How is he so hot?

He grips my hair with two hands as he begins to ride my mouth. "And you're going to swallow every fucking drop."

Henley

I wake with a jump. What time is it?

I scramble for my phone: 5:15 a.m. Thank god, I'm not late. I still have time to enjoy the view for a moment. I roll toward Juliet and watch her as she sleeps. Her honey-blonde hair is splayed across her pillow, her flawless skin almost glowing in the dark. I run my hand over her full breasts and down to her shapely hips. I run the backs of my fingers through her well-kept pubic hair and feel my cock harden to her softness.

Fuck . . . she's beautiful.

Her body is out of this world, and I just can't get enough. No matter how many times I fuck her, I still want more.

It took all my strength to not climb the fence last week. She's all I could think about. I'll be over this infatuation soon. One more time and that should do it.

I get a vision of the two of us last night in the shower. The ways she milks me so tight, her kisses, that fuckable mouth of hers . . . my balls contract.

Get up.

Have some self-control, for fuck's sake.

I sneak out of bed and quietly dress. I'll go home and shower before I go to see Dad. I tiptoe downstairs and out into the backyard. Fuck it. I'm sick of climbing this fucking fence, and it's only been once.

Maybe I should cut a gate in?

No . . . this is only happening one more time, remember?

I jump the fence and shower and then head off to go to the nursing home. I'm just pulling out of the street when I see the dickhead jogging.

My blood boils, and I slow down and lower the car window. "Mason, you're up early."

"Thought I'd go for a run." He smiles.

He's looking for her.

Well, too bad because she's safely tucked up in bed with a broken pussy, care of my cock. She thinks she's one up on me. Well, I'll show her.

I drive along beside him as I contemplate my next move. "We should go on a double date some time," I tell him.

"Yeah?" He frowns.

"Me and Taryn and you and a date."

"Yeah." He smiles excitedly. "That would be awesome, man."

Poor dumb fuck.

"I could get Juliet to come," he offers.

Not half as well as I can.

"Okay, then." I fake a smile. "I'll set it up and let you know."

"Thanks, man. You're a good guy."

I wave and drive away; I watch him in the rearview mirror.

"Good at fucking you up, asshole," I mutter under my breath. "Nobody touches her but me."

Chapter 13

"Good morning to the lovely Jenny." I smile as I walk through the reception area.

"Morning, Henley." Jenny looks over the top of her glasses at me. "Everything okay?"

"Everything's great." I walk into my office and begin to unpack my briefcase onto my desk.

I can feel Jenny watching me from the door. "Your voice mail is full," she says as she leans on my doorjamb.

"Is it?" I sit down at my desk and wince; I swear I have no skin left on my dick.

"You haven't asked for your messages for a while now."

I turn my computer on. "Haven't I?" I log in. "I've been busy, I guess."

She keeps watching me. "You're different lately."

I glance up. "How so?"

"Did you meet someone?"

I roll my eyes. "Because the only possible reason I could be in a good mood is if I met someone, right?"

"I think you should go through your messages. Vanessa has left several—she sounds frantic."

"Okay." I open my email and scan my inbox.

Jenny disappears and then walks in and puts my burner phone onto the desk in front of me. "Here, you can do it now."

I pick it up, turn it off, and throw it in my top drawer.

"Who is she?" she asks.

Ugh . . .

"Not now, Jen." I sigh. "You and I aren't dating. You do know that, right?"

"Of course I do," she snaps angrily.

"So why do you care?"

"I don't. I just think you should keep your options open, that's all."

"Okay." I open an email. "I will." I skim through my emails some more. "How's Martin?"

"He's good."

"Why don't you go and call him, organize his life?"

She exhales heavily. "I'll be at my desk."

I widen my eyes. *Like you should be.*

"Our new intern starts today," she reminds me.

"Okay, thanks."

She closes the door behind her, and I turn on my chair and wince.

Fuck, I'm sore. That damn tight pussy is like a cheese grater. I take out my phone from my pocket and text.

Good morning, Miss Drinkwater.
My cock is sore.

The dots start bouncing, and I smile as I wait for her reply.

Serves you right.
That thing is a lethal weapon.
At least you can walk.

I chuckle and type.

**I've made you an appointment with the Department of
Vital Records today at 3pm.**

I see the dots bounce again.

Why?

I swivel on my chair and smile as I type my reply.

**After last night I think it's appropriate to legally
change your name from Drinkwater to Drinkcome.**

The dots bounce once more.

**What can I say . . . there was a delicious drink on offer.
#thirsty**

Knock, knock. The door bursts open. "Hey," Antony says.

#thirsty

I smirk and put my phone screen down.
He flops onto the couch in the corner of my office.
My phone vibrates, and I turn it over to read.

**Seriously though.
Your dick is perfect!**

"I came to see how last night went," he replies.

I bite my bottom lip to stop myself from smiling. "It was okay. I guess."

"Just okay?"

I shrug. "Yeah."

"So . . . did you go over there?" He frowns.

"Uh-huh. And lucky I did too. That fucker Mason showed up and asked her out."

"I knew it." He smiles. "I was onto him. He was trying to tune her all night."

"Did you sort him out?"

"Not yet."

I reread her text.

Seriously though.

Your dick is perfect!

"What's so funny?" he asks.

"What?" I try to refocus. "Nothing, why?"

"You look all . . . creepy?"

Another knock sounds at the door.

"Come in," I call.

The door opens, and a young woman comes into view. She has long dark hair and is dressed modestly in almost Amish clothing. She has the most beautiful big brown eyes. "Mr. James, I just wanted to come and meet you, sir. I'm May. I'm starting today as the new intern."

She's sweet and innocent, young and naive.

"Hello, May." I stand and walk to her and hold out my hand. "We're very excited to have you with us. Welcome aboard."

"Thank you," she replies softly. Her eyes flick to Antony. "Hello." She smiles shyly.

Antony stands.

"This is Antony, one of my friends."

"Hi." He shakes her hand.

His tongue swipes over his bottom lip as he stares at her, and it looks like he wants to eat her whole.

Fuck.

"You come to me if anyone gives you any problems," I tell her.

"Yes, sir," she replies softly. "I will." She nervously looks at Antony, and I can smell his erection from here.

"Nice to meet you."

"The pleasure was all mine," Antony murmurs.

She walks to the door, and we watch her leave. The door shuts behind her.

He turns to me.

"Don't even fucking think about it," I snap. "You keep away from my intern."

He rolls his eyes and slumps onto the couch. I read Juliet's message again.

Seriously though.
Your dick is perfect!

"We should go celebrate with coffee," I tell him.

"What are we celebrating?"

"Juliet thinks my dick is perfect." I smile.

"Ugh . . . fucking hell." He rolls his eyes. "She must be desperate."

It's just now 8:30 p.m., and I flick through Netflix.

Owooooooooooooo. The coyote call sounds over the fence. And I roll my eyes.

That fucking mutt.

Juliet is on afternoon shift, and true to form, the dog is being a nightmare.

Owoooooooooooo.

He hates it when she's at work too . . . I mean, not that I do. I couldn't care less what she does.

He carries on some more, and I open my back door. "Shut up," I yell.

He barks again.

"Shut. Up!"

He goes quiet.

"That's more like it." I go back to Netflix. I need a new series or something. I begin to scroll through. *Yellowstone*. I pause and read the blurb. Maybe this. I press play and settle in.

Ten minutes later, I see something from the corner of my eye in the reflection on the glass. Huh?

Something's moving in the kitchen.

I peer around the corner and see the mutt standing outside my sliding glass door. He sees me and wags his tail. I open the sliding glass door in a rush. "What are you doing here?" I growl.

He wags his tail and pricks his ears up.

"Go home." I point to the fence.

He walks in a circle.

"I said go the fuck home!"

He lies down on the concrete.

"You are not sleeping there," I demand. "Go home."

He rolls over onto his back.

"No." I nudge him with my foot. "I am not scratching your belly. What the fuck do you think this is?"

He rolls over again and crawls toward me.

"Don't even try that crap. We are not friends. Go home."

He looks up at me, perplexed.

"The concrete is hard, you fucking idiot. Go home to your bed."

He barks.

Ugh, I hate this dumb dog.

Juliet

I walk through my house, straight to the back door, and I open it and look out into the backyard.

Silence.

Barry is usually waiting at the back door for me after he hears my car arrive home.

Hmm. He must be asleep. I close the door and walk back into the house. I turn the television on and put some bread in the toaster. I look out into the yard through my kitchen window. It is weird he hasn't come to see me.

I'll just check if he's okay.

I walk out into the yard. And using the flashlight on my phone, I walk to his doghouse. It's empty.

"Barry," I call softly.

Silence.

Fuck. I begin to get a little panicked. "Barry," I call again.

I hear a soft *bang, bang, bang* coming from over the fence . . . his signature tail wag.

I look along the fence and see a new hole that he must've dug.

Shit, he's in Henley's yard.

If he's destroyed it again, I swear to god, I'm going to kill him.

I walk out the side gate and duck around the fence. I let myself into Henley's backyard. His house is all in darkness. It is after midnight, after all.

I don't want Henley to wake up, so I tiptoe around to the backyard, and I hear Barry's tail thumping on the veranda. "Shh," I whisper. I shine the flashlight up to him and see him sitting on a makeshift bed.

"What the?" I walk up onto the veranda and shine the flashlight down; three pillows have been covered in a blanket.

Henley made him a bed.

I then notice a bowl of water set beside him.

I smile goofily and look up at Henley's bedroom window.

I feel like I know a secret, that I'm about to uncover a huge diamond stash that has been buried deep for years. Something valuable and precious. Priceless to its owner.

Henley James isn't a tyrant at all. It's his defense mechanism.

The man with the perfect dick may just also have the perfect heart . . .

I've just got to work out how to get him to show it to me.

I pour the first of the white paint into the roller tray.

Today's the day. I'm starting to paint my house, and I don't think I've ever been so excited for something. I bought the equipment I need and washed all the walls. I've taped all the windows and baseboards, and I'm ready to rock. I'm starting in the foyer hall; I roll up and I roll down.

Ugh, the paint is strong smelling. I open the front door to let the fresh air in and continue on my merry way.

An hour later, "Hey there, you" sounds from the porch.

I look up to see Mason standing at my front door. "Mason." I smile awkwardly.

"I came to visit, but looks like now I'm painting," he replies.

"Oh no." I shake my head. "I wouldn't do that to you. Thanks anyway, though."

"I insist. I'm ducking home and changing clothes, and then I'm coming back to help you."

"No, you can't," I blurt out.

Like really, you can't. *I'm trying to win Henley's trust. Having you in my house will only make him pull away from me.*

"See you in five minutes." He smiles before jogging home.

Fuck's sake.

This street is like the fucking *Brady Bunch*. Why is everyone so damn helpful?

Henley is going to come home and see him here and then ghost me again.

Ugh . . .

What do I do now?

I'll text Henley.

Help!
Mason just showed up here to help me paint.

I wait for his reply.

Tell him to fuck off.

I smile. Good answer.

I can't. He's being helpful and nice.

I see the dots bouncing.

My foot up his ass will also be helpful and nice.

I giggle and reply.

I didn't realize you had a foot fetish.

I wait for a reply, but one doesn't come.

Okay, at least he knows why Mason is here now. I feel better about it, having told him. I get back to painting, and just like he promised, Mason comes back. He's wearing shorts only: biceps and abs for days.

What the hell? He's cut like the Hulk. All that special-ops training sure pays off.

"Couldn't find an old T-shirt, so I guess it's skin." He throws me a sexy wink.

Nice.

I've got to give it to him, that's pretty smooth.

"Well then"—I smile as I go back to painting—"skin works for me."

"Skin always works for me too," he says. "Maybe you should paint in your underwear?"

I giggle. "Oh, you'd like that?" I tease.

"I would, actually."

You are never seeing me naked; I look like a jellyfish compared to you.

"White, eh?" Mason says as he pours some paint into his paint tray.

"Yeah, I am trying to make it all fresh and classic," I reply.

"I love this old house."

"Me too. So tell me about your work," I ask him as I paint.

"I'm a Navy SEAL."

"Have you always wanted to do that?"

"Pretty much. I loved scuba diving and the ocean when I was young, appreciated discipline, and loved to train hard."

I can see that.

"Those things kind of went together," he adds.

My phone beeps a text. It's from Henley.

What's happening?

I smirk and take a photo of Mason painting in his shorts, muscles on display. I send it to Henley.

Painting.

I wait for his reply. Nothing comes, so I go back to painting.

"So the guys you live with, are they close friends?"

"Aah . . ." He hesitates. "They are. We are close because we do the same job and understand each other. The housing is supplied through work."

He hesitated when he said that. I'm reading it as they get on his nerves sometimes.

"Have you always lived around here?"

"From New York originally."

"Really?"

"You seem surprised," he replies.

"I guess I am—not many New Yorkers go into the military."

"You'd be surprised. A lot of us just wanted to get out."

We keep painting for a while.

"What about you?" he asks. "Did you always want to be a nurse?"

"Um, yeah." I shrug. "I guess. I like to look after people."

"Must be a rewarding job."

"Some days are better than others."

"It looks good, doesn't it? Imagine when the entire house is done." He smiles as he stands back to look at our handiwork.

We chat for another forty minutes while we work. Mason is actually a really cool guy.

Not my type, but a cool guy nonetheless.

"Hello," sounds a familiar voice from the front door. I glance up to see Henley standing there. "What's going on here, poser painting?"

Excitement runs through me.

He came home from work!

This must be love.

Mason looks at him deadpan. "I didn't have an old T-shirt."

"Of course you didn't," Henley mutters dryly as he walks in past him. "I've got the day off; do you need some help?"

I say yes at the same time Mason replies no.

"Maybe I should drop my pants and paint naked," Henley replies casually as he looks around.

I smirk. That dick of his would definitely win any battle. "Ew." I act disgusted.

Mason chuckles.

"I'll have you know that I've been told before that my cock is perfect," Henley says nonchalantly as he picks up a paintbrush.

"I didn't know you kept chickens," Mason replies as he paints.

"I keep cocks," Henley replies as he rolls his roller in the tray.

"I prefer to keep pussies," Mason fires back. "Cocks don't interest me."

Touché.

Henley rolls his eyes, and I want to burst out laughing.

This is perfect.

"Hello," sounds an annoying female voice from the front door. We all look up to see Taryn standing there. "Lookee, lookee, what's going on here?" She smiles. "Henley, I saw your car drive in, and I was coming over to see if you were all right," she purrs.

"Nice to see someone cares about me, Taryn." Henley smiles sweetly over at me.

Fuck off.

Fuck right off.

"What are you guys doing?" Taryn asks in an overdramatic voice.

"Playing Monopoly," I reply deadpan as I keep painting.

Mason laughs. "Good one, Juliet."

Henley rolls his eyes. "So good," he mutters under his breath.

"Can I help?"

I say no at the same time Henley says yes.

"It's poser painting, Taryn. You better strip off," Henley says casually as he paints.

"Ha, ha. Oh, Henley, any chance you get to try and look at my body." Taryn laughs.

Fucker.

I bite the inside of my cheek, and Henley smirks at the wall he's painting.

"I'll slip home and get into something more comfortable," Taryn replies.

"This is a roller-skate-free zone, Taryn." I smile sweetly. "Don't want you getting hurt, now."

She laughs an over-the-top fake laugh, and she thinks I'm joking. I'm not. If she wears her roller skates, I'm 100 percent pushing her down my front steps, and I will not be resuscitating her.

She skips off across the street, and I'm left alone with the two men once again.

One buff and half-dressed, one completely covered up and simply irresistible.

"So where are we going on Saturday night?" Mason asks Henley.

I stop painting and look up. "What?"

"We're going on a double date. Henley and Taryn and you and I. Didn't Henley tell you?"

What the fuck?

My eyes flick to Henley. "No. He did not."

My blood boils. He's taking Taryn on a date . . . since fucking when?

"I've actually got a lot going on this week," Henley replies. "We'll have to reschedule."

"That's okay," Mason replies. "Juliet and I don't need chaperones; we can go alone. Can't we?"

Two can play that game, asshole.

"Sure we can," I reply. "Can't wait, Mason."

Henley looks at me deadpan, and I smile sweetly. *You are a fuckface.*

Bona fide.

"Here I am," Taryn says in a singsong voice from the doorway. We all turn to see her in tiny cutoff denim shorts and a white bikini top. Her boobs are huge and perfect.

"It seems I don't have any old clothes either," she says sexily.

Or any self-respect.

I really should have bought some chloroform for my tool kit.

"Hope I'm not too distracting, boys." She laughs.

Henley's eyes dance with mischief as he smiles at me. "I have good news, Taryn," he says.

"What's that?" she says as she picks up a paintbrush.

"We're going on a double date with Mason and Juliet in a couple of weeks."

"Oh goody." She jumps up and down, and her boobs bounce around like jelly.

Give me a fucking break. I stare at him deadpan, and he winks playfully.

You are going to die, fucker.

"Oh, I love this white, Juliet," Taryn says as she paints a little. "This is going to be the best house on Kingston Lane."

"I'm glad you like it," I reply.

214

You may be buried in the backyard under the rosebush soon.

I grit my teeth as I continue to paint. I shouldn't complain. I should be grateful.

Three very generous people are helping me paint my house.

A man who wants me to go on a date with him.

A man who I'm trying to make fall in love with me.

And a roller-skating sexiest woman alive who is putting on a private *Penthouse* Pet painting show.

Fuck my life.

"Okay, so what happens then?" Chloe asks.

"I don't know. This is a one-day-at-a-time operation." I shrug.

Chloe, Rebecca, and I are having coffee to strategize my disaster of a love life.

"So let me get this straight," Rebecca replies. "You told him that you don't want anything but sex, but you secretly do, and he agreed to it."

"Correct." I nod as I sip my coffee. I think for a moment. "But now he's pissed that Mason is hanging around, so he thought he would play games and arrange a double date with Taryn and me and him."

They both frown. "What?"

"The man is the biggest smart-ass I know." I roll my eyes. "And the hottest."

"Good?" Rebecca asks.

"Ridiculous."

"So what's this about a double date?"

"After the bonfire Henley came over to my house, and I was pissed about him talking to Taryn all night."

Rebecca cuts me off. "Rightly so."

"He and I are getting into it over that, and he tells me I have no right to be jealous and being all righteous, and he was pissing me off. Then in the middle of our fight, Mason turns up, and Henley hid in the cupboard under the stairs."

Chloe frowns as she listens. "Right . . ."

"Mason asks me out, and I know Henley can hear everything we are saying, and I was still angry with him after his I-can't-be-jealous-over-Taryn comment, so I said yes with no intention of actually going. But then Henley saw him and to one-up me, he organized a double date with Taryn," I blurt out in a rush.

"Jeez, this is getting complicated," Rebecca replies as she holds her temples.

"Oh, you think?" I stammer. "This is one colossal fuckup."

"It's too soon. You don't have him locked in enough yet to be going on double dates with other people. What happens if Taryn makes a move on him? And we know she will. What are you going to do then? Are you going to kiss Mason to get him back?" Chloe says.

I drag my hand down my face as I consider this possibility. "True. I hadn't even thought of that."

"And what happens if this Mason thing gets all too hard and Henley thinks 'fuck it' and walks away and does actually go for Taryn? He's got baggage, remember, and you are at a very fragile point in this relationship," Rebecca replies.

"It isn't even a relationship yet." I put my head in my hands. "Ugh, you're completely right. I didn't think this through at all. Why am I such a smart-ass?"

"I know what to do," Chloe says. "Put the date off for a while. Don't say never, but pretend to have things on this weekend. That way you will get some more time with him alone, but he still knows it may happen in the future."

"Yes," Rebecca gasps. "Perfect. That way he's still on notice of you trading him in."

I roll my eyes. "Henley James would never be traded in."

"Don't let him know that."

"Okay, I think this could work." I look over to Rebecca. "What's going on with John, anyway? Anything new happen?"

"He's going on a golfing weekend with the boys in a few weeks." She widens her eyes.

"Do you think he is?"

"Who fucking knows, but I figure that I'm not getting laid, so someone else must be. He's too highly sexed to just go cold turkey like this."

"You *actually* think he's cheating?" I ask.

"I don't know." She sighs sadly. "It's all I can think about, though. He always works late, and I thought it was just because he's a surgeon, but what if it's not?"

"I'm sorry." I take her hand over the table. "I'm sure it's going to work out."

"Hide an Apple AirTag in his car," Chloe says.

"What?"

"Hook up an Apple AirTag to your phone and hide it in his car. That way, if you do have suspicions on whether he's at work or not, you can see it in black and white."

"I don't want to be sneaky and deceitful," Rebecca replies.

"If I had suspicions my husband was fucking other women"— Chloe shrugs—"I'd do it."

"You just concentrate on snagging Dr. Grayson," I snap. "You can be so insensitive sometimes. This isn't just some guy she's banging. This is her husband, Chloe."

"Speaking of a guy you're banging—" Rebecca points to my phone on the table. A message has just come in.

Henley

A thrill runs through me at seeing his name light up my screen. I click it open.

Your turn to jump the fence tonight.

I smile goofily.

"What does it say?" Chloe asks.

"'Your turn to jump the fence tonight.'" I smile, excited.

"No, play hard to get, remember," Rebecca reminds me.

"But I want to see him."

"Then tell him to come to your house," Chloe says.

"Okay." I text back.

Come to mine instead.

I see the dots bouncing, and I smile as I wait for his reply.

No, it has to be my house.
I want to introduce you to my swing.

"What?" I whisper. "His dick is way too big for a fucking sex swing."

"He has a sex swing?" Chloe gasps. "Oh, fuck me dead. I always wanted to try one of those. I am so living vicariously through you right now."

I text back.

That's not happening.

"Why did you write that?" Chloe gasps.

"He'll break me in fucking half," I gasp. "Have you seen his dick?"

"No, but I want to," Chloe replies. "Can you take a photo of it tonight?"

My phone immediately rings. The name *Henley* lights up the screen.

"Dear lord, he's calling," Chloe stammers.

I answer as I try to sound cool. "Hello, Henley."

"Good afternoon, Miss Drinkwater," his deep sexy voice replies.

Butterflies swirl in my stomach. Just the sound of his voice does things to me.

I look up to the girls as they hang on my every word, and I get up and walk outside for some privacy.

"Hi." I smile goofily.

"Hi." I can tell he's smiling too.

"Why are you calling me?"

"To get my way."

I giggle. "Henley . . . we cannot do that." I lower my voice and look around to see if anyone can hear me.

"Yes, we can."

I lower my voice to a whisper. "You are too big for me."

"Nonsense. It's a perfect fit."

I feel myself blush. "We need more . . . practice."

"You actually think I'm going to hurt you?"

"I just . . ." I hesitate.

"You just what?"

"We're just new at this. Your body is a lot extra . . . I need you to be patient with me."

He stays silent, and I know he's considering my request. "I would never hurt you, Juliet."

"I know." I smile shyly. "I just want to get to know you better first in a more familiar environment."

He exhales but stays silent.

"So you'll jump the fence for me?" I ask hopefully.

"Only for you."

"I can't wait," I gush. "What time?"

"Ten minutes?"

I giggle. "About eight?"

"Okay . . ."

He hangs on the line, and I smile goofily.

"Goodbye, Mr. James."

"Goodbye, sweet Juliet."

I hang up and practically float back to the table.

"Well?" the girls ask impatiently.

"I think I won that round; he's coming over tonight. This hard-to-get thing is actually pretty fun."

Tap, tap, tap sounds at the back door, and my heart hammers in my chest.

He's here.

Oh man, will I ever become immune to his gorgeousness?

I open the door in a rush, and there he stands: blue jeans, white T-shirt, dark hair, large shoulders, and a look in his eye that could melt Antarctica.

"Hi," I whisper nervously.

He steps forward and sweeps me into his arms, his lips taking mine. "I've been waiting to kiss you all fucking day," he murmurs against my lips.

And there it is . . . the nine words that send me into heart palpitations.

"You have?" I smile.

His hands go to my behind, and he drags my hips over his erection, and I feel how hard he already is.

He's not joking.

I lick his lips. "Are you horny, Mr. James?"

His dark eyes hold mine, and he unzips his jeans and pulls his cock out. "I'll let you be the judge of that."

My eyes drop to his erection, engorged, with thick veins coursing down the length of it.

I feel a flutter down below.

Seriously . . .

Has there ever been a more beautiful dick in the history of human life?

"I thought you were coming over for conversation," I whisper.

He smiles darkly and pulls my nightdress off over my head and throws it to the side. His eyes drop to my bare breasts. "It's not your mouth I want to talk to."

He's so naughty.

"What do you want to talk to?" I play dumb.

He lifts me and sits me up on the kitchen counter. We stare at each other, and then he slides my panties down my legs and takes them off. "I want to speak to the supervisor." He circles his four fingertips over my clitoris.

Feels good.

He spreads my legs and then slides his finger deep into my sex and begins to pump me. Then he adds another finger, then another.

I close my eyes to deal with the pleasure. "That's a good place to start."

The sound of my arousal sucking him in echoes through the kitchen. Jeez . . . he's been here for all of two minutes.

We're like animals together.

He puts his mouth to my ear. "I fucked myself twice today, imagining doing this to you," he whispers.

I shudder at his dirty words and clench my sex around his fingers.

He smiles darkly. "You like the thought of me fucking myself?"

I whimper as he works me hard. My breasts begin to bounce, and he bends and takes a nipple into his mouth and bites me. Arousal surges through me as I lose control.

He lifts me, and we fall back onto the couch, and in one sharp movement he pulls me over and onto him. His thick cock slides deep and full in. We both moan in pleasure.

We lose control, fucking each other hard and loud.

My knees are up around his shoulders, and he's so deep inside of me, burning me up from the inside out.

I tip my head back and cry out as I come in a rush, and he holds himself deep.

An earth-shattering orgasm stealing sanity from us both.

And then he kisses me, soft and tender. As if he's been missing me all day.

Just like I've been missing him.

"Hi." He smiles, almost as if embarrassed at our lack of control.

"Hi." I smile shyly up at him.

He's disheveled and just fucked. His dark hair hanging over his forehead. His body still deep inside of mine.

"That was a great conversation." He smirks.

I giggle and put my head onto his shoulder, and then a thought runs through my head.

Fuck.

No condom.

Chapter 14

Henley

My heart is racing. The highest of highs tears through me, and I kiss Juliet's temple in a postorgasmic glow.

God, she's perfect.

I feel her stiffen. "What's wrong?" I whisper as I hold her face in my hands and kiss her softly.

"Nothing." She kisses me back. "I'm on the pill. It's okay."

What?

No condom?

What?

I pull out and take a step back from her to look down at myself, horrified.

The earth spins beneath me. "What do you mean?"

How the fuck did I forget a condom?

No . . . *Oh my god.*

I drag my two hands through my hair. The air has left my lungs.

"Henley, it's okay," she says in a soft voice, as if speaking to a child. "It's okay. We were just lost in the moment. It's okay."

"How is this fucking okay?" I stammer, wide eyed.

"I'm on the pill, and as long as you don't have an STD."

"I don't have a fucking STD," I spit angrily. I zip my jeans up with a sharp snap.

Juliet's eyes search mine. "Hen . . . ?"

"Don't." I turn my back, unable to look her in the eye. "I'm sorry." I struggle to find the right words. "I'm . . . that is not okay."

A large lump is nestled deep in my throat, and I close my eyes. My chest rises and falls as I struggle for air. "I have to go."

"Hen," she whispers. "Don't let this ruin our night. It's fine. I promise you I'm on the pill."

"Nothing about this is fine, Juliet," I snap. I stumble through the door.

"Henley," Juliet calls after me.

Before I know it, I am striding over to my house. I burst through the door and slam it hard behind me.

I lean up against the back of it as if hiding from the firing squad.

Maybe I am.

I look around my empty house, dark and silent. I don't want to be here, damn it . . . I really wanted to see her tonight.

You already got what you wanted.

I close my eyes in disgust.

Not even close.

Tuesday

I walk into the restaurant and look around. Blake spots me and gives me a wave. I make my way over to him and Antony.

"Hey," I sigh as I pull out a chair. They are in deep conversation.

"Hi," they both answer without looking at me.

"And then what happened?" Ant asks Blake.

"It's her."

"Who's her?" I ask as I try to catch up with the conversation.

"Guess who Holly is?" Blake raises an eyebrow.

"Who is Holly again?" I frown.

"The girl I've been seeing." He widens his eyes as if I'm stupid. "The hot one."

"I can't keep up; they are all fucking hot."

"This is true." Antony sips his beer.

"Supersoaker," Blake replies.

"What?" I frown.

"Supersoaker is Holly's sister," Blake snaps. "And now I'm totally fucked because I've had a million threesomes with her, and she's going to tell Holly every sordid detail, and Holly thinks I'm holier than God."

I pinch the bridge of my nose. "You hurt my brain, do you know that?"

"Wait . . ." Antony frowns. "How do you know?"

"Because Holly showed me photos of her sister on her phone, and it's the same nasty girl who squirts like a fucking fire hose."

I chuckle as I remember the finer details. "That's right. It's all coming back to me now."

"Does Holly squirt?" Antony asks.

"I don't know. I haven't slept with her yet," he scoffs.

"What?" We both gasp. That's unheard of.

"Holly is a"—he holds up his fingers and air quotes—"nice girl."

Ant's eyes and mine meet as we try to decide if Holly is also a squirter.

"I reckon it would have to be genetic," I say.

"Surely," Ant agrees.

Blake rolls his eyes. "You are not listening to me, you fucking idiots. We have bigger problems than if Holly is a squirter."

My mind goes to Juliet, and I exhale heavily. "You're right, we do."

"I don't think she will say anything. Nobody tells a family member that they gangbang," Ant continues.

But my mind isn't on this conversation.

It's off wandering with sweet Juliet, thinking about how perfect she felt the other night . . . of how badly I fucked it all up.

I wonder what she's doing right now.

Fifteen minutes later, my peace is interrupted, and I glance up. "Huh?"

"What the fuck is wrong with you today?" Ant snaps. "You haven't said a word all morning."

I shrug. "Sorry, distracted."

"By what?"

"Nobody," I snap a little too fast.

"Wouldn't have something to do with that hot little neighbor of yours, would it?"

"Nope." I cut into my breakfast and shovel in a huge mouthful. "We're done."

"Why? I thought you two were going to do the friends-with-benefits thing."

"I'm no longer interested."

"Bullshit."

I shrug as I try to act casual. "I'm serious."

Antony sits back in his chair. His assessing eyes hold mine. "Someone is going to swoop in and steal her from right under your nose, you fucking idiot."

"Don't care," I fire back.

"We'll see about that."

"She's not after a relationship anyway," I tell them.

"Until she finds someone else to be her friend and he falls desperately in love with her. You're a fucking idiot, man."

The conversation turns to Blake's work, and my mind goes back to her.

Always back to her, and I'm fucking sick of it.

I need her out of my system.

I sit at my desk and stare into space. The week has been long and depressing.

Every night before I fall asleep I tell myself that tomorrow I am going to go over to Juliet's and apologize and beg to see her . . . but then tomorrow comes, and I just don't.

Why am I like this? Or what could possibly be wrong with me to make me such a selfish prick?

Why do I torture myself the way that I do?

All I want to do is see her, to hold her in my arms and tell her that I missed her.

That shouldn't be hard. It should be the most natural thing in the world.

Logically I know that, so why can't I do it?

I open the top drawer of my desk and rustle through it, and I catch sight of what I'm looking for at the very bottom, buried under everything. I pull it out and stare at it in my hands.

AARON STEVENS

PSYCHOLOGIST

I've had this card for years. He's supposed to be the best of the best, supposed to be able to fix anyone.

Call him.

It won't help. What could he possibly say to make this all better?

Call him.

With shaky fingers I dial his number and wait as it rings.

"Aaron Stevens's rooms," a woman answers, and when I hear her voice, I immediately hang up the phone.

Fuck.

I drag my hands through my hair. I don't need that shit. I'm fine. I just need to stop thinking about her, that's all. If I'm not near her, then she can't make me feel this way.

Onward and upward.

Juliet

I carry the towels up the hall and slow down when I get toward the end of the corridor. I'm at the nursing home tonight. And even though I know that he doesn't remember his son, I know it's his dad.

I stop at the door and watch him through the window for a moment. He's lying in bed and watching the television, seemingly happy as a clam.

I mean, he is happy because, thankfully, he doesn't remember to be sad. I brace myself and then knock softly. "Come in," he calls.

"Hello." I smile as I open the door. "How are you, Mr. James?"

"Good." He keeps watching television. I glance up to see it's a football game tonight.

I replace his towels and straighten his blankets. "Have you had a good day?"

"It was okay." His eyes stay focused on the screen. "Better if that damn cat stopped scratching."

I smile and fold the blanket up at his feet. "He's annoying, isn't he?"

"You have no idea," he grumbles. "Getting on my last nerve."

I smile, and something about Mr. James makes me feel better. I'm really missing my parents this week.

The phone on the bedside rings, and I glance at it.

"Get that, please," he says casually.

"But . . ."

"Answer the damn phone," he demands. "Push the talk button."

I pick up the phone and hit speaker. I hear Henley's voice. "Hi, Dad."

Emotion fills me at the sound of his voice.

"Who's that?" Mr. James replies.

"It's Henley."

Mr. James's eyes light up. "Henley." He smiles. "Did you go to preschool today, son?"

"Not today, Dad," Henley replies.

My heart aches for him.

"Tell your mother to come and bring me home."

"Okay." Henley's voice is soft, sad.

"Ask him if he's all right," I whisper to Mr. James.

He frowns.

"Ask him if he's all right," I repeat.

"Are you all right, Hen?" he asks.

"Yeah, I'm okay. Had better days, I guess."

Tears fill my eyes. I can hear the sadness in his voice.

"What did you have for dinner?" Henley asks.

"They haven't fed me yet."

229

I look over to the empty dinner plates on the table that are still waiting to be collected.

"You would have had dinner, Dad. You just forgot," Henley tells him.

"Nope. I'm starving. Put your mother on the phone."

"She's busy right now."

"Is she coming to get me or not?" he snaps.

"Soon," Henley says.

I smile. He's so patient with him.

"I love you, Dad," Henley says softly.

My heart constricts.

Mr. James nods but doesn't reply.

"Say it back," I whisper.

"Huh?"

"Say it back," I repeat.

"Say what back?" he grumbles.

Fuck's sake . . .

"I'll let you go," Henley says.

"You go back to school, Hen. Be a good boy now. We'll build something when you get home."

"Okay. Sounds good."

I smile as I listen.

"Bye, Dad." The phone goes dead as he hangs up.

I slouch onto the bed, disappointed that Henley didn't get his *I love you* back. Which is ridiculous because, I mean, why should I even care?

He and I are in the world's most fucked-up relationship. He hasn't called me since he left in a huff the other night, and the sick thing is, I don't expect him to.

It's like I'm becoming accustomed to dysfunction and am now even expecting it.

I'll give us another couple of weeks, and then I have to decide where we go from here.

Nothing is ever easy, is it?

Thursday morning I stretch for my run. "Morning, Carol," I call.

"Good morning, dear." Carol smiles as she walks across the street toward me. "Beautiful day, isn't it?"

"Sure is."

Henley's front door opens, and he walks out. He glances up and sees us. His step falters a little. My heart somersaults in my chest. Fuck it. I hate that just the sight of him makes my heart race.

Why does he affect me so?

He waves and puts his head down.

Is he going to come over?

I watch as he walks around and gets into his car. And then, without making eye contact, he gives a quick wave as he drives past us down the road.

My heart sinks.

I get the feeling that it's not going to be okay between us.

I need to work out how I'm going to fix us, but then what if he's too far broken and will never be fixed?

Maybe there is nothing to fix. Maybe this connection we have is all in my head.

No.

I'm not imagining it. I know I'm not.

In fact, the only thing I do know for certain is the way that he makes *me* feel. It's real and raw, an earth-shattering addiction that I've never felt before.

And no matter how self-destructive I know that this is, I need to follow it through and see where it goes.

I want to try.

I take a long last look at myself in the mirror, wearing my green scrubs, with my hair in a high ponytail. I'm trying my very best to be hot nurse porn.

It's Thursday night, and without one single word from Henley, I'm taking matters into my own hands.

He better take the bait.

"Okay, this is it. I'm offering him an olive branch, and if he doesn't take it, then poof to him." I look down to my trusty little best friend. "Wish me luck, Bazza." I bounce downstairs and grab the key off the counter and head over to Henley's house.

I knock on his door.

Knock, knock.

Boom.

Boom.

Boom bangs my heart.

The door opens in a rush, and I come face to face with Henley James. He's wearing satin navy-blue boxer shorts and is shirtless, with his dark hair and perfect face. His ripped body only makes me more nervous.

There's a lot at stake here.

"Hi." I smile awkwardly.

"Hi."

"Umm." I frown as I try to get my practiced speech right before I say it out loud. "I'm on my way to work a night shift, and Barry seems jumpy today, and I'm worried that he might bark and keep you awake." I'm blurting the words out in a rush. "So I was thinking that if I gave you a key and he's being noisy, you could come over to my house and put him inside." I hold a key to my house out to him. "Because we're friends and all." I shrug nervously.

He doesn't take the key from my outstretched hand. Instead he gives me a slow sexy smile and leans against the doorjamb.

I swallow the lump in my throat as I wait for his reply. "What do you think?"

His dark eyes sweep down my body and then back up to my face. "I think that you should come inside for a moment."

"You do?"

He nods. "I do." He steps to the side, and I walk past him, and he closes the door behind us and then pins me up against it and puts his lips to my ear. "You should know better than coming over here looking like a walking fucking wet dream."

Butterflies dance in my stomach at his close proximity.

He takes my face into his hands and kisses me. His lips linger over mine with just the perfect amount of suction. "Hi," he murmurs against my lips.

"Hi." I smile shyly.

He kisses me again, and I feel his erection grow up against my hip. "What are you doing on Saturday night?" he asks.

Aah . . .

"Nothing." His lips take mine again as our kiss deepens.

Damn, he's good at this.

"I have tickets to the opera."

"You do?"

"Do you like the opera?"

I do now.

"We should go." He licks my open lips, and I feel it between my legs.

My brain has officially left the building. "Uh-huh . . ."

"But it would mean staying in town."

I'm literally a genius. This plan is working to perfection. He's asking me on a date—not just any date, a whole-night date.

"I suppose we can do that." I try to act casual.

We keep kissing, and he slides his hand down the front of my pants and slides his fingertips through the lips of my sex. He works me as we kiss, and I see stars.

Oh . . .

We didn't even make it inside. I'm still pinned to the back of his front door.

Animals.

He lifts me, wanting more.

"I have to go to work, Henley."

"You have work to do here." He carries me to the couch and throws me onto it. I laugh as I bounce. He crawls over me, his erection now peeking over the top of his boxer shorts. Pre-ejaculate is dripping from his end.

Gah . . . I want it.

This man . . .

Suddenly our kiss turns frantic. He holds my legs back as he rubs his erection over my sex.

We stare at each other as desperation runs between us.

So hot.

Wait a minute, what the fuck is going on here? I have no restraint at all when it comes to him. Who even am I? This is an intel mission only.

Go to work.

"Henley, I have to go."

"No, you have to come." He smiles darkly against my lips as he pumps me with his hips.

I so do.

No, play it cool.

"You're a fucking sex maniac, Henley James."

"You make me one."

I climb out from under him and stand. "Saturday."

His eyes hold mine. "Saturday . . . ," he whispers darkly.

The air swirls between us, and damn it, can he feel this? Whatever *this* is . . .

I kiss him quickly, and without looking back I walk out the door. I bounce down the steps feeling triumphant, and I just want to jump and punch the air.

Touchdown!

"Good evening, Mrs. Greenwell." I smile as I walk into the room. "How's my favorite patient?"

Mrs. Greenwell's eyes light up. "Here she is, my favorite nurse. Hello, Juliet, I've been waiting for you."

I fluff up her pillows and adjust her bed. I look over her chart. "You had extra pain management last night." I glance up to her in question.

"Yes, terrible night it was." She shakes her head. "And I don't like that Michelle. She's not very nice, is she?"

Michelle is a shift manager and no, she's not very nice. Not that I'll ever admit it.

"Behave, Mrs. Greenwell." I smile as I readjust the pillows some more.

"She has a terrible bedside manner, and seeing as I am in bed . . ." She raises her eyebrows sarcastically. "I think I should know."

I giggle. Mrs. Greenwell is in her late eighties and has a broken hip; she's been in the hospital for over a month now and is quite the character. I find myself thinking about her on my days off.

"How has your day been?" she asks.

"Fantastic." I smile. "I'm walking on air."

Mrs. Greenwell smiles. "Wouldn't happen to have anything to do with a certain grumpy neighbor, would it?"

"Maybe." I beam.

"I live for your stories." She pats the bed beside her. "Tell me everything."

"Well." I drop to sit on the bed. "Just quickly. I have to get back to work. I went over today to see him, and he asked me on a date to the opera on Saturday night."

"He did?" Her eyes widen.

"Yep." I smile proudly. "A real date."

She takes my hand in hers. "He's practically in love with you already, dear."

"Ha! I wish." I smile as I stand. "I'll be back in a while. I have to check on everyone. Do you need anything?"

"I'd love a glass of sherry."

"Now, you know I'm not allowed to give you any, even if we had any."

She lets out a deep sigh. "This place is no fun."

"Tell me about it." I leave Mrs. Greenwell and float down the corridor. After the week from hell, everything is finally working out.

I'm going on a date with Henley, not a booty-call-over-the-fence-in-the-middle-of-the-night kind of hookup. A real, bona fide date.

To the opera, no less.

I just hope it goes well. It has to.

"You look hot," Rebecca says from her place at my kitchen counter.

"He's toast," Chloe chimes in.

I look between my two friends. "I can't believe you two are hanging out without me."

Chloe has come over to stay with Barry for the night, and with John away, Rebecca is home alone. They are having pizza and cocktails on my front porch, without me.

"As if you won't be having more fun," Rebecca scoffs into her wineglass.

"I still think Henley's a weirdo," Chloe replies.

"I don't think it, I know it," I agree.

"I mean, who forgets a condom and then completely freaks out and leaves in the middle of it and then doesn't speak to you all week and then asks you to the opera on a date?"

"A weirdo," Rebecca and I say together.

"She's unpacking baggage," Rebecca chimes in. "Aren't you?"

"A truckload of it." I grab my boobs and boost them up into my bra. "Do I look okay?"

"You look great."

"Okay, I'm going to get going." We decided that I would meet him at the hotel. Carol doesn't miss a beat around here, and it's going to be awkward if anyone knows about us.

Although I kind of get the feeling that Blake and Antony already know. They seem to be really chatty lately, but that could be my guilty conscience talking.

I'm hopeless at keeping secrets.

"Have a great night."

"Good luck." Rebecca hugs me.

"Kick him to the curb if he's a dick."

I puff air into my cheeks. "It's Henley. We already know he's going to be a dick."

"True."

With one last wave I make my way out to the car and text Henley.

On my way.

A reply bounces straight back in.

Meet me in the bar downstairs.

Nerves dance in my stomach. Meeting a hot, mysterious guy in the bar of a hotel: it's all so exotic. Like a spy movie or something, hopefully one that ends well.

I take one last look into the rearview mirror at my face.

I'm nervous.

And I know it's stupid and that I shouldn't be because this isn't my first rodeo, especially not with Henley. But that's the thing: every time with him feels like the first time, and maybe that's why I'm so jittery . . . I know in my heart that this is something special, or at least it could be.

Nobody has ever made me feel the way that he does.

I need to remind Henley James of the chemistry we share.

Blow his fucking mind.

I get out of my car and make my way into the hotel. It's super fancy, with doormen in black suits standing around. The floors are a beautiful green marble, and huge oversize chandeliers are hanging from the ornate ceilings. I spot the restaurant and bar and make my way in, and instantly I feel more at ease. It's nicer in here, with a much more relaxed ambience. Timber-and-metal tables and chairs, and candles in small copper vases are on all the tables. The bar is a dark timber with old-fashioned stools lined up. Big copper light fittings hang low over it.

I smile as I look around. This is cool.

My eyes roam around the room, and then I see him, sitting in the corner booth.

He gives me a slow sexy smile, and excitement runs through me. All week I've thought of nothing else but him, and to be here now . . .

Play it cool.

I smile and, trying to be as casual as I can, make my way over to the table. "Hi." I pull out the chair.

"Hello." He taps the chair beside him. "Sit here."

My stomach flips, and I walk around the table and slide in beside him.

"Hi." He takes my face into his hands and kisses me softly. "You're late," he purrs.

And you're perfect.

Chapter 15

"Good things are worth the wait?" I pull out of his grip, trying my best to play hard to get.

He fills two wineglasses from a bottle that is sitting in ice on the table and passes one to me.

"Champagne." I smile. "What are we celebrating?"

"Well"—he taps his glass on mine and takes a sip—"we're here." He raises his eyebrow playfully.

"You mean, we made it through our first meltdown?" I smirk.

He breaks into a breathtakingly beautiful smile. "Did we, though?"

His smile does things to me. I get flutters all the way to my toes. "We did."

He leans in and kisses me again. His lips linger over mine, and I begin to lose sight of the mission.

What is it about this man?

He kisses me again and again, and my eyes close against my will.

Focus.

"Henley." I smile shyly as I break out of his grip. "We are in a crowded restaurant."

"I don't give a fuck where we are. I want to kiss you."

"And you will." I take his hand in mine and hold it against my other hand, resting on his thick quad muscle. "Later." I smile.

He exhales heavily. "I haven't seen you all week."

He missed me.

"I know," I reply as if I don't care.

"What have you been doing all week?" he asks as he sips his champagne.

Missing you.

"Working, painting."

"Did Mason help you?"

"No."

"What about the other fucking idiot?"

I giggle. "You mean my interior designer, the one you're jealous of, Joel?"

"I am not jealous of Joel," he fires back. "He's . . ." He pauses as if trying to choose his words carefully.

I cut in. "Touching your things."

He smirks at my analogy. "Yes."

"So I'm your thing now?"

His dark eyes drop to my lips. "Yes."

The air crackles between us as we stare at each other.

You are most definitely my thing.

He grabs my face and kisses me again, his tongue swiping through my open lips, and I feel it between my legs.

I remember where we are and pull out of his kiss. "Why is it that whenever we are together, we act like horny teenagers?"

"Because you make me fucking horny, that's why."

I smile and pick up my champagne glass. "Can we . . ." I pause. "Can we what?"

"Can we just have a normal date where we aren't trying to fuck each other at the table?"

"But I do want to fuck you on the table?"

I giggle. "You know what I mean."

"You want a normal date?"

"Yes."

"Okay." He smirks and sips his champagne. "Date me."

The thing about champagne is this: you are supposed to drink one or two glasses to celebrate an event.

Not drink three bottles until you are both laughing uncontrollably at the table.

The conversation never runs dry with us. We laugh and chat as if we are old friends.

And although we are completely different, we are on the same wavelength. We have the same sense of humor.

I'm not imagining it; this is way more than sex.

"Okay." Henley smirks. "Ten things."

"What?"

"Tell me ten things about you that I don't know."

"Hmm." I narrow my eyes as I try and think. "Umm." I twist my lips. "One . . . I love sex."

"I know that already. That doesn't count." He sips his champagne and smiles like a loon.

He likes this game.

I giggle. "Right." I think for a bit. "Two . . . I wanted to be a ballerina when I was a child."

"Why aren't you?" He frowns.

"Because I have two left feet and dance like a baboon."

"I did notice that."

I laugh out loud, and he does too.

"Three . . . I hate cilantro with a passion. I'm even in the I Hate Cilantro Facebook group."

He frowns as he listens. "There's a Facebook page for that?"

"Uh-huh." I giggle, and he does too. Why is everything we say to each other hilarious?

"Go on, seven more things," he says.

"Four . . . I've never had a lesbian fantasy."

"Oh . . . not a fan of that one." He screws up his face in disappointment. "Please lie to me and tell me you have."

"Okay, I take that back." I laugh again. "Five . . . every night I dream of having a threesome with a guy and another girl."

"Better." He raises his champagne glass toward me.

I smile goofily.

He's so fun.

I try to think of something else he doesn't know about me. "Six . . . never watched *Game of Thrones*."

He nods as he listens.

"Seven . . . I wish my dog wasn't called Barry."

"Don't we fucking all?"

We both burst out laughing again.

"Eight . . . I'm a great swimmer."

"Are you lying?" He refills my champagne glass.

"Totally."

"You're good at other things." He shrugs. "Can't be greedy."

"I know, right." I giggle, and he taps his glass against mine for our fiftieth cheers of the night.

"Come on," he coaches me, "I need more information."

"Umm." I look up to the ceiling as I try to think of something else to tell him. "Nine . . . I didn't like it when you left the other night."

He falls serious. "Why not?"

"You can't ask questions unless my answers count."

"Last question. Why didn't you like it when I left?"

"Because I liked having you inside of me."

His eyes darken and drop to my lips. He leans back and adjusts himself in his jeans.

He liked that answer.

"Your turn," I say.

"No, no, this was my quiz."

"Oh no you don't. Give me ten facts that I don't know about you."

He sits back in his chair as he thinks. "I also wish your dog wasn't called Barry because it reminds me of the Bee Gees."

I giggle.

"Never watched *Game of Thrones*."

"You can't just copy my answers," I tell him.

"Hmm." He twists his lips as he thinks. "Haven't had a vacation in a very long time."

"Uh-huh."

"I like to listen to true-crime podcasts. I could get away with the perfect murder if I wanted to."

"Don't kill me."

He raises his eyebrow, and I laugh.

"Let's see . . ." He thinks again. "I think about fucking you . . . a lot."

"I already know that."

"Oh, do you now?"

"Uh-huh." I smile goofily. "It's obvious."

He chuckles. "Is it? I thought I hid it well."

"Not at all."

"Umm, what else is there?"

I smile as I listen.

"Never been in love."

Oh . . .

"Well, don't fall in love with me," I tease as I tap his glass with mine.

"No chance of that." He smirks. "You're hideous."

"Facts." I giggle. "Come on, more."

"I . . ." He pauses.

"You what?"

He falls serious. "I didn't want to leave the other night either."

"So why did you?"

He twists his champagne glass on the table by the stem as he stares at it. "Because I'm fucked up."

Progress.

I take his hand in mine and lift it to kiss his fingertips. "I don't believe that."

He puffs air into his cheeks, and I know that was a lot for him to admit. Quick, onto the next question before he can think too much.

"Okay, last one . . . What is the *one* fact I don't know about you?" I smile playfully.

"The one thing?" he asks.

"The one thing."

His eyes hold mine. "It's my birthday."

"What? Today?"

He nods shyly.

My heart swells. He chose to spend his birthday with me.

Oh . . .

"Happy birthday, baby." I lean over and kiss him, and he kisses me back, and somehow this kiss is different. I don't taste a hint of the game we've been playing.

It's real and raw, somehow more.

Hand in hand, we walk up the corridor of the hotel and back to our room.

He glances down at my stilettos. "I like those shoes."

"Do you?"

His tongue slips out and runs over his bottom lip as if imagining something. "They're going to look great around my ears."

I know.

I smile up at my beautiful date.

This has been the best night in the history of all time. We've talked and laughed and kissed and made out in the elevator.

Henley James is the all-time ultimate date: handsome, funny, witty, intelligent, and let's not forget sexy as fuck.

The entire time we were having dinner tonight, I didn't know whether to laugh, swoon, or just bend over the table. This friends-with-benefits position definitely has its perks. There's no denying that spending a night with this god is like winning the jackpot.

But I want more.

And weirdly enough, my gut tells me that he does too.

He hasn't said so, of course, but I can hear the silent words hidden within his sentences. It's the things that he doesn't say out loud, the things he doesn't articulate, and I don't know how, but I already know what he's feeling.

He's right here with me, lost in a perfect moment of clarity. How could he not be? Together we're perfect, and it's not even about the sex—and trust me, the sex is a lot.

It's the conversation, the laughter, and the way we get each other's jokes. It's him wrapping me in his coat on the way home so I wasn't cold, the way he listens when I talk. The way he holds my hand, and the goose bumps I get when he looks at me.

He could have gone anywhere in the world tonight, and yet he chose to spend his birthday with me.

"How long is this corridor?" I frown. "We've walked at least five miles."

He gives me a sexy wink. "This is the warm-up."

"For what?" I play dumb.

"Bedroom Olympics."

I burst out laughing, and he does too, and then he stops at a door. "This is us." He fiddles around with the key as I run my hand down over his firm behind. His hands still, and I take it as a sign and unzip his jeans. He glances up the corridor and then back to me.

"I know what I want to give you for your birthday."

"What's that?"

I put my mouth to his ear for added effect. "I want to suck you off in public."

His eyes widen, and I drop to my knees.

"Juliet," he whispers as he looks up the corridor. "You'll get us kicked out of the hotel."

I pull his already-erect cock out of his jeans and take it in my mouth. "I don't care," I whisper around him.

"You'll get us arrested."

"We could do it in jail too."

He chuckles and shudders as I flick my tongue over his end. Then, as if losing control, he grabs my hair in his hands and slides deep down my throat.

Who even am I?

We fall into a rhythm. His eyes flick between me and the length of the hallway.

He's fucking my mouth with a hurried urgency, a desire so deep that he couldn't stop even if he wanted to.

And I take it all like a pro. His soft moans and ragged breathing turn me inside out as I watch him come undone.

"Fuck, fuck, *fuck*," he growls as he pumps me hard. His crazy eyes shoot up the corridor, and he tips his head back and comes in a rush with a deep moan.

I gag. Ugh . . .

He's a lot of man to take.

But then I see the look in his eye and I know it's all worth it, because it's Henley and I adore him and I want his birthday to be memorable.

I need to be burned into his brain like he is in mine.

Triumphantly I lick him clean, and the elevator dings, and he pulls me to my feet, and we both turn to face his door guiltily.

All flustered, he fumbles with the key and drops it. "Fuck it," he mutters under his breath.

I get the giggles. His dick is still hanging out the front of his jeans.

Two old ladies walk out of the elevator. They are chatting away. "Get the fucking key," he whispers.

"No."

He widens his eyes at me, and I laugh harder. "Show them your dick," I whisper.

He elbows me. "Get the key off the floor."

"No."

He gets the giggles too. What must we look like, facing the door, guilty as all hell, with the key on the ground in front of us? I'm laughing so hard, I couldn't bend down to get it even if I tried.

The grannies get closer.

Henley nods, looking as cool as a cucumber. "Evening, ladies."

"Hello." One lady smiles without looking at us closely. "We've just had the best night at the opera. If you get a chance, you simply have to go."

Henley's eyes flick to mine, and my mouth falls open in surprise.

We forgot to go to the opera.

We lie in the dark facing each other. It's late, and we have quenched our every desire. The night has been long and sweaty, our bodies well used. He's a god in bed. There's no other way to describe him.

We are freshly out of the shower and naked under the blankets.

I feel so close to him. There is no other way to explain our connection. It's magical.

A force to be reckoned with.

Henley's finger traces up my arm aimlessly, as if he still has to touch me, and we are both lost in our own thoughts.

I'm tired, but I don't want to go to sleep because I know that when I wake up, my beautiful and vulnerable Hen won't be here; Henley James the hard-ass will be in his place.

It's as if Henley knows it, too, and is fighting sleep as hard as I am.

"How was your birthday?" I ask.

"Perfect."

I smile softly over at him in the darkness as we stare at each other.

"Thank you for making it so special," he whispers as he leans over and kisses me softly.

His kiss is tender and loving, filled with so much feeling.

Every emotion comes to a head inside of my body as I feel my heart freefall from my chest.

I think I love him.

"Knock, knock. Housekeeping."

I wake with a start. Where am I?

"Housekeeping," a voice calls through the door. Shit, I'm at the hotel. I look over to see that I am in bed alone. Henley isn't here.

I jump up and run to the door. "Come back later, please," I call.

"Would you like the morning paper?" the voice calls.

"No thank you." Jeez, what time is it? Why is this woman waking me up for the daily paper?

I see a note on the side table.

Gone to the gym,
Back soon.
H x

I smile. He's visiting his dad.

What a beautiful man he is, spending every morning with his unwell father.

Gah . . . just when I think he can't get any better, he goes ahead and proves me wrong.

I float into the bathroom, still high from last night. Right . . . now to make myself simply irresistible.

I sip my coffee and read the morning paper, and my phone beeps a text. It's Henley.

Where are you?

Excitement runs through my body. Just a text from him sends me into overdrive. I reply.

In the restaurant having breakfast.
Come down.

Another text bounces straight back.

On my way.

I go back to reading my paper, pretending not to be the biggest fangirl in the history of life.

I have to be smart about this. If I want him forever, and I do, I can't mess this up.

"Good morning, Miss Drinkwater," his deep voice purrs as he slides into the booth opposite me.

I look up, and there he is: dark hair, square jaw, and the most beautiful face I have ever seen. "Good morning, Mr. James." I smile. "How was the gym?"

"Good." He smirks as his eyes hold mine.

He has that naughty look in his eyes, and I know he's still playful this morning.

Progress.

I pass him the menu. "I'm going to have the pancakes."

"Hmm." He frowns as he peruses the choices. "I'm going for the omelet."

The waitress walks over. "Hello, can I get you a beverage, sir?" she asks.

"Yes, please," he says as he holds the menu in his hands. "I would like a double macchiato, please."

She scribbles it down. "Are you ready to order your food?"

His eyes flick to me. "Are you ready?"

"Yes, I'll have the pancakes, please."

"And I'll have the omelet with a glass of orange juice." He passes the menus back to her. "Thank you."

She wanders off, and his eyes come to me.

"How does it feel to be a year older?" I ask him.

A trace of a smile crosses his face. "Satisfying."

That makes two of us.

It takes all my might not to climb onto his lap and kiss him stupid. "What's on today, boss?" I ask instead.

"Boss?"

251

I smile goofily. "Well, you are bossy."

"Only when naked."

"I beg to differ."

He smirks as the air swirls between us.

Everything is working out perfectly.

An hour later Henley walks me out to my car.

I don't want to leave him.

This hard-to-get business is killing me. I want to see him sooner than next weekend.

Quick, think of a plan.

We walk down the street toward my car. He doesn't hold my hand or show any affection, but it is there between us. I can feel it.

"I'm going to start watching *Game of Thrones* tonight," I announce.

"Are you?"

"Uh-huh."

He stays silent as we walk.

Shit . . . he was supposed to tell me that he wanted to watch it with me.

"Are you coming to watch it with me?" I act casual.

"That depends."

"On what?"

"On whether you're cooking me dinner."

I want to jump and punch the air. "I suppose I can do that."

"Okay, then."

I bite my lip to hide my goofy grin. A television date on a Sunday night? This is definitely love.

"Can you cook?" He frowns.

I wince. Jeez, don't ask me that. "Kind of."

"Define 'kind of' . . ."

"Well." I shrug. "I have a few dishes I'm good at."

He smirks. "I'll cook us dinner at *my* house."

"You cook?"

"Very well." He gives me a sexy wink.

Ugh . . . of course he does. He looks like that, he fucks like a demon, and now he cooks very well. Is there anything this man can't do with ease?

Fall in love with me.

My face falls as I remember something.

"What is it?" he asks.

"Can we eat at my house?"

"Why?"

"I haven't been home all weekend, and I feel bad for Barry."

He rolls his eyes.

"You cook at my house. Yes, that's a great idea." I smile hopefully. "Text me the ingredients, and I'll get them today," I offer.

He exhales heavily. "Your dog is annoying."

"I know." I bounce on the spot. "Please?"

"Fine." He sighs as we get to my car.

I open the door, and awkwardness falls between us for the first time. "Do I get a kiss goodbye?" I ask.

His eyes hold mine. "We're friends, Juliet."

Ouch.

"With benefits," I add. "Kisses goodbye is one of those benefits."

"Is it?"

I nod.

He smirks and takes my face into his hands. "Well, in that case . . ." He kisses me softly, and my feet lift off the floor. We kiss again and again, and damn it, I want all the benefits, but I know that I have to continue this hard-to-get crap, not that I'm executing it very well today.

"See you tonight?" I pull out of his grip.

"Tonight." He steps back and puts his hands in his pockets.

I look down and see his erection in his pants. "Better take care of that before you go back into the hotel."

He glances down at himself. "I'll call into the brothel around the corner on the way back."

My mouth falls open in horror.

"Kidding." He widens his eyes.

"Not funny." I get into my car and close the door. He taps on the window, and I wind it down. "Yes?" I say, half-annoyed at his hooker joke.

"I'll text you the shopping list."

"Okay."

"I had a great night." He smiles.

What if he really does go to the brothel on the way back to the hotel?

"We're just friends, Henley," I remind him to try and act tough.

"With benefits." He smirks. "Don't forget those."

I roll my eyes and start my car. How could I ever forget those? My vagina is broken.

With a casual wave, I pull out onto the road, and as I drive away, I watch him disappear in the rearview mirror. The farther I drive away from him, the more I want to turn around and go back.

Damn it . . . he's perfect.

"What about these jeans?" I take them off the rack and show Rebecca.

She twists her lips. "Too blue."

I exhale heavily. Chloe, Rebecca, and I are shopping. John is taking Rebecca away next weekend, and she wants some new clothes. She's trying to get the spark back in their marriage.

"I really think he likes me." Chloe smiles.

"Who?" I frown.

"Blake." She rolls her eyes. "Have you been listening to me at all?"

Not really.

"Tell me what happened again?"

"He was going out, and then he saw Rebecca and I on your porch, and he came over to talk to us."

"Yes." I listen as I flick through the rack of jeans.

"He ended up staying with us all night drinking cocktails on your porch, and Antony came over, too, and we played cards."

"So he didn't go out at all?" I frown.

"Nope." Chloe smiles hopefully.

"I wouldn't be getting excited over him," Rebecca says. "He's a serious player. Why would you want to set yourself up for heart-break with someone like him?"

"All bad men come good eventually." Chloe smiles hopefully.

I roll my eyes and keep hunting for jeans. "What about these ones?" I hold a black pair up.

"I've got black already."

"Why are we buying jeans? Why aren't we buying crotchless panties and lingerie?" Chloe says.

"True."

"You think?" Rebecca frowns. "Is that going too far?"

"He's your husband, and you said you wanted the spark back."

"I do."

"Well, jeans are not going to do that." Chloe rolls her eyes. "Dear lord, there is no such thing as too fucking far." She stomps off toward the escalator to go up to the lingerie floor.

Rebecca links her arm through mine. "So how was last night, anyway?" she asks.

"My god, Rebecca." I smile dreamily. "He is . . . so . . ." I pause as I search for the right word. "Amazing."

"Be careful with him," she warns. "This whole thing makes me nervous for you."

"I am," I lie. "He's cooking me dinner tonight."

She gives me a crooked smile. "I don't want you to get hurt."

"I won't."

Her phone beeps a text, and she pulls it out and reads it, lets out a deep exhale, and then stuffs her phone into her pocket. "Fuck's sake."

"What's up?" I ask.

"John is working tonight after golf."

"On a Sunday? Since when do orthopedic surgeons operate on a Sunday night?" I frown.

"That's exactly what I was thinking."

"You really think he's cheating on you?"

She shrugs. "My gut tells me he is. There's just too many anomalies in his stories."

God, I can't imagine being in her shoes.

"What are you going to do?"

"Try and save my marriage."

I put my arm around her and kiss her temple as we walk toward the escalator in search of Chloe. "It's going to work out, Bec. I'm sure there's a reasonable excuse for all of this."

She nods sadly. "I really hope so."

Showered, primped, and primed, with the dinner ingredients lined up on the kitchen counter, I am ready for my dinner date with the chef.

I peer through the kitchen window. "Where is he?" I wanted to get my washing off the line, but I've been waiting for him to arrive before I do it, and it's going to be dark soon. Guaranteed, the moment I go out into the backyard, he will knock on my front door.

I'll just have to wait.

I make another cup of tea and sit on the couch and wait.

My mind goes over our date last night and how perfect he is. He better show up tonight.

Damn it. I begin to worry about his whereabouts. He should have been here by now. He has stood me up before.

Tap, tap sounds at the back door, and relief fills me.

He's here.

I walk out into the kitchen to see him standing at my back door, in blue jeans and a white T-shirt and wearing that beautiful smile. I open the door in a rush. "Hello, Mr. James. You don't have to knock."

Mischief flashes across his face. "So I can just barge in whenever I want?"

"You do anyway." I step to the side, and he walks past me.

"When do I barge in?" he gasps, affronted.

"Whenever Joel is here."

"Because he's a fucking idiot."

"Who's touching your stuff?" I tease.

"Precisely." He kicks off his shoes and walks into my kitchen. "How did you do with the ingredients?"

"Good, I got everything."

He looks over the things out on the counter. "Where are the lemons?"

"Oh." I twist my lips. "Were they on the list?"

He widens his eyes. "Yes."

"Oh . . ." I shrug. "I didn't get lemons."

He stares at me for a beat. "I need lemons."

"For what?"

"To garnish."

I screw up my face. "It's only a garnish. Who cares, then?"

"It's in the recipe, Juliet."

"Oh my god, will you relax about the stupid recipe, just chuck shit in."

He inhales sharply as if frustrated. "I do *not* just chuck shit in, and for the record, this is probably why your cooking is ordinary." He glances over toward the door. "What are you doing?" he growls. "Do not eat that."

I turn to see Barry carrying his shoe around in his mouth. "Barry."

Barry looks up at us, completely clueless, and Henley walks over and takes his shoe off him. "This is not food." He walks into the kitchen and begins to get things ready. "Fuck's sake, dog, you're a liability."

"He's hungry too. Can you cook some extra for him?"

"Hard no." He fakes a smile and then drops his face.

I sit and watch him for a moment as he lines all the ingredients up and then lays out all the cooking utensils. Everything is done in a specific order. He's so methodical in the way he does things, the ultimate control freak. "I'm going to get the washing off the line," I say.

He flicks the tea towel over his shoulder as he concentrates on the task at hand. "Okay."

I walk out to my backyard and break into a huge goofy grin. The hottest man on earth is in my kitchen cooking dinner for me.

How is this real?

I take my time and get my washing off the line, and then I water my backyard. I keep glancing in through my kitchen window to Henley as he putters around, just to make sure that I'm not dreaming right now.

Nope, he's still there.

This is really happening . . . aah!

Eventually I carry the huge-ass washing basket inside, and the scent of garlic and herbs fills the house. "Oh, that smells good." I dump the washing basket onto the floor.

Henley glances up at it and then goes back to chopping vegetables.

"Do you want a cup of tea?" I ask as I flick the kettle on.

Henley glances back at the basket of washing. "No thanks."

"What about a glass of wine?"

"No." His eyes go back to the basket of washing. "What's happening over there?"

"What do you mean?"

"The washing. Why is it on the floor?"

"I just got it off the line."

"And?" He widens his eyes. "What are you going to do with it now?"

"Oh . . ." I pick up the basket of washing and carry it into the living room and tip it upside down and dump it on the couch.

His face falls in horror. "You did *not* just do that."

"Do what?" I frown.

"You don't . . ." He shakes his head as if he's about to explode. "You don't what?"

"You don't dump the washing on the fucking couch, Juliet," he blurts out in a rush.

I look around and shrug. "I do."

"Oh my god." He washes his hands and marches out into the living room in exasperation. He begins to fold the washing at double speed.

"What are you doing?" I frown.

"Folding your fucking washing. What does it look like?"

"Why?"

"Because it's triggering me. How it is not triggering you is the question." He folds a T-shirt and puts it onto the couch. He folds another shirt and puts it on top of the other. "You never told me you were messy," he huffs. "I don't do messy, Juliet."

"Washing on the couch is hardly messy, Hen."

"I beg to differ." He flicks a pair of jeans as he folds them. "What happens if we want to sit on that couch?"

"Then we throw it onto the floor." I shrug.

He closes his eyes and holds his hand up. "Stop talking." He picks up a pair of my panties and holds them up. They are full brief beige granny panties. "What in god's name are these?"

I get the giggles at his horrified face. "What does it look like?"

He marches out into the kitchen and puts the panties in Barry's bowl. "You have permission to eat these," he tells him. "Rip the fuckers to shreds."

Barry turns his head to the side in confusion.

Henley rolls his eyes. "Dumb dog." He marches back out to the living room. "I have to do everything around here—cook the dinner, fold your washing, *and* supply all the orgasms?"

I smile over at my beautiful grumpy man. "It works for me."

"What do I get for doing all of this?" He flicks a T-shirt before he folds it.

"Me."

His eyes rise to meet mine.

"You get me, Hen. All of me."

A trace of a smile crosses his face. "Well . . . all right, then."

He goes back to folding, and I walk over and wrap my arms around him from behind. "You're so adorable, do you know that?"

He keeps folding my washing. "Don't patronize me, Juliet."

"I'll fold the washing. You go and finish dinner," I tell him.

"You're going to put it away too?"

"Will that make you feel better?"

He nods.

I smile and kiss him softly. "Okay, I can do that."

He exhales heavily. "I just . . ."

"I know, baby. It's okay," I tell him. "You just tell me what you need to feel comfortable, and I can do it."

He nods as he realizes that he has just shown me a piece of his personality that he normally keeps hidden.

Another piece of the Henley James puzzle fits into place.

My man has OCD.

Four hours later . . .

"This show is shit," Henley huffs.

"Everyone says it takes until episode three before you get into it."

He exhales heavily.

After the most delicious dinner in history, we are in bed and watching episode one of *Game of Thrones*. Henley is on his side behind me. His naked body is snuggled up against mine; his erection is growing by the minute. "We should fuck," he whispers in my ear before grazing it with his teeth. Goose bumps scatter up my arms.

"We just had sex for an hour in the shower," I mutter dryly. "You could not need more."

The man is an animal.

"I can never get enough of you." He bites my earlobe once more. "Being inside of you is my favorite place to be."

I smile. "It's a personal favorite of mine too."

His big hand kneads my breast, and my phone beeps as a message comes through.

"Who is messaging me this late?" I frown. It beeps again as another message comes through.

My phone is on his side on the bedside table. "Something must be wrong. Can you pass me my phone, please?"

He reaches over and grabs my phone, and as he stares at the screen his jaw tics in anger. His furious eyes rise to meet mine. "Why the fuck is Joel messaging you at ten p.m. on a Sunday night?"

Chapter 16

"What?" I sit up in a rush. "What do you mean?" I hold my hand out for my phone, and he slaps it into my hand and gets out of bed in a rush.

I read the message.

Hi Juliet.
Can we catch up tomorrow?

I frown.

"What does it say?" Henley snaps.

"Umm . . ." I roll my lips, unsure how to answer.

"Well?"

"He wants to catch up tomorrow."

"The only thing he is going to be catching up with is my fist."

"About my house, Henley. This is work related."

"Bull fucking shit," he snaps. "It's ten p.m. He is hoping that you and he start chatting now in some kind of little Sunday-night sexting session."

I roll my eyes and return to concentrating on my show.

He begins to pace with his hands on his hips. "His plan is all becoming clear now."

"Will you get into bed?" I snap, annoyed. "I am not texting him back. He will get the message loud and clear that this is inappropriate behavior."

"Has he texted you before at night?"

"Yes. But it's been work related, just like this time is. It's completely innocent."

"Are you sure of that?"

"Ugh, Henley stop. It's Sunday night. We are supposed to be in relax mode." I drag my hand down my face. "Get back into bed."

He continues to pace.

"What are you worried about?"

He stays silent as he paces, and I know that he's trying to hold his tongue.

"Henley, you have me."

His eyes rise to meet mine.

"Nobody is going to steal me. I am yours."

"For how long?"

His little show of insecurity reaches right into my chest, and I smile softly. "For as long as you want me to be."

"What do you want?"

I tap the bed beside me, and he begrudgingly sits down. I take his hand in mine. "I want this. I like being here with you. I don't want Joel, I want you." I run my fingers through his dark hair as he looks down at me. He rolls his lips, and I know that once again he's holding his tongue.

"Now get into bed and cuddle my back before I kick you out."

He smirks. "I might leave of my own accord."

I flick the blankets back. "No, you won't."

"I'm just horny, that's all."

I smile into my pillow. The fact that he said that means he's here for other reasons. "I know."

He climbs in behind me and takes me into his arms. "I don't like him texting you."

"I get it. Tomorrow I'll tell him we are together and that it's inappropriate to text me in any way other than about the house."

He pulls me a little closer. "I don't want you to use him as an interior decorator anymore."

"Hen," I warn. "Don't . . ."

He stays silent.

"You have me," I reassure him again. "I'm yours."

Eventually he kisses my shoulder from behind, and I smile as I try to concentrate on *Game of Thrones*. Crisis averted.

We're getting better at this.

Henley

I wake gently to the sound of her breathing. My eyes drag open, and I reach over and turn the alarm off my phone.

Somehow I don't need my alarm when I'm with Juliet. I sleep so soundly that I wake before it goes off. She picks up my hand and puts it around her waist and immediately drifts back to sleep.

Why do we have to touch while we sleep? It's a weird concept.

I lean in and inhale her hair, soft and sweet. The warmth from her body is comforting, and I kiss her shoulder from behind.

Getting into bed with Juliet Drinkwater is easy. Getting out of her bed . . . not so much.

I run my hand up her thigh and cup her full breast.

She's fucking gorgeous.

My lips drop to her neck, and I slowly trail them up to her jaw, my cock rising to the occasion.

I can't get enough of her. Even this close isn't close enough.

And I should be sated, damn it. I spent most of yesterday inside of her. But the one thing I'm beginning to realize with Juliet is the more that I have of her, the more I need.

There is no quenching this thirst. In fact the opposite is happening.

My hunger for her is building at a rapid pace.

She moans softly as she stirs, and I know I have to let her sleep; with one last kiss to her cheek I drag myself out of her bed and dress in the dark. I watch her as she sleeps. Her honey hair is splayed across the pillow; her dark lashes fan across her face. Even in the semidarkness, her beauty emanates around the room. I've never known anyone quite like her.

I've been with gorgeous women before, sure. But none that affect me the way she does.

She's working tonight, damn it. I won't get to see her.

With one last look over the sleeping angel, I sneak downstairs and see Barry snoring in his bed. "Dumb dog." I walk out the back door and see that the sun is just rising, the birds are chirping, and it's a glorious day. Juliet's words from last night come back to me, and I smile as I make my way across her backyard.

"I'm yours."

"Good morning, Bernard." I smile to my father as I walk into his hospital room.

"Is it?" he grumbles.

"It is." I pass him the morning paper and open the blind. I pick up the remote and turn his television on to the morning news. "How did you sleep?"

"Not good," he replies flatly.

I smile at his grumpy reply. Always the pessimist. "Would you like some coffee?"

He looks at me blankly.

"You like coffee," I remind him.

"Do I?"

"Uh-huh."

He shrugs. "I guess."

"I'll make our coffee, and then we'll eat breakfast and get you showered. How does that sound?"

"I don't want a shower," he says as his eyes stay glued to the television.

"You love a shower and shave. Makes you feel fresh."

His eyes meet mine, and I can see the confusion rolling around in his head. "Do I?"

"Yep." I smile. I make my way down to the kitchen and brew us both a cup of coffee. I've done this so many times I'm almost on autopilot now. Every morning it's the same routine: I have to talk him into showering, remind him that he likes coffee, and put up with his griping. But I wouldn't change it for the world. This two hours with him is my favorite part of the day.

We sit and drink our coffee in silence. He watches the morning news, and I read the paper.

A nurse puts her head around the door. "Good morning, Henley. Morning, Bernard."

"Good morning, Alison." I smile. "Nice day outside."

"Is it?" Dad grumbles as his eyes flick out the window to the park below. "Doesn't look that good to me."

"Can't wait to see it," Alison replies as she puts the towels onto the end of his bed. "Have a good day." She disappears down the hall.

Twenty minutes later, I turn the shower on. "Come on, Bernard. Shower time."

"Why do you always want me to have a shower, for Christ's sake?" he snaps as he walks into the bathroom.

I smile as I readjust the temperature of the water. "Come on, clothes off."

He exhales heavily as if I'm the biggest inconvenience in the world and drops his boxer shorts and steps under the hot water.

I hold out the shampoo bottle. "Wash your hair."

"I just washed it ten minutes ago."

"I know, but it got dirty again."

He frowns as he stares at me. "Are you sure?"

"Positive." I squirt the shampoo into his hand. "Wash your hair." I put his hand up to his head, and he begins to wash his hair. Once he's doing an action, his body goes onto autopilot, and he remembers how to do it.

"Tell me about your family," I suggest to him.

He breaks into a broad smile as he stands under the water. The only time he's really happy is when he talks about Mom and me. "My wife is beautiful. A pain in my ass, but beautiful. She'll be here to collect me soon."

"Yes. She will." I smile. "How did you know that you were going to marry her?"

He keeps washing his hair as he thinks. "It wasn't so much that I knew I wanted to marry her."

I frown. "What was it, then?"

"I couldn't stand the thought of not seeing her, couldn't imagine not waking up with her beside me."

My heart twists as I stare at him. "You love her?"

"Very much."

I smile softly.

"And my son . . ." He smiles proudly.

"Tell me about him."

"His name is Henley, and he's the love of my life."

His silhouette blurs. "You're the love of his life too."

"He'll be home from preschool soon. Then he and his mom are going to come and get me and take me home."

"That sounds nice." I help him rinse the shampoo out of his hair.

I only wish it were true.

I walk into my office with a spring in my step. "Good morning, Jenny."

"Morning, Henley," she replies without looking up from her computer. "Vanessa called three times."

"Tell her I died," I reply as I walk into my office. I dump my briefcase onto my desk and begin to unpack it.

Jenny walks in and puts my burner phone onto the desk in front of me. "You need to call her."

"I'm not calling Vanessa." I throw my phone back into the top drawer. "I told you this already. Take the SIM out of that phone, I don't need it anymore."

"Who is she?" she asks again, insistently.

I roll my eyes. "*She's* none of your business."

"She's all of my business." She folds her arms and leans onto my desk.

I continue to open my computer.

"I don't like this," she says.

I glance up at her. "Like what?"

"This mystery woman you've met. Why are you so secretive about her? Who is she?"

"*She* is a friend." I widen my eyes. "Jenny, butt out. You are overstepping."

"I am looking out for your best interest, Henley. How do you know she is not after your money?"

"She is *not* after my money." I roll my eyes and open my emails. "Why don't you get back to work."

"I want to meet her."

"No." I open my first email.

"Do I know her?"

"Go away."

"I must know her."

"Why? Because you know everything?"

"About you, yes, I do."

I point to the door. "Out."

She scowls and storms out and closes the door behind her. Damn woman.

I really need a new PA.

Chapter 17

Juliet

Henley's eyes meet mine across the fire. He winks as he sips his beer before casually looking away. I drop my head to hide my smile.

Two weeks in heaven.

It's Friday night, and the street is gathered for a bonfire at Antony's house. Rebecca leans in. "You and Henley seem very loved up," she whispers.

"Not really." I shrug, but it's a lie. We are so loved up that it's not even funny and have not spent a night apart from each other in two weeks.

We kiss and cuddle and laugh, make love and fuck like animals. We pretend to watch *Game of Thrones* and eat snacks while naked at midnight.

This is it. I've found him.

Everything I've ever wanted in a man is right here in front of me, and I've never been so fulfilled. There's not one thing I would change about him.

Yes, he's got baggage, a lot of it. Every now and then he will have an inner freakout and tell me that we're just friends.

But we both know that's a lie.

This is something.

Something bigger than either of us can control.

The funny thing is we never make plans, but somehow, some-way, without fail, we see each other every day. Even if it's just for an hour before I go to night shift.

I ended up telling Joel that I wasn't doing anything with the house for a while. It wasn't worth the drama with Henley, and I want us to get to safer ground before I cross that bridge.

"There he is," Taryn's annoying voice calls from inside. "Henley James, I can see you," she calls in her singsong voice as she comes floating out the back door.

"Fuck's sake," Rebecca whispers under her breath. "Does she have no shame?"

Taryn runs over and plops herself down onto Henley's lap. "I'll sit with you, darling."

Henley's eyes flick up to me, and I raise my eyebrow.

No.

Don't you fucking dare let her sit there.

Henley bundles her up. "You're not sitting on me, Taryn." He jokingly pushes her off and pulls up a chair beside him and taps it. "Sit here."

"Oh . . . you're no fun." She pretends to pout. "I thought you would like my body weight on yours."

Blake, who is sitting beside them, laughs in surprise.

My blood boils.

"Seriously?" Rebecca whispers.

"Ugh." I try to change the subject. "So John's at work?" I ask.

Rebecca lets out a deep sigh. "Apparently."

"Why do you say it like that?"

"I don't know." She sips her wine. "We went away last weekend and had sex once, and even then I initiated it."

"Maybe . . ." I try to think of an excuse for his behavior. "Maybe his hormones are just out, and he isn't equipped to want it all the time. It happens to men, you know. Especially if they are under stress."

"Maybe," she agrees. "Whenever I ask him what's wrong, he tells me that exact excuse, that he's under a lot of stress and just isn't in the mood and that it has nothing to do with me because he loves me more than anything."

I watch her for a moment. "Do you believe him?"

"Whose footprints were in the back seat of his car, Jules? No matter how many excuses I can make for him, I can't deny what I saw."

"I don't know." I sigh. I don't blame her for being worried. I would be overthinking this, too, if I were in her shoes.

A voice sounds from behind us. "Ladies." We turn to see Mason slink into the chair beside us.

"Hi." I smile. I glance up to meet Henley's unimpressed eyes.

Ha. Now you know how it feels.

Henley

"Oh, Henley," Taryn says softly. "I've just been so . . . lonely lately, you know?"

Blake's eyes meet mine, and he raises a brow as he waits for my response.

"You should buy yourself a vibrator," I reply as I watch Mason talk to Juliet.

The fuck is he playing at?

Blake chuckles at my reply.

"What do you guys do when you're like"—she pauses for effect—"super horny and don't have a partner?"

273

"I find one," I reply. Across the fire Mason laughs and puts his hand on Juliet's leg. My skin bristles.

Don't fucking touch her.

"I'll get us some drinks." Taryn smiles. "What do you guys want?"

"Whatever," I reply, my eyes still locked on my girl across the fire.

Calm down.

Taryn takes off into the house, and I sip my beer as I try not to watch them.

Blake stares across the fire, his eyes not leaving a certain someone.

"You know, you really should stop staring at her," I whisper.

"Why?"

"Because she's fucking married."

"Do I look like I care?"

"You should," I snap.

"I can't help it," he whispers.

"Try harder."

Blake has a thing for Rebecca. Whenever she's close, he can't take his eyes off her.

And it's not good. She's married to someone who lives in our street. A colleague of his, no less.

"What happened the other week when you were drinking cocktails on Juliet's porch when we went out?" I ask.

"She was as tempting as ever." He rolls his eyes. "Their friend has fucked it for me, though."

"What friend?"

"Chloe. She's all over me like a rash, ruining my chances with her."

"There are no chances with her. Rebecca is married." I widen my eyes. "Don't fucking go there."

He sips his beer, unimpressed. "Where is her dickhead husband anyway? He's never around."

"It doesn't matter."

"Typical." He rolls his eyes. "The one woman I can't have is the only one I fucking want."

I sip my beer. "You only want her *because* you can't have her."

"Oh, fuck off," he huffs. "You just worry about Little Miss Across the Fire. Mason is making his move on your girl as we speak."

"Hmm." My eyes rise to watch them. "Not if I throw him in the fire first."

He chuckles as if imagining it. "How's things going with her, anyway?"

Great.

"Okay." I act uninterested.

"She wearing your balls for earrings yet?"

"Does it look like it?"

He smirks. "It does, actually."

"Fuck off." I sip my beer. "At least she's not married to someone else."

He fakes a smile and then drops his face dead. "You're fucking hilarious."

"I think so."

Mason keeps chatting to the girls, and I'm done watching this shit. I take out my phone and text Juliet.

I'm going.

I watch as she takes her phone out of her pocket and reads my message.

My house, half an hour?

I type my reply.

Make it ten.

Juliet

"Hello?" I call to Henley as I walk into my house.

Silence . . .

He must not be here yet.

"Hello, my little buddy." I smile to Barry as I scratch his chin. "Did you eat your bone?"

Barry walks back over to his bed and flops down. I'm taking that as a yes.

I make myself a cup of tea and head upstairs. I take my jacket off and dump it on the bed, kick my shoes off, and flick the television on. It's weird how quickly you get into a new routine. I've now gotten used to noise up here. I don't think I even turned the television on in my bedroom before Henley started coming over to watch our show. Now I seem to turn it on all the time. I sit on the end of the bed and flick through the channels as I sip my tea.

"What will we watch tonight?" I talk to myself as I concentrate on the channels.

I feel him before I see him. I glance up to see Henley leaning on the doorjamb with his shoulder. "Hi." His eyes drink me in.

My stomach flutters. I know that look. I live for that look. "Hello, Mr. James."

He's tall, his presence taking over the small space, or maybe it's just that his presence has taken over me.

He steps forward and takes my face into his hands. "I've been waiting to kiss you all fucking night."

I smile dreamily up at the god. "Have you now?"

"Uh-huh." His lips take mine with just the right amount of suction, his tongue slowly swirling against mine. "How was your day?" he whispers down at me.

"Better now." I smile up at him.

Without thinking, he turns, picks up my jacket, and opens the wardrobe and puts it on a hanger. He collects my shoes and puts them neatly into my wardrobe. He straightens the things that I've messed up. The first few times he cleaned up after me, I didn't like it. I took it as a controlling kind of behavior. But now I know that it's just him and what he needs to do to be able to relax and be in the moment with me.

The more I get to know him, the more his little idiosyncrasies become endearing. They melt me on a deeper level. Remind me just how real and raw my unfiltered man is.

I love that he is reacting to us on autopilot now, doing what is instinctive to him and feels right.

And let's face it, a man who cleans . . . What's not to love about that?

He takes me into his arms again. "Shower." His lips linger against mine as he kisses me, his hands pulling my hips onto his.

"Hen." I ease back from him. "Wrong time of the month for that, remember?"

He kisses me once more. "I know." His tongue gently coaxes mine to come out and play.

Oh . . . this man.

Behave.

I step back from him and head into the bathroom to take my makeup off. He follows me in and sits on the bathroom counter to watch me.

It's the weirdest thing. It's like he's fascinated with the mundanities of my day. He watches everything I do with the greatest of interest. I can't help but wonder if this is the first time he's ever been like this with a woman. He seems captivated by everything I do. "Tell me about your day," I say.

"I had meetings all morning, and then I went to lunch with Antony." He takes my scrunchie from me and begins to pull my hair up into a high bun on top of my head.

"Where did you go for lunch?" I ask as I stay still.

"Bellissimo." He tightens the bun on my head.

"Oh, Italian." I smile. "Yum."

"Have you ever been there?"

"No." I put some makeup remover onto a pad and wipe one eye.

"I'll take you there one day." He takes the pad from me and does my other eye.

I watch him concentrate on his task. "Are you always like this?" I ask.

"Like what?" He tilts my chin toward him and softly kisses my lips.

"Have you ever taken anyone's makeup off before?"

A frown flashes across his face as if he's surprised by the question. "Does it bother you?"

"No." I put my hands onto his hips as he sits in front of me. "That wasn't what I asked."

He stays silent as he wipes all my makeup off. "No. It's not something . . ." His voice trails off.

Progress.

"I like the way you look after me," I whisper.

And he does. The care that he looks after my body with is like nothing I've ever felt. He doesn't say how he feels . . . but he doesn't have to.

278

I can feel it in his touch.

He smirks down at me. "If I'm too extra . . ."

"You've got it just right." I lean up and kiss him.

He smiles against my lips as he takes my face in his hands. Our kiss deepens, and for a long time we stay lost in the moment, kissing, drinking each other in, my heart floating around my bathroom.

He undoes my jeans and slides them down, his fingers circling over my sex through my panties.

"Hen," I whisper against his lips.

"I know." His eyes are closed as we kiss.

"We can't."

"Why not?" he breathes.

"It's not . . ." I pause as I stop myself.

He pulls out of the kiss to look at me. "It's not what?"

"That's something you do"—I hesitate, embarrassed—"with your husband or boyfriend."

He frowns as he listens.

"It's . . . it's way too intimate," I whisper.

"You said you were mine."

"I am."

"So why can't I have that?"

"Why would you even want it?" I frown.

"I don't know." His lips take mine again. "I just do."

"Have you done that before?"

He shakes his head. "No."

"You're a clean freak. I don't think you're going to like it." I give him a lopsided smile.

His eyes search mine. "You said you were mine."

He wants the intimacy of the act.

And isn't that the point? Isn't that the entire reason we are here?

We kiss again and again, and damn it, I want to give it to him, but what if it backfires? What if he's so freaked out that he runs for the hills? I mean, I don't think . . .

It's pretty full on.

His lips take mine. "Please," he murmurs against me. "Do you want me to beg?"

The last of my resistance leaves my body, and I tug his T-shirt over his head and pull him off the counter to take his jeans off.

And he undresses me, and I know this is the precipice of something new. The good, the bad, and the ugly of what it means to be a woman.

"Get in the shower, and I'll go to the bathroom." I lead him in under the water and go to the bathroom down the hall and sort myself out. When I walk back into the bathroom, I see the beautiful man under the hot water. Wide shoulders, broad chest with a scattering of dark hair. Rippled abdomen, and lower, perfectly kept pubic hair, his thick cock hanging heavily between his legs.

But it's the look in his eyes that melts me.

He takes me into his arms, and we kiss in a moment of perfect clarity.

I *am* his.

I want this too.

He lifts me, wraps my legs around his waist, and slides in deep in one sharp movement.

The steamy room, the hot water, the extra lubrication magnifies the perfection between us.

His body stretches mine, and with our breath quivering, our hearts pounding, we make slow gentle love as we stare into each other's eyes. Millions of emotions swimming between us, those three sacred words swirling on the tip of my tongue.

This was written in the stars long before we met. It was inevitable and meant to be.

I'm totally and irrevocably in love with Henley James.

Henley

Juliet lies in bed with her back to me, naked, and I'm curled around her back.

Her gentle pattern of breathing is calming, like a balm to my soul.

Many nights over the last week I've stayed awake just so I could listen to it.

My hand roams up over her skin, and without thinking I drop my lips to her temple and kiss her softly. I tuck a piece of her hair behind her ear so I can see her face clearer.

Perfect bone structure, porcelain skin, and dark eyelashes that flutter as she sleeps. Her pink lips are big and kissable.

I've never known such a beautiful being, and I'm not even talking about the outside packaging.

Something happened tonight.

I can't put my finger on it, but I feel a storm brewing deep inside.

I've found myself swimming in a bottomless ocean, far, far from the shore.

Unsure of what to do.

Taken back to the fifteen-year-old boy who has lost his protector and his safe place to fall.

I rest my face against Juliet's just so I can be closer, hold her tighter.

She stirs while still sleeping and turns her head and kisses my cheek. "Hen," she whispers.

"I'm here."

She smiles softly, her eyes still closed. "I love you."

I close my eyes.

No.

Why did you have to ruin it?

Chapter 18

Juliet

I wake alone.

Nothing new—I wake alone every day, but because I know where Henley spends his mornings, I don't mind at all. What a beautiful man he is to care for his dad so well.

I smile up at the ceiling. Last night was incredible . . .

There are no words for how dreamy my man is. I get up and go to the bathroom and peer through the curtains over to Henley's house. I wonder if he's home yet.

Stop being clingy.

You are seeing him today, I remind myself. We have a date tonight, so I'll have to be patient until then. I make my way downstairs and see that Barry has been let out and fed his breakfast. I go to turn my kettle on and beside it see my pink teacup on a saucer with a teabag in it just waiting for me to make it.

I smile broadly. That's Henley's way of making me a cup of tea.

Damn it, I am done. Has there ever been a dreamier man on the face of the earth?

I don't think so.

With my cup of tea I walk out and sit on the back steps in the morning sunshine.

It's going to be a great weekend.

3:00 p.m., and I hold the dress up to my body as I look in the mirror. "Hmm, or this one." I throw that dress to the side and grab another to hold it up instead. "I want to look perfect tonight."

I slip on some nude strappy stilettos. Or would the black ones look better?

The doorbell sounds from downstairs. "Who's that?" It rings again. "Coming," I call. I bound down the stairs and open the door to see Taryn. "Taryn." I smile. "Hi."

"Hi." She beams. "Can I come in?"

"Sure." I step back to let her walk past me into the house. "What's up?"

She flops onto my couch. "What are you wearing tonight?"

Huh?

"Umm." I frown. "Sorry . . . What's tonight?"

"Our double date."

"What?"

"Yeah, Henley came over this morning and arranged it with Mason and I."

I stare at her as I try to get my brain to catch up. "So you and Mason are going on a date?"

"No." She rolls her eyes as if I'm stupid. "Henley and I are going on a date together, and you and Mason are hooking up . . . remember?"

"Oh . . . right."

What the fuck?

"Okay." I try to think on my feet. "Where are we going to, again?"

"Club SoHo." She frowns over at me. "Were you listening to Henley at all when he organized this with you?"

"Obviously not." I smile through gritted teeth.

"So . . . what are you thinking?" she says. "Pure, slutty, supermodel . . . What look are you going for?"

"Psychopathic works for me."

"Juliet, honestly." She throws her head back and laughs out loud. "You're such a hoot."

I'll hoot you in a fucking second.

"I don't know what I'm wearing. I'll play it by ear, I guess," I tell her.

"I'm going to wear my tight white dress. I really want to blow Henley's brains out."

That makes two of us.

"Sounds like a plan." I fake a smile. "I've got a lot to do, so . . ."

She stands. "I'll let you get to it. Mason is so excited to finally spend some time with you."

"Great, I can hardly wait."

Henley is dead fucking meat.

"See you at Henley's at six."

I frown. "Six?"

"We're having drinks there before we go, remember?"

"Right." I fake a smile as I begin to hear my angry heartbeat in my ears. "See you then." I close the door and march upstairs.

What the fuck is he playing at?

I wait fifteen minutes until the coast is clear, and I sneak over to Henley's through his side gate and into his backyard.

Damn this sneaking-around shit. I'm over it.

Bang, bang, bang. I knock on his glass sliding door with force. Silence . . .

Bang, bang, bang. I knock harder.

285

Eventually he saunters out of the hallway. He's wearing shorts with no T-shirt, his hair is messed up to perfection, and he is on the phone. "Hi," he mouths as he opens the door and steps back to let me in. I march past him into the house. He holds a finger up to me to symbolize he will be a few minutes, and then he walks back down to his office and sits at his desk.

"Yes, so you can see with the drawing on page two," he tells whoever he is on the phone to. "Scroll through to page eight, and I want to show you what I'm talking about."

Ugh . . . he's on a work call.

I walk out to his kitchen and open the fridge. "Fuck it, I'm having a glass of wine." I open all the kitchen cupboards as I look for his wineglasses and eventually find them in the last place I look. I pour myself a glass and take a huge gulp. I am furious with him. How dare he make a date with Taryn? And how dare I find out this information from Taryn herself?

Calm down.

I walk back out into the hallway and can hear him still deep in conversation, and I glance up the stairs. I've never even seen his bedroom. We are always at my house. I glance back down to his office, and then I sneak up the stairs.

The hallway is grand. Beautiful artwork hangs on the walls, and a marble side table sits at the top of the stairs with a vase of white lilies.

I feel a little deflated. Everything is so luxurious and perfect. What must he think of my disheveled home? I walk past a few guest bedrooms and a white marble bathroom, and then I get to the end of the hall: his bedroom.

It's huge and grand, with a four-poster bed. The carpet is navy blue, and the walls are a beautiful shade of taupe. Styled to perfection, and not a detail out of place.

An abstract painting of a naked woman in beautiful hues of blue and mauve is hanging above the bed.

"God . . . ," I whisper to myself as I look around. He is really slumming it at my dumpy house. I walk to his wardrobe and pause as I hold the door handle. I'm almost too scared to look, but I do anyway. I open the door and am surprised by the huge space of his walk-in wardrobe. It's another room.

Expensive tailored suits are all lined up and hanging, shoes all polished and in pairs. I pull out the top drawer and see ties all rolled up and on display. This is like a fucking Prada store or something. I pull out the second drawer to find a display of expensive designer watches. Insecurity runs through me, and I slam the drawer shut in disgust.

I walk back out into his bedroom and sit nervously on his bed.

It's a king size, with perfectly ironed white linen that has a navy stitching line about ten centimeters in from the edges. The only place I've ever seen this type of bed linen is in exotic house magazines.

I sit quietly on the bed as I look around his luxurious space. His bedside tables have neatly stacked novels and a crystal lamp on each side. Perfectly matched, like everything in Henley's world.

What on earth do we have in common?

A sense of dread fills me. Even if we do work out . . . how long will it be for? He belongs with someone as perfect as him, not a hot mess like me who has dog fur on everything she owns.

"There you are," his deep voice says from the doorway.

I force a smile. "Here I am."

He leans onto the doorjamb. "What's up?"

No kiss?

"Umm . . ." I pause as I try to get the wording right in my head. "Taryn just came over."

"And?" He raises his eyebrow as if impatient.

287

"She thinks we have a double date with them tonight?"

He breaks into a breathtaking smile. "Well . . . kind of."

"What do you mean, kind of?"

"They have been on my case, and I . . ." He shrugs.

"You what?" I snap.

"I thought tonight was a good opportunity to put it to bed and out of the way."

"What happened to *our* date? I want you to myself. I don't want to go out with Mason, and you are definitely not going out with fucking Taryn."

"Relax." He rolls his eyes and walks into his bathroom. "Blake and Antony are coming, too, with their girls." He turns the shower on. "It's a group thing. It's no big deal."

"Taryn thinks it's a big deal, Henley," I snap.

He drops his shorts and hops under the water. I'm instantly silenced by his beauty. He wets his hair and then begins to wash it.

"What happens if Mason makes a move on me?" I ask.

He smiles with his eyes closed. "Then I guess you handle it."

He's different.

"I don't want to handle it," I huff. "And what about Taryn? We both know she's going to try something on you."

He exhales heavily as if I'm inconveniencing him. "Juliet, I am not in the mood for your dramatics today. I'll see you tonight, okay?"

I stare at him. What's going on here? He hasn't touched me once.

"Okay, I'm going home," I announce.

"See you tonight," he replies casually. "Be here about six."

I stand at the side of the shower waiting for him to resurface into his old self, but he doesn't.

"What if I don't want to go tonight?" I snap.

"Then don't come." He shrugs as he soaps himself up.

"What's wrong with you today?"

"Nothing, why?"

"You're acting weird."

"Am I acting weird or are you acting clingy?"

I step back, affronted. Fuck this. I'm totally being clingy, not that I'll ever admit it.

"Goodbye," I snap.

"See you." He smiles casually and goes back to washing himself.

I march down the stairs and back over to my house in a fit of rage. I am not going anywhere tonight with them.

Taryn can have them both.

"Henley, your house is just divine, darling." Taryn smiles as she walks around his downstairs area.

Henley smiles like the cat that got the cream.

Ugh, this is the night from hell. I knew I shouldn't have come.

I sip my wine, unimpressed. *It will never be yours, bitch.*

We are having a glass of wine at Henley's before we head out tonight.

But what if he actually does like Taryn?

He doesn't.

"Did you see the backyard, Taryn?" I call. "Come and I'll show you."

She follows me into the backyard and sees the swimming pool. "Oh my god, I can see myself here," she calls.

Me, too, with cement blocks tied to your feet.

"It's nice, isn't it?" I look around while thinking of what to say next. "This is awkward," I whisper as I lean in close to her.

"What is?" she whispers back.

"This whole situation." I glance inside to where the boys are. "Promise you won't say anything," I whisper.

"What?"

"I think Mason likes you."

Her eyes widen. "What?"

"Yes," I whisper. "He can't keep his eyes off you."

"Oh." Her face falls. "Really?"

"I know, and he's so hot. Special ops and all. I'm so disappointed. I really liked him . . . and then to find out that Henley only organized this night out because he likes him too."

Taryn's eyes widen, and she looks toward the house and then back to me. "What the fuck?"

"I mean"—I shrug—"I'm only speculating, of course."

"You think Henley likes Mason?" she gasps. "He's into men?" she squeaks.

"Shh, keep your voice down," I whisper. "I don't know . . . maybe?"

"Fuck it. I had plans for him."

Cancel them.

"I mean . . . go for it if you want. I just thought I should let—"

She cuts me off. "No, you did the right thing."

"So what are you going to do?" I whisper.

Taryn looks into the house. "Maybe we should have a group thing? That way nobody gets left out. We can all get what we want and fuck each other."

I bubble up a surprised giggle. Out of all the things I thought she would say, that was not it.

Help!

Henley

I sip my beer. "Fuck . . . Taryn."

"I know." Mason nods. "Dude, I know she's your date . . . but, fuck me. Those tits."

I roll my lips to hide my smile. This poor dumb fuck has no idea. "I think she likes you," I tell him.

"Who, me?" He points to his chest.

"Yeah. She's checking you out every chance she gets."

"Really?" He frowns. His gaze flicks to the back door, to where the girls have gone.

"You could . . ." I shrug casually. "I mean, if she's into you."

"You want to swap dates?" Mason whispers.

"Not really . . . but, I mean, I see the way she undresses you with her eyes. I don't stand a chance."

Mason thinks hard. "But Juliet . . ."

"She's not that great," I lie. "I feel like Taryn is better suited to a guy like you."

Mason nods as he contemplates his perceived choices.

There are no choices, fucker. You can't have Juliet.

End of story.

"No. I want Juliet," he says defiantly.

Taryn interrupts us as she walks back in through the door. "We're ready to go."

Mason stands. "Here's my hot little date." He puts his arm around Juliet, and I stare at the two of them together.

Don't even fucking think about it.

Juliet

Our Uber arrives, and we walk out to meet it. "I'll sit in the front seat, Mason," Henley says as he opens the car door.

Taryn bends over to climb into the car. She's wearing a white wetsuit dress that leaves nothing to the imagination.

Honestly, where does she even buy this stuff?

Henley watches her ass and raises an eyebrow at me.

Don't even . . .

"No, sit next to me, Henley," Taryn calls out of the Uber.

Henley climbs in beside her.

I'm glad he's having fun. That makes one of us.

The drive is long. Taryn and Mason jabber on, but I can't concentrate. All I can think about is Henley's thick thigh muscles pressed up against mine.

"Ha, ha." Taryn laughs out loud as she tells a story.

"You are kidding me." Mason laughs.

"One time when I was in Bangkok," Mason continues.

"Do you ever wonder how that country got that name?" Taryn replies. "I mean, I do. All the time. *Bang cock*. Go figure. Like back in the day, I wonder, were the people of the country just banging cocks the whole time?"

"Never thought of it like that." Mason laughs out loud. "You're incredible, Taryn."

I roll my eyes. Seriously?

For fifteen minutes I listen to the most mundane stories of all time, and Henley hasn't even looked my way.

The Uber pulls to the curb as we arrive at the club, and we all climb out.

Mason and Taryn walk in front, and Henley puts his hand on my waist as he ushers me through the crowd. My hormones go into overdrive at just a passing touch from him.

Suddenly I feel off.

I want to be here with him but under much different circumstances. I want to be alone and on a date, just the two of us, with no lies or other people.

What started out as a fun playing-hard-to-get game has somehow lost its sparkle.

Fuck.

Stop overthinking it.

We walk through the super-crowded club. As Henley walks in front, he glances back and, sensing my mood shift, frowns down at me. "What's wrong?" he whispers.

"Nothing." I force a smile.

We arrive at a small table; it's high, with stools around it. "Here?" Taryn asks.

"Looks good." Henley smiles. "I'll go and get some drinks. What do you all want?"

"Thanks. I'll have a beer," Mason says.

"I'll have a vodka, lime, and soda." Taryn smiles. "Thank you."

"Um." I twist my lips as I think. I'm not sure what to have. "I'll just have . . ."

"Cocktail?" Henley asks.

"A margarita?" I ask hopefully.

"Sure." Henley gives me a swoony smile, and I melt a little inside.

"Where are the bathrooms?" I ask Taryn.

"Over to the far-left wall." She points.

"Okay, back in a minute." I make my way over to the far wall and then head down a corridor that leads to the bathroom.

I look in the mirror. The girl staring back at me doesn't look familiar. She looks flushed and flustered. Challenged, but more than anything, I can see a fear deep in her eyes. Because the girl in the mirror knows she's in over her head.

We just need more time.

Stop overthinking and enjoy it.

Just because our relationship isn't textbook doesn't make it mean any less.

Time. It's just a time thing. I know he feels this connection too.

I drop my shoulders as I give myself a pep talk. It's fine.

I make my way back to the others to find them laughing and talking. They actually get along great; they're the ones that should

293

be dating. I glance back over to the bar, where Henley is waiting in line, and I move over to the corner out of sight of the others so that I can watch him uninterrupted.

He towers above everyone around him. His thick dark hair is messed to perfection, and those black jeans hug his perfect ass. Broad shoulders, perfect posture, and a jawline that could cut glass. His skin is olive and tanned.

My eyes roam up and down his body as I drink him in.

I've never known anyone like him before: so attractive yet, like a mysterious quicksand, so unknown. It's the weirdest thing. I know him, but I also know that I haven't even scratched the surface of his personality.

He has this depth to him that I can't explain, an underlying darkness from within.

I'm not sure what it is or where it comes from or if it even truly exists. I mean, it could be a figment of my imagination. Just because he hasn't met the right woman doesn't mean he's necessarily damaged.

"Hey," a voice says from beside me, interrupting my spying.

"Blake." I smile as he kisses my cheek. "Hi."

Blake looks like he just stepped off a *GQ* magazine shoot: tall, with sandy hair and shoulders for miles. How are these men all friends?

"This is Sienna and Mikayla." He introduces me to two beautiful women who are standing beside him. One has long blonde hair and is wearing a strapless tight black dress. She's absolutely beautiful. The other one has long dark hair and is voluptuous and curvy. She looks like she walked straight out of Pornhub. Fuck . . . so hot that I almost want to do her.

"Hi." They each shake my hand with a smile.

"Hi," I squeak.

Did he bring these girls with him, or did they just run into each other? I need all the intel for Chloe.

A familiar voice sounds. "Hello, Juliet." I glance over to see Antony.

"Hi."

He smiles and stands his ground. Antony is shyer than the other boys. Dark hair and handsome European features, and he has the most beautiful smile.

"This is Rena." He introduces me to a beautiful girl with dark curly hair.

"Hello." I smile.

"Hi."

"Do you want a drink?" he asks her as he puts his hand on her behind.

Okay, they are definitely together.

She says something to him that I can't hear, and then he kisses her quickly before heading to the bar. I watch him disappear to the bar. Henley catches sight of him and laughs as he says something.

"This place is pumping," Mason says from beside me.

Ugh . . . please, go away. I really don't have the mental energy to play along tonight. "It is." I smile. I glance over to see Blake kiss the blonde girl while he's holding the brunette's hand; he then turns and kisses her.

What the fuck?

They share him.

Oh hell, now I've seen it all.

Blake heads to the bar, too, and I watch him chat with Henley and Antony. He says something, and they all burst out laughing. What the fuck are they talking about?

How great it is to have a menu selection of combination vagina?

Ugh, seeing Blake with those two girls boils my blood.

Fucking men are all dickheads.

"We should totally dance." Mason smiles sexily.

"Or not," I reply as I take out my phone. I have to call Chloe. "I've got to take this." I hold my finger up to Mason as I walk toward the doors to find a quieter place to talk.

"Hi," Chloe answers happily.

"Oh my fucking god," I whisper in a rush. "Blake Grayson is here with two women."

"What do you mean?"

"He was kissing one while holding the other one's hand, and then he started kissing her too."

"What the fuck? He's a gangbanger?"

"Looks like it."

"What's happening?" I hear someone say in the background of Chloe's phone.

"Blake is tag teaming two women tonight, and I officially hate all men."

"Who's that?" I ask.

"I'm with Rebecca. We are in the drive-through at McDonald's."

"Where's John?"

"One guess," Chloe mutters dryly. "Working late."

"I'm so off him." I roll my eyes. All men are legitimate assholes this weekend. "Henley is being a dick, too, and Mason keeps trying to talk to me because he thinks we are on a date. This is one big fucking disaster."

"What's Taryn doing?"

"Looking fucking hot," I snap.

"Taryn's looking hot," Chloe tells Rebecca.

"Of course she is," Rebecca replies.

"Ugh, I have to go."

"Are you sure Blake is with the both of them? Maybe one is just his girlfriend's friend or something."

I glance back over to the group to see Blake hand the blonde the drink with a kiss and then hand the brunette her drink with a kiss too. While he's kissing the brunette, his hand slides up the blonde's leg and beneath her short dress as she sits on the stool.

"Nope, he's fucking them both for certain." I puff air into my cheeks. "And they are so hot. What are they thinking? Un-fucking-believable."

"Ugh . . . damn it," Chloe snaps. "I hate that he has enough cock for two women."

I roll my eyes.

"Call me back. I need updates."

"Okay." I hang up and go to the bathroom and try to calm myself down, and then I make my way back over to the group. Without making eye contact, Henley passes me a drink and goes back straight to talking to Antony. "Thanks." I fake a smile to the back of his head.

Dickhead.

Damn it, Blake Grayson and his bimbo harem have rattled me. I'm suddenly feeling very naive and inexperienced. I thought he was a nice, respectable, kind doctor. Apparently not.

He's a porn star with a double-shot cock.

Stop it.

Just because this night is different does not mean there are problems with Henley and me.

We are fine.

He's different, an annoying little voice from my unconscious whispers.

He is different today. I can't deny it, but . . . ugh, perhaps it's just because things are going so great between us. *Try not to over-think this.*

His words from earlier come back to haunt me. *Am I acting weird, or are you acting clingy?*

Maybe I am being super clingy. I do feel very unhinged today, and I am hormonal.

It's fine. Everything is fine.

Blake can fuck whoever he wants, and if they want to share his dirty dick, more fool them.

I can't let it get to me.

Over the next hour I stand back as a spectator and let the night run its course.

Henley is being his swoony playful self to everyone but me. In fact, he hasn't even looked my way.

I'm not imagining it. Something is going on.

The music is pumping loud now. You can hardly hear over it. "Dance with me," Mason says as he puts his arm around me. I edge out of his grip.

"I'm not in the mood tonight," I call. I'm not even lying. I am so not in the mood to dance. In fact, I think I'm going to go home. Being alone in my bed is much better than being alone here.

Mason looks over to Henley. "She won't dance with me."

"Dance with him, Taryn," Henley calls over the loud music.

Taryn, who is well on her way to Drunkville, holds her hands up in the air and sashays. "Let's go, baby."

I sip my drink and look out over the dance floor.

"You should go and dance with him," Henley says as he comes to stand beside me.

"I don't want to dance with him, Henley," I mutter into my drink. "You know this."

"Why not?"

I frown over at him. "I think you know why."

"Because of our arrangement?"

I sip my drink.

"I've been thinking about that."

My skin bristles.

"And?"

"I want to explore this thing with Taryn."

"What?"

Did I hear that right?

"I'm into Taryn," he calls over the music. "I want to take her home tonight."

I step back from him, shocked.

I couldn't have heard that right.

"You want to take Taryn home tonight?" I ask to make sure I heard him right.

"You should take Mason home." He shrugs casually, as if we are talking about a drink from the bar. "He'd be a good fuck, I imagine."

Boom, boom, boom sounds my heartbeat in my ears. My stupid eyes well with tears, and unable to even form a sentence, I turn and march toward the doors.

He wants her.

I barge through the crowd, hurt like never before. What the fuck is he saying?

I thought we had something.

I angrily swipe my stupid tears away. "Excuse me," I yell. "Excuse me."

I burst out the front doors and onto the street. I look up and down the footpath. It's sprinkling with rain, and I begin to walk up the road.

I've never been so shocked by someone in my life. I've got to get the fuck out of here.

"Juliet," Henley's voice calls out from behind me.

I keep walking.

"Will you stop?"

I keep marching. Hot salty tears are running down my face.

Stop crying.

"Juliet," he yells. "Stop."

I stop on the spot, my face screwed up in tears.

I hate that I'm crying.

"Turn around," he demands.

I turn, and his face falls when he sees my tears. "I'm sorry."

My haunted eyes hold his.

"It's for the best."

"Why?" I whisper, my heart melting into a puddle out of the bottom of my dress.

How could he be so cold?

"I don't want this," he snaps. "This fantasy that you've built up in your head is not . . ." His voice trails off.

"I don't understand."

He throws his hands out wide. "I don't fucking love you, okay?"

The earth moves beneath me.

"I'm *never* going to love you."

Pain lances through my heart.

"We were just fucking."

"You don't love me?" I whisper.

He shakes his head.

Adrenaline surges through me. "If you don't love me . . . then that's just sad." I screw up my face in tears. And I wish I could articulate better words, something to make him understand what he's doing.

This is a tragedy. We are already in love.

"It's not sad, Juliet, it's life," he spits. "We were *fucking*. Just like we talked about, nothing more, nothing less."

"It was the everything in between," I sob as my heart breaks.

"I'm sorry. I wish I could say something more profound, but"—he steps back—"it meant nothing to me."

My eyes search his.

"Go inside and fuck Mason. It will make you feel better."

Oh . . .

I sob out loud and drop my head. How could he be so cold?

When I finally glance back up, I see him walking back into the club without a care in the world.

He's gone.

Chapter 19

I stand under the hot water with my head in my hands. I'm crying hard, my heart beating fast in my chest.

Did that really just happen?

I can't even bring myself to call Chloe and talk about it because if I say it out loud, then it has to be true.

His words come back to me. *Go inside and fuck Mason. It will make you feel better.*

I put my hands over my mouth, sickened.

Is that what he thinks of me? Is that how he saw us? I sob out loud, the pain in my chest hurting hard.

All this time I thought we were falling in love, he was just having sex with my body.

Using me to get himself off.

I thought he loved me.

He doesn't.

I set up this little fantasy in my head where he and I fell madly in love, we fixed up my house, and we lived happily ever after in our perfect little street.

It was all in my head.

Go inside and fuck Mason. It will make you feel better.

I screw up my face in tears and slide down the tiles and sit in the bottom of my shower, under the hot water, alone and heartbroken.

I let myself cry.

Henley

Sunday afternoon

I sit on my back porch and watch the rain come down. Thunder is rolling in the distance, and a storm is brewing.

The day is dreary and dark, like my mood.

I keep going over last night and its events.

Her tears . . . the way they made me feel.

I can't even comprehend what normal is anymore.

For a few weeks there, I was kidding myself that things were on the upswing, that everything had finally clicked and the darkness was over.

But reality has set in; it will never be over.

This is it for me.

I am the final product—there is no remodeling from here. Things are set in stone.

Today that's magnified, and I feel especially unhinged. I haven't slept. How could I?

The rain comes down hard, bringing me back to the moment. It's loud and angry. It begins to splash up and get my legs wet.

I see her tears again, and I close my eyes in regret. This is for the best anyway. She's better off with someone else. Someone who can love her properly.

I hear Juliet's car start, and I glance up at the fence and then at my watch. She's leaving for work, doing the afternoon shift.

And if I were a better person, I would go over and apologize, ask her to come back to me and make this right between us.

Beg for a second—no, third—chance.

But what's the point? I'll only ruin it later on down the road anyway . . .

I did do one thing, though; I proved a point to myself.

Now I know.

If the perfect woman can't save me, nobody can.

Thursday, 4:00 p.m.

I glance at the sign over the door.

AARON STEVENS

PSYCHOLOGIST

With a deep exhalation, I roll my eyes. "Here we fucking go." I push the heavy door open and arrive in the foyer.

"Hello," I say to the receptionist. "I have an appointment at four."

She fakes a smile. "Take a seat, Mr. James."

I glance over at the waiting couch. "Actually . . . I changed my mind. I won't be needing an appointment today."

The office door opens in a rush. "Henley," a blond man says in an English accent. "This way."

Fuck.

I walk past him into his office and stand, unsure what to do.

"Please, take a seat."

I unbutton my suit jacket and sit down. I cross my legs and then immediately uncross them. I sit back and then sit forward.

Aaron sits down and smiles calmly. "Nervous?"

I run my hand through my hair. "Nope." I stand. "This . . . is . . . was a mistake. Sorry to waste your time. Send me the bill."

"Sit down," he says in a stern voice. "You are here for a reason. Let's see it through."

I roll my lips, unimpressed, and look around before finally sitting down.

"Tell me about yourself, Henley. What do you do for work?"

"I'm an engineer."

"You work for someone?"

"I have my own company." I look over to the window as I plan my escape.

He nods. "I see."

"And you are single, married? Gay or straight?"

"Straight and single," I reply curtly.

"Okay . . ." He smiles and waits for me to say something.

I don't.

"And how would you describe yourself?"

I scratch my head in frustration. "I don't know." I shrug. "Normal."

"Okay, good." He smiles as he watches me intently. "And what brought you here today?"

"My friend." I shrug, embarrassed. "Made the appointment for me."

"And what's his name?"

"Blake."

"Blake who?"

"Blake Grayson."

"Yes, I know Dr. Grayson. He asked me to squeeze you in as a matter of urgency."

"He's rather dramatic."

"Does he have reason to be?"

"Nope." I look around the room—anywhere but at him.

"So there has been something happening that has made him concerned about you?"

"In his mind."

"And what was that?"

I shrug. "I stopped seeing someone. It's no big deal. He's overdramatizing it."

"This has upset you?"

I cut him off. "I really don't see what this has to do with anything."

"Answer the question, please," he fires back. "Are you upset by the breakup? What is her name?"

"Juliet."

I roll my lips, unimpressed.

Fuck this prick.

"Are you upset by the breakup?"

"Disappointed, yes."

"Who broke it off?"

I hesitate before answering. "I did."

He nods. "I see. You don't have feelings for Juliet anymore?" He shrugs.

Sadness comes over me like a heavy blanket.

"I adore her."

A frown flashes across his face. "And yet you ended the relationship?"

"It had run its course."

"Okay." He nods. "When was your last committed relationship before this one?"

I clench my jaw. Enough with the fucking questions.

"Take your time."

"I haven't had a committed relationship. I have"—I pause—"sexual relationships."

"Always?"

"Yes."

He sits back in his chair. "Since what age?"

"Fifteen."

"At what age did you become sexually active?"

"Same age."

"Was there a significant event that happened around that time?"

I roll my eyes. Here we go. "It's unrelated."

"But there was an event?"

"My mother died."

"I'm sorry."

"Me too."

He pauses for a moment as if collecting his thoughts.

"Do you have any siblings, Henley?"

"No."

He nods. "Is your biological father alive?"

"Yes."

"Are you in contact with him?"

I pause, unsure how to answer this question. "Yes and no."

Juliet

I sit on the floor of my living room and hold the remote up to the television as I skip through the channels.

No, no, no, no, no . . .

I let out a deep sigh. "Why is there nothing on television worth watching anymore?" I throw the remote onto the couch and lie back and look up at the ceiling.

It's been a long week. No contact at all.

So close but so far.

The sky has fallen. The world is gray.

And Henley James doesn't love me . . . just ask him, he'll tell you.

I shouldn't be this devastated. It was only two weeks. I should be over it by now, putting it down to a bad experience.

But that's the thing: How do you casually dismiss an emotion that you have waited to feel for your entire life?

It wasn't real for him, but it was *so* real for me.

Love in spectacular Technicolor, beautiful and raw.

Only it wasn't.

I get a lump in my throat, and my stupid eyes well with tears. I hate that he hurt me, and more than that, I hate that I let him. I knew exactly what I was walking into, and yet I went all in anyway.

This is on me. My fault.

The logical part of my brain is angry, furious that he got away with the perfect crime. I remember us laughing and rolling around in the sheets, dancing naked in the kitchen at midnight.

He hooked me good. I took the bait hook, line, and sinker.

My poor pathetic heart keeps reminding me of his baggage and pleading with me to forgive him for running.

Go inside and fuck Mason. It will make you feel better.

I close my eyes at the memory of his hurtful words. How could he even say that? He obviously doesn't respect me.

He never did.

I know what I need to do, but how do you forget someone who is so burned into your soul that they are all you can think about?

I lie on the floor and stare into space. I'll let myself wallow in self-pity for a few more days, and then I'll pick myself up and dust myself off. Just like the old saying goes, this too shall pass.

It's been five days without him now. It's going to get better soon . . .

It has to.

Saturday afternoon, I drive home from day shift at the hospital. It was hectic and ridiculously busy. Everything that could have gone wrong today did. I turn the corner into my street and see the boys in the middle of the cul-de-sac putting a golf ball onto a tee. They are drinking beer and laughing and joking.

Don't they ever get sick of that stupid game and hanging out together in the stupid middle of the street?

I drive past them with a fake smile and a wave.

Henley's not there.

Where is he? . . . *Is he okay?*

I'm currently suffering from multiple personality disorder. I flick between anger and worry for him. Raging one minute, crying the next.

Angry because he hurt me, but worried because I know that's not who he is.

Maybe I'm just a gullible idiot who got played by a player.

As I pull up to my house, I see that my lawn has been mowed. Huh? I pull the car into the driveway and get out to hear the lawn mower going in my backyard.

Who mowed my lawn?

I glance back out to the boys in the middle, and Blake dips his head and waves. "Hi, Juliet."

"Hi."

Ugh . . . stop acting nice, you gangbanger. Chloe's way too good for you.

I walk through my side gate to see Henley pushing the lawn mower at double speed over my lawn. He's walking so fast and pushes it straight over a garden bed and shreds the plants.

"What are you doing?" I cry.

He keeps mowing at double speed, his head down, his skin glistening with perspiration.

"Henley," I call.

He doesn't look up and mows over another plant.

That's it.

I storm over to him. "Stop!" I cry.

He looks up, and his step falters.

"What the hell are you doing?" I yell.

"Mowing your lawn. What does it fucking look like? It's a disgrace," he growls.

I put my hands onto my hips, infuriated. "You're running over my plants."

"Weeds," he yells over the lawnmower.

"Go home," I yell.

"What?" He pretends to be unable to hear me.

In a senseless rage, I look around at the carnage of my garden and the three plants he has chopped to pieces.

"Go home!" I point toward his house. "Do not mow my fucking lawn ever again."

I have never, ever met a more infuriating person. I'm so close to punching him in the face right now that it isn't even funny.

I push him away from the lawn mower, and he stumbles back, and I turn it off.

"Go home," I yell.

"What do you expect me to do? Your grass is ruining the entire streetscape. We are all sick of it," he spits through gritted teeth.

Something inside my brain snaps, and I want to lash out and hurt him. "You're a fucking controlling neat freak, and I will not stand for it."

His eyes bulge from their sockets. "What did you say?" he sneers.

"You heard me. Go the fuck home." I turn and march back to my house, and I realize my back door is locked. Damn it, my keys are still in my car around the front.

Ugh!

I storm around the front with him hot on my heels. "You did not just say that to me," he yells. "I am not a neat freak."

"Yes, I did, and yes, you are." I open my car and grab my keys. "Go away, Henley. You are a fucking nightmare." I slam the car door shut and march to the front door.

"Don't you fucking dare call me names." He follows me inside.

"I'll call you whatever I want."

He slams the door shut behind him. "Listen to me. You keep your fucking lawn in order or move the fuck out," he fumes. "I will not live next to a derelict house."

"What?" I explode. "My grass wasn't even long."

"Yes, it was." His eyes are bulging, and the veins are sticking out of his forehead. "You owe me a thank-you."

"For what?" I explode. "For chopping up my fucking plants?"

"They were weeds."

"You're a fucking weed. Go home!"

"Suits me fine." He turns toward the door. "You're an ungrateful wench."

"Henley," I call.

He turns back to face me. "You're a self-centered fucking asshole, do you know that?"

He narrows his eyes and steps toward me. "Do not blame me for your delusional little love affair."

"What the hell does that mean?" I explode. Adrenaline is surging through my body. My heart is hammering in my chest.

He screws up his face and in a whiny-little-girl voice says, "I love you, Henley." He glares at me, contempt dripping from his every pore. "You had to go and ruin everything, didn't you?"

I stare at him, shocked.

"Wow . . ."

His eyes hold mine, and he lifts his chin to the sky in defiance, as if goading me into a fight.

The stupid tears well in my eyes again. *Stop it.*

"At least one of us loves you," I whisper. "Because you sure don't."

His jaw clenches.

"Is this . . ." I try to articulate my words. "Is this how you treat people who care about you, Henley?"

He glares at me.

"Yes." I hold my hands up in surrender. "I won't apologize for being myself."

"Don't."

"Don't what? Don't be human? Don't hold someone dear who means something to me?"

He twists his lips in anger.

"I am about two minutes from walking out of your life forever. What have you got to say about that?" I snap.

His eyes rise to meet mine. They're cold and hard. "Don't let the door hit you on the way out."

Oh . . .

He turns and, without another word, leaves. I screw up my face in tears. My heart races out of control.

Fuck.

312

Tuesday night

I stare at my face in the bathroom mirror. The green mud mask needs to do miracles tonight.

I've never felt so bad.

Barry can sense my heartache and hasn't left my side. He's the best little friend ever.

I am officially sworn off men. I hate them all.

Knock, knock, knock sounds from downstairs.

Was that the door?

Knock, knock, knock sounds again.

What?

Who is that? I tiptoe down the stairs and see Rebecca at the front door.

What in the world? I open the door in a rush. "Hi. What's wrong?"

"Let's go," she snaps.

"What?"

"It's time. I put an AirTag in his car, and he's still not home from work. He's at a restaurant on the south side. Time to bust a move. Let's fucking go."

My eyes widen. "Oh shit." Okay. "I have to wash my face mask off. Give me one minute."

"I'll get the car," she snaps.

I take the stairs two at a time. Oh crap. This could be bad. *Please don't be doing anything wrong.* "Fuck, I hate men." I wash my face mask off at record speed and pull a sweater over my flannel pajamas. I pull on my sneakers. "Back soon, Barry." I run out the front, where Rebecca is waiting in her car.

I bounce in, and she takes off before I've even closed my car door. "What's happened?" I whisper as I look between her and the very quickly oncoming road.

"He's cheating, I know he is." She takes the corner, and we nearly lift onto two wheels.

I hang on for dear life as she drives like a maniac. "What's the plan?" My eyes flick between her and the road once more. "Do we have a plan?"

Please don't let us go to jail tonight.

"I just want to wait and catch him in the act. If I don't see it with my own eyes, I know he will never admit it."

"Okay." I nod as I cling onto my seat belt. "Probably should slow down, though, babe." We take another corner, and the tires screech. I close my eyes in fear.

Fuck, we're so going to die.

Twenty terrifying minutes later, we come to a standstill, parked across the road from the restaurant.

She turns the car off, and we sit in the darkness. "That's his car there."

His car is parked out front.

"Do you want me to go and see if he's in there?" I ask.

"No, I don't want him to suspect anything. He might see you."

"Okay."

"Do me a favor," she says.

"Anything."

"If he comes out and he's with a woman, film it on your phone for me."

"What?"

"I need to have photographic evidence that he's really doing this so I can look back on it to stay strong."

I nod. "Okay."

My heart is beating hard. Fuck.

Suddenly I'm given a new perspective. I think I've got problems? I was only with Fuckface Henley for two weeks, and I'm heartbroken. This is Rebecca's husband that she has spent twelve years with. The man who is supposed to love and protect her forever. I can't imagine what she's going through.

"What time does the restaurant close?" she asks.

I quickly google it. "It says eleven."

She glances at the clock. "Ten minutes."

Shit.

We sit in the darkness, not speaking. I mean, what is there to say?

The door opens, and we hold our breath. Two men walk out.

We both let out a sigh of relief.

I really hope this is innocent. I don't think it is, though.

The door opens, and a man and a woman walk out. "Is that them?" I frown.

"No."

We both sit back.

The door opens again, and this time John comes into view. He's holding a woman's hand. She's wearing a red dress and has long blonde hair. She's young and beautiful.

"Fuck," I whisper.

Rebecca watches, and I take her hand in mine.

They walk to his car. He opens up the passenger door for her. He pushes her up against it and kisses her deeply. He says something, and the woman laughs out loud.

"I know her," Rebecca whispers through tears.

My eyes flick to her. "Who is it?"

"Her name is Mia."

My heart sinks. "How do you know her?"

"She's his secretary."

We watch as they drive away, and sit in silence, both in shock.

"I'm so sorry, Bec," I whisper.

She starts the car. "Not as sorry as he's going to be." We pull out into the traffic and drive home in silence. I'm holding her hand in her lap.

"What are you going to do?" I whisper.

She shrugs as she grips the steering wheel with white-knuckle force.

"Stay at my house tonight, okay?" I squeeze her hand.

"No." She keeps her eyes on the road. "I'm dealing with this tonight."

"Just wait."

"For what?"

"For him to come home."

Oh hell . . .

We drive into our street and pull up in her driveway. She hits the remote, and the garage door goes up, and we drive in.

"You can go home," she says calmly. "Thanks for coming with me."

I feel like I shouldn't be witnessing this, that it's a private matter, but then I'm not leaving her alone with the douchebag.

"I'm not going anywhere," I tell her. "I'm waiting with you."

She gives me a sad smile and gets out of the car and walks inside.

Two hours later

Rebecca paces as I sit on her couch. The house is silent and sad, lit only by the lamp.

She doesn't want him to know she's still awake when he comes in.

Neither of us is saying anything. We both know that this is the end of her marriage, and what could you possibly say to make this better?

Rebecca stares into space. "He's having sex with her right now," she whispers.

I get a lump in my throat. "Don't think of it."

"I wonder if she gives him anal . . ."

My eyes well with tears.

"It's been going on for eighteen months," she says idly.

I've got a bad feeling about this.

"Why don't we go back to my house, deal with this tomorrow when we're fresh? I'll take a few days off. Maybe we could go on a girls' trip away to clear your head," I say hopefully.

"No." She walks into the office and returns with a baseball bat.

My eyes widen . . . *Fuck.*

"What . . . what . . . are you doing with that?"

Is she going to kill him?

I think I need to call Chloe for backup. I don't know what to do here.

"Rebecca, give me the bat."

The car pulls into the driveway, and before I can even look out the window, Rebecca is running through the front door toward him. "You fucking asshole," she screams. She takes a run up and smashes the bat into his windshield, shattering it into a million pieces.

"Fuck." I run out after her. "Rebecca, stop."

The lights in the houses all go on.

"How could you?" she screams like a crazy person. Her screams echo for miles, and she lifts the bat back again and smashes his car once more.

"What are you doing?" John cries.

"How is Mia?"

His eyes widen.

"Bec, don't. Please," I beg. "He's not worth it."

317

She smashes the car again. "I leave all my family and friends, move across the country for you, and this is how you repay me?"

"What's happening?" Blake calls as he runs toward us from his house. He's in boxer shorts and disheveled. "Rebecca," he yells. "What are you doing? Stop."

"How could you?" she cries.

"Rebecca." Blake struggles with her to take the bat out of her hand as she fights him.

"He's sleeping with his secretary." She's hysterical and crying, and eventually Blake fights the bat from her hands.

John gets out of the car. "What have you done to my car?" he yells.

Blake's murderous eyes rise to John. "Leave."

"This is my fucking house. I'm not going anywhere."

Blake pushes Rebecca to the side. "I said . . . fucking leave. *Now.*"

Oh no. I look between the two of them. If Rebecca doesn't kill him, Blake actually will.

"What the hell is happening?" Carol cries as she runs across the road. "Are you okay, Rebecca?"

Rebecca is sobbing in my arms, and I look up to see Henley has come out to the commotion. He's in his boxer shorts too.

"It's not what you think," John yells. "Rebecca . . . I love you."

"It's exactly what I think," she yells. She's lost all control. Tears and snot are all over her face.

"Let's go inside and talk about this in private."

"No," Rebecca yells. "Go back to your whore. She knows me. She talks to me every fucking day. I pay her fucking wages. How could you?"

"She means nothing. I'm not going anywhere. I love you."

Blake pushes him by the chest, and he stumbles back. "You get in your fucking car and disappear before I kick your fucking ass." He pushes him again, and he falls down onto his back.

Blake is now going to kill him for real. This is getting out of control.

"Henley," I yell. "Do something."

Henley steps in and pushes Blake back from John. "That's enough. Leave, John."

"This is none of your business," John growls.

"Leave before I call the police," I yell.

"You're my fucking wife, Rebecca," John calls. "She means nothing."

Rebecca is hysterical, and Blake takes her into his arms to protect her from John.

John, realizing that it's the whole street against him, eventually gets into the smashed-up car and drives away.

Rebecca is heartbroken, crying uncontrollably on Blake's chest. We all stand around, shocked to silence, unsure what to say. Rebecca's cries echo through our sleepy little street.

"How could anybody ever want to be married?" Henley mutters under his breath.

I look over at him, my faith in men completely and utterly ruined.

"Fuck. Off."

Chapter 20

Henley

Rebecca cries against Blake's chest as we all watch, unsure what to say.

"Come on, Bec, you're staying at my house tonight," Juliet says.

"That's a good idea." Blake nods. "Okay?" he asks her softly.

Rebecca finally nods. "Okay."

With her tucked safely under his arm, they follow Juliet over to her house. I trail behind them, unsure what to say.

They walk up the front steps, and Juliet opens the door. Blake and Rebecca walk inside, and I go to follow them in, and Juliet steps in front of me, blocking the doorway.

"No."

I frown.

"The door did hit me on the way out, Henley, and it knocked some sense into me."

My eyes search hers.

"You're not welcome here anymore. Stay the hell away from me."

I step back and nod. "Fine." I'm shocked but not surprised.

Juliet closes the door in my face, and I hear Rebecca start to cry from inside. I wait for a moment, unsure what to do. Unsure where to go.

You're not welcome here anymore.

I close my eyes in disgust at myself. *What did you expect?*

Eventually I drag myself home, and I sit on my front steps in the darkness.

And to the sounds of Rebecca's heart breaking in the distance, mine does too.

"Henley." Aaron smiles. "Come in. Please take a seat."

I walk past him and sit down. "I don't know why I'm here. This is a waste of fucking time."

He smiles and sits behind the desk opposite me. "How have you been?"

"Okay."

"Anything new happen since I saw you last?"

"Nope." I roll my lips and look around. I just want this over with.

"Henley." He pauses. "I know you are only here because Dr. Grayson is making you come."

"I told you before, he's dramatized the entire thing. I'm fine. I don't need to be here. You are wasting your time. Spend it on someone who really needs it."

"Okay." He nods casually. "That's good to hear that you are doing well." He scribbles down some notes while I wait.

"So . . . let's pick up where we left off, shall we?"

I shrug.

"Have you thought any further about Juliet since we spoke last?"

"She's all I fucking think about."

"That's good." He sits back with a smile. "You care about her."

I roll my lips, choosing to stay silent.

"Are you and her getting along well?"

"No."

"Did something happen?"

You're not welcome here anymore.

"Ahh . . ." I shrug. "She told me that she never wants to see me again."

"What caused her to say that?"

"I . . ."

"You what?"

"Every time I see her, I"—I shrug, ashamed by my behavior—"I become very nasty toward her. I say things." I wring my hands together. "Terrible things."

"You try and hurt her?"

I nod.

"Like she hurt you?"

I clench my hands into fists. "I don't know why I do it . . . I can't seem to stop myself. Horrible things just blurt out."

"I see." Aaron watches me for a while. "Why are you angry with her?"

"I'm not."

"Did she sleep with someone else?"

I frown. "No," I snap. "She's not like that."

"She's not a nice person?"

"She's the best person," I fire back in disgust.

"She lied to you?"

I nod. "Yes."

"How so?"

I puff air into my cheeks. "She told me that she wanted a sexual relationship only."

He frowns as he listens. "Go on."

"And then . . ." My voice trails off.

"She made you fall in love with her?"

My eyes drop to the floor, and I nod.

"You're uncomfortable with those feelings?"

I stay silent, unable to answer.

"Why do you think that is, Henley?"

"I don't know," I reply softly.

"Do you want to be in a loving relationship with Juliet?"

"No."

He goes silent, and eventually I have to look up at him. He gives me a reassuring smile. "This is a safe space. You can express your feelings freely in here. But I think we both know that you do."

"Trust me, I don't."

"Have you told Juliet how you feel about her?"

"No."

"Why not?"

"Because I like being on my own."

"It's easier this way?" he asks.

"Yes."

"In a perfect world, where you aren't you, how would your life be?"

I pause as I contemplate his question.

"Would you be married with children? A large family of your own?"

I nod. "I guess."

He smiles. "Let's make that a goal."

"I gave up having personal goals a long time ago."

"When your mother died?"

323

"Leave her out of this." I sigh in frustration. "My mother has nothing to do with being in love."

"Because she died?"

"Stop saying that." I close my eyes to try and block him out.

"Do you remember what we talked about on your last visit, Henley?"

I roll my lips. I just want this fucking over with.

"Let me refresh your memory. We went over the day your mother passed away and the trauma you have suffered over it."

I inhale with a deep shaky breath as that dark day floats back.

The young boy sobbing over his mother's body, unaware that she's already passed over.

Mom, it's okay. Dad's coming, Dad's coming, he's going to take us to the hospital.

Wake up, Mom, please wake up. Mom, I need you to wake up . . . please.

"Henley." Aaron's voice brings me back to the present moment, and my eyes rise to his blurred silhouette. "It's an upsetting memory, isn't it?"

I wipe my eyes with the backs of my hands. "Yes."

"Have you ever talked about that day with anyone?"

I shrug. "Umm . . ."

"Take your time."

"My two best friends are the only . . ." I frown, unsure how to carry on the sentence. "They came over that night, and . . ." I shrug. "We were young. I don't know what we talked about."

"Are you still in contact with them?"

"Blake Grayson." I shrug. "You know, him and Antony Deluca are still my best friends."

"Do you see them often?"

"Every day. We all bought houses in the same street."

He smiles. "You look after each other."

"I guess." I shrug.

"It sounds like you have a good network around you."

I nod.

"Do you ever think about death, Henley?"

I swallow the lump in my throat as my eyes rise to meet his. "I don't care if I die."

"What about others?"

My breath begins to shake again. "It's not something I dwell on."

"What about inside a relationship? Does it ever cross your mind?"

"No," I snap.

"But"—he pauses as if collecting his thoughts—"if you do love another woman . . . she might die and leave you, couldn't she?"

I clench my jaw. His words strike a chord in the pit of my stomach.

"And you couldn't possibly go through that pain again, could you?"

I close my eyes. This topic is too real. "Shut up."

"Because where would you be if another woman you loved left this earth before you? Is that where your thought process has taken you?"

"*Shut. Up,*" I snap, infuriated. "This is not helping. Just fucking fix me. I don't go over this shit. It doesn't fucking help. All it does is upset me again."

"Your reaction to relationships is completely understand-able," he says calmly.

"What the fuck is wrong with me?" I spit.

"In my opinion, you have posttraumatic stress disorder brought on by an apocalyptic event. The human mind has an intelligence of its own. It will do whatever it takes to protect you from future harm."

I clench my jaw so hard that I feel like my teeth may crack.

"It's called self-preservation, Henley. Your mind is unconsciously protecting you from harm. If you don't love someone with your whole heart, you can never feel that pain again."

The floor moves beneath me as I stare at him.

"But this behavior no longer serves you, Henley. It's now sabotaging your happiness and future. You need to make a conscious decision to let it go."

"Let it go," I huff. "Like it's that fucking easy? You think I want to be like this?"

"Unconsciously, yes."

"Fuck you."

"The first step of recovery is acknowledgement of this behavior."

"You have no idea what you're fucking talking about," I spit. "I'm not listening to this shit for one minute longer." I stand and march from the office. I've had as much of this fucking idiot as I can take. "I won't be back."

"Henley," he calls after me. "We are not finished."

With my heart beating out of my chest, I push out through the heavy doors and storm to my car.

Fuck . . . just get me home.

Juliet

I watch through the kitchen window as Rebecca lies on a blanket in the morning sun in the back garden with Barry.

She's strong.

It's been days since that ungodly night where we caught her husband out. He's begged for forgiveness and tried to force his way back into their house.

Blake won't hear of it, won't even let him drive in the street without waylaying him and threatening to kick his ass.

The joke of it is, after John got caught out that night, he went straight back to his mistress's house. He's still staying there now, clueless that, thanks to the Apple AirTag, we know his every move.

Rebecca has been staying with me, still not up to staying alone. If I'm honest, it's helping me too. While she's being brave, I still feel like my world is about to end.

I miss Henley. I miss the laughter we shared and the way he made me feel.

Rebecca is finally meeting with John this afternoon to discuss the future. She wanted to be stronger before she properly talked to him.

Hopefully now she is.

Knock, knock sounds at the door.

I flick the tea towel over my shoulder and open the door. "Blake." I smile.

"Hi." He smiles back. "You guys okay? I'm heading to the hospital to check in on some patients. Just wondering if you need anything."

"We're good." Recently I've been seeing exactly what Chloe sees in the good doctor. He has a swoon factor of one thousand. "You know, for a gangbanging player . . . you are surprisingly attentive, Mr. Grayson."

He chuckles. "Just checking in on you both." He turns and walks down the front steps, and I follow him out. "How's she doing . . . really?" he asks.

I shrug as we get to the mailbox. "She's okay. I guess she's had time to get her head around this long before it was actually confirmed as true."

He nods as he listens.

"She's meeting with him this afternoon to discuss what's happening with them, so I guess she will know more after that."

"What a fucking idiot he is." He shakes his head in disgust.

"I know."

Henley's front door opens, and we both look up. He walks out, wearing a perfectly fitted navy suit and a crisp white shirt. His back is ramrod straight. He glances over at us and nods but then keeps walking to his car. With my heart in my throat, I watch as he drives past us without so much as a wave.

My heart sinks. *He really doesn't care.*

"Don't mind him . . . he's . . ." Blake shrugs. "Sorting through some stuff right now."

I roll my lips so I don't say something snarky.

"He's a good man, Juliet."

My eyes search his. "Is he?"

"Don't give up on him."

"He gave up on me."

"Henley is"—he exhales heavily—"complicated."

Suddenly I want all the information I can get from Blake. "How so?"

"It's not for me to elaborate on . . . but just"—he shrugs—"give it some time."

"Is there someone else?" I ask.

"God no." He screws up his face. "It's nothing like that." He kisses my cheek. "Call me if you need anything."

"Okay, thanks." I watch as Blake crosses the cul-de-sac and gets into his new silver Porsche. It purrs like a kitten as he starts the engine. He waves happily as he drives off into the distance, and my mind wanders over his insight.

Don't give up on him.

I wish it were that easy.

At 5:00 p.m., a text bounces through. It's from Rebecca.

Can we go out for dinner and drinks.
I need to vent.

Shit. It must not have gone well. I reply.

Sounds good, I'll book and call Chloe.
Seven ok?
Margaritas are on the menu.

I watch as her dots bounce.

Sounds great.

8:00 p.m.

I walk into the restaurant and see Chloe and Rebecca already at the table with margaritas in their hands. I did a four-hour shift at the retirement home this afternoon to cover for someone and am running late. They have started without me.

"Hey." I smile as I take a seat.

"Welcome to the Man Haters Anonymous table." Chloe holds her margarita up to me in a toast. "All men are fuckers," she slurs.

I giggle and pick up the margarita that is waiting for me on the table. "How long have you two been here?"

"Long enough to establish that we hate men," Chloe says in a way-too-loud voice.

Rebecca holds her glass up too. "Hear, hear."

I giggle. "Well, just so happens I am the president of man hating, so I'm glad to be in good company."

We clink our glasses in a toast.

"So . . ." I widen my eyes. "What happened?"

Rebecca rolls her lips. "He cheated because I wouldn't give him anal."

"What?"

"What a fucking idiot," Chloe gasps. "I'm going to give him anal with a fucking mop handle."

"What do you mean?" I stammer. "Explain everything to me. Where did you meet?"

"Okay." Rebecca sips her drink. "We went to a coffee shop that we always go to. I wanted somewhere public that would force us to have a civilized conversation."

"Sounds fair." I listen intently.

"I told him that I needed complete honesty and that if he gave me that, then we may possibly work through this."

"Right." I frown. My eyes flick to Chloe, and she pulls her finger across her throat. "What happened?"

"He has been sleeping with her for over a year."

"Fuck."

"He says it's just sex and that he is completely in love with me and had no intention of ever ending our marriage."

"What a fucking idiot," Chloe gasps. "I fucking hate this guy. Can we cut his dick off and feed it to the feral cats?"

I bubble up a giggle but try to hold it in. "Right." I try to stay focused on being a good listener for Rebecca. "How did it start?"

"Get this," Chloe slurs. She points her drink to me, and it sloshes over the side.

Rebecca leans in toward the table. "He said that he had always wanted anal sex."

"Right." I roll my lips. "Is that true?"

"It is, and to be fair, I wouldn't even try it."

"Okay."

"He said that one day he was in the lunchroom with Mia, eating their lunch. They had become friends over time, and Mia said that she was having sexual problems with her boyfriend."

I frown, and my eyes flick to Chloe, who is giving an overexaggerated eye roll. "Give me a fucking break," she spits.

I giggle as I sip my drink. "Right. What kind of sexual problems? I'm-a-whorebag problems?"

"Exactly," Chloe splutters.

"He said that Mia was upset with her boyfriend because he wouldn't try anal sex."

"What?" I explode. "Who tells their fucking boss that in the lunchroom unless they want to fuck his brains out? This woman is the living end."

"I know, shameless," Rebecca whispers angrily. "Anyway, that opened the conversation for them to talk about sexual fantasies, and yada, yada, and two months later they decided to have one night together at a work conference."

My eyes widen. "Their first time was anal?"

"Apparently."

"Fuck off," I snap. "He is using anal against you to justify him being a fucking sleazebag."

"Exactly," Chloe spits. "If he was good at sex, she would have given him anal, wouldn't you, Bec?"

Rebecca shrugs as she sips her margarita. "Who knows, but he's not the fucking porn star he thinks he is, that's for sure."

"God." I drain my glass and gesture to the waiter for another round of drinks. "Then what?"

"He said that it was never emotional, that they fell into the habit of having sex, and that she has a boyfriend she is in love with too. They told each other every time that this was going to be the last time."

"What?" I gasp. "Fuck her."

"That's exactly what he did," Chloe snaps.

I'm shocked to my core. "What do you even say to this?"

"He said that he thinks that we met too young and that he just needed to do some sexual exploration but he knows that it's me who is the love of his life."

I stare at Rebecca. "How do you feel about this?"

"Heartbroken."

"What are you going to do?"

"Can we kill him?" Chloe chimes in from the sideline. "Let's kill him and bury his body in your backyard, Jules."

I giggle. "Tempting, although Barry would probably dig him up."

"Good old Bazza." Chloe smiles. "He can chew on his bones and shit."

"He told me he fired her from work," Rebecca says.

"Is that true?"

"I don't know. I haven't been into his office, obviously, but I would assume she would have resigned in case I did go in there."

"True." I sip my drink. "What must the other secretaries think of her?"

"They probably all knew. I feel like such a fool."

"Don't," I snap. "He's the fool. You remember that."

"And then he did something that really broke my heart," Rebecca says sadly.

"What?"

"He said that he hadn't seen her since I found out and that he was never going to see her again."

My eyes hold hers. "Why did that break your heart?"

"Here we are, laying our hearts out on the table, discussing his infidelity in great detail, anal and all. He's telling me that I'm the love of his life, apologizing and telling me it's the biggest regret of his life, and yet . . . he's still lying about seeing her. I know for a fact he is staying at her house. I've driven past and seen his car there."

My heart sinks.

"And then while he was talking and begging for forgiveness, I had an epiphany."

"What was it?"

"He's always going to lie about seeing her. Even in a conversation about saving our marriage, he's still lying. I can never trust him again. We can't save this. It's too far gone." Her eyes well with tears. "My marriage is officially over."

"God, Bec." I take her hand over the table and hold it in mine. "I'm sorry."

"Me too," Chloe says sadly.

The waiter arrives with our new round of drinks. "Thanks." I smile.

Rebecca takes one and holds it up for a toast. "Tonight, we're celebrating." We smile and hold our drinks up to hers. "To new beginnings."

Wednesday morning

I walk down the corridor of the nursing home. I'm just about to clock out from the night shift.

I'm on autopilot now.

Nothing could surprise me anymore. My faith in the male sex has been utterly and irrevocably ruined.

Rebecca's heart is broken. My heart is broken.

The whole world is fucking broken.

I get to Bernard's door and glance through the window and stop still on the spot.

My heart breaks all over again.

Henley is lying on his back in the hospital bed. His father is lying beside him. Bernard's head is on Henley's chest, and Henley's arm is protectively around him. Henley is watching television as his father sleeps.

My eyes well with tears . . .

I know he doesn't love me, but he sure loves his dad.

Lucky him.

Chapter 21

They say time heals all wounds. I don't think that's necessarily true.

But it sure gives you some perspective.

It's been four weeks since Henley and I last spoke, three weeks and six days since I felt swept away and in the moment.

Five minutes since I've thought about him . . .

But I don't care because I am completely and utterly over him. Henley who?

I mean, it's not like we had a grand love affair. It was a few weeks. I got up, dusted myself off, and got over it.

It was the best grand love affair of all time . . .

Stop it . . . focus!

Barry runs to the front door, and then I hear a gentle *knock, knock*. I open and step back in surprise when I see him. His dark hair just messed up, still wearing his suit from work, he is the epitome of fuckable.

Why does he always smell so damn good?

"Henley."

He gives me a lopsided smile. "How are you?"

"Good." I look out into the street. Is he here alone?

"I . . . ahh . . . I just . . ." He's tripping over his words and clearly nervous.

"Yes." I act brave. "What is it?"

"I bought you some new—" He gestures to six potted plants lined up on my front porch.

I cut him off. "Weeds?"

"Apparently they're plants." He smiles, as if relieved at my joke. "Who knew?"

You did.

I roll my lips to hide my smile.

"Anyway, I wanted to apologize for calling your house names."

"Anything else you want to apologize for?"

"A lot, actually." He shrugs. He tries to continue, but I cut him off.

"What else do you want to apologize for?"

"Aah." He swallows a lump in his throat. "My . . ."

I widen my eyes as I wait.

"The way you told me to sleep with Mason?"

He winces. "Yeah . . . about that . . ."

"Yes?" I wait.

"That didn't come out exactly right."

"It didn't?"

"No, it was just . . ." He shrugs.

"You're terrible at apologizing, by the way."

"I'm well aware."

"Carry on," I reply flatly. Acting tough is fun.

"I just don't want a relationship, that's all."

"Okay, you could have just said that instead of trying to throw me to the wolves."

He smirks at my analogy. "Mason is hardly a wolf. He's more like a greyhound."

"Jealous, are you?"

"Of him?" He screws up his face. "No."

"Ha." I tut as if I don't believe him. Although his story is credible—Mason could totally be a greyhound.

We stare at each other some more as the air does that stupid thing between us, and I want to yell and scream and be a complete drama queen for him not falling madly in love with me because damn it, we have something.

But I won't . . . I'm keeping my cards close to my chest from now on.

"I just wanted you to know that I would like us to be friends, seeing that we *are* neighbors," he says with a soft smile.

It has been awkward around here with us ignoring each other.

"Okay." I nod. "I agree. I would like that too."

"Good." He smiles as if proud of himself.

"Good."

"So . . ." He hesitates. "What are you doing now?"

"Nothing."

"Oh . . . me neither."

"Okay."

His eyes search mine. "Okay . . ."

"Okay." I fake a smile. "Goodbye."

His face falls. "Goodbye?"

Why is he repeating everything I say?

"Goodbye," I say flatly. What does he think is going to happen?

He tells me that he doesn't love me and to go sleep with someone else, kills half my garden with a lawn mower, and then buys me six crappy plants and has the gall to think all is forgiven?

No, Mr. James, I don't think so.

"See you later." I close the door in his face. I lean up against the back of it and smile in relief.

Thank god that's over with.

An hour and a half later, I'm freshly showered and in my robe.

Knock, knock, knock. At the door, Barry is wagging his tail, so I know it's someone we know. I open the door.

"Henley," I say in surprise.

He gives me a beautiful broad smile, wearing navy satin boxer shorts and a white T-shirt. He smells like soap and heavenly man, and I get a vision of my legs around my ears . . . yeesh.

He's holding a coffee mug in his hand.

"What's up?" I try to act casual and not impressed at all.

"I was wondering if you had some spare milk?"

I frown. "What?"

"I want a cup of coffee, but I'm out of milk."

"Oh . . ." I shrug. Not what I thought he was here for, but whatever. "Sure, come in."

I go to the fridge and take out the milk. I go to take the coffee cup from him, and he pulls it out of my reach. "What are you doing?" He frowns.

"Getting you some milk."

"Not cow's milk."

"Huh?"

"I want breast milk."

He did not just say that.

I bubble up a surprised giggle. "You want what?"

"Breast milk. Happy to extract myself." His teeth catch his bottom lip in that naughty way he does.

"I don't have any breast milk."

"Why not?"

"Because I'm not a lactating mother, you sicko."

He gives me a slow sexy smile. "In exchange, I could give you some cream for your coffee?"

"Really?"

"Uh-huh."

"Do you have enough?"

"Ample. Two big vats of the stuff."

I try to keep a straight face. *I like this game.*

"I don't like cream in my coffee. It curdles."

"It's a delicacy."

I know.

"Are you sure?" He raises an eyebrow.

"Positive."

"Oh . . . shame." He gives me a cheeky smile, and it's all I can do not to drag him upstairs. Playful Henley is so very hard to resist.

"So . . ." He rocks up onto his toes.

"Actually, I do know where you could get some of the milk you're after." I act serious.

"You do?" His eyes flick around. "Where . . . upstairs?"

"Across the road at Taryn's. Huge milk factory, full production."

He looks at me, deadpan. "That's not the milk I'm after, Juliet."

"That's not what I heard."

"I'm after a specialty boutique kind of milk only served here."

"This boutique is members only."

"Seems a shame to put a label on the factory, therefore nobody gets to drink it."

"Oh, you needn't worry." I fake a smile. "There's people lining up for a membership."

"Like who?"

"My milk is no longer any of your concern, Mr. James."

He rolls his eyes, and I push his shoulder toward the front door. "I only said that—"

I cut him off. "I know."

"It's just such a waste . . ."

"Too bad." My smile does break free this time. "The shop is closed."

"What about a fifteen-minute window? It would be record speed."

No kidding.

"No." I push him out my front door, and he turns around to face me.

"Happy milking." I smile sweetly as I close the door in his face. *Dick.*

Things are getting better. I've been going out with the girls, I got a new hairdo, and today, Joel is coming over. I've saved some more money and am finally getting back to decorating my house.

The entire house is painted internally now, and it's time to look at outside colors and themes. I'm still enjoying it here, but I'm not sure if it's my forever home.

I mean, it's great and all, and maybe one day when my brain finally lets me forget the man next door, I will fall in love with the street again.

The car pulls up, and I peer through the curtains. That's Joel here now.

I smile and open the door as I wait for him. He gets all his swatches and carries a big box inside. "Hey, stranger." He smiles as he walks past me into the house. He stops and pecks me on the cheek. "You look gorgeous. I've missed seeing you."

Oh . . .

"Hi, come in."

Henley

I sip my beer, unimpressed, and stare over at her house. That fucking idiot Joel has been at Juliet's for over two hours.

"I don't know if they are going to win," Blake says casually as he lies back on my couch watching the game. "If I lose this bet over these fuckers . . ."

I stand at the window, peering through the curtains, my eyes still glued over the fence.

My temper hangs on by a thread. "Shut the fuck up about your bet and just watch the game." I drag my hands through my hair.

"What's so interesting out the window?" he asks.

"Nothing."

"What is this . . . the third or fourth time the interior designer has been over to her house this week?"

I roll my lips, infuriated.

Fifth.

"Who knows and who cares," I lie.

I've been baiting her with all my might, and not even a nibble. I've fucked this up well and good.

"She's practically in love with him already," Blake says casually.

"Shut up." I begin to pace back and forth. It's all I seem to do lately. "I don't give a damn what she does."

"Sure you don't."

If she falls for him . . . I swear to fucking god . . .

Damn it, I don't have time to be worrying about her all the time.

I just want this over with.

"What are we doing tonight?" he asks.

"I don't know." I peer through the curtains again. *Hurry up and leave . . . fucker.*

Before I break your face.

"I'll hook us up with some girls, blow some steam off," Blake replies.

My eyes stay glued on Juliet's house. "Sounds good."

341

11:00 p.m.

The bar is loud, the company is hot . . . but my mind isn't on the scantily dressed women around me.

It's at home.

With her.

It's been weeks, and it's not getting any better. If anything, it's getting worse.

The more I see her, the more I want her.

She's all I fucking think about.

I've ruined everything with Juliet. I need to work out how to change her mind.

I feel a hand slide up my thigh, and I glance up as I remember where I am. "What are we drinking, Henley?" the hot little redhead purrs.

What *is* her name?

I exhale heavily. Ugh . . . "I . . ." I pause as I reconsider my options. "I have to get going."

Blake raises an eyebrow in question. "What?"

"I just remembered something I have to do."

"Oh no," the girls sigh. "Don't leave, the night is young."

"Sorry."

"You fucking kidding me right now?" Blake widens his eyes.

"More for you." I stand and put my hand on his shoulder as I walk past him. "You want them all, admit it."

"You're fucked," he mouths.

I chuckle. "I agree." I smile to the girls with a nod. "Good night. Have fun."

"It's getting late," I say to Joel. "I have to work early in the morning."

"I'll get going."

"Okay."

It's the weirdest thing. Joel has been here all week. He's telling me that we need house-planning time, but the reality is that we don't talk about my house at all; he just wants to hang out.

Which is fine. He's a great guy, and in any other circumstance I should be interested. I'm just . . . off men.

"I'll walk you out," I say. We walk out the front and down to his car, which is parked on the street. We stop beside it, and his eyes come to me. "Would you like to go out some time?"

I stare at him.

He answers my question before I have a chance to ask it. "Like on a date."

"Oh . . ." I shrug. "I'm not really"—*fuck*—"wanting to get into a relationship right now."

"It's just dinner, Juliet." He smiles. "Not a marriage proposal. Relax."

"Right." I smile, feeling embarrassed by my dramatic reply. "Sure, why not?"

"Great."

I step back from him. *Please don't try and kiss me goodbye.*

"Next Saturday night?" he asks.

I nod. "Yep. Sounds good."

Henley's car pulls into the street and into his driveway. His car turns off.

Don't look.

"Okay. I'll see you next week," I blurt out in a rush to end the conversation. I really don't want Henley to see me here with Joel. "Goodbye."

"Bye." Joel smiles.

I quickly walk inside before Henley gets out of the car. I close the door behind me and lean on the back of it for a moment. Even the sight of his car sends me into overdrive.

Maybe I really should consider moving house?

With a deep sigh I walk into the kitchen and flick on the kettle to make myself a cup of tea.

Knock, knock sounds at the door.

It's him.

Don't ask me how I know; I just do.

On autopilot I open it in a rush, and there he stands. Six foot four of hard ass. His dark hair is just mussed to perfection. The pull to him is instant.

"Hi." He smiles softly.

I stare at him, unsure what to say.

His eyes search mine. "Can I come in?"

My stomach flutters at his proximity, and we stare at each other.

"So . . . can I come in?" he asks again.

I step back to let him walk past me.

Fuck.

I don't know if I have it in me to resist his milk requests tonight.

"I, um . . ." He shrugs. He's wearing blue jeans and a gray T-shirt. His shoulders are wide, and his chest is broad. Regardless of how things have worked out between us, I know there has never been a more beautiful male specimen on the face of the earth.

"I just . . ." His eyes hold mine, and once again, I can tell that he's nervous.

"You what?"

"I just wanted to see you," he murmurs. His eyes drop to my lips.

It would be so easy to kiss him right now.

"Why?" I act brave.

"I . . ." He pauses. "I wanted to . . ." He shrugs as if feeling stupid.

I frown. "What is it?"

"Can I have a hug?"

"What?"

Oh, gentle Henley is here . . . the one that I love.

"I just . . ." He swallows the lump in his throat, and unable to help it, I take him into my arms.

We hug, tight and close, and my eyes shut as I lean against his shoulder.

"Do you ever think of me?" he whispers.

I get a lump in my throat. "Yes."

He nods as if processing my answer.

"Why do you ask?"

"Because I think about you. A lot."

I can pretend that I don't care about our demise, but the reality is that we really should be together.

Why doesn't he get it?

My nostrils flare as I try to hold in my emotions. Why does he affect me so much?

"I just wanted you to know that"—he frowns as he articulates his words—"it's not that I don't want to be with you. This has nothing to do with you."

Wow, that old chestnut.

"'It's not you, it's me'?" Annoyed, I pull out of his arms. I give a subtle shake of my head. "Is that what you're saying?"

He nods.

Frustration sets in. Seriously, is that the best he's got?

"Is that it?" I ask.

His eyes hold mine. "Do you want it to be it?"

Come out with it. *If you want me, have the balls to say so.*

"What do you want, Henley? Why are you here?"

He exhales heavily. "I don't know."

Wrong answer.

I can't fix this for him. I'm not giving up what I want so that he gets what he wants.

I deserve better than to be his booty call, and he knows it.

"Look, I have to work in the morning." I walk to the door and open it. "I'll see you later."

He pauses, and I get the feeling he wants to say something else . . . but he doesn't.

"Goodbye, Juliet." He brushes past me and walks out.

I roll my eyes and close the door behind him. *Stop fucking with my head.*

"How are we feeling today, Mrs. Potter?" I smile as I take her blood pressure on my morning rounds.

"Okay, I guess. I would be a lot better without that racket." She gestures to the woman in the bed opposite her. The woman is asleep and snoring like a Mack truck.

"Now, now, be nice, Mrs. Potter." I readjust her bed and fill out her chart.

Tom puts his head around the door. "Delivery just arrived at the nurses' station for you, Jules."

I glance up. "What kind of delivery?"

"The romantic kind." He winks and disappears.

"Oh." I hunch my shoulders up in excitement. "Call me if you need anything, Mrs. Potter."

"I need some peace and quiet."

"Let her sleep a little longer, please." I make my way down to the nurses' station and see the biggest bunch of red roses I have ever seen.

"Somebody is sucking up big time," Rosemary says.

I smile goofily. "And so he should."

346

I open the envelope and smile as I read the card.

Can't wait to see you on Saturday.

Joel.

Oh . . .

They're not from Henley . . .

"What's wrong?" Rosemary asks.

"Nothing." I fake a smile and stuff the card into my pocket.

Wrong man.

"Beautiful, aren't they?" I exhale heavily . . . jeez.

I take out my phone and text Joel.

Thank you for the Roses,
They are beautiful.

A reply bounces back.

Like you.

Ugh, this is getting complicated.

A beautiful man is sending me roses, and all I feel is disappointment that they didn't come from an asshole.

What the hell is wrong with me?

I put the roses onto the shelf. "They can stay here so we can all enjoy them."

"You don't want to take them home?"

"No." I shrug. "Nicer here. I need to get back to work."

I trudge down the corridor and roll my eyes in disgust with myself.

Move on, Juliet.

Chloe leads our toast. "To Rebecca. May she find a hot man to have hot rebound sex with tonight."

We all giggle and sip our drinks.

Club Nero, also known as the meat market.

This is the place to come if you want to pick up, and tonight . . . Rebecca does.

She's no longer the damsel in distress; she's the angry bitch from hell, and god help anyone who stands in her way.

She wants revenge on her sleazebag husband, and Chloe and I have decided that the best way to get over him is to get under someone else.

It's 10:00 p.m., and with way too many cocktails under our belts, we are on the prowl. Our eyes scan the club for any suitors.

"Maybe I need to get under someone else too," I mutter.

"Definitely," Chloe agrees. "Me, too, probably."

Rebecca hunches her shoulders up in excitement. "This is actually kind of fun."

"How long since you've had sex with anyone else?" I ask.

"I've only ever had sex with John."

"What?" I gasp. "He's the only one?"

"I know." She rolls her eyes. "Don't even get me started on how pathetic I am."

"Who's pathetic?" a voice says. We all turn to see Blake Grayson standing beside us. He's in a suit. My eyes instantly flick around to look for his friends, and the masochist in me is excited to see Antony and then Henley. "Hi." They nod.

Henley's eyes hold mine for a beat longer than they should. Nerves dance around in my stomach, and I try to act casual. "Hello."

The night just got interesting.

348

"What are you guys doing here?" Chloe asks.

"We had a charity thing we had to go to and bailed early," Antony replies.

"So who's pathetic?" Blake smiles over at us with his best sexy, boyish charm.

"Rebecca is having rebound sex tonight," Chloe announces.

"Chloe." Rebecca laughs. "Don't tell them our secrets."

Blake's face drops as he looks between us. "What?"

"She is going to get it good tonight." Chloe laughs. She punches her hand with her fist to simulate hard fucking.

Henley and Antony glance at each other and then chuckle at some kind of private joke.

"This is a terrible idea," Blake replies.

"No. I need to do this," Rebecca replies. "I've thought it through."

Blake puts his hands on his hips as he stares at her, completely perplexed.

"The best way to get over a man is to get under another one," Chloe says.

"Enough talking, Chloe," Blake snaps. His eyes lock onto Rebecca; he takes her drink from her, sips it, and winces. "This is too strong for you."

She snatches it back off him. "Wimp."

Henley and Antony are really finding something funny in the background. Henley says something to Antony, and he bursts out laughing.

"Fuck off," Blake whispers as he elbows him swiftly in the ribs.

Wait a minute . . . does Blake have a thing for Rebecca?

Surely not?

"It's too soon," Blake tells us. "Nobody is getting their hands on you this early. I'm making sure of it."

Henley mutters something under his breath, and Antony throws his head back and laughs hard.

What *is* so funny?

Okay, I think I've been reading the room completely wrong. I thought Blake was into Chloe, but now, watching this interaction, I actually think he's into Rebecca. It would make sense. He hangs on her every word.

Fuck . . . wait until Chloe finds out. Nothing is easy, is it?

There's always a fucking problem.

I like Henley; Henley is an unobtainable asshole. Joel likes me; I don't like Joel that way. Chloe likes Blake; Blake is a serial gangbanger who now also has a thing for our friend Rebecca whose husband is fucking his anal-hungry secretary.

Ugh . . . just thinking of this sordid web is making my head spin.

"I'm going to the bar." Antony heads off in that direction.

Chloe sees someone she knows across the dance floor. "Back in a minute." She dances off through the crowd toward them.

I glance back and lock eyes with Henley. In slow motion, his eyes drop to my toes and then rise up to rest on my face. He licks his lips as if imagining something.

My stomach flutters. I know that look.

It would be so much easier to get over him if the sex wasn't so mind blowing. Our bodies were like the perfect jigsaw puzzle, fitting together in every way.

He filled every fantasy I ever had.

Dominant, powerful, and hung.

I get a vision of him holding my legs back, his thick cock, creamy with want.

The perspiration sheen on his muscular skin, the way his stomach muscles rippled with his thrusts.

The look in his eyes as he fed his body from mine.

My sex flutters at the memory.

Dear lord . . .

A thousand drinks and a million dirty thoughts later . . .

"Let's dance," Blake says. He grabs Chloe's and Rebecca's hands and pulls them onto the dance floor. My eyes flick over to Antony, who is talking to a group of men he knows by the bar.

"Alone at last," Henley murmurs. His eyes linger on my lips, and without thinking, he adjusts the spaghetti strap on my dress. His fingers trail down my arm as he takes them away.

Goose bumps scatter up my arms at his touch.

I can't stand this any longer. "What do you think about?" I ask him.

He frowns in question.

"You said you think about me a lot."

"I do."

"What do you think?"

He puts his mouth to my ear. "Dirty things." His fingers trail a circle on my thigh as he stands close.

"Do you miss me?"

He leans closer. "Do you miss me?"

Arousal heats my blood at the feel of his touch, every cell waking from a dormant sleep.

"You know I do."

His lips drop to my neck, and he kisses me there. "How do we get around this?" he murmurs against my skin. My eyes instinctively close.

The feeling of his large body towering over mine, standing so close that I can almost taste him . . .

This is primal.

The kind of physical attraction you only read about. I can't fight it anymore; I can't even pretend to want to.

"You kiss me," I murmur.

His eyes hold mine, and he takes my face in one hand and licks my lips. The fire starts.

I feel it between my legs.

He puts his mouth back to my ear. "You're all I can think about." He bites my earlobe, and shivers run down my spine. "I dream of you in my sleep."

"Like a nightmare?" I smirk.

"Exactly." He grabs a handful of my hair and holds my face to his. The dominance of the act sends my pheromones into overdrive. "There isn't a day goes by that I don't fuck myself while I imagine it's you."

The sanity rubber band snaps, and I don't care who sees us—I kiss him with everything that I have.

My tongue swirls against his. His hands snap around my behind as he holds me close.

And right here in the middle of the club, we forget where we are.

Kissing like our lives depend on it.

His hands drag me over his hardened cock in his suit pants, and I whimper.

It's going to be so good.

"I need you beneath me," he growls into my mouth as he bites my lip. "Right fucking now."

"Let's go," I pant.

He grabs my hand and drags me out of the club, and once outside, he drags me around to the side alley and slams me up against the wall and kisses me again.

Like animals we dry hump each other, desperately trying to get more of each other in the shortest time possible. His hands slide up and down my bare legs. His thick erection nudges firmly against my stomach.

"You're going to make me blow right here, baby girl."

I stare up at him, lost somewhere between heaven and hell. He runs his hand up my thigh and under my dress. His fingers slip underneath the side of my panties, and he inhales sharply as he feels my creamy sex.

"So fucking wet for me." He slides two of his thick fingers into my sex, and I shudder around him. "I'm going to fuck you so good," he growls into my ear.

My head tips back with a moan. His fingers pick up the pace as he begins to work me with them, and I spread my legs to give him greater access.

My eyes flick up the alley toward the club. Anyone could walk around the corner right now and catch us.

The sound of my wet body sucking him echoes around us, and I see stars.

All the beautiful stars: the whole galaxy and then some.

"I knew you'd come around," he murmurs against my neck. "Finally see us for what we are."

Huh?

"And what is that?" I pant. His fingers become almost violent.

God . . . that's good.

"This is when we are at our best." He twists his fingers, and we both cry out on the cutting edge of an orgasm.

So close we can taste it.

"Sexual soulmates. We don't need a relationship; we just need to fuck each other's brains out." He jerks his hand. "Take care of each other's needs."

My arousal fog evaporates, and my eyes snap open.

"What?" I push his hand away. "What do you mean?"

"Juliet." He grabs my behind to drag me back over his cock. "Get on it."

"I still want the same thing, Henley," I snap. "Nothing has changed for me."

He steps back from me, panting as he struggles for control. "What are you saying?"

"What are *you* saying?"

"We miss each other. We need to fuck," he snaps.

I blink, shocked. "I don't want to be your fuck buddy, Henley. I want to be in a relationship. I want you to love me."

He rolls his eyes. "Here we go a-fucking-gain. Will you drop this bullshit?" he spits. "It's never going to happen. Why would you want to ruin what we have? What we have is perfect."

I take a step back from him. "Because I deserve better."

He pants. His eyes are wild. "You said you missed me."

"Because I'm in love with you," I spit. "Because I know what we have is special. I know you feel the same. I can feel it. Do you think I can't feel it?" My voice rises as I begin to lose control of my emotions.

"I can't give you that, Juliet. I'm not fucking capable of it," he fires back. "How many times do I have to tell you?"

"Can't or won't?" My eyes well with tears.

"If I could, I would." His eyes are wild; his stance is crazy.

And there it is . . . spelled out in black and white.

"I want to be in a relationship, Henley. I want a man who is proud to call me his," I whisper through tears. "I don't want to be your booty call whose only currency is orgasms."

He puts his weight onto his back foot. "Then move on."

That's it.

That *is* it. I am so over this self-centered fucking asshole.

"You know what?" I screw up my face in tears. "I'm going to. Tomorrow night I'm going on a date."

"With him?" he snaps.

"Yes. With Joel." I throw up my hands in surrender. Suddenly I want to hurt him the way he hurts me. "And guess what, Henley? I'm going to sleep with him, and I'm going to be the best damn fuck he ever had. Because Chloe is right: the only way to get over one man is to get under another. And I need to get the fuck over you . . . because all you do is think of yourself and hurt me."

"Don't you dare sleep with him," he growls.

"You had your chance." I shake my head in disgust. "Ha! You've had about a hundred chances, and you've blown them all."

"Enough with the dramatics," he spits angrily. "You belong with me."

"Only on your terms. Guess what? I'm not some wimp who will take anything you give me."

"You sure about that?" he sneers.

"Fuck you." I turn and storm off.

"Don't come crying back to me when he can't get the job done," he calls after me. "Nobody can make you come like I can."

I hate that he's right.

I storm up the alleyway, and with my ovaries screaming at me to go back and take whatever he is offering, I put my hand up for a cab.

One pulls up, and I get in and stare out the window.

Last chance.

Henley

I stand in the darkness. From my place at the upstairs front window, I can see it all.

It's 7:00 p.m. on Saturday night, and he's at her house.

355

And after the worst twenty-four hours in history, I don't know why the fuck I need to see this. It's like salt in the wound, but I can't look away.

Juliet's front door opens, and she walks out. She's wearing a tight black dress and high heels. Her hair is up, and she's laughing and talking to him.

No.

He opens the car door for her. She says something, and then he leans in and kisses her.

My fists clench at my sides; murder crosses my mind.

I turn, and I punch the wall as hard as I can. The drywall explodes under the impact, and then next thing I know I'm out in the street, marching toward them.

"What are you doing?" Joel stammers, wide eyed.

"Don't make me hurt you," I warn him.

I open the passenger-side car door where Juliet is sitting. "Get the fuck out of the car. Now."

Chapter 22

Juliet

I exhale heavily as I stare out of the car at the maniac. How did I know this was coming?

Stay calm.

"Henley," I sigh.

"We need to talk." His chest is rising and falling as he struggles for control.

"It's too late."

"No, it's not," he fires back.

"Do not dare throw a childish tantrum, Henley. I'm warning you right now," I yell. "We have nothing to talk about."

"But . . ." His face falls. "We have everything to talk about." His voice softens, and I know that somehow the gentle version of Henley James's personality has shown up.

The one I can't resist.

"Please . . ." His eyes search mine.

"Henley . . ." I drag my hand through my hair. Damn it. He doesn't make anything easy, does he? "Now is not the time."

"Now is the only time." He stands in front of my open car door so that we can't drive away. "Please. Can we just talk about this?"

I exhale heavily.

"What's he doing?" Joel says, unimpressed, from behind the wheel.

"Just . . ." I sigh. What do I even do here? This is so fucking awkward for Joel.

"Last night . . . I don't know why I say the things I do," he stammers in a panic. "I don't mean them. I'm sorry."

Fuck's sake. He's had all day to apologize, and he chooses now to do it?

Of course he does.

I put my hands over my eyes. "Henley," I snap. "Honestly . . . you're so infuriating. I am going on a date, and I am not talking to you about this." I gesture to the road. "Just drive, Joel."

"Last night . . . you said you loved me . . . Is that still true?" he stammers.

Joel's eyes flick to me in question. "You love him?"

Fuck.

I close my eyes, ashamed of myself. "It's . . . complicated."

"Get out of the car." Henley takes my hand. "Please."

"Damn it, Henley," I snap in frustration. "You *don't* love me."

"Who says?" he spits angrily.

I roll my lips, unimpressed.

"I'm trying to get better for you," he blurts out in a rush. "I swear I am."

Fuck . . .

What do I do?

"You should"—Joel rolls his eyes, sensing that our date is over before it began—"go . . ."

"Joel . . ." I look over to him. "We are not together."

"We *are* together," Henley interrupts. "You just haven't realized it yet."

Who hasn't realized it yet, fucker?

"Henley, god damn it!" I snap. "Get into the house now."

"Are you coming?"

"Yes, I'm fucking coming," I snap. "I have never known a more infuriating man than you."

He stands his ground.

"Now." I point to the house.

He walks over and stands on the curb and folds his arms, defiantly waiting for me.

"I'm so sorry, Joel." I sigh. "This is unacceptable."

"I knew he liked you." We both look over to Henley as he stares back at us through the windshield. "I didn't know he loved you."

I let out a deep breath. I'm not even excited by this revelation. In fact, I'm pissed. "I'll call you during the week?"

"Okay." He starts the car.

I walk past Henley and into his house. He follows me with his tail between his legs.

I'm so pissed that I can't even bring myself to say one word to him—not one fucking word.

I sit on the couch. He tentatively sits down beside me.

"Start talking," I say.

"Well, firstly . . . I want to apologize. I've been out of line." He pauses as if collecting his thoughts.

You think?

"My behavior last night was just . . . terrible," he continues. "I didn't mean *any* of it. I don't know what came over me, and I don't know why I acted like that."

"Like what? Aggressive and abusive?"

His gaze drops to the floor.

Silence . . .

My heart sinks.

Why do I feel bad for upsetting him?

"Why do you act like this?" I ask him.

"I don't know . . . ," he whispers. "It's like . . . my feelings for you bring out the darkest part of my personality."

What?

What do you even say to that?

"You said you were trying to get better?" I eventually ask.

"I am," he says hopefully. "I go twice a week, and Aaron says I'm making progress."

"Aaron?"

"The psychologist."

"Making progress with what?"

He hesitates . . .

"Hen." I look him square in the eye. "Now is the time for honesty," I say softly. "You at least owe me that."

He nods. "I . . ." He licks his bottom lip. "I know." He wrings his hands nervously on his lap. "The thing is . . . and there is no easy way to say this, but . . . I'm fucked up."

No shit, Sherlock.

"How so?"

He continues to twist his hands together on his lap . . .

"Hen?"

"Well, I always thought I was like this because I hadn't found the right woman and I'm happy on my own. It's never bothered me."

Where is this going?

"Right . . ."

"But then I met you, and I wanted more, but . . ." His voice trails off.

"But what?"

"But I couldn't do it."

"Do what?"

"Commit to a relationship."

I frown. "But you committed to a friends-with-benefits situation with no problem."

"I did." He takes my hand in his. "Because it killed two birds with one stone."

"What birds?"

"I got to spend time with you without weirding out."

"Weirding out?" I repeat.

He shrugs, embarrassed. "I'm totally fucking weird. Don't worry, I am well aware."

I fight to hide my smile. *You got that right.*

"What does your psychologist say about this?"

"Aaron thinks that my mind is trying to protect me, so it blocks my emotions."

I frown, not understanding. "Why?"

"I don't understand it myself."

"So you don't have any emotions?"

"No, I do." He shrugs. "With you, I do."

"And what are those emotions?" I ask.

He frowns as if perplexed. "Love is a strong word."

"It is."

"So . . ." He pauses as if choosing his words very carefully. "You say you loved me."

"Uh-huh."

"What does that feel like?"

"What?"

"If you love someone, what does it feel like?" He continues. "I mean, when do you get that light bulb I'm-in-love moment?"

I smile at his immaturity on this subject. "It's not one light bulb moment. It's a million little things."

His eyes hold mine as he listens.

"It's looking forward to seeing someone. It's thinking about them all day. It's missing them when they go home, even though you've just seen them all night. It's laughing and conversations and sexual attraction, and most of all it's a sense of belonging to that person."

"Belonging to that person?"

"Like you don't want to sleep with anyone else, you only want one person, and nobody else will do. The thought of giving your body to someone else is sickening."

He nods as if finally understanding.

I wait for him to elaborate on the subject, but he remains silent.

"Well?" I ask. "Any of that sound familiar?"

He swallows the lump in his throat as if bracing himself for the worst thing possible. "Maybe . . . I do . . . somehow—I mean, I don't know, but I think I . . . love you." He stares at the ground, unable to make eye contact.

Empathy fills me at his botched-up declaration of love.

"And that's a bad thing?" I whisper.

"No, I think it's a . . . good thing." He rolls his lips. "It's just brought up a lot of baggage for me."

"What kind of baggage?"

He hesitates before answering. "I struggle with intimacy."

"Why?"

"I don't know."

But he does know.

"What does Aaron say the reason is?"

He stares at me as if processing the question. "That I won't rely on anyone as a form of protection."

"Protection from what?"

"If you leave me."

Oh . . .

My heart . . .

"Hen," I whisper softly.

"But I don't think that's true. I mean . . . big deal. My mother died. A million people's mothers die every day, and they don't walk around fucked up like this."

"Henley, on our first date you told me that your mother dying was a catastrophic event in your life." I squeeze his hand in mine. "Don't play it down. Grief affects everyone differently. You were at a very vulnerable age when she died."

His eyes fill with tears as he stares at a spot on the carpet, unable to bring himself to look at me.

He *is* fucked up.

"So . . ." I frown as I try to work out where we go from here. "What do you want to happen now?"

"I want to be with you," he replies without hesitation. "In a . . ." He swallows again.

I cut him off. "Relationship?"

He nods. "I want to try."

Silence . . .

Still not a commitment . . . but maybe *a promise*.

I know I shouldn't, but I see him, the beautiful man I fell for, lost as he tries to navigate the world. Henley is a good man, deep down. I've always known that. He doesn't want to live like this. He's had no other option.

I cup his face in my hand. "On one condition."

"Anything."

"You be honest with me from here on in."

His eyes search mine.

"I need to know what's going on in your head, or we won't make it, Hen."

A trace of a smile crosses his face as he takes my hand in his.

I smile, too, and in that moment, I know it's going to be okay between us.

"Kiss me," I whisper. He leans over and kisses me. His face screws up against mine as if overwhelmed with emotion.

My beautiful, tortured king, so messed up.

So fucking lovable.

An ocean of vulnerability swimming between us.

"Henley." I put my hand under his chin and bring his face to mine. "We can do this."

He closes his eyes as if to block me out.

"Hen," I demand. "Open your eyes and look at me."

He drags his eyes open.

"Love me back," I whisper. "Like I know you can." I kiss him softly. My tongue gently swipes through his open lips, and I kiss him again. "I just need you to always be honest with me. If something is bothering you, just tell me."

His kiss deepens, and then, as if remembering something, he pulls back to look at me. "Are we starting the honesty thing right now?"

I nod. "Uh-huh."

"Then take it off."

"What?" I frown.

"The makeup that you put on for him."

It bothers him that I'm all dressed up to go on a date with another man.

I would be too.

"You mean the makeup I put on while I was thinking of you?" I smile softly.

He points upstairs. "Wash it off. *All* of it."

"I'm going to need to take a shower."

"Probably." He narrows his eyes as he acts serious.

Excitement rushes through my veins. "You're going to need to get in with me to help."

"Definitely."

We stare at each other, excitement buzzing between us, the air crackling with promise.

"I'm going to fuck you so good that you don't remember your name." He bends and, in one swift movement, picks me up and throws me over his shoulder. I laugh as we take the stairs.

His step falters halfway up.

"You regretting this decision to carry me now, Mr. Strong?" I smile as I hang upside down with my hands on his behind.

"Little bit," he puffs.

I laugh out loud, and he slaps me on the behind. "No talking."

"I'm laughing."

He slaps me again. "No laughing either."

We get to the bathroom, and he slides me down his body. We fall silent as we stare at each other.

And this is it, the beginning of us, *the real beginning*.

At least I hope it is. It better fucking be.

He takes my dress off over my shoulders and throws it to the side. He undoes my bra and then slides my panties down my legs. His eyes drop and linger on my naked body, and I want to please him so badly. Do everything I can to make it up to him, because I hate that I have makeup on for another man too.

I pull his T-shirt off over his head and then slide down the zipper on his jeans. I'm blessed with the sight of his large cock as it springs free.

Then all control is lost. He pulls me in, under the water, and we kiss like long-lost lovers.

Because that's how it feels.

The last six weeks have been a living hell without him in my arms.

He pins me to the wall, and as we kiss, his body instinctively slides deep into mine. We both moan deeply as arousal takes over.

I thought the first time we did this it was going to be this big mad foreplay session with all the bells and whistles . . . but every time with Henley is all the bells and whistles.

"I love you," I whisper.

He smiles against my lips and pumps me deeper. "You fucking better." I laugh, loud and free, and he does too.

We're back, baby . . .

We lie in silence. *Exhausted* doesn't come close. We made love in the shower, all tender and sweet, and then we fucked like animals as he showed me exactly who I belong to.

It's him. *It's always been him* . . .

"It's the little things," he whispers as we stare up at the ceiling.

I look over to him in surprise.

"It's the way your smile drops my stomach."

Oh . . .

"The way you crunching ice with your teeth infuriates me, but I never say anything because somehow I find it endearing."

I smile into the darkness.

"It's the way you glow in the refrigerator light at midnight when you're looking for ice cream," he murmurs as his eyes stay glued to the ceiling.

"How do I glow?" I ask.

"Just-fucked and perfect."

My heart swells.

"It's the way I think about you all day." He pauses for a moment. "It's the way I watch for your car to come home all night."

Is he being romantic?

"The way I kind of like your dog, but I can't tell you because then you will know that you have me in the palm of your hand."

Unexpectedly, emotion overwhelms me, and I get a lump in my throat as I watch him.

He rolls on his side, and his eyes finally meet mine. "It's the way I can't stand the thought of sleeping with anyone else."

"I like that one." I smile.

He smiles too. "Oh . . . that's the only one you like?"

I giggle and kiss his big, beautiful lips. His arm comes around me, and I snuggle my head into his chest.

"It's the way I was so upset that you didn't want to see me anymore that I ran over your plants with the mower."

"You had to go ruin it and bring that up . . . didn't you?" I mutter dryly. "You were going so well."

He chuckles and kisses my temple and holds me close.

"Don't let me fuck this up," he says softly. "Tell me if I get too close to the line."

"Oh, I will, and for the record, if you ever run over a plant of mine with the mower again, I'm running over you with it."

"Deal." He smiles.

We lie in silence for a while, both lost in our own thoughts.

"Good night, my beautiful Juliet," he whispers. "Thanks for waiting for me to get here . . ."

My heart swells at his newfound vulnerability. "You were worth the wait."

Midnight, the magical hour

I lie and stare at the man beside me as he sleeps.

He's on his back, the white blanket pooled around his lower stomach. His broad naked body is on display.

I watch as his chest rises . . . holds, and then gently falls. I've been lying here watching him for two hours. My protective

367

instincts have kicked in, and I just want to care for him. To make him feel loved and safe.

How must it feel to be so traumatized that you can't let yourself be loved? And his dad is sick too . . .

I feel so sad for him.

I push the hair back from his forehead and kiss him softly.

How is it possible that tonight my attachment to him is deeper than ever?

Is this what it feels like?

Where nothing else matters, and to hell with the consequences. Because there are consequences for being with Henley. I know that.

I'm twenty-seven years old, and at a time when I want to relax into a drama-free and easy relationship, I know this will be anything but. How could it not be? He's never had a girlfriend, much less a serious relationship, and these things take practice. Years and years of practice. I'm in for a rocky ride.

I lean up onto my elbow, and hope fills me as I smile over at him in the darkness. His dark hair, big eyelashes, and kissable pouty lips. Out of all the men I've ever met in my life, Henley James is the one I compare everyone else to.

He's the set point.

The last few weeks have been a nightmare—for both of us, I now know.

But he's here with me, revealing his vulnerability and declaring his love.

It's weird. In reality, we hardly know each other, but our attraction is so deep that it's cellular. It's as if my body was always his, as if he was always meant to be mine. He has this special ingredient. Every whispered word, every touch means so much more than it should.

I let out a big yawn and know I need to get some sleep. I roll onto my side, facing away from him, and his hand comes out and pulls me back to be snug against his body, still asleep. He kisses my shoulder blade, and I feel his manhood against my behind, the warmth from his skin.

I smile into my pillow. I think maybe . . . it's going to be okay.

Chapter 23

I wake to an unfamiliar scent permeating my bedroom, and I frown. *What is that?*

Pancakes.

Huh? My eyes snap open. What's happening right now? Has someone broken in to make me food?

I've never even woken up with Henley before, let alone had him cook me breakfast. I jump out of bed, throw on my robe, and go in search of my man.

I find him in the kitchen, standing over the frying pan, a tea towel slung over his shoulder as he concentrates. I lean against the doorjamb for a moment and watch him. He's wearing a white T-shirt and pajama bottoms, and as he flips the pancakes I can see the muscles in his shoulders contract underneath his shirt.

So fucking hot.

He glances up, sees me, and gives me a slow sexy smile. "Good morning, my sweet Juliet."

His sweet Juliet . . . has there ever been a more swoony good morning in the history of life?

I don't think so.

I smile goofily. "Good morning, Henley."

He walks over and puts the spatula down to my sex and flips air.

"What are you doing?" I laugh as I swat him away.

"Flipping my breakfast. What does it look like?"

"You want it done both sides?"

"Only the best are flipped both sides." He smiles against my lips as he kisses me.

"What are you doing here, Mr. James?" We kiss again as his hands slide up underneath my robe.

"Putting in the effort." He winks.

"Oh, breakfast is your effort?"

He bends me over backward. "Once you taste these pancakes . . . you're never going to let me go." He bites my neck, and I laugh and try to escape him.

Who said I was ever going to let you go?

"Behave." He stands me up. "My pancakes are burning." He goes back to flipping them over.

"I've got an idea," I say as I watch him.

"What's that?"

"Let's go away and do a total reset. Relax into this new stage and each other properly without any outside noise."

"I can't." He turns back to his pancake duties. "I have responsibilities here."

"I'll get Chloe to visit your dad every day to check on him."

A frown flashes across his face as his eyes flick to me. "How do you . . ."

"I work a second job at the nursing home. I've met your father. He's a lovely man."

"And you didn't think to tell me this?" he snaps.

"Henley, you haven't spoken to me in six weeks," I fire back. "When have I had the chance to tell you?"

He rolls his lips and thankfully holds his tongue because he knows I'm right.

He snakes his hand in under my bathrobe to hold my behind, and I look up at him. "Can we go away?" I whisper. "Just the two of us?"

"I . . ."

"You need a break," I tell him. "You've never been away since your dad has been sick."

"He needs me."

"What he needs is for you to be happy and relaxed."

He drags his hands through his hair as if conflicted.

"We could go somewhere hot—sun, sand, and the ocean." I smile hopefully.

"Well, what about Barry?" he replies.

I smile, realizing he is close to giving in. "Chloe can watch Barry. She can come and stay with him. He loves her. We want to start again, and this could be the perfect opportunity to leave all our crap in the past."

His eyes hold mine, and I know that he thinks it's a good idea too. "I'll think about it."

"Okay." I kiss him softly, my lips lingering over his. As we kiss his eyes close, too, and I know he feels every bit as lost to this as I am. And it's there again, the crazy chemistry we have. It takes me over every time we're alone.

"My body ached for you," he murmurs against my lips. "You're all I could think about." Our kiss deepens. He turns off the griddle and sits down on a chair and pulls me over his lap. He begins to rock me over his body as we kiss.

"Let's go back to bed," he breathes.

"We have to eat."

"We have to fuck," he whispers. "I can't get close enough to you." He kisses me again. "I need more."

Oh . . .

372

"How did I ever think I could live without this?" I murmur against his lips as he rocks me onto his body. He pulls himself out of his pajama pants and positions himself at my entrance and slowly slides in.

"Mm," he moans softly as he grabs my hair in his hands, pulling me down onto him harder. "You feel so fucking good on my cock."

An earth-moving shudder runs between us. Face to face, we stare at each other.

Rocking, kissing, aching for each other in a way that nobody else could understand.

Primal and urgent.

No matter what problems we face, no matter how fucked-up things are, nobody can take this away from us.

When Henley and I are naked, the world is ours.

We walk up the street hand in hand, and I'm really hoping the paparazzi are snapping the shit out of this and are about to post it all over the internet.

I have breaking news.

Henley and I are on a date . . . in our own neighborhood . . . on a Sunday night.

Miracles do happen.

After breakfast today he went and visited his father while I did my washing, and then this afternoon we lay by his pool. It's been the best weekend of all time . . . except the hurting-Joel's-feelings part, but I'll handle that tomorrow. God knows what I'm going to say to him.

There is no excuse for my and Henley's behavior.

We push open the heavy glass door and walk into the Italian restaurant. "Hello," Henley says to the waiter. "We have a table booked in the name of James."

The waiter looks through the bookings. "Ah yes." He smiles. "This way, Mr. James." We follow him through the restaurant toward our table.

James.

I love that surname.

Juliet James . . . hmm, certainly has a ring to it.

I smile at my own private joke as Henley pulls my chair out for me and I sit down.

"Can I get you any drinks to start?"

Henley opens the menu to peruse the choices. "I'll have a glass of sparkling water please?" I ask.

Henley's eyes shoot up. "No wine?"

"Not for me, thanks. I'm not in the mood for drinking."

The waiter smiles over at me. "And you, sir?"

"You know what?" Henley closes the menu. "I'll behave too. Sparkling water as well."

The waiter leaves us alone.

"You can have wine. Don't not drink just because I am."

"It's no fun on my own." He smiles as he takes my hand over the table. "Looking at you gets me drunk anyway."

My heart swells . . .

"You know, I love this version of you."

"What version of me?"

"The one who doesn't watch what he says."

He chuckles and looks away as if embarrassed. "Well . . . it's been . . ." He shrugs.

I cut him off. "It's been good for us."

"How so?"

"Well, I honestly believe everything happens for a reason."

He leans on his hand and steeples his pointer finger up the side of his face as he watches me. "And what do you think was the reason?"

"It was a lesson."

"On what?"

"Life."

He frowns. "How so?"

"For me, the lesson was to not let go of what I truly want and deserve. I knew that we were more and had a real shot at a future together. It would have been so easy to keep being friends with benefits just so that I could have you."

He nods as he listens.

"What did you learn?" I ask him.

He thinks for a moment. "That I missed you."

I smile softly over at the gorgeous man in front of me and take his hand in mine. "I missed you too. What else did you learn? What was the lesson in all of this?"

He exhales, unsure how to answer my question.

"I'll tell you what I think the lesson was."

"Please do. I'm clearly hopeless with lessons." He smirks.

"When the chips fall down and things get hard, you lean into the light."

"What do you mean?"

"You lean into the light, Henley."

"What's the light?"

"Love. Love is the light."

His face falls as he listens.

"Love used to scare you, but it's a shield. It will protect you. I . . . will protect you."

His nostrils flare as his eyes hold mine.

"I love you."

He squeezes my hand in his.

"When things get hard, you lean into the light."

"And what a beautiful light you are," he whispers.

The waiter comes back with our two glasses of sparkling water. "Here you go." He places them down onto the table.

"You know what?" Henley says. "I've changed my mind. Can we order a bottle of the best champagne you have, please? Two glasses. We're celebrating."

"Of course, sir." He disappears once more.

"What are we celebrating?" I ask.

His eyes twinkle with a certain something. "You."

Aftershave brings me out of my coma, the heavenly scent permeating the bedroom. I drag my eyes open, and as my vision centers, I see Mr. James dressed in his suit, ready for his day. "Good morning." He leans down and kisses me softly, his lips tenderly hovering over mine. "You look angelic in my bed." He cups my face in his hand and smirks. "Optical illusion," he mouths. "I know better."

I smile sleepily. "What time is it?"

"Time to get up." He stands and walks to the dresser and puts his expensive watch on. "I brought you coffee." He gestures to the side table, and I look over to see a steaming cup of coffee sitting beside me.

I pull myself up to lean against the headboard and pick up my coffee.

"What are you doing today?" he asks as he hangs my robe up in the bathroom.

"I have the day off."

He walks around the bedroom tidying. "And what do you have planned for your day off?"

It boggles my brain to watch him. This is why his house is so immaculate. He cleans it at five thirty in the fucking morning. Ugh, do we have anything in common at all?

"I'm having lunch with Joel."

376

He stills, and his eyes meet mine.

"To apologize for Saturday night," I say in a rush. "This lunch was planned already because we are going over roofing options. It has nothing to do with us going on a date."

"No."

"What?"

"No!" he replies. He goes back to tidying the bedroom.

I put my coffee down. "What do you mean, *no*?"

"No, you're not going out with Inferior Interiors." He flicks a T-shirt before he folds it. "There is no need to go to lunch. You text him and tell him that you are with me now."

"What?"

"If he doesn't respect that, then he will have to answer to me." He fumes as he walks around organizing his room.

"Henley, I need to tell him in person."

"Tell him what, exactly?" he snaps impatiently.

"That I'm going out with a caveman now who thinks he can tell me what to do."

"I don't think it." He glares at me. "I know it."

"You *know* that you can tell me what to do?" I gasp, offended.

"Listen," he snaps. "That prick interior decorator has been after my girl since day one, so don't act offended when I refuse to put up with it."

Calm, calm . . . *keep fucking calm.*

"First, I have only been your girl since yesterday because *you* refused to admit your true feelings. That is not *his* fault. Joel is an innocent bystander in all of this."

He opens his mouth to say something.

"Let me finish," I snap, cutting him off. "Second, I am an adult. I do not ghost people like an immature child, unlike some people we know."

He narrows his eyes. "Careful."

"You be careful, Henley," I snap. I get out of bed in a rush and walk into the bathroom and close the door. I sit down to go to the bathroom.

He walks in. "You're not going to lunch with him. End. Of. Fucking. Story."

"Do you mind? I'm using the toilet," I snap, infuriated.

He puts his hands on his hips and raises an eyebrow. "So?"

"So I am not having this conversation midpiss."

He marches back out and slams the door.

Fuck my life. I don't need this bullshit. It's not even 6:00 a.m. yet. I take my time, trying to calm down my temper.

This is all new for him, I remind myself. He doesn't know how to handle jealousy. Be patient.

Okay . . .

This is fine. I can handle this . . . keep calm.

I wash my hands and walk out to see the bedroom spotless and the bed made.

He's like a fucking drill sergeant.

I hear something bang downstairs in the kitchen, and I put my robe on and walk downstairs to see him making a protein shake with his back to me.

I put my arms around him from behind. "Okay." I kiss his shoulder.

"Okay what?"

"Okay, I won't have lunch with him. I will come and have lunch with you instead."

He turns in my arms and looks down at me. I kiss his lips. "*After* I tell him in person, over a cup of coffee."

He opens his mouth, and I put my finger over his lips. "Henley. This is nonnegotiable. He has been a friend and my interior designer. I *am* telling him in person."

He twists his lips, and I know he's trying his hardest not to react.

"A quick ten-minute cup of coffee, and then I come and have lunch with you." I smile up at him. "I owe him this much. He likes me."

"I know he fucking likes you."

"But that's too bad, because I love you."

"I don't like it."

"You don't have to." I kiss him softly. "But you do need to understand."

He exhales heavily and unwraps my arms from around his waist. "I have to go."

"Okay."

He holds his protein shake in his hand and stares at me as if contemplating his next sentence.

"Do I get an *I love you* this morning?" I smile teasingly.

"When you get to my office and it's done, you will."

"We need some time alone. Can we go on our vacation?"

"I have a million things on."

"Hmm." I try to sweeten the deal. "A week in the sun and the ocean with me in a string bikini, my big buff boyfriend rubbing suntan oil all over my body. Making love on the beach under the moonlight."

"Sounds terrible." A trace of a smile crosses his face, and I know our fight is over.

I smile and kiss him. "So can we?" I really want to reset away from here and all our crappy memories.

"When do you want to go?" he asks.

"Next week?"

"Next week?" he gasps. "I can't pack up and go away in a week."

"Why not? Aren't you the boss?" I smile hopefully. "If I can organize someone to cover my shifts next week and Chloe can look after Barry and check on your dad, can we go?"

He exhales heavily.

"Chloe is a nurse. She can check on your dad every day. She will call us immediately if you are needed here, and we can come straight home."

"I'll think about it."

"So . . . I'm taking that as a yes. I'm an optimist, you know."

He rolls his eyes. "Goodbye, Juliet."

I grab the lapels of his suit and pull him to me. "Goodbye, my grumpy, hot boyfriend."

He screws up his face in disgust. "I don't like that term."

"Grumpy?"

"Boyfriend."

I giggle. "Hurry up and marry me, then, so you can be my mister."

His face falls.

"Joking!" I laugh at his horror. "Relax, it was a joke."

"Not a funny one, Juliet."

"Yeesh . . ."

He walks to the door and looks back at Barry and me. "You need to wash the coffee cups before you leave."

I widen my eyes and point to the door. "Go to work."

I sit in the café with my heart in my throat. I feel like shit. This is not Joel's fault. This is a circumstance of very bad timing. Joel comes into view, and he waves and smiles when he sees me. "Hi." He bends and kisses my cheek.

I'm an asshole.

"Hello." He smiles as he falls into the chair opposite me.

"I already ordered us coffee." I shrug. "Hope that's okay."

"Sure, coffee before lunch. I'm down."

I stare at him. There's no easy way to say this. "I'm sorry for Saturday, Joel," I say softly.

"Me too."

I try to explain. "It was the worst timing."

"It wasn't bad timing," he huffs. "He knew exactly what he was doing."

"What?"

"He's had you on ice the entire fucking time he's lived next door, Juliet, and as soon as you meet someone else, he comes in like a spoiled child wanting his toy back."

"Oh," I reply, surprised by his venom. I wasn't expecting this reaction.

"So . . . let me guess," he says sarcastically. "You organize a date with me, and suddenly he realizes that you are the one for him, and he's miraculously over his commitment issues, and now thinks he's in love with you . . . but he didn't say it straight out; it was in a roundabout way."

I frown.

"How am I going with my prediction?"

Surprisingly fucking accurate.

"You don't need to be like this."

"But I do, because you're being an idiot and letting him play you like a fiddle."

I exhale heavily. "I'm in love with him, Joel."

"Because you have good sex?"

I stare at him as I roll my lips. I'm not even replying to that.

"There's a lot more to a relationship than sex, Juliet, and if you want a life with someone like that, go ahead."

I've heard enough of this shit.

I throw my napkin onto the table. "Thanks, I will." I stand. "Goodbye, Joel." I walk out of the restaurant.

I hope Henley really knows how to decorate fucking houses.

The elevator rises as excitement bubbles in my stomach. I'm on my way up to Henley's office to have lunch with him. My coffee date with Joel didn't go as planned, but after calming down a little, I do understand Joel's disapproval.

I chose Henley, and no matter how sweetly I wrap the delivery, the message is still the same.

The elevator doors open to a large reception area, and I walk in. It's all modern timber with beautiful apricot marble floors. A huge gold sign is on the back wall.

HENLEY JAMES

ENGINEERING

Oh . . . bougie as fuck.

A lot fancier than I expected.

"Can I help you?" a woman's voice asks.

I look over and see a gorgeous brunette sitting at a desk: long dark hair and perfect bone structure. "Um, yes. I'm here to see Henley."

"Are you?" She fakes a smile and looks me up and down. "And what's your name?"

What's with the condescending tone, bitch?

"I'm Juliet, Henley's girlfriend, and you are?" I fire back.

She looks at me, deadpan. "Strange, I've never heard of you before."

"Your name?" I repeat.

"Jenny," she replies flatly.

Jenny . . . I remember fucking Jenny; she was the witch who blew me off all those years ago. So she's still around, eh? Nobody told me she also happened to be a bombshell. "Hello, Jenny." I smile through gritted teeth.

"Hello."

"Where is Henley?" I assert. *Don't give me your crap, Jenny. I will end you.*

"He's in his office."

"Which is where?" I begin to get annoyed with this woman and her outright rudeness.

"Take a seat, and I'll let him know you're here."

I roll my lips and take a seat on the couch. I text Henley.

Who the fuck is this receptionist?

A door instantly opens, and Henley comes into view. "Hello." He smiles. He throws Jenny a quick glance and gestures into his office, and I stand and make my way over.

Jenny pretends to look at her computer, not even looking up.

I walk into the office and turn toward Henley, and he closes the door behind us.

"How did it go?" he asks.

"It was a five-minute conversation. I left before his coffee even arrived." I cross my arms in front of myself. "The deed is done."

Satisfaction flashes across his face before he takes me into his arms. "Good." He kisses me softly.

"Forgot to tell me a small detail that your hot receptionist is in lust with you?"

He chuckles. "She's just a bit—"

I cut him off. "Rude."

"Protective."

I roll my eyes, and his hands drop to my behind, and he bumps our hips together. "What do you want for lunch?"

"You . . . on Jenny's desk sounds good," I huff. Why the hell is his receptionist so hot?

"That could work." He smiles.

I roll my eyes. Seriously, I need to get ahold of this jealousy thing. Why do I think every woman alive is after Henley James?

Because they are.

"I called Chloe, and she can help us out next week."

He looks down at me.

"Can we go?"

"Juliet."

I bounce on the spot. "Tell me we can go."

"All right." He widens his eyes as if I am a huge inconvenience. "We can go."

I smile broadly.

"On one condition," he says.

"What's that?"

"You let me organize it."

"Why, because you're a control freak?"

"Precisely." He gives me a slow sexy smile, and I feel it to my toes.

"Okay." I pull him close and kiss him. "I can't wait to have you all to myself."

His hands go to my behind. "You already do."

Knock, knock sounds at the door. Henley steps back from me. "Come in," he calls.

A man opens the door. "Hen." He looks up and sees me. "Oh, I'm sorry to interrupt."

"No, no, please come in." Henley smiles. "This is Juliet. Juliet, this is Ronan."

"Hi, Ronan." I shake his hand.

"Hello, Juliet. Lovely to meet you." His eyes flick to Henley. "I'm having some trouble getting into the new program."

"Did you put in the password?"

"Yeah, but it's asking me for some code or something that is going to be sent to your phone."

"Ah, okay." He grabs his phone. "I'll come and sort it out with you. Back in a moment, Juliet." He sits me in his chair behind his big fancy desk before leaving with Ronan.

I sit and look around his big office and smile. Wow . . . he really is successful.

I mean, I knew it, but until I saw how swanky his offices are and all his staff buzzing around, it hadn't really sunk in.

I run my hands over the glass-topped desk and glance down to the drawers. I wonder what he keeps in there. I pull the top one open and instantly see something I don't want to.

His burner phone.

Ugh, I hate this fucking phone. I pick it up and look at it. How many women are just waiting in here for him to call them?

"What are you doing?" a voice snaps.

I glance up to see Jenny standing at the door. "Oh . . ."
Fuck.

"Don't go through his things," she snaps before marching over and snatching the phone from my hand.

"I beg your pardon?" I frown, shocked.

"Do not come into Henley's office and touch his private things," she repeats. "I will not have it."
What the fuck?

"Jenny, I'm his girlfriend. We have no secrets."

She smiles sarcastically. "Of course you don't."

Fuck off . . . Jenny.

"I don't appreciate your tone," I say.

"You don't have to." With another fake smile, she walks out with his burner phone in her hot little hand.

I officially hate Jenny . . . ugh, I'm infuriated. I can hear my angry heartbeat pumping blood through my body.

She's been with him a long time. I have to be calm about this and play my cards right, or I'm going to look like a jealous psychopathic girlfriend.

Game on, Jenny. Don't fuck with me.

Henley

"What do you mean you're taking a week off?" Jenny gasps. "Since when?"

"Since now." I sit back down at my desk and turn to my computer.

"Your schedule is way too busy this month to take a vacation."

"Cancel my appointments." I open the spreadsheet.

"I've been putting off your visit to Dubai for over twelve months. The only place you should be going is there," she huffs as she comes and stands beside my desk. "It's just not possible," she adds.

My eyes rise to meet hers, impatience getting the better of me. "Jenny . . ."

"Yes, sir." She folds her arms.

"I do not need your permission to take time off."

"This is untoward . . ." She rearranges the papers on my desk. "You are acting out of character."

I narrow my eyes as I stare at her. "Are you referring to Juliet?"

"I . . ." She pauses.

"You what?"

"I'm not sure you are thinking clearly, sir."

I lean back in the chair, my pen between my fingers. "And why is that?"

"Well, you hardly know this woman. How do you know she's not after your money?"

"We dated three years ago, well before she knew about my money."

Her eyes hold mine.

"I know her a lot better than you think."

"I don't like it," she snaps.

"You don't have to."

"I'm just concerned . . ."

"Enough, Jenny," I snap, cutting her off. "I am *not* explaining myself to you. I heard you were rude to her yesterday." Juliet didn't tell me this, but I'm reading between the lines. She was definitely ruffled about something after I returned to my office. Knowing Jenny like I do, I know something happened while I was out of my office.

She steps back onto her back foot, affronted.

"You treat Juliet with utmost respect at all times, or you will have *me* to deal with. Do I make myself clear?"

She twists her lips, annoyed. "Yes, sir."

I exhale, frustrated. Seriously . . . is everyone purposely trying to piss me off?

She walks toward the door and turns back to me. "You have a visitor waiting in the lounge. Michael Swartz."

"Send him in."

"Yes, sir." She disappears out of the office.

Juliet

I turn onto my street, deep in thought. My eyes instantly go to Henley's house. It's in all darkness. It's after midnight. He's obviously asleep.

We didn't speak today.

It's fine. He's going to call me tomorrow. *Stop overthinking everything.* I exhale heavily. God, I hate this. The man has me jumpy. His past behavior has been so sporadic that I have no idea if his craziness will return to ruin my love life.

I walk in and go straight to my back door. Barry is wagging his tail like the best friend that he is. "Hello, my little man," I coo. "Come inside, big boy."

He runs in and dives in his bed, all excited. I think I'm going to get him a companion. I hate that he's here alone while I'm at work.

But what if I get him a friend and they hate each other and fight all day while I'm gone? Hmm, I'll have to think some more about that one. I peer through my kitchen window over to Henley's house. Maybe I should text him?

No.

Stop being needy.

Ugh, I hate that he didn't call me today. I want him to miss me like I miss him.

I make myself a piece of toast and sit down and watch the late news. Eventually I drag myself from the couch. I grab a towel and take a shower in the downstairs bathroom. The water pressure upstairs is killing me, and I seriously do not have the patience for a pissant dribble of hot water tonight.

I want fire hose pressure, hard enough to strip this shitty feeling that I have on my skin.

I really thought he would call; damn it, why hasn't he?

Didn't he miss me at all today?

I get out and dry myself off, and with a towel wrapped around myself, I open the back door so that I can look over the fence at his house one last time, just to be sure he's not awake and waiting for me.

Darkness.

Honestly . . .

What the fuck is wrong with me? Why am I overthinking everything? Being in love with this man has me jumpy as all hell.

It is late . . .

Tomorrow is a new day.

I make my way upstairs and into my bedroom and walk into the bathroom to brush my teeth. I flick the light on. I jump with fright. "What the fuck?"

Henley is in my bed, lying on his side, the blankets pooled around his waist.

He's here.

His eyes fixed on me.

"You scared the hell out of me."

He gives me a slow sexy smile, the kind that sends shivers down my spine. "Get in here."

He flicks the blanket back, revealing his naked, muscular body. My eyes roam down his hardened torso and then come to rest on his large erection.

My sex flutters.

"Been helping yourself while you wait for me?" I murmur as I look at it, engorged and angry, ready to blow.

His eyes darken, and he gives himself a slow hard stroke. I see the shimmer of pre-ejaculate on his tip in the filtered light. "Maybe . . ." He strokes himself again, hard, long, and slow.

I clench, arousal filtering through my system.

The moonlight catches the muscles in his arm as he strokes it again. With his dark eyes locked on mine, he speeds up, pumping himself. His hips rising to get a deeper connection.

My breath catches as I watch him.

So fucking hot.

"Get over here," he growls.

I drop the towel and walk to the bed. He rolls on his side and lifts one of my legs onto the bed, his tongue lifting to lick me there.

Oh . . .

My hands go to his hair as he pulls me apart with his thumbs, his tongue licking me deep, his teeth grazing my clitoris.

Goose bumps scatter up my spine, and he throws me onto the bed, his strong hands on my inner thighs holding my legs open wide. His tongue takes no prisoners as he licks me deeply, sucking, moaning into me as if this is the best thing he's ever done. As if he will die if I don't come on his tongue.

I begin to writhe beneath him. His cock hangs heavily between his legs as he goes down on me. The sound of his slurps of my arousal, hearing his moans of ecstasy . . . feeling the want in the room between us.

Every cell is on fire.

Damn, if this isn't the best homecoming of all time.

I reach for his erection, and he pulls it out of my hand. "I don't need any help tonight, angel. I'm going to blow from the taste of you." With my eyes fixed on the pre-ejaculate dripping from his end, I clench hard.

Oh . . .

My back arches from the bed. "Hen." My hands fist his hair as I begin to ride his face.

The need to orgasm takes me over.

The burn of his stubble, his strong tongue, teeth grazing. And then he slides three thick fingers into my sex, and I shudder as I come hard.

He pumps me hard and fast, working every cry out of me, the muscles in his shoulders contracting.

I pant, gasping for breath. And then he keeps licking . . . cleaning me up. His face glistens with my orgasm. His dark eyes hold mine. "I need more."

I stare at him in the filtered light, at a loss for words. For the first time since we met . . . I wonder if I can handle him. I've never met someone so virile. This is primal mating in its ultimate form.

Henley James was born to fuck, his body unlike any I have ever known.

My temple.

He rises up my body, bringing my legs up over his forearms until they are up around his shoulders. "Tell me if I hurt you." He licks my neck, his teeth grazing my jawline.

I nod.

He kisses me aggressively.

"Okay," I murmur against his lips.

Fuck . . .

There's a darkness to him tonight, an intensity that I haven't felt before.

He slides in deep in one sharp movement.

I close my eyes at the domination. In this position, I am completely at his mercy.

He circles his hips to loosen me up, first one way and then the other. His breath is quivering, and I know that he's hanging on to his control by a thread.

He pulls out slowly and then slides back in, his dark eyes locked on mine. "Are you okay like this?" he whispers, his teeth skimming my neck once more.

I nod, grateful that even as aroused as he is, he's aware of how big and strong he is.

How much damage his cock could do.

He widens his arms, his biceps and shoulders bulging as he holds himself up. And then he pulls back and slides in hard, knocking the air from my lungs. "Take it all," he whispers darkly. "You take every fucking inch of this cock." He pumps me hard. "Do you fucking hear me?" he whispers angrily.

I close my eyes in the hope of blocking him out. He's too intense . . . too big.

Just way too much of fucking everything.

My feet are up around his shoulders as he holds my legs back. The sound of my wet sex sucking him echoes around us.

"Open your fucking eyes," he growls.

I drag them open to see him staring down at me, perspiration beading on his skin. His cock works at piston pace as it takes what it needs.

Feeding from my flesh.

I cry out, afraid of the orgasm he's about to rip out of me. "Henley . . ."

He slams harder and harder, the bed hitting the wall with a deafening sound. His hands on the backs of my thighs near painful as he holds me open with force.

I shudder hard, screaming out loud. He moans and holds himself within the depths of my body as it sucks him in.

I feel his cock jerk as it comes deep inside my body.

We stare at each other, hearts racing. His body still deep inside mine. He pumps me slowly as he completely empties his body into mine.

I pant as I try to bring myself back to earth. What the hell?

I've never . . . there are no words . . .

He pulls out and falls onto his back beside me, his chest rising and falling as he gasps for air.

I look over at him in question. Something is clearly bothering him. "What is it?" I whisper. "What's wrong, baby?"

"I love you."

Chapter 24

I chuckle as I pant up at the ceiling. "Good."

"Good?" He's struggling for air, his breathing labored. "Doesn't feel good, feels terrifying."

"Well . . ." I shrug casually as if I have this type of conversation every day. "You love me . . . I love you . . . the rest of it is semantics."

He frowns over at me in question.

I get out of bed to collect the blankets that are all over the floor. "It's going to take you a while to get used to, Hen. Relying on one person isn't easy."

He leans up on his elbow as if interested. "Do you feel like this?"

"Yeah, I guess." Now I'm really acting hard. I go to the bathroom and clean myself up. I walk back out to the bedroom to see the tortured man in my bed. I apply my face moisturizer as he watches me.

"Did you plan our trip?" I ask him to change the subject. He's two seconds from having a full-on meltdown. "We're going to the snow, right?"

His eyes flick over. "You said the beach."

I giggle. "Just checking you're listening to me. How much do I owe you for this trip? Tell me so I can transfer it over."

"This is my surprise for you."

"I don't want you paying for everything. That's not fair."

He reaches over and pulls me toward him. He arranges my body over his and holds me tight. "Shut up, I am."

I relax against his chest. "You know, breaking and entering is a crime, right?"

I feel him smile above me. "You gave me a key."

"When?"

"When your dog was barking and you told me to put him inside if he didn't calm down."

"Aah." I smile as I think back. Seems like ten years ago that we had that conversation. "Keep it—put it on your key ring." I kiss his chest. "This is my new favorite thing."

"Me waiting in bed for you like a puppy?" He sighs, disgusted.

"Being punished for you loving me."

"Yeah, well, shut up, or I'll fucking do it again." He pokes me in the ribs, and I laugh as I try to get away from him. He rolls over the top of me and kisses me tenderly, his erection growing against my leg once more. His lips linger over mine as a moment of perfect clarity runs between us. We're the perfect storm, where normality feels wrong and the forbidden feels hot.

I want to lighten the moment, remind him that it's okay to be us.

"I'm sorry, I've been a bad girl, Mr. James," I whisper as I play with him. "Please don't hurt me, sir."

I see fire flicker in his eyes as he spreads my legs with his knee.

I roll my lips to hide my smile. Dirty talk is his kryptonite, the one thing that I know brings him out of his own head and back into the moment with me.

"What would my father say if he knew his closest friend was about to take liberties with his untouched daughter? I'm barely of age."

He chuckles, his teeth grazing my neck as I feel his arousal teeter on the dangerous.

"Please don't mark me, sir . . . I beg you."

He surges forward, claiming every inch, pinning me to the bed. "Giddy the fuck up."

Henley strides in front of me through the airport terminal. He's wheeling our two suitcases and taking charge of everything. Amused, I follow him along.

We've had a big day, and he's been in drill sergeant mode. Organizing Chloe, Barry, his father, our houses, his business. Everything has been planned with perfect precision.

This is who he is.

Henley James likes control; nothing is left to chance.

The more vulnerable he feels, the more organized and structured he gets, and that's fine with me. He can be that enough for the two of us. I couldn't care less about things being perfect the way he does.

Every night this week, he has been waiting in my bed for me. We've fucked. We've made love, laughed, and talked into the wee hours. It's been the perfect week that's brought us closer.

When we're alone, he seems to have gotten his head around us . . . although that could be only because of all the dirty talk I'm doing.

All aboard the slut bus.

However, when we're in public together, it's a different story. He struggles with the couple thing, and I get it.

Henley James is a work in progress—a very entertaining work in progress.

We walk up to the check-in agent. "Hello, we're checking in for a flight today, please," Henley says as he passes over our two passports.

"Thank you." She looks at our passports and types into her computer. "Here you are, two tickets to Thailand."

His eyes flick to me, unimpressed, and I smile goofily. He didn't tell me where we are going. It was supposed to be a surprise.

I grab his hand, and he rolls his lips; I know he desperately wants to give her a hard time for ruining his plan.

"There you go, Mr. James." She smiles. "Pop your wife's luggage onto the conveyor belt."

He clears his throat as if holding in a fit.

"Now yours, sir." He puts his suitcase on, and she weighs it and then hands us our boarding passes. "Have a great trip."

"Thank you." He turns and gestures for me to walk in front of him.

"We're going to Thailand?" I whisper excitedly.

"Yes."

I beam at him and link my arm through his. "I'm so excited. You are so getting laid tonight."

"Like I wasn't anyway." He widens his eyes as if I'm stupid.

"Whereabouts in Thailand?" I whisper as we walk through security.

"Koh Samui."

"Oh," I gasp. "I always wanted to go there."

We walk along, my arm linked through his. "We can get massages on the beach, drink cocktails, and oh my god, Hen, this is going to be the best week of all time."

He smirks as he listens to me raving on.

"I was listening to what she was saying and hoping that she would let it slip, and when she did . . . ," I continue as we walk along to the airport lounge.

"There was only one thing I heard her say throughout that check-in," he replies.

"What?"

"When she called you my wife."

"Oh . . ."

His eyes hold mine. "I liked it."

My stomach flips as we stare at each other. "Me too."

I want to say something playful and fun, but it doesn't seem to fit here.

He liked it.

We are taking steps forward in leaps and bounds here.

We arrive at the airport bar and take a seat. "What do you want to drink?" he asks.

"I'm celebrating with a margarita." I smile.

"Good idea." He disappears to the bar, and I sit alone at the table and have a mini meltdown. I can't believe that just happened.

He liked me being called his wife. This is progress.

This is big!

Huge.

He arrives back at the table with our two drinks and slides mine over to me and holds his up. I clink my glass with his and take a sip. "Thank you."

I mutter into my glass, "I don't know if you realize what you've gotten yourself into by taking me to Thailand."

"Why is that?"

"I'm a stripper in Thailand, you know?"

His eyebrow raises as if impressed. "Really?"

"Uh-huh." I smirk, proud of myself.

He sips his margarita. "Well, anal with a stripper, I'm good with that."

I cough-snort my drink through my nose. "Aah . . . no. Your stripper does not do that."

His eyes twinkle with mischief. "Why is that?"

"I've never done that."

"What?"

I shake my head.

"What . . . never?" He frowns, fascinated.

I shake my head, and I get the feeling I just put a target on my ass . . . literally.

He smirks and holds his glass up in a silent toast to me, and I feel myself blush as I imagine him going there. He's way too big for that . . . I can't even . . . I would end up in the hospital, surely.

Jeez.

I need to change the subject. "Where are we sitting on the plane?"

"Up front, business."

"We're flying business class?" I squeak.

He kisses my fingertips. His sexy eyes linger on mine. "Only the best for my wife."

I look to the gate impatiently. "We're going to miss it." People have been lining up and getting on our plane.

Henley is reading the paper, in no rush whatsoever. "We are not going to miss it."

"If we miss it . . ."

He rolls his eyes and keeps reading.

I watch as more people board. "Henley . . ."

"I don't like boarding a plane too early."

"Why not?"

"Because you are on there long enough. Have patience, woman."

I exhale heavily. If we miss it, I'm going to go feral. Over the next fifteen minutes, I watch as the line dwindles. "Last boarding call for flight 282 to Phuket."

I widen my eyes impatiently.

"*Now* we can go." He stands and leads me over to the boarding gate; we pass the flight attendant our tickets, and she scans them. "Hello, Mr. James, welcome aboard." She smiles at me. "Hello."

"Hi." I beam. *Thank god. Just get me on the plane already.* We walk down the corridor to the plane. "I'm nervous," I whisper as I grab Henley's hand.

"What for?"

"I've never flown business before."

"That makes you nervous?" He frowns as we walk onto the plane.

"Uh-huh."

"Weirdo," he mouths.

"Mr. James, this is you." She gestures to a chair in the front. "And this is you, Miss Drinkwater." I look down at the two wide leather seats in their own cubicle thingy. There's a fancy screen between our two chairs.

"Thank you." I smile. She goes to serve someone else, and my eyes flick to Henley.

He frowns in question.

"There's a glass screen between us," I whisper as I look around at the other seats.

"Yes, some planes have this seating configuration," he replies.

"I would've rather been in cattle class, where I can sit next to you."

He takes my bag from me and puts it in the overhead. "I'll be on top of you for ten days. Enjoy the peace." He kisses me quickly and sits me down. "Fasten your seat belt," he instructs.

I roll my eyes and do as I'm told.

He takes his book and sits in the seat beside me. Even though he is close, I can't touch him at all.

Ugh . . . stop it, Juliet. Can you hear how needy you're being? The world won't fall apart because you can't touch your boyfriend for one measly flight.

Boyfriend.

A thrill runs through me. I still can't believe everything that has happened in such a short time, but then it feels like we've been together forever at the same time.

Strange but surreal.

The flight attendant comes around with a silver platter. "Can I offer you a glass of champagne or an orange juice?"

"Oh." *In a real glass too.* "Champagne, please." I take it and hunch my shoulders in excitement. I glance over, and Henley gives me a sexy wink.

I sit back and smile. *Bring it on.*

The drone in the background is a constant hum. Everyone else on the plane seems to be in deep relaxation mode.

Me, not so much.

I've watched two movies and tossed and turned. I attempted to watch a third movie but was unable to concentrate, so I stopped it after fifteen minutes.

I hate sitting still.

I look over at Henley; he's still reading the same book he has been for hours. He turns the page, completely absorbed. How does he concentrate for so long?

Ugh . . .

I lie back down and toss and turn some more . . . fuck's sake. I sit back up, and Henley glances over. "What's wrong?" he mouths.

I shrug, feeling dejected.

He puts his book down and taps his lap. I walk around and lean over and kiss him.

"What's happening?" he asks softly as he brushes the hair back from my forehead.

"I can't sleep."

He pulls me down onto his lap. "Sit with me for a moment." I curl up on his lap, and he spreads the blanket over the two of us. "I missed you too," he murmurs against my temple with a soft kiss.

How did he know?

With his big arms around me, finally safe in his arms, I feel myself begin to relax.

He holds me tight as he closes his eyes too.

Now, we sleep.

Henley scans the key, and the door to our cabana clicks open.

Holy . . .

"Oh my god," I whisper as I look around. It's so beautiful that I don't know where to focus first.

Henley smiles, proud of himself. "Not bad."

"Not bad?" I gasp. "Are you kidding? It's spectacular."

The back wall is all glass, looking over the most breathtaking view I have ever seen.

Blue ocean, palm trees, and white sand.

Built on the beach, it's a timber cabana with a huge deck, private swimming pool, and spa. My eyes roam around the interior. It's all white, with light wood furnishings. It looks like something straight out of a beach house in a magazine. I walk into the bedroom and see a huge four-poster bed and an en suite with a sunken bathtub. "Oh my god," I gasp again. "Henley James." I laugh out loud.

"How'd I do?" He smiles as he takes me into his arms.

"You did good." I kiss him softly. "You did really good."

He chuckles and lies on the bed and taps it beside him.

"No way in hell." I wheel my bag into the bedroom. "If we lie down now, I'm going to fall asleep, and I don't want to get jet lag. We have to stay awake until tonight."

He exhales heavily. "And how are we going to do that?"

"We're going to the beach."

"What, now?"

"Right now."

The waves gently lap at the shore, and the sound of the seagulls echoes in the distance. "I'm in heaven."

"You said that already."

"Just making sure you know how much I love this place."

"I do."

"Do you also know how much I appreciate you booking everything?"

"Yep."

"And the business class, I can't even believe we flew business." I think for a moment. "I just wish I changed into the pajamas, you know?"

"Next time." He smiles.

I grab Henley's hand and kiss the back of it. "Thank you." I kiss his hand again. "You've thought of everything."

Henley props himself up onto his elbow as he lies on his side, his body resting against mine. "You need sunscreen."

I glance down at myself. "I'll be fine."

He sits up and pours some suntan lotion into his hand and rubs it across my back. I smile at the sensation of his hands on my skin. He slowly begins to rub it into my upper thighs. His fingertips skim down over my sex. "Careful, we are in another country," I murmur. "You'll get us arrested."

"What would the charge be? Orgasming in public from rubbing sunscreen on my girlfriend?"

"Exactly that." I smile sleepily. "See, I told you you'd get used to it."

"Get used to what?" He slides his fingers beneath my bikini top and tweaks my nipple. I squirm at the sensation.

"Saying the word *girlfriend*."

"Meh." He smirks as he concentrates on his task. "Still an ordinary word. *Wife* is more of a flex."

I open my eyes and look up at him. Big brown eyes. His dark hair is messy from the salty sea. His rippled skin already golden and glowing from being in the sun today. How can someone be so utterly gorgeous?

"*Wife is* much more of a flex," I whisper, distracted by his beauty.

His gaze follows his hand as he continues to rub the lotion in. "Where do you see yourself in five years?" he asks.

"Married to the love of my life," I reply without hesitation. "Hopefully pregnant—that's if we're blessed with children. If we don't have children, traveling the world with my husband sounds pretty good too."

His fingers keep roaming over my skin.

"Where do you see yourself?" I ask.

He opens his mouth to say something and then closes it as if second-guessing his thoughts.

"Tell me . . ."

"I don't know."

I watch him. "Yes, you do. You at least have an idea."

"Recently"—he shrugs, his eyes still following his hands—"I've been seeing a very different future from what I always thought I would have."

I reach up and run my fingers through his dark stubble. "And how does that make you feel?"

He shrugs again, remaining silent . . .

"Terrified, horrified, or just plain petrified?" I smirk.

His eyes rise to meet mine. "Excited."

I smile softly up at my beautiful man.

What?

"We have so much to be excited for, Hen. Don't we?"

He nods.

"So who's the lucky girl, then?" I tease.

His eyes dance with delight. "A threesome-loving chick I met at a swingers' party a while back."

I laugh. This man kills me. "She's a lucky girl."

"Maybe." He leans down and kisses me, his lips lingering over mine. "We should fuck now."

I smile against his lips. "We're waiting until we get back from dinner tonight, or I'll fall asleep and won't go out at all."

He exhales in disgust and rolls onto his back. "My three-some-loving swinger wouldn't say that. She'd be all for it, blowing me, right here, right now."

I giggle. "Who, the future Mrs. James?"

"That's her."

"Maybe you'll find her back at the hotel."

He slaps me hard on the behind. "Let's go."

Henley

I sit out on the deck overlooking the ocean. What is she doing in there? I glance at my watch; she's taking forever to get ready.

I have never felt so relaxed and sated. This trip really was needed. I didn't realize how much I needed to get away.

The wind whips through my hair, and I smile into it. I glance at my watch again.

We are going to be late. What the hell is she doing in there?

I walk back into the bedroom and open the bathroom door; I take a step back. What the . . . ?

Juliet is wearing a long dark wig and has a full face of sexy makeup. She's in white sheer suspender stockings and a matching sheer bra.

My eyes drop down her body, and my mouth falls open.

This is so unexpected . . .

She's bending over the sink, and my eyes meet hers in the mirror as my cock begins to throb.

She turns and drops to her knees in front of me. "Threesome-loving swinger at your service, sir." She unzips my trousers and takes me into her mouth as she fists me hard.

My head tips back in ecstasy. "Fuck." I grab her face between my two hands and slide deep down her throat. I stare at her beautiful face, so innocent and sweet, yet the dirty, dirty whore that I need.

I know exactly where I'll be in five years.

Married to her.

Chapter 25

What?

She sucks me hard, and I clench my cock down her throat as my body takes over.

The need to fuck ravages my soul.

This is a trap.

The walls begin to close in around me: her dark wig, the lingerie.

Her perfect mouth. Her eyes flutter shut as she slurps and sucks me loudly. "You taste so good."

She wants to get married.

Her legs spread wider on the floor, and I drag her to her feet and spin her toward the mirror and bend her over. I rub my finger over her perfect asshole.

I want her here. I want her to feel as vulnerable in this as I do.

She whimpers as she throws her head back in pleasure.

I hate that I have no control over myself with her.

When we are in the moment, which is all the fucking time now . . . she owns me.

And she fucking knows it.

I hear my heartbeat in my ears as arousal takes me over.

I lift her leg and rest it up on the sink and slide my finger deep into her ass.

My cock is weeping in anticipation.

Her eyes darken as they hold mine in the mirror.

I grab a handful of the dark acrylic hair. "Stop acting fucking innocent, Juliet."

She throws her head back and moans.

"You want my cock so far up your ass." I jerk her hard. "Don't you?"

She whimpers.

"Say it," I growl. Something has come over me, something dark and sinister, my old traits returning. I can't play gentle with her anymore.

I am who I am. I want her here like this.

Right now.

I position myself at her back entrance.

"No," she cries.

My eyes meet hers in the mirror.

"Not like this."

She brings me back to the moment.

"Fuck it." I bend her over and slam into her sex. The muscles deep within her body ripple around me. I see stars.

All the fucking stars . . . and I hate them.

And in this moment, I hate her for how weak she makes me.

I take her to the bed and give it to her, good and hard like she deserves.

She cries out as I bring her to orgasm again and again, and damn it.

I hold myself deep as an earth-shattering orgasm runs through me. I'm breathless, panting, covered in perspiration.

I pull out and roll off her.

We lie in silence, both gasping for air.

I eventually get up and walk into the bathroom and turn the shower on.

I need to get my head around us . . . and quick.

Juliet

I wake with a start. The room is in darkness, and feeling disoriented, I look around.

What time is it?

My stomach growls. I'm hungry . . . starving.

We didn't make it to dinner. Exhaustion set in. I don't remember anything after . . .

I look over to the man beside me, sleeping peacefully on his back.

My stomach growls again. I need to find something to eat. I get out of bed, grab my robe, and tiptoe out of the bedroom and softly close the door behind me.

The cabana is lit up. It's a full moon, and light is dancing across the walls as it reflects off the ocean. The sound of the gentle lapping of the ocean is echoing so loudly.

So perfect.

I flick the lamp on and find a big bowl of fruit in the fridge. I'm going to eat this entire thing. I open the sliding door and peer out into the darkness, still and quiet.

A little bit scary, if I'm honest.

I'm not sure if it's safe to sit out here alone at night. Who knows what's out there? I glance at the time on my phone: 3:00 a.m. The witching hour.

Being in another country is unsettling. I'm sure it would be fine, but . . .

I decide against sitting outside and come back in. I lock the screen door and sit on the floor in front of it, cross-legged. I peel my banana and look out to sea as I eat.

My mind is in overdrive.

Something happened tonight . . . last night.

It was all going fine, and then . . . Henley pulled away, retreated back to his old habits. Guarding himself at all costs.

Damn that stupid check-in agent calling me his wife. I knew right then and there that it was going to freak him out. But at the time, he said he liked her calling me that . . . and not surprisingly, I did too.

I think back to my little dress-up skit. Was it that?

Did I go too far?

He seemed to love it . . . physically, he was all in. Emotionally, he wasn't even in the same building.

It's his heart that I want, and some days we are there, but how the hell do I get to it every day? Every time we get closer, he puts his walls back up.

I know he's trying. We're away together on a vacation that he organized. He's come such a long way in a very short time. It's only been a couple of weeks; this is eighteen years of a behavior pattern that we have to break down. Of course it's going to take him some time to adjust.

I'm overthinking this.

I slowly eat my fruit and sit on the floor in the darkness, contemplating a life with Henley James.

Is this what it's always going to be like with him? Three steps forward, one step back.

I mean, how can I complain? His sexual dominance is so perfect.

I lie back on the floor and listen to the ocean. It's so loud. Like an amphitheater, the sound echoing off the beach. There's a feeling of melancholy that has fallen over me, which is weird because I knew what I was getting into with him.

Yet when he pulls away . . . it hurts.

What happens if he never gets over this? What happens if I spend the next ten years trying to make him let me in, only for him to turn around and leave me anyway?

The bedroom door opens, and Henley appears. He's naked, hair disheveled, and he frowns when he sees me sitting on the floor. Without a word he comes and sits beside me, and we both stare out to sea. The feeling between us is thick with regret.

He knows.

He knows how he makes me feel when he checks out during sex.

For a long time, we sit in silence, both lost in our own thoughts. To be honest, I felt better when he was still asleep, because at least then I thought this was all in my head. Now I know for sure it's not.

"Why are you like this?" I whisper.

"I don't know."

Silence . . .

"Do you want to be like this?" I ask.

"No."

"Talk to me." My eyes search his. "Tell me what's in your heart."

"My heart isn't the problem."

I frown as I listen.

"My head just gets in the way."

"What happened tonight?"

He stays silent . . . his jaw clenching as if he's holding himself back.

"Hen, if we are going to work out, you need to talk to me. We need to have a clear and open line of communication."

He listens but still stays silent.

"What was the trigger tonight? What set you off?"

He gives a subtle shake of his head.

410

Seriously . . . this is pointless.

I'm beating my head up against a wall here.

He lies on the floor and puts the back of his forearm over his eyes to cover his face. "I had a fleeting thought where I knew where I wanted to be in five years," he murmurs.

Oh no . . . he doesn't want this. Scared of the answer, I ask the question. "And where was that?"

"Married . . . to you."

I frown. Not the answer I was expecting. "And that . . . ?"

"Fucked with my head."

I nod as I begin to understand. "You're processing."

"Processing what . . . that I'm a complete fucking asshole?"

I smile softly as I lie down beside him. "That things are changing."

We lie in silence for a while.

"I don't know how to turn my head off." He sighs.

"So don't."

He frowns.

"Henley, just because you have feelings for me doesn't mean that you are out of control."

"It sure feels like it."

I roll onto my side so I can see his face. "What does it feel like?"

He thinks for a moment as he tries to articulate this. "Like the floodgates have finally opened, and as a consequence, I'm about to drown."

"Because you've been holding yourself back from everyone for so long?"

He nods.

I stay silent as I try to think of the right thing to say here.

"I'm an all-or-nothing kind of person, Jules. As far as relationships go, I've always been nothing."

I listen.

411

"It's just . . ." He lets out a deflated sigh. "I'm moving too fast. This isn't . . ." He cuts himself off. "I shouldn't be . . ."

"You're afraid that your all . . . is too much?"

His eyes search mine, and I know that's it. That's the answer I've been looking for.

"Your all is not too much for me, Henley. It's what I want too." I pause. Should I say this out loud?

Fuck it.

Lay it all on the table.

"I know that you're the one for me. I've known it for a while now. I want marriage, I want to see you in my children, and most of all, I want what I deserve, what we both deserve—the happily ever after."

He frowns. "But we hardly know each other. It's not normal to feel like this so quickly."

"Says who?" I kiss him softly. "Since when do you want to be normal?"

His arm tenderly slides up my back as he stares at me.

"For the record, you cannot move too fast for me. I am all in, all yours. I'm here, Hen. Ready and waiting."

He takes my face in his hands and kisses me, his tongue slowly sliding through my lips. "I truly love you," he whispers. "I'm trying to be better; I know it doesn't seem like it, but I am."

The emotion behind his words brings tears to my eyes. "I know, baby." I kiss him softly and want to lighten the mood. "So what time are we getting married tomorrow?"

He breaks into a breathtaking smile. "Don't even joke. I'm feeling unhinged enough to actually want to do it."

We fall serious as we stare at each other, the air swirling between us.

So ask me, then.

"Promise me something," I whisper.

"Anything." He kisses me softly.

"If you have a moment where you freak out . . . you just say, *Juliet, I'm having a moment.*"

His eyes hold mine.

"That way, I'll know where your head is at, because when you pull away from me in the middle of things . . . it's upsetting."

He thinks for a moment and eventually nods. "Okay." He rolls onto his side, facing me, his fingers sliding through my sex.

His touch is different now. My Henley is back, his tenderness returned. "I'm sorry. I'm sorry," he whispers as if pained. "I didn't mean to . . . Did I hurt you?"

"Shh," I soothe him. I kiss him softly. "It's okay, baby. No, you didn't. I've got you."

He rolls over me, and his body slides deep into mine. "Let me make it up to you," he murmurs against my lips. "I'm sorry." He slowly pumps me.

And right here on the floor, in the middle of the night, Henley James makes sweet slow love to me for the first time.

"I love you too."

I was scared before . . . but now, I'm terrified.

This has to work out because I can't lose him.

Ever.

The night markets are abuzz with activity, and Henley and I amble along, soaking in the atmosphere. It's been a great day, the best.

We walk into a shell stall and look around; Henley picks up a huge white shell and smiles as he looks down at it. "My mom used to love these shells."

"Did she?"

That's the first time he has ever mentioned what she was like.

"Yeah." He puts it back on the shelf.

"Can we get it?" I ask.

"Why would you want that?"

"Because your mom would love to have a shell at my place," I say casually as I keep looking around.

He scrunches his nose.

"I'm going to get it." I take it to the counter and pay the lady as he waits outside the store. Eventually I join him. "I got it." I smile.

He nods. "Okay." We start ambling back up the street.

"Can I ask you a question?"

"Yeah."

"Have you ever been to grief therapy . . . you know, specifically about your mom?"

"No point," he says as he looks around. "My mom died. Lots of people's moms die. I've done enough therapy already."

"You know, I've done some research. There's a place called Camp Angel. It's a specific facility where they treat grief." This place is hardcore. They don't let you out until you are on your way to a full recovery.

"Why would I want to go there?"

"So you can face your demons."

"I don't need to go to a camp to do that." He smiles, amused. "I face them every day."

Oh . . .

"Just a thought." I shrug.

He puts his arm around me, and we keep shopping. He digs into his pocket and answers his phone with a smile. "Hi, Jen."

Ugh . . . fucking Jenny. She's called him every day, and it has had nothing to do with work.

"Yeah?" He listens as I pretend not to. "Beach day today." He listens again and then laughs.

My inner jealous bitch rears her ugly head. We walk through the shops as he happily chats away with her while holding my hand.

I know he's innocent. He wouldn't be so happy to talk to her with me here if he wasn't.

Her . . . I don't trust for a second.

I wind my finger in the air to signify to wind it up.

"I've got to go, Jen."

"I miss you," I hear her say.

"Yeah, you too." He smiles as he hangs up.

She misses him.

Ugh . . . fuck off, Jenny.

"You think you know someone," I call up the hill.

Henley chuckles as he turns back toward me. "Come on, woman."

"Why didn't you tell me you were an extreme sportsman?" I pant and puff as I drag myself up the hill.

"Athlete." He winks. "I'm an elite athlete."

"Ugh." I put my hands on my hips to try and make the hill feel less steep. You know that lying-in-the-sun-and-relaxing vacation I had planned out in my head?

Turns out it isn't this one. Henley James can't relax.

"I need a vacation to get over my vacation," I puff.

"Stop whining, or I'll stuff your mouth."

"With what?" I call as I climb.

He grabs his crotch. "Dick."

I giggle. We've been motorbike riding, kayaking, mountain climbing, parasailing, bike riding. You name it—we've done it.

We get up in the morning and have a relaxing breakfast and go for a leisurely swim. Then somehow, he talks me into being some extreme-parkour kind of person.

We do random adrenaline things all day until finally we get to relax on the beach in the late afternoon.

He walks back down the hill and grabs my hand and begins to pull me up along with him, and I smile goofily.

Who am I kidding? This is the best vacation of my life.

Action hero all day, making sweet love all night.

"It's just up here," he says as he looks at a map on his phone.

"What is?"

"A surprise."

"Oh." I hunch my shoulders in excitement. "I do like surprises."

He turns back toward me and pulls a black silk eye mask out of his pocket. "Put this on."

My heart skips a beat.

"What?"

He puts the eye mask on me and takes my hand and leads me up the hill some more.

What's happening?

"I love surprises." I smile.

"Do you?" He plays along.

Oh my god, is this . . . this is the best day of all time.

What's the surprise?

Is he going to . . .

"Ta-da." He lifts the mask.

I look around. There's a sheer cliff face and a zip line. A man is waiting with two harnesses.

My face falls in horror. "No, no, no." I step backward. "Henley, you are on drugs if you think I'm doing that."

His eyes twinkle with mischief. "You can do it."

"I could," I splutter with bulging eyes. "But I don't want to."

He chuckles and takes my face in his hands and kisses me softly. "You said you love surprises."

When I think you are proposing, you dickhead.

"Not. This kind," I splutter.

"Babe, it's fine. This is going to be amazing."

"Why, because I'll be dead in a ditch in the middle of a rain-forest somewhere in the Pacific Ocean?"

"The Gulf of Thailand, actually."

I look down over the cliff and get dizzy. I take a big step back. "Nope. No way in hell."

"Do you trust me?" He takes my two hands in his. "Because I'm trusting you. I'm following you over the cliff every day."

"Metaphorically." I widen my eyes at him. "Not actually."

"Loving you is way scarier than this."

I swallow the lump in my throat. When he puts it like that, damn it . . . now I kind of want to do it.

"If I die . . . ," I warn.

"I'll take care of Barry."

"Henley," I splutter.

He laughs out loud. "I'll go first." He steps into the harness. "Come on, babe." He holds his hand out to me. "Let's do this."

I twist my fingers as I look to the guide, who is patiently waiting with the harness. "Do you check the harnesses?" I ask.

"Yes."

"How often?"

Henley chuckles and fastens his buckle. "Will you relax?"

"Says the boy who is afraid of a girlfriend," I whisper angrily. "You are peer pressuring me into an early grave."

Mischief is all over his face.

"Juliet." He leans in and kisses me tenderly. "I love you. I wouldn't let anything happen to you. Trust me."

"Fine," I whisper. "Just so you know, I am putting this on the scorecard, and you better pay up big."

He chuckles and pulls me into a hug.

"Like five carats big," I grumble against his shoulder.

He tips his head back and laughs out loud, and it echoes through the valley.

And somehow, I just know everything is going to work out.

With my heart beating hard in my chest, I get my harness on and listen to the instructions. Together we stand at the edge.

"You ready?" He smiles over at me.

"Maybe six carats," I mouth.

He chuckles and dives over the edge. He goes flying down into the valley, the sound of his laughter bouncing off the rock faces.

Thump, thump, thump goes my heart.

Fuck.

Just do it.

I close my eyes, and against my better judgment, I let go of the edge.

I'd follow him anywhere.

Chapter 26

Juliet

The plane hurtles down the runway, and I let out a deep sigh. All good things must come to an end. Our perfect vacation is over.

We are so in love; our little speed bumps while we were away only cemented our bond even further.

This is it for us, and we both know it.

Henley's learned that he can still be his sexually dominant self and be in love with me.

There are no lines, no one or the other.

Somehow in his mind he thought he had to choose, love me . . . or dominate me in bed, and he was struggling. Unable to choose between the sex that he needs and the love that he wants.

We've finally found our happy place where we can have it all.

He loves me so much and yet now has the freedom to fuck me like he hates me . . . and it is so fucking good.

I glance over to my traveling partner; he smiles and gives me a sexy wink.

Ugh, he's infuriating. How does he look so good even after a stupidly long flight? I look like roadkill, and he's over there looking all *GQ*-model-like.

"Welcome home to Los Angeles International Airport. Local time eleven fifteen p.m. Thank you for flying with us, and we look forward to welcoming you again very soon," the voice says over the loudspeaker.

We leave the plane and go through customs on autopilot. "I can't wait to get into bed." I sigh. "I'm so exhausted."

"I know, babe." Henley puts his arm around me and pulls me close to kiss my temple. "Soon."

I sleep in the car on the way home. "We're home." Henley wakes me up before he wheels our bags inside. I try to finish waking up enough to get out of the car. Damn, I'm wrecked.

Barry is jumping around and excited to see Henley as he opens the door. "Hello, pain in my ass," he says as he pats his head.

I roll my eyes. He can act tough all he wants, but I know the truth.

Chloe went home today, knowing we would be here tonight.

I owe her a kidney for doing this for us. I can't wait to catch up with her tomorrow.

Barry jumps up all excited-like. "Hello, hello," I sing to him. I lie on the couch and hug him hard. "I missed you, did you miss me?"

"I didn't miss your Barry baby talk voice, that's for sure," Henley mutters dryly.

I giggle. It's true. Barry does bring out the baby talk in me. He and I speak another language to each other.

Puppy talk.

"Bed." Henley grabs my shoulders and faces them toward the stairs. "I'll have something to eat and then be up."

"Okay." I put my arms around his neck and kiss him softly. His hands go to my behind. "Thank you so much. I had the best time."

"So did I." He smiles against my lips.

"Can we go back next year?"

420

"Okay."

"I love you."

"I love you too. I'll be up soon."

I walk up the stairs, and I hear his voice. "Hey, yeah, I just got back."

I frown. Who's he talking to?

I stop on the spot as I try to listen. Who would call him this late?

Jenny.

He talks to her as he walks around organizing things. Why is she calling him at night at all?

He lets out a low chuckle. "Yeah, I know."

And why is he fucking talking back to her as if she's his long-lost friend?

Ugh, after the best week of my life, I come home to the reality that my boyfriend's PA is after him.

Is she, though . . . or am I just being insecure?

Probably a bit of both.

"You, too, hey?" I hear Henley's hushed voice reply. *You too* what? "Bye, Jen."

I quickly tiptoe up the stairs and jump into the shower. I don't want him to know that I heard him on the phone, and the last thing I want to do is to fight with him over her . . . but I do need more information. I quickly shower, get into bed, and pretend to read my book as my mind runs a million miles per minute.

Eventually he comes to bed. "Hey." He smiles as he walks into my bedroom. "I thought you would be fast asleep by now." He sits on the side of the bed and kisses me and tucks a piece of my hair behind my ear.

"I woke myself back up." I hold my book up. "Thought I'd read a little."

"Okay." He kisses me again and plugs his phone in to charge on the bedside table and walks into the bathroom. I hear the shower go, and I glance over at his phone. I wish I knew the code so I could see how many times she calls him a day.

Stop it.

Don't be this person.

I will not be the jealous, insecure girlfriend, no matter how in love I am.

Henley showers and walks into the bedroom with the white towel around his waist. "Are you looking forward to getting back to work tomorrow?" I ask casually.

"Yeah, I guess," Henley replies as he walks around tidying. He folds my clothes that were on the floor and lays them on the chair.

"How long has Jenny worked for you?" I act uninterested in the answer.

"I don't know, twelve years."

"Twelve years?" I gasp. "You've owned your business for twelve years?"

"No, she and I worked together at another company, and then we both left to work at another company before I asked her to come and work for me." He puts my shoes in the bottom of my wardrobe. "We need to remodel this wardrobe. It's doing my head in. Way too hard to keep organized."

I could give a rat's ass about organizing the fucking wardrobe.

"So you've worked with her at three companies?"

"Uh-huh."

"You must be close . . ." I twist my lips to hide my disapproval.

"She's a good friend." He crawls into bed beside me.

"Do you trust her?"

He frowns. "Of course I trust her."

That makes one of us.

"What's with the sudden interest in Jenny?" he asks as he slides his arm around me.

"She just . . ." I pause as I try to get my thoughts together. "She calls you a lot."

"She worries about me. For a long time she's been the only woman in my life."

I blink, shocked. "I'm the only woman in your life now, Henley."

He smiles and snuggles up to me. "I know, babe." He kisses my arm. "It's cute that you're jealous of her. But you have no need to be. I am yours and only yours."

"I am *not* jealous of her," I lie.

Green with fucking envy, actually.

"Good night, sweetheart," he says as he lies down. He switches his bedside lamp off and closes his eyes. "I'm beat." He glances over at me. "How are you still wide awake?"

Because I'm imagining the ways to burn Jenny alive at the stake.

"Not tired." I fake another smile. "Good night."

Within five minutes Henley is fast asleep, and my mind is racing.

I hate that he has this friendship with her and that he works with her . . . and that she sees him every day and that I know she's not on my side.

But more than that, I hate jealous and insecure girlfriends.

I have to let this fear go. This isn't who I am.

"So I guess that's it." Rebecca shrugs.

We're having drinks at my house before we go over to the street party.

"I mean, what did he expect me to do?" she continues.

Chloe and I listen intently. Rebecca met with John today, and she asked him for a divorce.

"What happened then?" Chloe takes Rebecca's hand in hers.

"He cried and begged for another chance." She exhales deeply. "And the pathetic thing is that if I didn't know for a fact that he was still seeing her, I probably would have tried to forgive him."

We fall silent, lost deep in our own thoughts.

"I feel like a shitty failure of a person." Rebecca sighs.

"You've done nothing wrong, Bec. You know that, don't you?"

"I put a tracker in his car. That's not okay. I'm not innocent in all of this. I was spying on my own husband. I still am."

"Because he was sleeping with somebody else," Chloe gasps. "Give yourself a fucking break. What were you supposed to do, just believe the lies and stay married to an adulterer for all of your life? And as far as not telling him now, you're damn lucky you didn't. You would have forgiven him only to have your heart broken again when you caught him out. He's never stopped. He's been seeing her the entire time. Sure he's fired her from work, but he's still going around there every night. It's not just sex—they obviously have some kind of relationship going on here."

"I know. I can't believe after all this . . . he's still lying." Rebecca's eyes fill with tears. "I just never saw myself as a divorcée kind of person, you know?"

"I know, honey." I smile sadly. "I don't think anyone ever does. But the good thing is, this is a great lesson as to what you don't want in life."

Rebecca widens her eyes. "You got that right."

Chloe charges her glass in the air. "No more sleazebags."

"None." I smile over at Rebecca, so beautiful even when she's so broken.

"That's it . . . I'm done with men, so done."

Chloe scrunches up her nose. "I wish I could be done . . . problem is, I like dicks."

We all giggle.

"What's with Henley having the street party tonight?" Rebecca frowns. "It's so unlike him to play host."

"I know, I thought the same thing." I shrug and glance at my watch. "We should go over soon."

"One more drink." Chloe refills our wineglasses.

"You're going to be okay, Bec," I tell her.

"Am I?" Rebecca smiles hopefully.

"We'll make sure of it."

Henley

"Okay." I look around my living room. "Cocktails are done, canapés are out." I rub my hands together. "I think we're all set."

Blake looks around as he sips his drink. "Where are the girls?"

"Juliet's. They're having drinks before they come over."

"Rebecca is still coming, right?"

Antony's and my eyes meet, and I give a subtle shake of my head. "Yes. But you're not allowed to talk to her."

"I can talk to her if I want," he snaps, indignant.

I fake a smile and then drop it immediately. "Go for Taryn."

"I don't want fucking Taryn."

"Rebecca doesn't like you." Antony rolls his eyes into his drink.

"That's half the fun of it," Blake says matter-of-factly as he looks around.

"Knock, knock," says a voice from the front door.

"Come in, Winston," I call.

The door opens, and he saunters in. I roll my lips to hide my smile. Winston is at least eighty and super skinny with gray hair that he combs over in a very bad attempt to hide his bald

425

patch. He's in tight blue jeans and a white polo shirt. "You're looking spiffy tonight, Winston." I smile.

"Thanks." He smiles proudly as he looks down at himself. "Thought I'd dress up for the occasion."

"Good for you," I reply.

"Wait." Blake frowns. "There's an occasion?"

"Yes, there's an occasion." I widen my eyes. "Do you listen to me at all?"

"Clearly not." He frowns. "What the fuck is the occasion?" His eyes dart to Antony. "Wait a minute, this isn't your wedding, is it? Like . . . you're not doing that dumb surprise thing, are you?"

"Oh my god." I pinch the bridge of my nose. "Nobody even knows Juliet and I are together," I whisper angrily. "How could this be a fucking wedding, you idiot."

He puts his hand over his heart. "Thank god for that. I thought you'd really lost it for a second there."

"Hello, boys," Carol calls as she walks through the door holding a tray of quiches. "This is so lovely of you, Henley. I've made your favorite, dear."

"Hello, Carol." I kiss her cheek and take the tray from her. "Thank you. I'll put this on the table out back."

"Hey, Dr. Grayson," Winston says as he comes over. "Can I talk to you for a minute?"

"Call me Blake," he replies.

Winston's eyes flick to us. "In private."

Blake frowns. "O . . . kay." They step to the side, and Winston begins to whisper in his ear.

"What's that about?" Antony says as he watches them.

"I have no idea." I take out my phone and text Juliet.

"Henley," Taryn gushes as she walks over and hugs me. "Oh, I love coming to your house. It's like coming home. This house is just so me."

Hard no.

Antony tips his head back to sip his beer with a subtle scrunch of his nose.

I peel Taryn's arms from around me. "You should get a drink, Taryn."

"Are you coming?" She bats her eyelashes. Why she thinks that is attractive is beyond me.

"Sure, give me a minute, and I'll be over."

She toddles off, and Blake returns to us.

"What was that about?" Antony asks him.

Blake leans in close so that nobody can hear us. "Turns out Winston is a freak in the sheets."

"What?"

"He wants a script for Viagra."

"You're shitting me," I reply, fascinated. "Who the hell is Winston fucking?"

"No idea, he said he has a lot of options." He taps his beer bottle with mine and then Antony's. "Goals."

Antony's eyes are locked on Winston as he talks to people. "What kind of options?"

Blake looks around casually. "I don't know. He's pulling granny fanny left, right, and center, apparently."

I snort my beer up my nose, and Antony bursts out laughing. "There's a sentence I never thought I'd hear."

"So did you give it to him?" I ask.

"What?"

"The script."

427

"I have to examine him first. Don't want the fucker to die of a heart attack in the middle of the deed."

"Good point."

Mason appears at the door. "Hey," he hollers as he makes a grand entrance.

"Hi, Mason," everyone calls in reply.

"Fuck me," Blake mutters under his breath. "Why does he talk so fucking loud? We're not deaf, you idiot."

"Hadn't noticed that before, but . . ." I shrug. "You're right, he does."

"Just be grateful that he doesn't have his shirt off," Antony mutters as he looks him up and down.

I chuckle. "Feeling inferior, Ant?"

"Nope." He sips his beer. "Just skinny."

"Who's that?" Blake frowns over to the door as someone walks in. My eyes roam over to the good-looking guy who just arrived.

"Oh, that's Liam, Juliet's brother. Remember the one I thought she was engaged to? Turns out he's not a bad guy."

"Where's his girlfriend?"

"She died."

Blake curls his lip in disgust as he looks him up and down. "What did you invite *him* for?"

"Because he's Juliet's brother." I widen my eyes. "Behave."

"If he tries to pick up Rebecca, you are so fucking dead," he whispers angrily. "Girls love that grieving bullshit."

"You are so fucking dumb I can't even stand it," I whisper. "She doesn't like you."

"Give me time." He rolls his lips as he looks around the room.

"Fuck me." Ant rolls his eyes. "I've just had to live through Henley's shitshow with his neighbor." He gestures to me. "If

428

you want to date Rebecca, I'm moving out of the street. I can't deal with the drama."

"Good. Fuck off," Blake replies. "You're boring anyway."

"What do you mean my shitshow?" I snap, affronted.

"Oh, let me think . . . you can't stop thinking about her, but you don't want her. You don't want her, but you keep jumping the fence. Her dog thinks he lives at your house. You hate her, but she's the best sex of your life—do I need to go on and on and on?" He rolls his eyes in a dramatic fashion.

I smile. It was a bit like that, actually. "Well . . . now I love her. So my shitshow turned out exactly how it was meant to."

"You got lucky," Ant fires back. "I don't know how she put up with you for so long."

I smirk. "I know. Me neither."

"Speak of the devil," Blake whispers.

We turn to see Juliet walk through the door. She's wearing a flowing white dress, her hair is up in a messy bun, and she's wearing big gold hoop earrings. She laughs and kisses Winston as she greets him.

And it's the best laugh; happiness is just oozing out of her every cell. I can feel it all the way to my bones.

As I watch her, my heart nearly beats out of my chest. It's like she has this pink glowing aura around her, so filled with love and tenderness. I've never met someone who is as beautiful on the inside as they are on the out.

She glances over, and our eyes meet. She breaks into a big, broad smile, and time stops. "She's so fucking perfect I can't stand it," I whisper to my friends.

"Oh god." Blake rolls his eyes. "Don't put me through it. Who are you, and what have you done with Henley? I think I liked you more when you were fucked up."

I chuckle.

"You're fucking pathetic, man. Get a grip on yourself." Ant winces.

Where Juliet is concerned, I am *totally* pathetic. I can't deny it.

Nor would I want to.

"Pussy whipped," Blake mutters under his breath.

I smile, because never has a truer word been spoken. "Happily so."

Juliet

My eyes meet with Henley's, and he gives me the best come-fuck-me look in all of history. I feel it all the way to my toes. He immediately strides over. "Hi, Chloe. Hi, Rebecca."

"Hi." They both smile.

"Hello, Miss Drinkwater." His eyes flicker with naughtiness.

"Hello, Mr. James."

His eyes drop down my body and back up to my face. "You look lovely."

"Thanks." I beam.

He leans in and puts his mouth to my ear. "Lovely enough to eat."

I giggle.

"We should go upstairs," he whispers.

I just got here.

"Why is that?"

"I have an appointment with your mouth."

I giggle in surprise. "My mouth?"

"Hmm." He frowns as if imagining it. His hand subtly brushes against my leg.

"Why are you so obsessed with fucking my mouth?" I whisper.

"Because it feels good." His breath tickles my ear and sends goose bumps down my spine. "Later." He taps my thigh and disappears into the kitchen.

"Hey you." I feel someone put their arm around me from behind. I turn to see my brother. "Liam." I smile, surprised. "What are you . . ."

"Henley invited me."

"He did?"

Oh . . .

"Liam, this is Rebecca, and you know Chloe."

Liam smiles. "Of course I know Chloe." He kisses her cheek, and his eyes come to meet Rebecca's. "Hello."

"Hi." She beams.

"Do you guys want a drink?" he asks us.

"Yes, please." I smile.

"Me too."

"And me."

He saunters off to the bar, and Rebecca leans in. "You didn't tell me that your brother is a total babe."

"Isn't he?" Chloe agrees. "Too bad I'm not allowed to touch him."

"Eww, he's my brother. Nobody is allowed to touch him. Gross."

"Not even me?" Chloe raises her eyebrow.

"Especially you. Concentrate on Dr. Grayson."

Our eyes all float over to Blake Grayson as he stands in the corner. Tall with ruggedly handsome good looks. "God damn it, he's a gorgeous piece of man meat," Chloe whispers.

"Too bad he's a total man whore," Rebecca replies.

"That's half the appeal," Chloe says, her eyes fixed on Blake.

Rebecca turns up her nose in disgust. "Not appealing to me at all."

431

From the corner of my eye, I see Taryn throw her arms around Henley's neck, and I feel my hackles rise. Henley unpeels himself from her grip, and his eyes come to me. Ugh, he knows it annoys me when she touches him.

"What's your brother's story?" Rebecca asks. "Married or . . . ?"

"He had a girlfriend for years, and she was killed in a car accident three years ago."

Her face falls. "Oh no."

Henley hits his glass with a spoon, and everyone quiets down. "Dinner is just about ready, guys, but before we head out back to eat, I have something I want to say."

Everyone falls silent as we wait for his smart-ass joke.

"I just . . ." He pauses as if collecting his thoughts.

"You what?" Blake says impatiently.

"I wanted to tell you . . ." His eyes come to meet mine.

What is he doing?

"So a few months ago I got a new neighbor." He raises his beer to me. "And I didn't realize how much I was in dire need of . . ." He tips his head to the side. "Her friendship."

"I thought you hated each other," Antony says. Everyone chuckles.

"We did," he agrees. "What you don't know is that Juliet and I already knew each other before she moved in. In fact, years ago we went on a date."

"Oh no," Taryn sighs. "Where is this going?"

Rebecca, Chloe, and I get the giggles.

"Spit it out," Blake says.

"What I'm trying to say is that Juliet and I are . . ." His eyes float over to meet mine, and I smile at my beautiful man. "I'm very happy and extremely blessed."

"For fuck's sake, spit it out," Blake sighs. Everyone chuckles once more.

"Juliet and I are together." He holds his arm out for me, and I walk over and join him. His arm slinks around my shoulders, and he kisses my temple.

"Like together, together?" Taryn gasps, horrified.

"Yeah." Henley smiles proudly down over at me. "Together, together, and you don't know what a relief it is to finally fess up to you all."

Carol bursts out laughing. "This is a joke, right?"

"What?"

"You honestly think we didn't know?"

"Wait . . ." Taryn frowns as she looks around. "You all knew about this?"

"Of course we knew. It's so obvious. You jump the fence every night." Carol taps her nose.

"Oh." Henley laughs. "Neighborhood watch . . . right."

Henley kisses me softly, and everyone cheers. His eyes twinkle with a certain something. "Let's eat. Dinner is served."

He grabs my hand, and we walk out into the backyard with everyone behind us. "What the hell?" Henley yells.

My eyes widen in horror as I look around. "Oh no."

The food is everywhere, muddy footprints are on the white tablecloth, and Barry is sitting up on the white couch eating a whole cooked chicken.

"Barry," I cry. "What did you do?"

Henley looks around and assesses the damage and inhales deeply before saying anything. "Who wants pizza?"

Three months later . . .

Henley

I walk down the street with Blake and Antony. It's Tuesday, and we're on our way to lunch.

"You should just go for it," Antony says.

"I can't just fucking go for it," Blake snaps. "She's not even divorced yet. The bed hasn't even gone cold."

I roll my eyes, unimpressed with Blake's obsession with Rebecca. "Do me a favor and never go for it."

"Why?" he snaps.

"Because she is Juliet's friend, and we live on the same street, and we all know that you will completely fuck this up and I will never hear the end of it."

"That's a very good point," Antony agrees.

Blake rolls his eyes. "I just want one night."

"You can't fucking have it. Find someone else to lust over. Rebecca is off limits to you. Permanently." We pass a jewelry store, and I stop and peer in. Blake and Antony keep walking, turn to see what I'm looking at, and walk back. Blake puts his hands into his suit pockets as he looks in at the jewelry through the window. "What are we looking at here?"

"Engagement rings."

"Why?" His eyes widen.

"I'm going to ask Juliet to marry me."

"Again, why?" He winces, horrified.

"Fuck me." Antony drags his hand down his face. "You've been with her for two fucking minutes. Calm down."

"Right?" Blake agrees. "Why would you want to get married?"

"Because I love her. It's been the best three months of my life. I've thought long and hard about this. I want her as my wife."

Juliet and I are inseparable.

Blake grabs my arm and pulls me away from the window. "It's too soon. I'm not letting you act fucking crazy. If in twelve months you still want to do it, be my guest. You don't ask someone to marry you after twelve fucking weeks."

We trudge down the street. "If I want to do it, I'm doing it."

"In twelve months," he snaps.

"Just concentrate on not sleeping with Rebecca," I fire back. "Stay out of my business."

"She's concentrating on that enough for the two of us," he replies flatly.

"She seriously has zero interest in you," Antony adds.

"I'm aware." Blake sighs. "Dumb. Doesn't she know what she's missing out on?"

"Clearly not," Antony mutters.

We walk into the restaurant and wait to be served. A sexy voice sounds from the left. "Blake." We turn to see a red-hot brunette. She's wearing a skintight dress that leaves nothing to the imagination.

"Hey, Cleo." He smiles; he kisses her cheek. "You're looking fucking amazing." He holds her hand up as his eyes drop down her body so he can inspect her properly. "When are we catching up?"

"Tonight?" She smiles sexily.

"Sounds perfect."

She saunters off, and we all stare after her.

Wow.

"Weren't you just telling us that you want Rebecca?" I raise my eyebrow.

"I believe that's true," Antony replies.

Blake rolls his eyes. "A man's not a camel. I need to feed the beast. I'm here for a good time, not a long time."

I chuckle at his answer. *Typical Blake Grayson.*

2:46 a.m.

The phone buzzes on the nightstand, and half-asleep, I glance over.

Who would be calling me at this time of night?

Nursing home.

What?

I snatch it up and walk out of the room. I close the door behind me so that I don't wake Juliet. "Hello."

"Hello, is that you, Henley?" Her voice is calm and unwavering.

"What's wrong?" I snap.

"Unfortunately, your father has had a fall and taken a turn for the worse. We are not sure if he had a spell first that caused him to fall out of bed or if he fell out of bed and that set off the events. He's hit his head rather badly, and the ambulance is here. They are taking him to the emergency room."

"Do you think he needs stitches in his head?" I ask as I walk downstairs.

"Henley, he's unconscious."

I stop midway on the stairs. "He didn't wake up after he hit his head?"

"No, he didn't."

The world spins . . .

"I'm sorry."

The air leaves my lungs.

"He's headed to Memorial Hospital."

"I'm on my way."

I run home and get dressed as fast as I can. I pull out of my driveway at record speed.

Please, be okay.

I grip the steering wheel with white-knuckle force as I drive, my mind a clusterfuck of confusion.

It's 3:00 a.m. How long was he lying on the floor before someone found him?

Was he calling for help and nobody came?

My stomach twists with regret. Here I was, having the best night ever, tucked safely in bed with Juliet, and he was lying on the floor in a cold nursing home.

The traffic light turns yellow, and I drive straight through. I glance up to the rearview mirror to see if a camera flashes.

I drive faster.

I'm sorry, we did all that we could.

She didn't make it.

The road blurs, and I wipe my tears with the back of my forearm. Suddenly I'm a fifteen-year-old boy again, reliving my worst nightmare.

I'm sorry. We did all that we could.

I can hardly see the road anymore; I angrily wipe my eyes again.

I speed up.

We just need to get on with it, son. It's just you and me now.

His words of wisdom come back to me, yet they bring me no comfort.

"Don't leave me, Dad." I screw up my face in tears. "Not yet. I'm not ready. You can't leave me yet."

After the longest drive in history, I finally pull into the hospital. I park in a spot reserved for doctors and run inside at top speed. The security guard looks me up and down.

"My father was just brought in by ambulance?"

"Head to the emergency department." He points down the corridor. "Follow the red arrows."

"Thank you." I run down the corridor and up to the check-in desk. "Hello. My father was just brought in by ambulance."

She gives me a kind smile. It's only then I realize what I must look like.

"Hello," she says calmly. "What was his name, dear?"

"Bernard James."

She types his name in and then reads her computer screen and twists her lips as if not liking what she's reading.

"What is it?" I stammer. "What's happened?"

"Just take a seat, sweetheart," she says softly. "Someone will be out to get you soon."

"Is he okay?"

"I can't see any information, only that he's arrived. I do have a note here for me to let them know when next of kin arrives. What was your name, sir?"

I stare at her. "Henley James."

"Take a seat." She gestures over to the chairs in the waiting area. "I'll let them know you're here."

"Okay."

I take a seat and lean my elbows on my knees. My heart is racing.

Next of kin.

The kind receptionist calls someone, and I watch her with my heart in my throat.

Who did she call?

The double doors open, and a man in scrubs with a stethoscope around his neck comes into view. "Henley?"

On autopilot, I stand. "Yes."

"This way, please." He turns and walks down the corridor, and I follow him down to the ward where an empty bed sits in a private room.

"Where is he?"

"Having a scan. He had a significant blow to the head and is unconscious."

"Still?" My eyes are wide. "He's been out for how long?"

"Over an hour now." He gestures to a chair. "Take a seat. I need to talk to you."

I drop to the chair.

"I just need to go over your father's health plan."

"I'll cover everything. You don't need to worry about payment. Just give him the best treatment that there is."

"Henley." He pauses. "He has a do-not-resuscitate order on his file."

"What?"

"He has specified that if something happens, he doesn't want to be resuscitated."

The doctor's silhouette blurs.

"That's ridiculous," I spit. "You have to do all you can."

"You need to respect his wishes."

"You do it," I spit angrily. "He's just knocked out; he's going to be fine." I stand. "You go to that scan room, and you do your fucking job and fix him." I'm outraged. "Why are you wasting time in here blubbering this nonsense to me when he needs you in there?"

The doctor stands. "He'll be back from the scans soon."

"And I'll be here waiting for him." I don't know why, but I'm furious with this doctor. "He'll be awake soon. He's a fighter," I tell him.

The doctor gives me a sad smile and leaves me alone.

I begin to pace back and forth. Back and forth.

He doesn't want to be resuscitated . . . Why? Why would he say that?

Aren't I enough to live for?

I drop to the chair in the corner, my mind floating between the now and then.

I see my father and mother, so happy and in love. Our family vacations and the house filled with noise and laughter. The love between them in Technicolor brightness, so over the top that it could be felt by all who knew them.

I'm sorry. We couldn't save her.

And then . . . his life without her.

The long days and endless nights of deafening silence.

Suddenly, it becomes all too clear why he doesn't want to be revived.

He wants to be with her.

And who can blame him? . . . I want to be with her too.

Where the love and happiness are so fulfilling. The light from her happy heart, so bright that it eclipses anything and everything.

A nurse appears. "Here he is." Coming behind her are two orderlies wheeling my father on his bed. He's asleep . . . unconscious, whatever the hell he is. He has a bandage around his head. I stand in the corner and watch as they hook him up to all the machines. The gentle beep of his heartbeat now sounds through the room.

Beep . . . beep . . . beep.

"The doctor will be in soon." The nurse smiles as she leaves us alone.

"Thanks." I pull my fingers through his hair to smooth it and take his hand in mine as I stare at him. His skin is smooth. He looks peaceful.

"I understand now, Dad," I whisper as I cup his face in my hand and brush my thumb back and forth over his stubble. "Now that I'm with Juliet, I understand."

He doesn't move.

"I know why you chose to forget everything . . . to forget me." I brush his hair back from his forehead once more. The lump in my throat is so big that it's painful. "It was too hard to remember her, wasn't it?"

He lies still. His chest rises and falls as he softly breathes.

"It's okay, Dad." His silhouette blurs. "You can go now."

Beep . . . beep . . . beep.

"Thank you for looking after me so well," I whisper. "It can't have been easy to live with someone for all those years who was just like her . . . but wasn't." I screw up my face in tears as I take his hand in mine. "I love you so much, Dad. You did a good job on your own. I'm so proud to be your son."

His eyelids flutter, and I smile through tears. He can hear me. He's in there somewhere.

"I know you love me, Dad," I whisper. His eyelid flickers again, and I smile through tears. "You can go now. It's okay. I understand."

The doctor walks into the room holding a clipboard, and I stand back and wipe my eyes; he gives me a sad smile. "Okay, the scan results are back."

"And?"

"He's had an aneurysm."

"When he fell?"

"Most likely before, and that's why he fell."

I nod.

"I'm sorry, Henley. Unfortunately, there was no brain activity detected."

"Meaning what?"

"It's highly unlikely he will come back from this."

I already knew.

"So what happens now?" I ask.

"The next twenty-four hours are critical. We will make him comfortable."

I nod as I stare at my father. "Okay."

"I have other patients to see. I'll come back in a little bit." The doctor puts his hand on my shoulder. "I'm sorry the news isn't better."

"Me too." The lump in my throat is back.

The doctor disappears out the door, and I pull a chair up beside the bed and sit and hold Dad's hand. Like I've done so many times before.

Only this time it's different.

I'm savoring every second, listening to his breathing, trying my hardest to soak in every minute detail.

For five hours I watch him, reminiscing on our life together. Going over every single little detail of his personality and what I love about him.

He takes a deep breath and holds it.

Beeeeeeeeeeeeeeeeeeeeep.

The heart-monitor line goes flat.

No . . .

I screw up my face as I hold his hand. His silhouette blurs.

The long beeping sound of the heart rate machine is echoing through the room.

But I'm not here. I'm having an out-of-body experience, hovering above as I watch my father die.

Two nurses come to the door.

"Leave us alone," I ask. "Give us privacy, please."

I hold his hand as I watch the life drain out of him. The man that I love the most in the world is leaving it.

It doesn't seem dramatic enough, big enough, worthy enough. It's all too simple, yet the hole that he will leave in my heart is immeasurable.

"I love you, Dad," I whisper through tears. If only he could say one more sentence to me.

Just one.

I watch him as I wait for something, some earth-shattering sign that he's okay, that Mom has come to take him to their next life. That he knows how much he is loved.

That he loved me.

I wait and I wait.

But no sign comes . . .

I rest my head on his chest and cry.

Chapter 27

Juliet

"Come on, Bazza." I stand at the door with the leash. I slept like a log, didn't even hear Henley leave this morning. He must have had an early meeting or something. He left much earlier than usual. I walk out the front door and stretch on my veranda. Carol sees me and comes walking across the road.

"Morning, Carol." I smile.

"Good morning, dear. Is everything all right with Henley?"

"Yeah." I frown.

"I was up getting a glass of water, and when I saw him speed down the street at three this morning, I got a little worried."

"What?"

"Yes, he went somewhere in a hurry in the middle of the night."

"Oh."

What the fuck?

"I'll check on him. Thanks, Carol." I go to walk back inside, and Barry pulls his leash in the other direction. "Let me get my phone."

"I'll watch him. You go get your phone," Carol says.

I run inside and grab my phone off the charger and quickly call Henley. It goes straight to voice mail.

"Hello, you've reached Henley James. Leave a message."

Hmm, he's either on the phone or it's turned off.

I glance at the time: 6:30 a.m.

Why would his phone be turned off at this hour of the day? I walk out front again.

"Any news?" Carol asks.

"He's not answering," I reply, distracted. "Maybe he had an early Zoom meeting or something."

"Yes, of course. That would be it," Carol agrees. "Can't be easy running a multinational company with all those different time zones."

"Yeah," I reply, but I get the feeling something is off. He didn't mention an early meeting last night. Maybe he just forgot. "Thanks, Carol. I'll go for my run and try him again later."

"Let me know if everything is okay, won't you?"

I smile. Forever the neighborhood busybody. "For sure." I begin to walk up the road with Barry. "Come on, Baz. Let's go."

It's 10:00 a.m., and I am getting worried.

Henley still hasn't turned his phone on. Something is off here. I call his office.

"Hello, Henley James Engineering. Monica speaking."

"Hi, Monica, it's Juliet. Can I speak to Henley, please?"

"He's not in today, Juliet."

I frown, taken aback. He distinctly said he was working today. "Can I speak to Jenny, please?"

"Sure, I'll transfer you now. Have a good day."

I wait.

"Hello, Jenny speaking."

"Hi, Jenny, sorry to bother you."

"Hi, Juliet. What's up?" Her tone is abrasive.

"Sorry to bother you, but have you heard from Henley today?" I ask.

"He emailed this morning to say he had external meetings all day and that he wouldn't be in to the office."

"Oh, yes. I completely forgot about that." I hold on the line while I think. She obviously doesn't know anything either. "Okay, thank you. I just couldn't reach him. I'm sure he will call me back soon."

"He's a very busy man, Juliet."

"I know," I reply through gritted teeth. *Don't mess with me today, Jenny.*

I am not in the mood.

"Thanks, Jenny."

Thanks for nothing, bitch.

I do some cleaning and vacuum the floor. And then I prep my dinners for the week. I'm working afternoon shifts and want to try and be organized and healthy.

Where could he possibly be?

His father.

Oh fuck, I hadn't even thought of that. Shit, shit, shit.

I scramble through Google to look for the nursing home's phone number, and I call.

"Hello. San Sebastian Nursing Home."

"Hello, can I be put through to the level-two nurses' station, please?"

"Transferring you now."

"Hello, level two. Christine speaking."

I wince. I don't really know Christine. I've never worked with her before. "Hi, Christine, it's Juliet Drinkwater calling. We've never actually met, but I've seen your name on the roster. I do one shift a week."

"Yes, hello, Juliet. I've seen your name on the roster too. How are you?"

"Good." I pause. I know she can't tell me anything.

"This is a random question, but I was wondering how Bernard James from room 206 is?"

"Oh . . . um." She pauses.

"Off the record, of course," I say. "He's actually my boyfriend's father, and I can't get ahold of my boyfriend and am getting worried. His name is Henley James. Have you seen him?"

"Oh . . . ," she replies. "You might want to come down here."

"What's happening?"

"Mr. James's room is being cleaned out."

My eyes widen. There's only one reason someone cleans out a room.

No.

"He died?" I gasp.

"You didn't hear it from me."

My heart stops.

No.

"I'm on my way." I hang up, grab my keys, and run for the door.

I walk down the corridor with a deep sense of dread. I have no idea what I'm about to walk into.

Only that Henley hasn't called to tell me and his phone is now turned off.

Henley being Henley, I'm assuming he wants to deal with this alone.

Tough titties. He's got me now.

I get to the door and stand outside as I peer in through the glass window.

Henley is methodically taking clothes out of the closet, folding them, and putting them into a box.

He's emotionless, collected.

His silhouette blurs as the lump in my throat closes over.

I knock softly, and he glances up and sees me. Before he stops himself, I see a fleeting flash of anger across his face. "Come in," he calls in a clipped tone. He continues to fold the clothes without looking up.

He's on autopilot. Cleaning is his way of controlling the situation.

I brace myself; I don't even know if I've done the right thing by coming. I just knew I didn't want him to be alone while doing this. I open the door, walk in, and close it behind me. "Hi," I say softly.

"You've heard the news, no doubt," he snaps as he angrily flicks a pair of pants.

I stay silent as I watch him.

"You can go home. I'm fine." He flicks the pants again as if to get something off them.

My heart breaks.

"It's for the best, anyway." He keeps folding the clothes. "He had no quality of life for a long time."

I go to sit on the bed.

"Don't sit there," he barks.

I quickly stand back up.

"I want to . . ." He opens and closes his hands by his sides, highly agitated. "I need to change the linens."

He's skating along the edge of sanity.

I stand still, unsure what to do. "What happened?" I whisper.

"He's dead. But you already know that." He flicks the pants again.

"How did he die?" I ask a little stronger.

"He had an aneurysm."

My heart is racing as I watch him. He's like a bomb about to explode.

"I'm so sorry, Henley."

"Don't be." He flicks the pants again without even looking at me. "I just need to clean out this room, and then I can move on."

"Come here." I go to hug him.

He pulls away from me. "Don't. The last thing in the world that I want is to hug it out. Go home, Juliet," he snaps in frustration.

God, how do I deal with this?

"Okay, I will," I whisper. "Can I help a little before I go?"

"No." He flicks a T-shirt in the air. "I've got it."

Maybe coming here wasn't the right thing to do.

"I'll clean the bathroom," I offer.

"No, Juliet," he yells. "How many times do I have to tell you? Go the fuck home."

He's angry.

My eyes well with tears for him. He is feeling so out of control in the situation. I don't blame him. I'm feeling pretty out of control here myself.

"I'm not going anywhere, Henley," I fire back. "If you think I'm leaving you alone right now, you are sadly mistaken."

His furious eyes rise to meet mine. "Leave or I'm calling security."

What the hell?

"Hen."

"I mean it. I'm fine. I want to do this alone." He flicks a T-shirt. "I'll come over later when I've dealt with all of this."

"Do you promise?"

"Yep." He puts a pile of T-shirts into a suitcase.

I watch him for a moment, unsure whether to leave. He wants to do this alone; I think I need to respect his wishes and give him some space.

"Okay." I walk over to him. "Can I have a kiss goodbye?"

He pecks me quickly on the cheek.

"You'll be over later?" I ask.

"Yes." Without making eye contact, he goes back to folding.

"I'll cook us dinner."

"Okay. Thanks."

He's coming over afterward. I feel a little better, but I really don't want to leave him here. "I love you."

"You too," he says, distracted.

With one last long look at my dear heartbroken man, I walk out the door. This is a complete nightmare.

I peek into the oven and then at the clock: 7:46 p.m.

Where is he?

He hasn't returned from the nursing home—hasn't been home at all—and I'm trying so hard to give him some space, but I'm really worried about him. It's a fine line between caring and smothering. I'm going to call him; I dial his number and wait as it rings.

"Hello, you've reached Henley James. Leave a message."

My stomach drops. Fuck.

Why did I leave him at the nursing home? What on earth was I thinking?

I should have been there to support him. I should have stayed. *He was going to call security.*

I feed Barry and fuss about some more. It's 8:30 p.m. now, and still no sign. I call him again, and he answers on the first ring. "Hi."

I close my eyes in relief. "Hi, babe, are you close?"

"Yeah, around the corner."

"Okay, see you soon." Thank god. I've been having a minor panic attack all day.

Ten minutes later, he drives onto the street and pulls into his garage. I peek through the curtains as I watch him walk over. I open the screen as he solemnly walks up the front veranda. He kisses me quickly as he walks past me into the house.

I roll my eyes as I pretend not to notice. He's here. That's all that matters.

He walks into the bathroom and washes his hands and comes back out. "Something smells good," he says as he looks everywhere but at me.

"Hope you're hungry?"

"Starving. I haven't eaten since yesterday."

My heart sinks. "Sit down, sweetie." I pull a chair out for him, and he sits at the dining table. I begin to serve our dinner. I don't know what to say or do. Do I bring it up, or do I pretend it hasn't happened, like he is? "Did you do everything that you wanted to today?" I ask.

"Uh-huh."

"We can go through the things over the weekend and sort them."

"I've donated everything to charity."

"What?"

"I dropped it off at the Goodwill store around the corner on the way home."

My eyes well with tears as I serve the peas. He gave away all his father's things.

"The photo albums?"

"Gone. I don't want them."

How could he?

He didn't. Surely, he didn't. Nobody is that cold.

Just stay calm . . . he's pushing you on purpose. This is dysfunctional Henley James at his very best.

I put the plate of food onto the table in front of him.

"Thanks."

I sit down at the table with my plate, and he begins to eat in silence. He really is hungry. He'll feel better after he eats. I'm sure.

I chatter on through dinner about every single subject on earth. I haven't brought up his dad . . . I don't know how to, and I don't want to trigger him.

I just have to be patient; he'll talk to me about it when he's ready.

We finish dinner, and I load the dishwasher. "I made you some chocolate pudding." I smile hopefully.

"Thanks, babe." He kisses me softly. "I'm just . . . tired. I'm going to go straight to bed." He kisses me again, his lips lingering over mine. "I'm exhausted."

"Okay." I smile, feeling a little better.

He goes to walk away, and I pull him back by the hand. "You know how much I love you, right?"

He nods. "I'll eat the pudding tomorrow."

"Okay."

He trudges up the stairs, and I hear the shower turn on. And for the first time today, a sense of calm falls over me. I think it's going to be all right.

I wake with a start. Henley is gone.

He seemed to have slept well, while I tossed and turned all night before falling into an exhausted sleep around 3:00 a.m. I didn't hear him get up and leave because by then I was out like a log.

I think he's gone to work, but honestly, who knows?

There is one comforting thing, at least. I know that Henley does autopilot like a pro. And if autopilot is what he needs to do for a while, then that's totally fine.

Keeping busy is probably the best for him at the moment. If he needs to be a workaholic this week, then so be it. I just wish I wasn't on fucking afternoon shift this week. I'll swap my shifts or take the week off.

I need to be home for him this week.

I get up and get into the shower. First things first. I'm going to Goodwill to get his father's things back. I'm going to hide them in my attic, and I know that one day Henley will be grateful that I got them.

Or maybe not . . . but I can't stand the thought of his family photo albums being thrown into the trash. They are way too valuable; I'll keep them for myself if he doesn't want them.

I glance at my watch. "Damn it, Henley." It's 2:00 p.m., and I've called him twice, and he hasn't called me back. I can't imagine the torture going on in his head right now, and I know I need to give him space, but seriously? He can't even return my call?

Fuck.

He's gone onto autopilot and is blocking me out. I know it. I can feel it in the pit of my stomach.

A car drives into the street and pulls into Henley's driveway. Who's that? I peer through the curtain; the relatives must be turning up.

Maybe he's been at the funeral home all day today. Yes . . . that's it. Of course that's where he is.

I keep spying through my curtains, and to my surprise, Jenny gets out of the car.

What the fuck is she doing here?

I watch as she walks up to his front door and opens it with a key.

She has a key?

Adrenaline surges through my system, and before I can stop myself, I find myself marching over there. I walk in without knocking, "Hello?" I call.

Jenny walks out of his office and exhales heavily when she sees me as if I am a huge inconvenience to her. "Hello, Juliet."

"What are you doing here?" I ask.

"Getting Henley's passport."

"Why?"

"He's going to Dubai tonight."

"He's not going to Dubai alone," I snap, infuriated.

"He won't be alone. I'm going with him."

Chapter 28

"What?" I step back from her in shock. *I can't have heard that right.* "What are you talking about?" I snap, infuriated. "Henley can't go anywhere. He has a funeral to plan."

Jenny rolls her eyes in an overexaggerated way. "If you knew him at all, you would know that his father didn't want a funeral."

Her sarcastic tone lights a fire in my temper, and I lose all control and point to the door. "Get out."

"What?"

"Get out of this fucking house before I call the police on you for trespassing."

"You cannot call the police on me," she scoffs. "What do you think you're doing?"

"What I should have done a long time ago: exposing you for the nasty piece of work you are."

"Go to hell," she fires back. "You think you are so important, but we all know that you'll be gone soon."

"Henley is grieving, and at a time like this he needs support, not to be talked into ridiculous travel plans."

"He wants to go to Dubai," she spits. "Working is his happy place."

"Working is not his happy place," I yell, infuriated. "He needs time to process his loss. Get off his back about work."

Fuck this bitch.

She rolls her eyes. "You know nothing about this situation." She marches past me and out the front door.

"Oh yeah, Jenny. That's not entirely true," I call after her. "I know you need to look for a new job."

She glares at me and gets into her car, and I slam the front door in fury.

You are so getting fired . . . stupid bitch.

Ugh!

I am infuriated.

I wait for her to drive away, and I storm over to my house to get my phone. I call Henley.

Ring, ring . . . ring, ring . . . ring, ring . . .

"You've reached Henley James. Leave a message."

"Damn it, Henley." My heart is racing. He wouldn't leave for Dubai tonight, would he?

Surely not?

He wouldn't. I know he wouldn't.

He's in self-destruct mode. Anything is possible.

Fuck.

What do I do?

I call him again.

Ring, ring . . . ring, ring . . . ring, ring . . .

"You've reached Henley James. Leave a message."

"Henley, it's Juliet. Come home, babe. I'm worried about you." I hang up and close my eyes as I imagine the nightmare this could turn into.

If he goes with her, if he turns away from me in a time of crisis . . . we can never recover from that.

I drop to the couch and put my head in my hands, tears welling in my eyes. "We worked too damn hard to be together. Don't ruin it now."

I'm panicked for what's about to come. I'm scared for Henley.

He's grieving and alone, and I want to go to him at work, but then if he is on his way home . . .

What do I do?

"Blake." I dial Blake's number.

Ring, ring . . . ring, ring . . . ring, ring . . .

"You've reached Dr. Grayson. I'm unable to come to the phone right now. If this is an emergency, dial 911. Alternatively, you may call my office at (650) 944-9494."

"Fuck." I dial the number of his office.

"Hello, Dr. Grayson's rooms."

"Hello, this is Juliet Drinkwater. I'm a friend of Blake's, and I'm unable to reach him. Is he there in the office today?"

"Dr. Grayson is in an appointment today. He won't be out until later tonight. Can I take a message for him for tomorrow?"

I close my eyes. *Fuck.*

"No, that's okay. Thanks very much." I hang up and scroll through my phone until I get to Antony's number. I quickly dial it.

Ring, ring . . . ring, ring . . . ring, ring . . .

"This is Antony Deluca. I'm in court today. Leave a message."

"For fuck's sake, why do his friends have to be off ruling the world?"

I begin to pace back and forth. My heart is in my throat, and I feel sick to my stomach. "Come home, baby. Please come home."

Henley

The buzzer sounds on my desk. "Your four o'clock appointment is here, Henley."

I buzz back. "Thanks, Jenny. I'll be out in a minute."

With a deep sigh, I stand and walk to the window. I put my hands in my suit pockets and stare out over the high-rise skyline.

There is no brain activity.

I clench my jaw as I stare out over the skyline. My beloved father is gone.

Nobody to visit, nobody to care for.

There's an emptiness that I can't explain. A void that nothing else can fill.

I go to my desk and look around for my phone. Not on my desk, not in my drawers. I rustle through my laptop bag. I haven't been able to find it all day. Have I left it somewhere?

"Where the fuck is it?"

I buzz Jenny. "Jen, have you seen my phone?"

"No, sir. Do you want me to come and help you look for it?"

I scratch my head as I look around. "No, it's okay. What time is my next appointment?"

"She's here now."

"Okay, send her in."

"Thanks for coming. It was great to finally put a face to the name." I shake Erica's hand on our way out of my office. It's the end of a day that has been booked with back-to-back appointments. Exhausting doesn't come close.

"You too. Have a nice night." She smiles. I watch her walk through the reception area and get into the elevator. Jenny is sitting at her desk, working away.

"Go home, Jen." I sigh. "Thanks for today." I walk back into my office and begin to pack up my computer.

A soft knock sounds at the door. I glance up to see Jenny coming in.

"Come in," I reply. "What's up?"

She walks in and closes the door behind her. "I just wanted to check in on you."

"I'm okay."

"You work too hard."

"Someone's got to pay the bills around here." I smile as I begin closing down my emails.

She walks closer and leans on my desk. "I'm here for you, Henley. You know that, don't you."

Something about her tone makes me look up at her. She undoes the top button on her blouse. "Anything that you need . . . I'm here for you."

What?

I lean back in my chair as I stare at her. "And what is it that you think that I need?"

"To relax." She undoes another button on her blouse; a hint of a white lace bra comes into view.

"And how will you help me do that?"

"You know you can trust me . . ." Her voice trails off as she undoes another button. "I know how hard your heart is breaking right now."

Huh?

"Remember that time in Germany at the conference where we spent the night together?"

"That was eleven years ago, Jen, and a one-off."

"It doesn't have to be." She undoes another button. "I can satisfy you, Henley. You need to just forget the world, lose yourself physically. I can be your safe place to fall."

She opens her shirt to reveal a perfect set of perky breasts. Her stomach is toned, and her body is perfect.

She walks around to my side of the desk and sits on my lap; she cups my face in her hand. "I can make you forget everything. We can leave for Dubai tonight and get away from everything."

"Jen, what the fuck are you doing?"

"You need this." She looks down at my lips. "You need me."

And in this moment, I see it. Clarity.

Crystal clear clarity.

Who I belong with . . . belong to. I've known it all along, but still, the realization comes through again.

"I'm in love with Juliet."

Her eyes search mine.

"I'm sad, Jen. My heart is broken, and I appreciate all that you do for me. But it is not like that between us."

"We have something, Henley."

"We do. I know we do. It's called friendship. A very special friendship."

"I've booked us on the red-eye to Dubai. The flight is at ten."

"What?" I screw up my face. "What on earth would make you think we're going to Dubai tonight?"

"You said you wanted to go to Dubai as soon as possible."

"Not fucking tonight," I gasp as I throw my laptop into my bag. "I've got to get home."

"To her?" Jenny folds her arms angrily.

"Yes, to her. I told you a million times, Jenny. I'm in love with Juliet. We *are* getting married."

"Then what the hell am I doing here?" she cries.

"Right now . . . you're being the most selfish person I've ever met." I throw my hands up in the air in surrender. "My father fucking *died* yesterday, Jenny, and here I am dealing with you carrying on and trying to kiss me and get me to fly to the other side of the world away from my family."

"You don't have a family," she spits.

The venom.

"Yes." My anger rises. "I do. I have *my* family, the one I chose: Juliet and Blake and Antony." My eyes hold hers. "And I used to have the best PA in the business."

Her eyes well with tears. "Used to?"

"I'm done, Jen." I shrug. "You can't work for me anymore. I'm transferring you. This is not acceptable behavior." I walk toward the door.

"You can't leave me. I quit," she yells.

I keep walking and hold my hand up in surrender. "Good."

Fuck off.

Juliet

I sit on the front steps in the darkness, my optimism slowly fading.

I keep picturing Henley in that hospital bed that day, his father lying beside him, asleep with his head on his chest, Henley's arm protectively around him.

I get a vision of Henley carefully shaving his father's face and whipping him with the T-shirt as he helped him dress. The way he used to help him shower and read him the morning paper.

The way he visited him every single day. The way they laughed together about everything and nothing.

Never to happen again . . .

I know his dad didn't remember him, but that doesn't make it any easier or any less significant. The loss is still so great.

My poor beautiful Henley.

I can't imagine what he's going through. I can't even pretend to.

I'm so worried that I feel sick in the stomach. What if Henley does something crazy? Like, really crazy . . .

Fuck.

I drop my head into my hands in despair. I can't stand the thought of him on the other side of the world. He can't go. This can't be happening.

A car comes into the street, and I glance up to see that it's a black Range Rover.

What?

He's home.

He pulls into my driveway, and with tears in my eyes, on auto-pilot, I stand. He gets out of the car, and his face falls as he sees my tears. "What's wrong, baby?"

"Are you okay? I've been so worried."

He pulls me into his arms. "I am." He kisses me softly. "Now that I'm with you." He holds me tight, and I can't help but cry tears of relief against his chest.

My big, beautiful man, after all he's been through.

He did it.

He leaned into the light . . . and made it home.

Epilogue

Twelve months later

I sit at the kitchen counter and smile into my coffee like the cat that got the cream, because I did just that.

Henley James, the biggest prize of all. The most beautiful man with the biggest heart. He adores me as much as I adore him.

What a whirlwind of a year, the happiest year I have ever had. My name is Juliet James, and I am married to the love of my life.

We got back just yesterday from our honeymoon, a month in Italy.

It was incredible . . .

Filled with love and laughter; the sun, the moon, and the ocean; and everything in between.

And I thought things couldn't get any better, but fate has other ideas. They just did.

It just did.

Henley's car pulls into the driveway, and I bounce up to greet him at the door. "Hello, Mrs. James." He smiles sexily as he pulls me into his arms and kisses me. His tongue gently swipes through my open mouth.

"Hello, husband." I smile against his lips.

His hand grabs me roughly on the behind as he walks me backward into the house. "Today was long without you."

"Without sex, you mean?" I smile as he kisses me.

"Yep." He throws me backward over the couch, and I bounce with a laugh. "Wait."

"Wait what?" He smiles darkly as he takes his suit jacket off and throws it over the chair.

"I have news."

"I already know it. You're about to be fucked."

"No." I laugh, and I hold up the pregnancy test to him.

He stills and looks down at it.

"You're going to be a father, Hen."

"What?"

"Our own family has already begun." I take his hand and put it over my stomach. He splays his fingers out tenderly.

"Are you sure?" he whispers.

I nod.

Through tears, his eyes search mine. "Oh, Juliet . . . I love you so much."

"And I love you . . ."

When one door closes . . . another one opens.

The circle of life is a mystical thing. As an elder is lost . . . a new soul is created.

Magic in the making.

If I've only learned one thing in this life, it's this . . .

If you lean into the light, love will always find you there.

NOTE TO READER

All my love,
Tee
Xoxo
Thank you so much for reading.
You are adored.

x

ACKNOWLEDGEMENTS

There are not enough words to express my gratitude for this life I get to live.

To be able to write books for a living is a dream come true. But not just any books, I get to write exactly what I want to, stories that I love.

To my amazing publisher, Montlake. Sammia and Lindsey, thank you for believing in me. You make me better.

To my wonderful team, Kellie, Alina, Lauren, and Christine. Thank you for everything that you do for me,

You are so talented and so appreciated.

You keep me sane.

To my fabulous beta readers, you make me so much better.

My beautiful mum who reads everything I write and gives me never ending support.

My husband and three beautiful kids, thanks for putting up with my workaholic ways.

And to you, the best most supportive readers in the entire world.

Thank you so, so much for everything.

I live my dream life because of you.

All my love,
Tee xoxo

ABOUT THE AUTHOR

T L Swan is seriously addicted to the thrill of writing and can't imagine a time when she wasn't. She resides in Sydney, Australia, where she is living out her own happily-ever-after with her husband and their three children.

Follow the Author on Amazon

If you enjoyed this book, follow T L Swan on Amazon to be notified when the author releases a new book!
To do this, please follow these instructions:

Desktop:

1) Search for the author's name on Amazon or in the Amazon App.
2) Click on the author's name to arrive on their Amazon page.
3) Click the "Follow" button.

Mobile and Tablet:

1) Search for the author's name on Amazon or in the Amazon App.
2) Click on one of the author's books.
3) Click on the author's name to arrive on their Amazon page.
4) Click the "Follow" button.

Kindle eReader and Kindle App:

If you enjoyed this book on a Kindle eReader or in the Kindle App, you will find the author "Follow" button after the last page.